JUST
LIFE

Also by Neil Abramson

Unsaid

Available from Center Street wherever books are sold.

JUST LIFE

A NOVEL

NEIL ABRAMSON

CENTER
STREET

NEW YORK   BOSTON   NASHVILLE

Center Street
Hachette Book Group
1290 Avenue of the Americas
New York, NY 10104

www.CenterStreet.com

Printed in the United States of America

RRD-C

First edition: May 2016
10 9 8 7 6 5 4 3 2 1

Translation of "Magic Words" on page xi used by permission of Edward Field.

Center Street is a division of Hachette Book Group, Inc.
The Center Street name and logo are trademarks of
Hachette Book Group, Inc.

The Hachette Speakers Bureau provides a wide range of authors for speaking events. To find out more, go to www.HachetteSpeakersBureau.com or call (866) 376-6591.

The publisher is not responsible for websites (or their content) that are not owned by the publisher.

Library of Congress Control Number: 2015960090

ISBN: 978-1-4555-9104-6 (hardcover), 978-1-4555-9103-9 (ebook)

For my angels—Amy, Madeleine, and Isabelle.

Acknowledgments

My wonderfully wise editor at Center Street, Christina Boys, told me after *Unsaid* that "first novels are a gift in that they often find a way to break out of you whether you want them to or not; second novels take work and more than a little courage." She was so right. I thank her for her tireless efforts on *Just Life* and her belief in this story. I could not have completed this journey without her.

With *Just Life*, I was very fortunate to be able to return to the remarkable people at Center Street and Hachette Book Group. In addition to Christina, my profound gratitude to publisher Rolf Zettersten for his support and vision. Huge thanks to Patsy Jones, vice president of marketing; Andrea Glickson, marketing director; Karen Torres, vice president, account marketing; Katie Broaddus, publicist; Billy Clark, vice president, sales; and Gina Wynn, channel director, sales for their extraordinary skill, integrity, dedication, and creativity. My deep appreciation as well to the members of the *Just Life* editorial, marketing, sales, and production teams, especially Melissa Nicholas, Katie Connors, Virginia Hensley, Tareth Mitch, and Jody Waldrup.

I am forever grateful to Jeff Kleinman and all of the folks at Folio Literary Management. Thank you for everything.

Many thanks to my colleagues at Proskauer and the brilliant people in the Labor and Employment Department for their continued support and friendship. I really don't know what I would do without them.

More thanks to the teachers and families at HVWS for providing a community of boundless creativity, warmth, learning, and fun.

To all the animals who first opened my heart and then kept it open, I am blessed to have known you; I always received much more than I gave.

My gratitude to Liza Margulies, for her incredible photography, Chris Cassidy for his masterful videography, Adrian Alperovich for his always-sage advice, and publicist Laura Mullen for her hard work and guidance.

Thanks and love to my mother and siblings for their support, and to my dad for his pen. I miss him.

And to Amy, Isabelle, and Madeleine. You are the beginning, middle, and end of all things for me.

JUST
LIFE

"In the very earliest time, when both people and animals lived on earth, a person could become an animal if he wanted to and an animal could become a human being. Sometimes they were people and sometimes animals and there was no difference. All spoke the same language. That was the time when words were like magic."

—"Magic Words," Nalungiaq, translated from the Inuit by Edward Field

Book I

Cages

I

Samantha Lewis woke in a panic as she most often did these days. This was not a "damn, the Klonopin has worn off" slow ascent to anxious wakefulness; this was full-on, deer-in-the-headlights, "holy shit I've left the dog under anesthesia too long" or "I nicked the cat's liver when I removed the spleen" alarm. She could hear an incessant beeping like an enormous clock ticking off the time that she would never get back.

No, not a clock. The alarm-like ring tone of her phone.

She reached it just before the call went to voice mail.

"You up?" Kendall demanded in his bear-like growl of a voice.

He never called her this early. "What's wrong?"

"I need help. Central Park Lake near the 108th Street entrance."

"But—"

"Please."

"I can't keep doing this, Kendall. I don't want to anymore."

"You know I got no one else," Kendall said, and disconnected.

Sam thought about ignoring him, but couldn't do it. Kendall was one of the few good guys left.

Sam glanced down at the bottom of the bed, where Nick, her giant husky mix with ghostly blue eyes, looked back at her with concern. There was a time when he would have been the first one awake, pacing with his leash in his mouth, urging Sam to start their morning run in Central Park. But that was history; Nick no longer tried. Even a strong dog will eventually surrender to the stillness of his human's doubt-induced lethargy.

A wave of nausea suddenly coursed through Sam. *Control it*, she pleaded with herself. *Think about something else.* "Breathe," she muttered.

No use. She threw off her blanket, ran into the bathroom, and puked up her dinner of red wine and brown rice (mostly wine) from the night before.

With her head still hanging over the toilet bowl, Sam's pendant escaped from its permanent spot under her T-shirt and swung into view. She grabbed it and ran her fingers over the nineteen metal dog tags. She felt for the names she knew so well. Those names usually brought Sam the comfort of clear purpose. This morning, however, the pendant felt particularly unsympathetic, heavy and cynical.

Sam flushed the toilet and eyed herself in the bathroom mirror. When had her face become so skull-like? When had the hollows under her eyes become so dark? When had she stopped looking twenty-nine? "Snap out of it," she told her reflection. Self-pity was for the end of the day, not the start. Otherwise she wouldn't be able to trick herself into getting out of bed at all.

Sam returned to the bedroom and grabbed her journal and a pen out of the nightstand drawer. She quickly scrawled the date on a fresh page, and wrote beneath it, "Panic 1, Numbness 0." Her therapist said that these were merely flip sides of the same problem—her inability to address her anger. Turned outward, this anger became extreme anxiety; inward it was cold detachment. Sam thought this was a load of crap and a sign that she really needed to find a new shrink. Still, she kept the journal because she figured if the day ended with the numbers low and roughly equal she was doing OK. That, however, was becoming about as rare as a comma in her bank account balance.

Nick trotted into the bedroom and dropped his leash on Sam's feet—further confirmation that the day was moving forward whether she wanted to be a part of it or not.

She threw on sweat pants and sneakers and clipped the leash to Nick's collar, and together they ran down three flights of stairs and across four blocks to the Central Park entrance.

Sam kept running until she saw Sergeant Jim Kendall's towering presence. He stood a few feet back from a ninety-pound pit bull mix with penetrating eyes and a badly scarred muzzle. Kendall kept his long arms out in front like he was trying to placate an emotionally disturbed perp. "It's OK. I just wanna help you," he told the dog.

The pit, a female, snarled and snapped at Kendall, pacing in a circle around a smaller terrier-type dog that Sam guessed was either dead or dying.

A few early-morning joggers stopped to gape. "Just keep moving," Kendall told them. They didn't argue with the big cop.

Sam tapped Kendall on the shoulder and he jumped. "Crap, Sam. Don't do that!"

The pit bull growled at Nick, lips pulled back over her teeth. Nick sniffed the air and dropped to the ground at Sam's feet, ignoring the challenge.

"I wasn't sure you'd come," Kendall said.

"Yeah, right. What happened?" Sam asked.

"No idea. A jogger called it in."

Sam could now see the little dog's gruesomely broken jaw. "This was batting practice."

"Probably got too close to the work site."

A hundred yards deeper into the park, work crews were busy constructing a massive stage and fifteen-foot scale replicas of the White House, the Lincoln Memorial, the Washington Monument, and the Capitol building. These were the preparations for the Central Park Gala to honor the governor of New York after he accepted his party's almost certain presidential nomination at the convention scheduled for the last week of September.

Sam nodded to the construction. "Man has come to the forest, Bambi," she said.

"More like assholes. Ever since they found that rabid raccoon near the site, the hard hats have been pretty aggressive with anything that crosses their path."

"That's a bad excuse for animal abuse. There's been rabies in the park before," Sam said. "No one's ever been bit."

"Yeah, but we've never had the governor and ten thousand of his closest black-tie political friends partying in the park before." Kendall shook his head. "But today's problem is that the little dog is still breathing and I can't get to it. I'm supposed to call animal control for every incident near the site, but..."

Kendall didn't need to finish the sentence. Not with Sam. They both knew "animal control" these days meant a one-way trip that ended with a body bag. Kendall could never be a part of that—whether it was for the president or the pope—just as he could never bring himself to remove the photo of his long-dead K-9 patrol partner, Phoenix, from his wallet.

"Let me try," Sam said, and handed Kendall Nick's leash. Kendall and Nick usually did well together. Nick sniffed Kendall's shoes, but quickly lost interest.

Sam stepped forward, showing the pit bull her open palms. The pit looked from Sam to Kendall and then to Nick, but remained silent. Sam took another cautious step.

"Careful, Sam," Kendall whispered behind her. "This one feels different."

Sam nodded without turning around. "It's OK," she said, more to herself than to Kendall. "I got—" Before she could stop herself, Sam locked eyes with the pit bull. *Damn*, she thought. *Rookie mistake.* Locking gaze with a dog was a challenge. She mentally cursed her own stupidity. The pit bull growled deep in her throat.

Sam tried to look away, but the big dog's dark eyes were too powerful. She saw fear, anger, and something else in them. The word *grief* darted into Sam's head, but that feeling was never very far from her own thoughts, so she couldn't be certain of its source.

Sam tried to clear her mind of everything except the big dog staring at her. "I won't hurt him. I promise," she said.

"I'm not liking this," Kendall called. He wiped away the beads of perspiration that had suddenly formed on his dark-brown skin. Sam heard the fear in his voice and tried to ignore it while she stood motionless, waiting.

The pit bull finally dropped her gaze and retreated, coming to rest on the grass a few feet away. Sam finished the distance to the injured terrier and carefully cradled it in her arms while the scarred pit looked on. The little dog didn't make a sound. Sam knew this was a bad sign; dogs are supposed to make noise. Kendall moved forward to help, but Sam quickly waved him back.

The pit bull slowly got to her feet. She appeared exhausted and defeated, all her menace gone. She whined and glanced backward, as if something waited for her in the dense woods of the park.

Sam probably could have corralled the big stray, but she thought about all the dogs in cages in her shelter. Sure, she could provide them with food, safety, and even love. But freedom? True sanctuary? A place with sky, grass, trees, and wind? That was off the table for now and probably forever. She just couldn't bring herself to fill a cage with another unwanted creature. She couldn't pretend any longer that keeping something alive was the same as giving it a life.

Sam lowered her arms so the terrier was at eye level with her companion. The pit bull sniffed the terrier, licked him on the muzzle, and whimpered. After ten silent seconds, the pit bull turned and ran back toward the woods.

As Sam watched the dog run off, she recalled other recent partings, and an aching sadness pierced her chest so forcefully that it threatened to knock her over.

Kendall put his huge hand on Sam's shoulder. "The shelter?" he asked.

Sam shook her head. "We need to get to a real operating room to have any chance."

"Morgan then."

"She won't like it. I'll need a big cop to convince her."

"Least I can do."

2

New York City is overwhelmingly huge, but real New Yorkers don't live in New York City. They live in their neighborhoods—a handful of contiguous streets holding their apartments, schools, places of worship, and essential stores. The neighborhood is the art of juxtaposition brought to life and can make city living personal, tolerable, and, often, peculiar.

The streets that made up the working-class neighborhood called Riverside were already heavy with pedestrians hurrying to get to the subway or the downtown buses, while shop owners raced to open in time to grab a piece of the morning rush. The presence of the six-foot-five African-American cop carrying the body of the dog in his arms, running next to the pretty five-foot-eight white woman leading a wolf-like dog on a leash, was odd even by city standards. People slowed to look.

"Coming through!" Kendall shouted, and lowered his shoulder like the high school football star he had once been. The pedestrian traffic reluctantly parted to let them pass.

Four minutes later they stopped before the imposing glass-and-chrome structure of the Hospital for Advanced Animal Care. Sam tried the front door. Locked. She rang the buzzer. Kendall was less patient and kicked at the door. "We've got an emergency," he yelled. "Please open up."

Footsteps, and then Dr. Jacqueline Morgan opened the door. Morgan was a handsome woman who, because of her Chanel outfit and perfectly highlighted blond hair, looked far younger than her real age of fifty-five.

"Sorry, Jacqueline," Sam said, and pushed past her into the empty waiting room. "This one won't keep." Kendall followed, carrying the injured dog. Nick trotted in last and sat by the large reception desk.

"What are you doing here?" Morgan demanded.

"Police emergency, Dr. Morgan," Kendall said.

"I'm sorry, Sergeant." Morgan spoke as always in the polite tone of a well-mannered maître d'. "I am not able to accommodate you." She smiled, but her teeth remained hidden behind her tightly sealed lips.

"This dog's in shock," Sam said. "He'll die. You have to let me try to save him."

Although Morgan's smile never wavered, her *sanpaku* eyes narrowed when she turned to Sam. "You of all people should understand that what you ask is simply not possible."

"Don't make this about us," Sam said.

"Of course it is not about us," Morgan replied calmly. "My insurance policy prohibits any work on these premises by non-employees. That, of course, would be you."

"Then you can do it," Sam said. "At least start an IV, open him up, and stop the bleeding."

"Why don't you take him to your little shelter and work on him there?"

"Because, thanks to you, I don't have a surgery room or any equipment."

"I'm not responsible for the terms of your city lease."

"No, that's right. You only make sure they're enforced by

threatening…" Sam shook the rest of the sentence out of her head. She didn't have time to argue. "Can you just look at the dog?"

Morgan glanced at the terrier in Kendall's arms for less than a second. "Another stray. Oh joy. This one looks hopeless at this point," she said.

Sam felt herself losing control in the face of Morgan's genteel obstinacy, knowing that every lost second put the dog's life further out of reach. "God, you are such a bitch!"

Nick rose at Sam's tone and took a step toward them. Nick and Morgan were not buds.

"You are so much like your father, you know?" Morgan said. "Once you get past the self-righteous indignation, there is so little substance."

Even though Sam knew Morgan was pushing her buttons—as usual—that understanding didn't help. "Leave my father out of this." Sam grabbed the injured dog from Kendall and brushed past Morgan to the bank of exam rooms in the rear of the hospital.

"Where do you think you're going?" Morgan demanded.

Kendall fished a credit card from his pocket. "You can put all the charges on this." He tossed the card onto the reception desk.

Morgan reached for the phone on the desk. "I'm calling your precinct captain."

"Damn, Morgan. Why can't you just be a decent neighbor for once?" Kendall asked.

"But that's exactly what good fences are for, Sergeant."

Sam sensed an almost imperceptible shift of energy from the dog in her arms. In the movies she had loved growing up, death always came in one of two ways—with an agonal breath and then a panicked, desperate grab for the last vestiges of life, or with a deep, peaceful exhalation followed by a contented sigh. Either way, the act of dying was a remarkable moment that commanded the attention of all those in proximity. But Sam had learned the truth about death in vet school: it wasn't special at all. It wasn't even an event. Death was only the failure of life. It crept into the vacuum created when you couldn't beg, cajole, or push life out any further. This was why death always eventually won; the act of fostering life requires constant diligence and we tire or get distracted far too easily. That was true, Sam knew, whether the dead thing was a mutt in shock or a parent who happened to end up on the wrong side of a windshield.

Sam wrapped the still dog in a towel that she grabbed from a pile and returned to Kendall. "Let's go," she said.

"Wha—?" Kendall started.

"He's dead." Sam opened the towel and shoved the body into Morgan's face so that his fur almost touched her nose. "Take a good look! I want you to recognize him when you see him again. You have no idea how many little eyes are waiting for you!"

Morgan didn't even blink as she continued to hold the phone to her ear, waiting. She was frighteningly good at maintaining composure and restraint. "Hello, Captain?" she said smoothly into the receiver. "It's Dr. Jacqueline Morgan... Yes, we have another issue..."

Nick growled again, low and guttural. Sam sensed that this time it wasn't just for show.

Kendall stepped in front of Sam and her dog. "Not here, Sam. Not now." Part of Sam understood that she was only making things worse—and they were bad enough—but a larger part just wanted to unload on Morgan in every human dimension they shared. "Sam?" Kendall gently touched her arm. "Let's just go."

Sam nodded in defeat and whistled for Nick. In a moment she was on the sidewalk holding a dead dog.

Kendall came up beside her. "Sorry about all this," he said. "I really didn't have anyone else."

"Yeah, well." Sam struggled for calm. "I figure people come into each other's lives for a reason, you know?" She noticed a group of grade school children walking toward her on their way to Riverside Elementary School. Six of the youngest kids were sporting surgical masks over their tiny noses and mouths. "What the hell?" Then she remembered.

The virus.

The CDC had reported the first case at the beginning of the week, and soon there had been four. The disease started like the common flu, but then the symptoms became frighteningly neurological: tremors, memory loss, speech deficits, followed by paralysis. All the victims were kids and all the kids lived in Riverside. Besides those two facts, the children had no other obvious connection.

Kendall followed her stare. "You heard the first kid died early this morning?"

Sam shook her head. "How old?"

"She was only four."

"Christ. Those poor parents. Did you know them?"

"Just by sight at the playground. They seemed nice enough. Regular folks...you know?" Kendall shrugged.

Sam did know—not the kind of people who deserved to experience an unimaginable life-altering loss. No words would offer comfort, let alone hope. Their lives, like their hands, were now forever shrouded in the odor of freshly turned soil.

Kendall brought her back. "Another case reported too."

"What the hell is this thing?"

Kendall often learned things at roll call that wouldn't break publicly for hours, if at all. Some of it was just gossip and rumor, but the "blue telegraph line" was usually accurate and Kendall had realized long ago that he could trust Sam. "State department of health thinks it's zoonotic." Kendall dropped his voice. "They're assuming avian source. I wouldn't want to be a pigeon in Riverside right now."

"You mean like West Nile?"

"Something like that. But I'm hearing lots more questions than answers. They're thinking about closing the schools in Riverside for a few days until they've got a better idea about the source."

"Sounds a lot bigger than the city is letting on."

"They're always worried about panic. Me too. The timing sucks with the convention coming to town in two weeks. People might start making poor choices if they think the virus poses a serious risk to their little presidential show."

"Yeah," Sam agreed, feeling the weight of the dead dog in her arms. She had seen too often that frightened people do frightening things.

"I'll stop in later and let you know what I hear." Kendall dropped a hand down to Nick's head. The dog licked it. "You watch her back," he told Nick, and headed down the street.

Sam watched him go and experienced a deadening fatigue that she knew no amount of coffee could relieve. She really believed what she had told Kendall—people did appear in your life for a reason. What she questioned, though, what made her grind her teeth through the night so hard her jaw ached in the morning, what made her furious when she passed the Mother's Day card section at Duane Reade, and what regularly sucked the life right out of her, was the utter lack of reason for all the exits. Sam had yet to find any logic on that side of the life equation and feared she never would.

But she did know one thing for certain—the day was still coming to get her, whatever she believed.

3

A New York City subway station is a dirtier, darker (in both light and energy), warmer (in temperature only), and smaller microcosm of the street above. There are shops, cops, riders, beggars, thieves, con men and women, preachers, schoolchildren, roaches, rats, performers, and lost pigeons. It is both an overwhelming and a numbing country, where all interactions explode against a soundtrack of rattling trains and a melody banged out by some musician praying for a few dollars dropped in a case, box, or hat.

Most humans do not linger in a subway station unless they hope to be saved, need to be saved, or are trying to do the saving. Andy was none of these today. His short blond hair, lanky frame, smooth face, high-top sneakers, and bulky backpack could have put him in high school, but something about his vaguely feral demeanor, piercing green eyes, and assured gait made him seem older.

Andy was about to exit the station with five hundred other self-absorbed riders when something familiar but wrong caught his eye.

The beggar with the one leg who often sat on a mat near the stairs had a new addition—a sickly-looking dog with a narrow face and dirty-blond coat from its Doberman/yellow Lab ancestors. A soiled rope that served as both leash and collar secured the dog to a railing while a sign on its neck completed the humiliation: "Help feed my dog! Please!!!"

The dog was panting hard, but not from thirst—the beggar had at least thought to provide the animal with a plastic dish of water.

"Your dog's sick," Andy said.

"Nah, man, just hungry."

Andy shook his head. He knew the dog was ill as surely as he knew his own name.

"C'mon, kid. Help feed him and a Vietnam vet. I fought for your freedom."

"I know you, don't you remember?" Andy said. "The closest you've been to Vietnam is the noodle shop on the corner."

"Leave me alone, kid...not bothering anyone."

"Where'd you get the dog?"

"A guy I know couldn't take care of it anymore. So he gave it to me."

"*Him*, not *it*," Andy corrected.

"What?"

"Never mind. You're only keeping him because he helps bring in the cash, right?" The beggar shrugged and looked away. "Well, now he's sick. I need to take him."

"But it's mine. We...we care for each other."

"Right. So what's the name of this dog that you care for so much?"

The beggar hesitated for a moment. "I call it Brutus, and if you lay a finger on it, I'll start screaming."

"And assuming I don't put my foot down your throat first, what do you think that's gonna accomplish?"

"The cops'll come."

"Yeah..."

"And when you can't prove you own it, they'll take Brutus away."

"Then you won't get to keep him either. So nobody wins."

The beggar shook his head in mock sadness. "'Cept we both know that in the pound they'll kill Brutus. And I think that might weigh heavily on a nice young man like you."

Andy wouldn't be put off. "I know people. I could get him saved before that happened."

"Go ahead then. Take the chance."

Andy didn't need to do the math. Although good and caring people worked at the regular city shelters, it was a question of overwhelming numbers. Once the dog went into the central system, he would be lost for days or longer in a river of creatures flowing downhill to the garbage chute. Andy knew about that too well from his own journey down a parallel course. He leaned into the beggar close enough to smell his urine. "You know I can end you right now and no one would even care."

"Oh, I know you could. But I know you wouldn't. You got the smell of the system all over you. You don't wanna go back, do you?"

At the beggar's words, Andy heard the clang of cold steel doors locking for the night. He saw himself shivering on a mattress so thin he could name each bedspring. He smelled the slightly sour odor of overcooked vegetables and undercooked meat. He felt hard and unforgiving hands on tender skin.

Andy had a problem with memory. His entire personal history since the age of eleven was a constant physical presence in his life. He could recall specific memories with photographic clarity at any moment—what he'd worn to school on November 12, 2009, where he'd had lunch on June 5, 2010, and what he'd eaten, the combination of every lock he had ever used, and the number of stairs in every foster home that had swallowed him. He "saw" his past the way other people watched old movies. And because each memory connected to another, he often became lost in the theater of his history, like some musician trapped in an infinite loop of a twisted version of "And the Green Grass Grew All Around." When that happened, it required all of Andy's emotional and physical strength to return to the present.

The scientific name for Andy's rare condition is highly specific autobiographical memory or HSAM. Andy just called it "piking." HSAM sounds like a remarkable gift...unless your life has sucked. Then, as Andy would have quickly acknowledged, it was like being trapped in a cage made out of razor wire.

Andy bit into the top of his own hand to bring himself back to the present. He left new teeth marks, but stopped before breaking the skin. These would quickly fade. Other marks he had previously posited on his hands and elsewhere would remain with him forever.

Andy's eyes found the dog's. He saw intelligence there, as well as pain and desperation. He was about to make a move for the dog that undoubtedly would end with yet another police interaction, when the beggar said, "Of course you can also buy it from me."

"Right," Andy answered. "Because he means so much to you." The beggar smiled in response, showing his gray teeth. "How much then?"

"Fifty."

Andy clenched his fists, but forced himself to remain still. He knew he couldn't allow this to end in violence. Too many people were starting to slow as they passed him. A few had stopped, waiting to see what would happen. He dug his hands into his pockets and pulled out three five-dollar bills and four singles. "All I got is nineteen. You're gonna take that." It wasn't a question.

"No. I'm not." With one eye on the growing crowd, the beggar announced, "You can't take my dog." Then louder for the audience, "It's all...he's all I've got in the world."

Andy knew the bastard had him. He was down to one choice. He shook off his backpack, pulled out an old, battered violin case, and removed his violin and bow. Then he yanked an almost clean paper bag from the nearest garbage can and propped it open at his feet. "Not the Mendelssohn," Andy mumbled. "Please not the Mendelssohn."

Andy lowered the bow to the strings and closed his eyes, bracing himself for the searing pain of recollection.

The Mendelssohn. Of course.

Many believe that the first movement of the Mendelssohn Violin Concerto in E minor is one of the most beautiful pieces of music ever written. Although perhaps not as technically challenging as the Bartók, it is more melodic, more layered, and more inward-looking. For Andy, for reasons having little to do with the piece itself, this particular composition was transporting; the music turned him into a tourist in his own ruins.

Memory blasted through the thin veil of Andy's reality. Every note drew him away from the station with its petty cruelties and toward the edge of a large lake floating in the purple dusk of winter. Andy stopped resisting the pull of time and gave in to the power of remembrance.

Huge snowflakes drifted down and covered him, but they were oddly warming. She was beside him and soon covered too, laughing at how incredibly soft the snow felt in her hands. Then she wrapped her hands in his. Andy and the girl both held the bow. The notes belonged to the two of them, alone in the world, as the snow swirled about. She kissed him.

Those in the station heard those same notes and they found they couldn't move away. They opened their purses and wallets and dug inside their pockets to offer coins, dollars, and even fives. People who had never given a dime they didn't owe threw fistfuls of change into Andy's paper bag.

In less than ten minutes, the strings stilled and Andy opened his eyes. The lake and snow were gone. The girl had returned to her home in his past and he was back at the station alone among the fetid odor of underground Manhattan and pressed bodies. He tasted blood; he had chewed his lip open again.

The crowd stared at him. He noticed the violin and bow in his hand and tried to remember how they'd gotten there. This temporary lapse in his immediate short-term memory often occurred after he played, sometimes even accompanied by a brief inability to form words. It was as if his mind could not simultaneously hold the embers of his past and the ashes of his present, forcing his most recent memories to give way.

An elderly man with round spectacles and a white beard approached him. "You cannot keep this gift to yourself," he said, and gestured to the violin. "You owe it to him."

"Who?"

"The One. He gave you this talent—Elohim. Adonai. The Creator."

"Oh. Him," Andy said dismissively as he returned the instrument to its case. "No, I don't think I owe him anything anymore."

Ignoring the stares of the old man and the others who had watched him play, Andy grabbed the bag of money, took out twenty for cab fare, and tossed the rest to the beggar. Andy waited, but the beggar didn't try to count the money or even meet Andy's stare.

Andy shoved the violin case back into his pack and untied the dog's rope. "C'mon, Little Bro. I'm gonna take care of you," he said.

The boy and his dog climbed the filthy stairs out of the subway and onto the trash-strewn street.

4

Kendall was terrible at names, but he had a knack for faces. As he walked back to his precinct house, he constantly scanned the sea of eyes, mouths, noses, cheekbones, foreheads, chins, and eyebrows for those he had seen before. There were many. These were Riverside faces…his faces…comforting faces, except for the ones obscured by surgical masks.

Riverside had been a good move for him. After he lost Phoenix, he could not bring himself to partner with another dog. The guys in K-9 understood, but no one else did—not even his wife, Ellen. He was too young to retire, too old to start over at the bottom, and too self-aware to pretend he didn't understand the gap between the two. So Kendall had bounced around from one precinct to another, never quite finding that fit he was seeking.

He had landed in Riverside two years ago as part of a new patrol initiative for recently gentrified areas. The mayor and the NYPD top brass were establishing small, dedicated units under the street supervision of an experienced cop to help certain neighborhoods deal with the complex issues created by socioeconomic change. Kendall couldn't speak for the other community units in the city, but for him and his team, the concept had worked. He felt as if he belonged again, and believed the neighborhood had accepted him. He had a good team of patrol cops under him, liked most of the people he met, and enjoyed the steady rhythm of the neighborhood at daybreak. He had even moved his wife and nine-year-old daughter from Brooklyn to a co-op in Riverside.

Once Ellen had called him her "Jedi Knight." When he looked at her quizzically, she added, "You know, you go around resolving disputes and dispensing street justice before things escalate. Just don't forget that you can still get shot."

And, as stupid as it sounded, in his own head Kendall began thinking of himself in that way. But finding that dog today in the park, together with the virus hurting his people, brought him too close to the guilt-ridden stairwells and sudden silences of his memories.

Kendall and Phoenix had been together for six years when they were called out to a domestic disturbance in Brooklyn. As they charged up to the top floor of the five-story walk-up, Kendall heard a man yelling and a woman and children screaming. He remembered the woman's voice: "Just put it down."

By the time they got to the fourth floor, he heard only the sound of kids wailing.

They made it to the fifth floor as the fullness of the silence hit.

Kendall crashed through the door, his gun drawn, shouting, "NYPD." His voice was the only sound, but there were blood-spattered little bodies everywhere. Phoenix pulled out of Kendall's grip and leaped for the man who had just murdered his family. The murderer dropped his knife and raised his arms in surrender.

Kendall immediately gave Phoenix the order to return to his side. He had given this order a thousand times before. Phoenix always complied. Compliance was not just about obedience; it was part of their bond. On duty, they were one integrated whole. And after six years together, their off-duty relationship was little different. Phoenix began where Kendall ended—and sometimes, with an ever-growing frequency, it was the other way around.

Except this time.

Phoenix growled as he dived for the man. When the man raised his arm in defense, Phoenix bit down on it so hard Kendall heard the bones crack. The man screamed but Phoenix held on.

Kendall yelled the return and stop commands, but Phoenix ignored him. Maybe the dog got lost in the scent of blood, or perhaps whatever separated the dog from his human counterpart had finally dissolved and Phoenix in that instant became a vessel of Kendall's honest but base desires. Whatever the reason, voice commands would not work. Kendall grabbed Phoenix by the neck with his free hand and pulled. The dog finally released the arm.

Phoenix backed up, disoriented, like an epileptic just coming out of a seizure. The dog glanced around the room and whimpered. The man on the floor bled heavily from his arm and moaned.

Before Kendall understood what was happening, Phoenix lunged again, this time for the murderer's throat.

"Nooo!" Kendall screamed.

Kendall had no choice. This was his training. Human life over animal life, even if it meant killing your own partner. Even if it meant killing your friend. Even if it meant a lifetime of guilt.

He fired. Phoenix yelped and slumped to the floor.

Kendall often wondered whether, given what he now knew, he would again pull that trigger. He had spent the last six years attempting to outrun that particular appointment in Samarra, but he knew it was out there, just waiting for the right confluence of events.

Suddenly weary, Kendall climbed the cracked concrete steps to his precinct station house. At the front door, he turned and surveyed his neighborhood. He promised those faces he would help them get through this. Then his eyes shifted to the rooftops, summoned by movement on an ancient six-story apartment building. A figure in full department of health protective gear peered over the side at the street below.

"And so it begins," Kendall said to no one, and stepped inside the building for morning roll call.

5

Father Gabriel O'Connor, a gaunt seventy-year-old with a once-handsome face creased by cigarettes and alcohol, stared out at his morning congregation. The word *congregation* was an embarrassing overstatement—just eight of the diehards who had stopped in for a quick Mass and a few words of inspiration before starting their work-day. On a good Sunday outside of football season, he could maybe get up to thirty people, but rarely double digits on a weekday morning these days. He couldn't blame those who had stopped coming; he would have liked to join them.

And, Gabriel was certain, he soon would.

Gabriel stretched his back. He had almost made it through another Mass without any incident. He just needed to deliver the homily and he would be done until evening. As a precaution against a repeat of the day before, he brought his notes up to the chancel with him. That was a significant concession to his condition; he had never before used notes. But so what? A few notes, a few naps. Maybe he was just making too much of the lapses. Perhaps the doctors were being alarmist. He had been doing this for a very long time, and everyone got tired, didn't they?

"Have I ever told you about the legend of the Just?" he asked. The congregants shook their heads and settled in for one of Gabriel's stories. Of all the many aspects of being a priest, Gabriel had always loved this part the most—trying to establish a connection between God and the everyday lives of his faithful. He felt that if he could do that—keep it relevant, bring God beyond the doors of his church—then perhaps he would have left something positive behind.

"The legend, which dates back to the Old Testament, states that a small number of completely righteous beings are chosen to be born into every generation to maintain the balance between good and evil. They bear the burden of the world's sins, hold back the darkness, and serve as physical and personal proof of goodness in the world. The Just must always share this burden for the world to continue as we know it. If even one of the Just stumbles, the balance will be lost, the souls of even the unborn will be forfeit, and humanity will suffocate under the weight of its own despair."

Gabriel took stock of his house of worship as he spoke. The sanctuary of Riverside Church was large—too large for the level of service he now provided—with twelve pews on either side of a narrow aisle and a simple altar on a low chancel. A modest wooden sculpture of Christ on the cross oversaw the room from a spot just below the ceiling. Gabriel kept the sanctuary extremely clean and organized in the hope that this created a sense of the peacefulness he could no longer personally project through his words.

One of the stained glass windows—the Old Testament story of Abraham and the sacrifice of Isaac at Mount Moriah—needed repair because a carefully thrown rock had shattered half of it.

"They are sometimes called the *Lamed Vov*, the Hidden, the Pillars of God, and a hundred other names in a hundred other languages. These chosen are unknown to themselves and to each other because their humility prevents them from understanding their own significance. They act not because they are aware of their responsibility to the world, but because they see and hear what the rest do not; our need moves them in ways we are now too broken to understand. And when they scream in anguish at what we have become, we hear only whispers or, worse, nothing at all."

Most of Abraham and some of Isaac were now gone, boarded up in anticipation of the repair that had never come. Still, enough glass remained to see that the scene depicted was awful—Isaac looked backward in terror at the elaborate dagger held by his tormented father while the glowing face of an approving God watched the act of sacrifice.

Gabriel stared at the window and shivered, recalling other faces he had seen at that same dark moment when realization and helplessness combined.

"The Just could be anyone, anywhere, and, at this moment, doing anything or nothing. Their actions define what they are—not their occupations, their incomes, their education, or their voice—if, indeed, they even have a voice at all.

"And what are those actions that according to the legend have saved the world from the abyss time and again? The simplest of all actions: the offer of sanctuary. From the Latin *sanctuarium*—a holy place. But make no mistake; the meaning of *sanctuary* is not limited to this room or any church or temple or place of worship. What makes a place holy? What creates *sanctuarium*? The answer is so obvious that it often remains hidden in plain sight.

"Intention. Your intention to imbue the space between you and another being with the spirit of God. Your intention to care. That is the stone and mortar, the architectural drawings and the building permits all rolled into one. It is the only required ingredient. That is the definition of a just life.

"This is why we must never ignore an opportunity for unlikely friendships; why only at our great peril do we numbly walk past an outstretched hand: anyone we meet might be one of these beings upon whom an unimaginable burden rests. A burden you can ease by creating a sanctuary simply by accepting that outstretched hand in kindness and with an open heart . . . simply by being present."

Gabriel's gaze dropped back to the waiting faces of his faithful. They shifted uncomfortably in their seats, coughing nervously into their hands. A few spoke to each other in hushed tones. Why weren't they listening? Were his words now so meaningless that his congregation couldn't even afford him the courtesy of their attention? That was the whole point of his sermon! Pay attention because hands are reaching out for you all the time. Opportunities for sanctuary . . . presenting themselves and then dissipating into the ether because you are lost in your iPads and iPhones, your Kindles and BlackBerrys . . . your judgment and gossip, your distractions . . . your inability or unwillingness to remain present . . .

"Excuse me?" Gabriel finally asked his congregation irritably. "Is there some problem?" He heard his powerful voice reverberate in the beams above and knew with heartbreaking certainty the answer to his question even before one of his congregants meekly raised her hand.

"Um . . . Father? We were sort of . . . um . . . waiting for you. You asked us if we had heard about the legend of the Just and then you just sort of stared back at the broken window. Are you all right?"

Gabriel grabbed his notes. He could feel the flush of embarrassment bloom in his cheeks. "Yes, thank you," he said. "Just collecting my thoughts. But please forgive me. I see I have kept you good people too long." He forced a smile. "I will offer my remarks when next I see you."

Gabriel dismissed the congregation with a quick blessing. They could sense his discomfort and were happy to leave as the priest, his eyes never rising from the floor, retreated to his office.

6

Sam passed Riverside Church and walked another thirty feet to the cheap laminated sign screwed beside the entrance of a squat concrete building: "Finally Home Animal Shelter—A Safe Place." She glanced down at the body in her arms and recalled how much she hated irony.

Sam shoved open the door and Nick trotted inside, following the sound of human voices and muffled barking. After a few deep breaths that didn't make her feel any better, she followed him.

Finally Home was one of only two city-assisted no-kill animal shelters and adoption centers in Manhattan. And Sam knew that if she didn't figure something out with the city, soon there would be only one. In her case the city assistance came in the form of a meager stipend for personnel costs and a very valuable no-cost multi-year lease. Morgan had ensured that the lease prohibited Sam from offering outside veterinary care and, thus, any competition—a battle Sam had fought and lost.

Sam was at the very end of the lease period and so far, all efforts to convince the city to renew or extend it had been unsuccessful. The worth of the shelter property in these days of fiscal restraint simply dwarfed the importance of keeping some dogs alive.

The shelter currently housed twenty-four dogs of various breeds (often within the same dog) and varying sizes. Most of the dogs had been with her for months and a few for over a year—drop-offs, rescues, or leave-behinds.

Sam was long past believing that she would ever find loving adoptive families for most of her shelter dogs, but she still said a little prayer every time someone came into the shelter to look—and held back tears and anger when they left empty-handed. Her dogs were too old and too damaged—physically and emotionally—to compete with the beautiful and energetic puppy mill traffic. The whole situation was all the more tragic because she knew those same cute puppies that now inspired such *oohs* and *aahs* likely would walk through her door—or that of a less compassionate shelter—a few years from now. She just prayed the city would let her continue to be present for them when that happened.

Sam had been living on the hope that she would be able to start an animal sanctuary. She dreamed about buying an abandoned farm someplace where these and other creatures who had seen the worst of humanness could live out the rest of their lives in safety and peace, beyond the ever-present shadow of cages. Cages sucked. They were better than the needle these dogs certainly would have faced at the other city-run shelters, but in the world of a no-kill shelter, cages were an unacceptable ending.

The promise of a sanctuary was starting to look more and more self-delusional. The equation was straightforward. A sanctuary required land. Land cost money. After Sam was done paying for those shelter expenses the city didn't cover, there was precisely enough money left over for absolutely nothing. *Frustrating* did not quite capture her situation. Sam knew she had become a vet and started this shelter for good and honorable reasons. It was just that, as of late, she found it hard to remember those reasons at all. And when she did remember, those reasons more often than not simply failed to overcome her feelings of inadequacy and failure.

Two of the shelter's longest-term residents greeted Sam, their tails wagging so hard that their entire back ends shared in the movement. Blinker, the golden retriever, had come to Sam a year ago with one eyeball lost to infection. Kendall had brought in Scrabble, a shepherd-Rottweiler mix, at about the same time. Scrabble took his name from the letters someone had carved into his back. Sam was always a bit pragmatic when it came to naming her charges.

Sam usually gave Blinker, Scrabble, and a handful of other dogs free range of the shelter during the day. This was a poor antidote to the cages and an inadequate remedy for the guilt that came from knowing she couldn't bring all the shelter dogs home with her. Daily time out of the cages was simply "the best she could do"—a phrase that Sam had grown to hate. Sam gave the dogs rubs, scratches, and hugs until they calmed down.

Greg Wright, a tall black man in his forties with the lithe body of the professional dancer he had once been, threw Sam a distracted wave from the reception desk. "I understand, sir," he said into the phone. "Yes... The moment I see her... I said I understand... English is my first language, sir," Greg snarled. "And my hearing is fine, so you don't need to repeat it a third time." Greg slammed the phone down and turned to Sam. "Wow. You look like shit."

Greg had come to Finally Home from Morgan's hospital as Sam's only full-time employee—part vet tech, part office manager and accountant, part protector, part therapist, and constant reality check. Sam thought of the news of the dead child as she lifted the bundle in her arms. "Bad morning. Don't start."

Greg's tone softened. "Sorry. Anyone you knew?"

Sam shook her head. "Can you call to have him picked up? Round trip, OK?"

It is illegal to bury a dog body in New York City, so Sam had the shelter animals cremated once they passed. The ashes came back to her in little colorful metal canisters that would have been more appropriate for jelly beans than for the small discarded envelopes of enormous souls. She kept all these stacked on a shelf in her office and their collar tags around her neck with a promise that she would bury the canisters and the pendant in a meadow at her imaginary sanctuary. Until then, the ever-growing pendant and line of canisters provided a stark and constant reminder of her promise.

Sam stared at the pile of papers sitting in front of Greg.

"You want to know?" he asked.

"No."

"Overdue invoices, nasty-grams from the city followed by super-nasty-grams from the city, your insurance payment must be wired within twenty-four hours or it will be canceled, and a denial of your appeal of the appeal of your denial of a hearing before the city council. Oh, and Morgan's lawyer just called."

"I thought I said no."

"Sorry, but here on earth"—Greg grabbed a handful of papers and waved them in the air—"they don't seem to take no for an answer."

"It'll work out."

"Really? You're going with that?"

"Why not?"

"Because you always say that, and it's never true."

"Never?"

"Never," Greg confirmed.

"Then think of it as aspirational."

Greg shook his head. "I met all my own aspirations as of last week and I'm not due for any more until the next decade."

Sam knew she couldn't keep up with Greg this morning. "Is our new community service assignment here yet?"

"Mother Teresa? Oh, yes."

"Let me guess. You had words?"

"Just one word. 'Fuck you.'"

"That's two words."

"Not the way I say it. Judge Allerton's little con enrichment pro-gram didn't do you any favors this time."

"Where is she?"

"Look for the large mass of white flesh with the evil attitude in the break room. And please find us some money, dear child."

Sam carried the dog's body to the small room toward the back of the shelter that functioned as the staff break room, television lounge, kitchen, and emergency bedroom for those nights when someone got stuck because of a sick dog. She was far beyond annoyed even before she saw the handwritten note on the closed break room door: "Do Not Enter. Absolutely No Admittance. Procedure in Progress." And under that, in large block letters: "THIS MEANS YOU!"

Sam ripped the note off the door and pushed into the room.

Beth Cohen's generous form, enrobed in a New York University sweat shirt and sweat pants, was flopped on the lounge couch. The television blared some news channel, but Beth ignored it; she was plugged into her iPhone, reading *People* magazine and making her way through a box of Dunkin' Munchkins and a can of Tab balanced on her sweat shirt. She looked at least ten years older than her real age of thirty-four. From the amount of crumbs and powdered sugar on her chest, Sam guessed Beth had been at this for a while.

"Is this yours?" Sam shook the crumpled sign at her.

Beth removed an earbud, but didn't look up. "Yep. I see it didn't quite work, though."

"And what procedure exactly are you referring to?" Sam asked, each word separated by a hostile beat or two. If Sam had been a dog, she would've flattened her ears and drawn her lips back over her teeth.

"Eating," Beth said. She grabbed another Munchkin and popped it into her mouth. "You have to be very careful when you eat these round things lying down. Don't you think—and here I'm asking you as a medical professional—they should've made these square?" Beth eyed another Munchkin. "That way they wouldn't be able to roll away from you when you stick your hand in the box. Little bastards."

Sam yanked open the refrigerator door and tossed old ice cream cartons and frozen pizza boxes into the trash, clearing a spot in the freezer section. She gently placed the stiffening shrouded body into an open spot between two of her microwavable frozen dinners. The little bundle looked so pathetically alone in the makeshift morgue, just like...

Sam slammed the door and spun on Beth. "Clearly you don't understand the terms of this arrangement."

Beth finally met Sam's glare. "My understanding, Doctor, is that it was this or cleaning garbage off the side of the highway in an orange jumpsuit. Not a flattering color for me. Makes me look like a pumpkin. So here I am."

"I expect you will act as professionally here as you would in front of your own clients."

Beth laughed.

"That's funny to you?" Sam asked.

"Hysterical, actually. My clients walked into my office on Park Avenue and held their hand out to be kissed by the doorman. They carried Prada bags and wore Christian Louboutin shoes. They wouldn't even get their dry cleaning done in this neighborhood." Beth put the bud back in her ear and closed her eyes.

All of Sam's anger from the morning's events suddenly had a single focus and it was personal. Before she knew what she was doing, Sam had yanked out both of Beth's earbuds.

"Yeow!" Beth's eyes flashed open.

Sam lowered her face to an inch above Beth's. "You'd better be prepared to do your job or explain to Judge Allerton why you violated the terms of your probation. If you screw up, you'd best go home and pack your toothbrush, because I'll be sure he gives you back your time. Now, you've got five minutes to get off your butt and be useful."

Luke, the other shelter employee, stepped into the room. "Need you up front, boss," he said in his gravelly voice.

Luke was sixty-seven years old, with a pockmarked face, mischievous blue eyes, a long white ponytail braid down his back, and still-powerful arms covered in ink. At a quick glance, the tattoos appeared to be a meaningless jumble of colors and letters. But if you took the time and asked him a few pointed questions, you would learn that Luke's arms were layered with the history of his life. On his right arm, the symbol of his marine unit in Vietnam mingled with the address of his apartment in Haight-Ashbury during the seventies, his prison inmate number, and a portrait of the Dalai Lama. On his left arm, the name of his daughter shared space with "God Loves Dogs and Brooklyn" and the word *Empyrean*, which Sam understood to be the name of a computer program Luke had been working on for years with some of his old war buddies but never spoke about.

"Can it wait?" Sam asked.

Luke shook his head. His face seemed particularly drawn and dark this morning. Sam's stomach lurched. Despite his appearance, Luke was usually the most upbeat of their group.

When Sam arrived at reception with Luke and Greg, she immediately knew this was going to be a particularly bad day in her life.

Men in suits. They had never—not once—brought her good news.

The three men introduced themselves and gave their titles too quickly for Sam to process. After she heard "Office of the City Attorney," her attention remained focused on the papers in blue legal backing they carried.

The one who looked like a turtle cleared his throat. "Can we speak someplace privately?"

"If this is about the shelter, it involves all of us."

"Very well," Turtle said. "As you know, Dr. Lewis, your final appeal regarding the lease has been denied."

"Yeah, I just heard," Sam answered. "I guess I'll be filing another appeal."

"There are no further appeals to file," Turtle said, handing her the stack of papers. "I am sorry, but this shelter will be closed thirty days from today. You will need to place all dogs presently in the shelter by that date or they will be relocated to the general city shelter population."

The papers trembled in Sam's hand. "But that will put them on a fourteen-day adopt-or-euthanize schedule."

"That is correct," Turtle responded.

"That's a death sentence for these dogs," Luke said.

Turtle suddenly took a great interest in his own shoes. "I'm not happy about this either. You've had plenty of notice. We were all hoping you were making other arrangements for these animals. This result was inevitable. The city cannot sustain your use of this property."

Inevitable? Sam thought she had been trying to manage the line between hope and denial, and only now realized that she had been traversing the artificially verdant land of the latter the whole time. "I'm going to need more time to place the dogs. Please." She heard and hated the desperation in her own voice.

"I'm sorry," Turtle said. "I really am. But the decision's been made. I have no more time to give you."

Turtle and his friends quickly retreated from the shelter in silence. Sam thought of undertakers leaving the grieving family to mourn in private.

"I'll call your lawyer," Greg offered. "Let's get him over here and strategize. Maybe a new lawsuit."

Sam shook her head. "I had to let him go after the last appeal. There's no more money."

"I have some money," Luke said.

"Me too," Greg added.

That was when Sam really wanted to cry. It was more than just losing the shelter and the dogs. It was the fact that they continued to believe in her when she knew how misplaced that belief was. "Thank you both for offering. Really, it means so much to know you'd do that," she said, trying to swallow her misery. "But I think they've got us. We just need to admit that the city is going to do this."

"What about the sanctuary then?" Luke asked. "Maybe this is an opportunity for you to—"

Sam cut him off. "Even if we found the right farm, we would still need to raise over half a million dollars to buy it and set up operations. All of us working full-time couldn't raise that in five years, let alone thirty days."

"Wow," Greg said, and slumped against a wall. "You really sound like you're giving up."

"I guess I am."

"You're just having a bad day," Luke volunteered. "It will pass."

How could she make them understand that it would not pass? That this was where all of her experiences had brought her? That she was so angry at being tired and tired of being angry, of losing this fight every damn day, of expecting the people out there to care and being disappointed when they didn't, of the flow of the unwanted and rejected, of all the goddamn cages? Maybe her ex-boyfriend Charlie had called it correctly after all. We are just schmucks and everyone out there is laughing at us because we've deluded ourselves into believing we're making a difference. "If we can improve just one life, make one human-animal connection, then we will have accomplished real change," she had always said. Such blah-blah. A rationalization to redefine success in the face of obvious failure. What a crock.

Still, there was no point in dragging Luke and Greg down to her reality. They would find out soon enough. In the meantime she would work to get them new jobs and confirm the continued viability of Plan B. It was the best she could do.

"Maybe you're right," Sam told Luke with as much of a smile as she could muster. "I'll start making some calls and see what new options we have." That answer appeared to satisfy them for the moment and they left her.

Sam locked herself in her office and placed the call she never thought she would need to make.

"Bill Ackerman, please," Sam said into the phone. Bill was Sam's counterpart at the only other city-supported no-kill shelter in Manhattan. Sam and Bill also had a little personal history together that made anything more than rare interaction uncomfortable.

After a few seconds, a deep voice came on. "This is Bill."

"Bill, it's Sam. There's something I need to know."

"OK, I am not currently in a relationship and yes, I still have the hots for you."

"I'm serious."

"Me too." Sam didn't respond and Bill dropped the banter. "OK, Dr. Lewis, shoot."

"Do we still have our deal?"

Bill was quiet for a moment. "So it's true? They've pulled your lease?"

Will not cry. Will not cry. "Yup. Looks like it's final this time. Thirty days." *No cry. No cry.*

"Bastards. Yeah, we've still got a deal. I'll take whoever you can't place. You can come and visit whenever you want. Do you have another job lined up?"

"Not yet."

"I'll keep my ears open."

"Thanks, Bill. This is a big load off my mind."

"You would do it for me. That was the deal...You maybe want to get a drink later to talk about it?" More beats of silence from Sam. "Can't blame a guy for trying."

"Maybe sometime soon. Just not tonight."

"I won't hold you to that. But it's nice to know."

Sam hung up just before the body-racking sobs she'd been holding back finally exploded.

7

Gabriel said an Our Father and unlocked the door at the rear of the sanctuary, directly beneath the hanging wood crucifix. He trudged down forty stairs, constructed with pride of prewar cement when they'd first built the church foundation.

The priest flipped on a light switch at the bottom step, illuminating the cavernous room. The only items in the entire space were a metal chair, a bookcase filled to overflowing, and an old wooden desk supporting an ancient table lamp and a large cardboard storage box.

The books, some of which were quite old, provided physical evidence of a decade-long search. Books on the kabbalah, Ezekiel, and the Talmud competed for room with volumes on Sufism, Buddhism, Rosicrucianism, Gnosticism, and Hinduism. The writings of Rudolf Steiner leaned against those of Padre Pio, Francis of Assisi, Thomas Merton, and William James. Except for an incongruous first edition of T. S. Eliot's *Old Possum's Book of Practical Cats*, all the books were nonfiction. Most of them displayed well-creased spines. Post-it notes written in Gabriel's hand jutted out of their pages. These volumes obviously were not for show.

The books had great personal value, not only for what they said, but also because of the journey through which they had been obtained. Gabriel could not look at the books without thinking about Channa Gold, the woman who had managed the used bookstore, and their conversations (debates, really) through the years over religion, purpose, and, eventually, the meaning and limits of platonic friendship. Gabriel now thought of the books as Channa's living breath—the continuation of a dialogue ended years too soon. He needed that breath with increasing frequency these days.

After the books, the box on the table was now Gabriel's most significant possession. The box contained his visual memory.

He turned on the lamp, pulled the lid off the box, and removed a handful of photographs. These were in no particular order—a photo of himself at his seventh birthday party, of his mother near the end of her life, of his dorm at the seminary, of a softball game he had sponsored a year ago against the temple three blocks away. He went through the photos very slowly, trying to imprint each memory into his failing brain.

The last photo in his hand had been taken at that game. Gabriel had been covering first base when Channa hit a clean single. They were both on the bag, leaning forward toward the camera. Channa had draped her arm casually around his shoulder. Gabriel was grinning like an idiot. Someone, probably her husband Sidney, had snapped the picture. Sidney, in addition to owning the local hardware store, was the neighborhood's historian and photographer. He had taken more than a few of the photos in the box.

Gabriel traced Channa's photographed features with his finger. "Am I destined to forget you too?"

He heard the gentle footfalls on the stairs and saw her just as she saw him. The cat ran to Gabriel and leaped into his outstretched arms.

"Oh, Molly." Gabriel squeezed her tight. "Have you come to help save me from myself?" Molly purred and pushed her orange tabby head hard against his chest.

"Is that what you're really worried about, Gabe?" Channa stood next to him, her hand on his arm. "Forgetting?"

Gabriel let the question hang.

"Tell me," Channa pressed.

Gabriel lowered Molly to the floor and the cat rubbed against his legs. "Forgetting is better than never knowing. I just want to see His face, Channa. I want to feel His countenance shine down upon me before I can no longer recognize it. I want to look upon Him before they put me in the home for old priests where I can drool in my oatmeal and mumble incoherently without embarrassing anyone. I want to be sure He is not that leering voyeur from the broken window upstairs."

"Surely you have seen Him before now," Channa insisted.

Gabriel shook his head. "I've felt His breezes and shadows, but nothing more. That is not enough after forty-five years."

"Perhaps not, but whose fault is that?"

"You of all people know that answer. I have never witnessed my reflection in my own child's eyes. I've never seen the sunlight break through a bedroom window and touch the face of a woman I love sleeping next to me. I've never known anything more than a platonic touch or experienced the mind-numbing exhilaration of flesh in flesh."

"Those are all just sensory stimuli, Gabe. Those feelings don't last."

"No! You're wrong. It is in these things—the living things—where the face of God truly resides. He does not dwell near the stale wafers and sour wine I have dabbled in."

"So you believe your vows have kept Him hidden from you?" Channa snorted. "Were you always such a self-pitying ass, Gabe? Or did the collar do that to you too?"

"For a mere projection of my own rotting mind, you talk a tough game. Why don't you go haunt your beloved husband?"

Channa waved him off. "Don't be petty. You really want to see God? Look closely and without blinking into the faces of the forgotten, the frightened, and the unforgiven. Bear witness. Get down on your knees with them, spend time in their presence, hear their stories however they are told. Otherwise it is far too easy to believe they deserve their hell."

"I have tried. I search for Him in their eyes just before the needle, but He never arrives. All I see is my own pathetic reflection."

Channa placed her finger on the spine of the *Book of Practical Cats*. "Do you still remember what I said when I gave this to you as a Chanukah present?"

"Yes. You called me 'Old Deuteronomy.' And I still don't get it."

"Because you choose not to. Just accept what you by now must know; you have helped others, you have eased their pain. For that you have His blessing."

"I have done nothing!" Filled with a sudden rage, Gabriel grabbed the box of photographs and threw it to the floor at Channa's feet. "I have helped no one! I have mattered less than one dust mote in God's eye."

Channa shook her head sadly. "Then you really are lost to me."

"Hey, Father Gabriel?" Andy yelled down from the top of the stairs. "You OK?" Andy shouted Gabriel's name two more times and was halfway down the stairs with the dog before the priest realized what was happening.

"I'm coming up," Gabriel called back as he quickly stuffed the photographs into the box and closed the lid.

Gabriel led Andy and the dog to the empty sanctuary. "Who's this?" He dropped a gentle hand to the dog's head. "Not a face I know."

"A friend I met in the subway. I call him Little Bro."

"I'm guessing there's a good story there?" Gabriel said kindly. This wasn't the first time Andy had brought a "friend" to the shelter or into the church.

Andy grinned and Gabriel saw the young boy that remained within him. "No better than the others you already know," Andy said.

"Was afraid of that."

"I promise you no people were hurt in the rescuing of this animal."

"Then I am comforted...slightly. What brings you by?"

"I heard shouting. Wanted to make sure you're OK."

Gabriel waved him off. "Just the television on too loud. Old ears," he said, and pointed to the sides of his head.

"You don't have a television in the church, Father."

"Don't call an old priest a liar to his face in his own sanctuary. Bad for business."

"So let it go?" Andy asked.

Gabriel nodded. He and the boy had been through their share together and had come out of it connected in some comfortable way. "But it's good to know that some shouting is all it takes to get you to stop by. Sam was also asking of your whereabouts."

"I'm taking that as a question?"

"No offense meant."

"And none taken," Andy replied. "Classes, mostly."

"Ah. 'Mostly,'" Gabriel repeated wistfully. "One of my favorite words. I'm not trying to pry."

"You are, but that's OK," Andy said without rancor.

"I actually call it caring."

"I know and I appreciate it. But..."

"But you don't want it. I get it."

"It's not that. I'm in a good place now. Working hard. Studying. You guys don't need to worry so much anymore."

"I think it's more that we miss you."

"Right," Andy answered. "Me being such good company and all."

"Compared to Greg?" They both had to laugh at that one. "I'm also more than a little worried about this virus."

"You need to have faith, Father."

"I believe in catastrophic thinking." Gabriel's eyes darted to the broken window.

Andy followed the priest's gaze. "Not every hill is Mount Moriah," Andy said. "Besides, I'm not a kid anymore."

"You're all kids to a decrepit relic like me. At least just check in once in a while."

"I will be more mindful. I promise."

"That's all I could ask for."

"Nope, but that's all you're gonna get, old man." Andy winked at the priest.

Little Bro lifted his leg shakily and peed on the edge of a pew before Andy could stop him. "Sorry, Father. I'll clean it up."

Gabriel didn't seem to care. He focused on the dog's face—the confusion, disorientation, and shame. Gabriel recognized the look from his own mirror and it scared the crap out of him. "No, it's OK," he said. "I'll mop it up. You should get him to the shelter and have Sam check him out."

"Thanks."

Gabriel offered a silent prayer for both boy and dog as he watched them leave.

8

In the small room that served as her office, Sam examined a very
young mutt—a cross between border collie, husky, and probably
half a dozen other breeds. Sidney Gold, a seventy-year-old gentle bear
of a man with Coke-bottle glasses and a gray buzz cut, looked on like a
proud parent. The dog had arrived at the shelter a few days earlier. Sid
saw him and it was love. Sometimes, rarely to be sure, but enough to
sustain hope, it actually all worked out.

"I can tell you in my professional opinion he is one of the damn
cutest things I've ever seen," Sam said.

"Isn't he though?" Sid beamed. "You know I always wanted one."

"I know."

"But Channa with her breathing trouble . . . it just wasn't possible."

Sam had attended the funeral and had never seen one human
grieve so deeply for another. Certainly not her father. Not even herself.
During the recitation of the kaddish, the Hebrew mourner's prayer,
Sid had collapsed to his knees and begged God for more time, screaming that "forty years together is not enough." Sam still held out hope
that one day she might find that kind of connection with someone who
had hands and feet instead of paws, but the prospects were looking

increasingly dim. "He will be good company for you between visits from the kids. Did you pick out a name yet?"

"Louis. After Channa's father. She would've liked that."

"No," Sam said. "She would've loved that." She placed the stethoscope on Louis's chest and listened for a moment while the puppy nibbled on her fingers. "What can I say? Everything looks perfect."

Sid grinned, but then a shadow clouded his face. "What am I going to do without you?"

"Whatever happens, I'll still be around."

"You know it won't be the same. Isn't there some other—"

"I've tried everything I could. I called in every chit that I had. I guess it just isn't meant to be."

Sid wiped something from his huge doe-like eyes. "Tell me, do you know a sadder phrase?"

"There'll be time enough for dark days. Today we need to celebrate that you have a new family member."

Sid kissed Sam on the forehead, gathered Louis, and almost bumped into Beth on his way out of the office.

Once Sid departed, Beth cornered Sam. "Nobody wants my help."

"Wow, I'm shocked," Sam said with a hand to her mouth in mock surprise. "You being such a caring person and all."

Beth's most expressive form of communication appeared to be her shrug. In the half day they had been together, Sam had observed an "I don't know" shrug, an "I don't care" shrug, a "don't blame me" shrug, an "I'm not impressed" shrug, and perhaps a dozen more. Now Beth showed Sam her "Popeye" shrug—a mildly embarrassed elevation of the shoulders with palms open and upward that said, "I y'am what I y'am."

Sam led Beth to the back of the shelter. "Don't take it personally," Sam said. "They really care about the animals and they don't trust you. They assume you're a screw-up."

"Well, as long as it's not personal."

They found Luke kneeling before the open door of one of the larger cages. Inside, a big, handsome mix of Lab and collie waited.

"What's her story?" Beth asked Sam.

"His. We found him a year ago," she said. "Pelvis was crushed. Some kids took a bat to him. Sweet guy, though. We call him Hips."

"C'mon, boy. Time for your walk," Luke called to him kindly. Hips raised himself up on his front legs; his back end didn't move. "Can someone grab me his chair?"

Greg brought forward a device that looked like a cross between a small wheelchair and a luggage cart, with two wheels connected by an axle. Instead of a seat and back, a wide sling of stretchy material dropped down from a bar over the wheels.

Luke took a wide leather strap, slipped it under Hips's waist, and gently lifted the dog so he was standing on all four legs. Luke carefully fit Hips over the sling so that his useless hind legs were lifted off the ground. When Hips was secure, the wheels supported his back end while his two front paws made contact with the floor.

"Jesus," Beth whispered.

"He's figured it out OK," Sam said defensively. To the dog, in a much softer tone, she said, "Haven't you, sweetie?" Sam slipped a hand under Hips's collar and scratched a spot on his neck. The dog pressed back hard against the kind contact. Despite what some humans had done to him, Hips never displayed a moment of hostility or aggression. Sam wanted to learn how to forgive like that, but so far Hips wasn't talking. "Why don't we let Beth take him out today?"

"Me?" Beth responded as if she'd been picked out of a lineup.

"Andy'll be pissed," Greg said. "He takes Hips."

"Andy's late," Sam replied.

"But I don't know how to handle him," Beth protested.

"Not much to do," Sam answered. "Put a leash on his collar. He knows how to do the rest."

"But what if—"

Sam cut her off. "Just be a helpful human."

Hips whined and Luke reluctantly stepped aside. "Just walk next to him," he said. "Simple."

Beth reached for the nearest leash, an extend-a-leash lying on a counter. As soon as her fingers touched the device, Greg grabbed it out of her hand. "That's my leash."

"It's just a leash," Beth said. "What the hell's the big deal?"

Luke stepped between them. "No, no. It is never 'just a leash,'" he said solemnly.

"Oh boy," Sam muttered. "Here we go."

Luke adjusted his ponytail. "The leash is not 'just' anything. It is the sacred source of the bond between the human and the animal in her care. It is the symbol of trust between the caregiver and the care receiver, that control and discipline will be used wisely and not merely to secure obedience when it is not otherwise necessary. The leash defines who leads, who follows, and, ultimately, who must be left behind. This is true whether it is the tether to a chopper flying low along the Mekong or an extend-a-leash wielded by a firm but caring hand."

Sam, Greg, and Beth stared at him. "IMHO," Luke added self-consciously, and then pressed his hands together and bowed. "*Namaste.*"

Beth sighed. "OK, Gandhi, so what the hell should I use?"

Sam pulled a Gordian knot of leashes from a drawer. "Just grab one of these and take him to the park before he pees on himself."

Beth freed a leash from the tangle while Hips waited patiently. She attached the leash and pulled a little too hard. The dog stumbled and yelped in surprise.

"You need to take the brake off," Luke said, and pushed a lever on one wheel of the device.

Beth threw Sam a pleading glance. "I'm not very good with living things."

"You'll be OK," Sam said. She thought about trying to be more encouraging, but rejected the idea; Beth hadn't earned that type of gratuitous kindness yet.

Beth pulled on the leash again and this time they made it to the shelter door without incident.

Following his injury, Hips no longer had the ability to wag his tail. The dog had learned to show affection in other ways, most often by leaning into his human companion. He did that now to Beth. Although she might not have known what it meant, Beth seemed to understand that it was a good thing; she smiled down at the dog.

Sam watched them leave and felt a tiny tug of jealousy.

After Beth and Hips were gone, Sam turned to Luke and Greg. "You're going to need to give her a chance."

"Why?" Greg challenged.

"Because she is us yesterday and maybe again tomorrow," Sam said.

"Nope," Greg said. "I was never a large white woman and don't intend to become one. Try again."

"Then because I said so," Sam answered.

"OK," Greg yielded. "If that's the best you can do."

"It is," Sam said.

Andy arrived, a dog at his side. "Hey, Doc, got a new one you need to take a look at."

"Christ, Andy. Not"—*one-more-living-thing*! she almost screamed, but she stopped herself when she noticed the dog's long-suffering face and Andy's hopeful smile. "Take him to my office. I'll be there in a minute."

Sam closed her eyes against the day, but instead of total darkness, she saw that enormous digital clock again. It was now in countdown mode.

Thirty days.

9

A ndy found Beth asleep on a bench under a large Central Park oak with Hips standing guard beside her. Hips trotted over to Andy and rested his head in the boy's hand.

"Don't bother my dog," Beth said with her eyes still closed. "I don't know if he bites."

"He doesn't," Andy said. "This is one of the sweetest creatures God has ever made."

"Yeah, well, I'm not taking any chances. And God's not here to vouch for him at the moment, so go away, please."

Andy didn't move. He was close to piking again, recalling the moment when he first found Hips, broken and bleeding in the park. He could see the bone jutting out of torn flesh, the unnatural twist of the dog's body, the huge brown eyes pleading for an explanation. Andy chased the bastards who did it deep into the park and made sure they understood what an aluminum bat felt like. They whimpered just like—

"Look," Beth said as she finally opened her eyes. "You're sort of creeping me out here, kid, so if you've got something to say…"

"Sorry." Andy rubbed his forehead with the heel of his hand. "Brain fart. Didn't mean to be rude." He removed his backpack and sat down on the bench next to Beth. "I'm Andy. Dr. Sam sent me over to make sure you didn't get lost or fall asleep."

"Well, I guess I didn't get lost."

An ancient black man with short silver hair, dark eyes almost lost in a deeply etched face, and a long black coat walked past the bench. The man paused for a moment and nodded at Andy. Andy shivered and the old man quickly moved on.

"So you're the shrink?" Andy asked.

"Was," Beth said. "Not my job anymore."

"Good."

"You don't care for mental health professionals?"

"Not really."

"Me neither. What do you do at the shelter?"

"I volunteer when I can. Sort of paying off a debt."

"Yeah, I know the feeling." Beth nodded to the violin case showing out of the top of the backpack. "Gun?"

"Some days. But today it's a violin."

"How do you know which one it's going to be?"

"Depends on which Andy I feed the most."

"Ah. So you just carry it around or do you use it?"

"The gun or the violin?"

"Both."

"Sometimes I use the violin."

"I was a musician too."

"Really?"

"No. But I used to play the bells in marching band in high school."

"That counts. Notes is notes."

"Not really. I never learned to read music, so I just kept hitting the same note over and over."

"Did anyone notice?"

"Yeah. They finally took my mallets away, so I just marched with the bells and pretended to hit them. Then they took my bells away.

That's when I took up the bass drum. Bad conduct followed. The usual 'girl loses glockenspiel' hard luck story."

Andy laughed. He usually wasn't good around new people—particularly shrinks—but he recognized another inhabitant of the island of misfit toys when he saw one. He always experienced a "mashed potatoes and mac and cheese" sense of comfort on those rare occasions when he found someone at least as screwed up as himself. And laughter was like kryptonite to piking—the two could not exist in the same space because laughter, like hope, was forward-looking. Andy had also found, however, that laughter was far too fleeting; his memories always returned and hope did not linger.

"Where do you—" Beth started to ask, but a human steroid advertisement texting on his iPhone rounded the path. Hips couldn't maneuver fast enough and the man stumbled over the dog. Hips yelped.

"Hey, watch it!" Andy shouted. The man continued without apology or even acknowledgment. "Dickhead!" Andy called after him.

That got the man's attention and he turned. "What'd you say, kid?"

Andy rose and stepped forward to meet him. Even though the man was several inches taller and about forty pounds heavier, Andy didn't seem to care. "I said, 'Get your head out of your ass, moron.' If you can't even pay enough attention in the world to avoid stepping on a crippled dog, what are you really doing here?"

"You gonna do something about it, faggot?" the man challenged.

Beth joined Andy. "Maybe we should just get back," she told him.

"Yeah, maybe you'd better," the man sneered, jabbing his finger into Andy's chest with each word. Hips growled at his tone.

Fingers . . . hands . . . dirty nails . . . a brutal touch. Andy felt the pull. Heat spread from his chest up through his neck to the top of his skull. His head throbbed and his eyes narrowed as he became completely quiet. All his muscles knotted. Someone looking at Andy objectively would have seen something older, larger, menacing—an animal balanced on an unpredictable precipice of violence.

The man must have seen something dangerous too because he faltered, took a step backward and then another. Andy advanced.

"We're cool," the man offered hopefully.

Andy shook his head slowly. "No." His voice was calm, a whisper. "We're not."

"I'm sorry, OK?" The man backed off another two steps.

"Let it go," Beth told Andy. "He said he's sorry."

After one last frightened glance at Andy, the man turned and walked away from them at a pace just short of a jog.

Once the big man cleared the corner and disappeared, Andy's shoulders dropped and his eyes widened and cleared. He had returned.

"Sorry. I don't like bullies," Andy confessed.

"Yeah, I got that," Beth responded. "Just curious. What would've happened if the guy hadn't backed down?"

Andy shrugged. "I'm sure we would've worked something out."

Beth appeared to ponder that answer. "So, just between us, are you dangerous?"

Andy laughed. "Were you a good mental health professional?"

"No. Not really."

"OK then. Just between us? Only on days when it's a gun."

Beth nodded. "Actually, I'm oddly comforted by that," she said.

As they walked back to the shelter with Hips between them, Andy worked hard to forget the memory of hands reaching out for him in the darkness.

10

At seven that evening, Sam ran into the shelter's break room and found Beth on the floor with Hips nestled in the crook of her arm. The dog looked so comfortable in the shrink's company that Sam hesitated. But delay was not possible. "I need another pair of hands," Sam said.

"Huh?"

"I let everyone else go for the night and I need some help."

"But I just—"

"Now, Beth!" Sam snapped.

Beth rose shakily. "You are such a bully . . . but I can see how some men might get turned on by that."

Sam grabbed her by the arm and tugged her into the first open room.

Beth gasped. Little Bro flailed on a metal table, heaving uncontrollably. Bloody vomit sprayed from his mouth. "Holy shit," Beth muttered.

"Beth, meet Little Bro. An Andy special."

Without any further argument, Beth pushed up her sleeves. "Just tell me what to do."

"I shot him up, but it's not doing crap. Hold him still. I need a vein."

"This I can do." Ignoring the bloodstained vomit, Beth threw her arms around the dog's body in a massive bear hug, pinning the dog against the table.

Sam inserted the needle end of the IV line into the dog's front leg. "You're pretty good at this," Sam said.

"Rotation at Bellevue," Beth explained. "Sometimes you need to hold a patient until help arrives. Plus I'm actually freakishly strong."

"OK, I'm in." Sam secured the IV needle with tape and checked the line to make sure the saline solution was flowing properly. When she was certain the line was set and working, she filled a syringe from a small vial and injected it into a port in the IV. "Just another minute for this to work."

In less than sixty seconds, the dog's movements under Beth's body began to slow. "We're good," Sam said. "You can get off him while I examine."

Beth stood upright and stretched her back. She glanced down at her bloodstained front. "I feel like a human Tampax. Will anything get this out?"

"It's very goth. I'd leave it."

Another Beth shrug—this one apparently meaning "OK with me."

Sam felt the dog's abdomen, looked into his eyes with a penlight, and then listened to his chest with the stethoscope.

"Is he going to be OK?" Beth asked.

"No," Sam answered, and tossed her stethoscope on the table. "He crapped out."

"What?"

"He's gone."

"He's dead? You're sure?"

"The fact that his heart's stopped and he's not breathing is really the giveaway. I went to vet school and all."

"But it was so quick." Beth's voice trembled. "I expected there to be...I don't know—"

"Angels blowing golden trumpets? A celestial light dropping down from the ceiling?" Sam asked with a bitterness that surprised even her.

"No. Just…more, I guess."

Sam saw the confusion in Beth's face and felt some of her armor loosen. "That's all there is. They are here, and then they're not. If they're lucky, it's a sudden stillness, nothing more."

Beth ran to the nearby sink. Her lunch came up in a rush. She rinsed her mouth and the sink and turned back to Sam. "Well, that was professional, wasn't it?" Beth said with a weak smile.

Sam smiled back sympathetically. "At least you made it to the sink. I often don't. Come on. I'll buy you dinner. A nice bloody steak. Put you right on your feet."

Beth gagged at the word *bloody*. "You really are a pleasure, aren't you?"

In the booth of a diner a block from the shelter, Beth worked her way through a burger, fries, and a vanilla shake while Sam largely ignored her salad and nursed a beer. Beth had changed into a large T-shirt that said, "Forecast tonight: Drugs, followed by impaired judgment, ending with poor decisions. Forecast tomorrow: More drugs…"

Between bites, Beth said, "Sorry I was such a bitch this morning. I spoke to my lawyer today. I do prefer avoiding the orange jumpsuit on the side of the parkway and he tells me you had a lot to do with that. So thanks."

"I just needed the hands. It's not personal." Sam took a long pull from her bottle and noticed Beth watching her swallow too closely. The recognition hit her mid-gulp. "Does the beer bother you?"

"Nah. I was never a beer kind of girl. Mine was a terrible struggle between eating something salty to get the sweet taste out of my mouth and then eating something sweet to get the salty taste out of my mouth. Witness…" Beth popped a French fry in her mouth and then washed it down with some shake. She made a slight bow. "Ta-da!"

"Yeah, but they don't give you probation for that."

"No. They don't. But you'd be surprised how slippery the slope actually is. One day you're sitting around watching *Ellen*, alternating between Mr. Peanut and the M&M man, and the next day you're playing with Mr. Vicodin and Ms. OxyContin. Before you know it, you're entering a plea deal, giving up your license, and enjoying all the comforts that probation has to offer."

"If you believe the probation report, your fall from grace was a little more complicated."

"Sure it was," Beth said. "We'd all like to think we're complicated, but ninety-nine percent of the time, the entirety of the difference between hero and pariah is one, maybe two, well-timed decisions."

"I don't believe that," Sam said.

"Maybe you just haven't faced those decisions yet. Nevertheless, here I am—your newest blood-soaked probie."

"Sorry I had to drag you into that scene back there. That's never pretty."

"What do you think happened?"

"An old, neglected dog who had spent too long on the streets eating all sorts of garbage. Probably a gastric hemorrhage. Don't worry, you can't catch it."

"I wasn't worried. Just wondering."

"Don't think about it too hard. You might start to care."

"Unlikely. So this shelter, what are you, like some Statue of Liberty for the mentally ill?"

"Just your usual urban mix of depressed, anxious, overburdened, grieving, insecure, obsessive-compulsive, socially avoidant upstanding citizens. I thought you'd feel right at home."

"I do. But usually I'm sitting in a comfy chair and they're lying down on a couch."

"Just care for the animals and be pleasant and understanding. You'll be fine."

"So basically, you want me to be something I'm not."

"Exactly. Think of it as a growing experience."

"I'm big enough."

"Then think of it as something you need to do to avoid cleaning up garbage on the Cross Bronx Expressway in that orange jumpsuit."

"Much clearer, thank you." They chewed in silence for a few moments. "I just don't want you to expect too much from me...I disappoint people."

"You handled Hips pretty well. I think having you with us will be helpful." *At least for the next thirty days*, Sam thought about adding, but she saw her internal TMI light blink on and held back. She grabbed for her beer. Vodka to follow at home later once she was alone. In a month she wouldn't even need to pretend to be functional.

"For a bright woman, you really are pretty dense." Beth leaned forward. "There's a reason why the government takes your license away for life. That's a pretty big deal, you know? I'm a danger to my patients, my judgment has been impaired—or didn't you read that part of the probation report?"

"I read it. I also read that you were really brilliant once. They took away your license to prescribe meds, I get it. But they didn't suck out your brain, did they?"

"No, but all they left me were words to work with, instead of my arsenal of psychopharmacologic friends."

"Words matter. Sometimes even just one," Sam countered.

"Maybe once they did, once they held power. But we don't believe in them anymore. They're just filler until you get out the prescription pad."

"Your cynicism feels a bit practiced to me."

"Funny. My ex used to tell me the same thing. It's only slightly less annoying when you say it."

"You were married?"

"Surprising, isn't it?"

"No, I just meant—"

"There's a seat for every ass. And there was a time when my ass wasn't nearly so big. How about you?"

"How about me what?"

Beth pushed her palms out. "It's OK. We don't need to get personal, Doctor."

"Good. I don't do personal anymore."

"Thank God. I was worried we might start having the same menstrual cycle." Beth scrutinized Sam's face. "Besides, I can already tell—you're a dumper, not a dumpee."

"How's that?"

"You're surrounded all day by dogs that adore and depend on you and give you unconditional love. No man can compete with that. It's like using a vibrating personal massager: everyone else is somewhere between slightly and very disappointing. Anyway, you do have that coldness just around the eyes."

Sam suddenly found the composition of her salad intensely interesting. It wasn't the first time someone had called her cold. Charlie had made it his mantra toward the end, alternating that with the word *angry*. But it was impossible for Sam to pretend it didn't sting. "See?" Sam said without looking up. "You're not as dumb as you look."

"Oops." Beth leaned back. "I was just joking. I didn't intend to hit a real nerve."

"You've just made my point—words do matter."

"Nope, you've just made mine—I'm an instrument of damage."

"No real damage. It's just that I didn't realize I was so easy to place."

"Don't feel bad. This is New York. We're all one-dimensional stereotypes. It's what makes us so unique."

Sam's cell phone rang. She checked the number and debated whether to answer it.

"Take it," Beth said. "I've got to pee anyway." She left the table.

"Hey, Bill," Sam answered. "Can I call you back tomorrow?"

Sam knew the answer when she heard the tone of Ackerman's voice. "It's important," he said. "Something's going on. They won't let me take your dogs."

"I don't understand."

"I put in the order for the additional cages and supplies to handle your dogs. I got a call back that the request was being denied."

"Probably just about what's in the budget. I'll find a way to get that stuff for you. We'll work it out."

"That's not the end of the story. I made some inquiries to find out why. I think this is personal, Sam. You must've really pissed someone off. They aren't going to allow me to take your dogs. They're being very aggressive. If you don't find them homes, they will all end up in Central."

The appeal, Sam thought. She knew she had angered some people at the city, but would they really take it out on her dogs? That was just so wrong in so many ways.

The ceiling of the diner suddenly felt too low. The walls too close.

"Sam? Are you there?" Bill asked.

She managed a barely audible response.

"I'm so sorry," he said. "I'll keep trying."

She disconnected the phone in a daze.

Beth returned to the table. "What's wrong? Now you look like the one who's gonna hurl."

"I've got to get back to the shelter."

"Because of what I said?"

Sam shook her head. She didn't trust herself to speak over the one thought pounding in her head—she would not be able to save her dogs.

II

A ndy stopped in the little supermarket on 109th for his evening
supplies and then headed east toward Central Park.

Near Columbus Avenue he felt someone tap him on the elbow. He
turned and peered down into blue eyes surrounded by a porcelain face.
"Andy, right?" she said, extending her hand. Andy took it. "Catherine.
My friends call me Cat. We're in—"

"—Music theory together. Oboe, right?"

"Right. You live around here?"

Andy shook his head. "The dorms."

"Me too," she said brightly. "But I don't think I've seen you outside
of class."

"I haven't spent a lot of time on campus," he said quickly. "Between
work and practice . . . you know."

"You work too?"

"Yeah. Part of my deal at the school."

"Must be hard to get it all done. No wonder I never see you around."

"It makes for some late nights."

"So what do you think of Professor Morrison?" Cat asked.

"He's alright. I think he tries too hard to convince us that dissonance is beautiful…I mean some things are just painful to hear…they should be." He almost added that there is power in that pain, but didn't want to come off sounding like some freak.

Cat seemed to ponder his answer and then came to a decision. "Hey, you feel like getting a cup of coffee or something?" she asked. "Go over some stuff from the class?"

Andy shifted uneasily. "Um?"

"There must be a Starbucks somewhere around here. I mean if you don't need to be somewhere or…you know…meet someone."

"I'd like to, but I'm, uh, sorta seeing someone."

Andy saw a flash of disappointment, but Cat recovered quickly with a smile. "Kinda, sorta, maybe, huh?" she said playfully. "It's complicated?"

"Yeah. And I don't think she would like it so much if I was late because I stopped for coffee and what I'm sure will be great conversation with a beautiful girl."

"You do know how to let a girl down easy, I'll say that for you. See you in class. If you change your mind…" Cat touched his hand and turned in the other direction.

Andy felt that touch. He couldn't deny it. But he quickly put the girl out of his mind. There was no point in dwelling. That could not be his future anymore. He just kept walking.

Outside the entrance to a five-story walk-up on Columbus Avenue, a blue-and-white police sawhorse barricade manned by two cops blocked Andy's path. Another barricade fifteen feet away halted pedestrian traffic coming from the other direction. Two police cars with flashing bubble lights sandwiched a nondescript white van on the street.

"Hold up a sec," one of the cops told Andy and the twenty others on his side of the barricade waiting to continue down the street.

Two men in blue vinyl hazmat suits complete with protective hoods, heavy gloves, and the department of health insignia emerged from the walk-up carrying a rectangular object five feet by four feet by two feet and wrapped in a blue tarp. Andy heard the panicked coos and the desperate flapping of wings coming from beneath the tarp and realized that this was one of the pigeon traps he'd heard about. Since the current belief was that the virus sickening Riverside kids was avian, the city and state departments of health had placed traps on the roofs of several neighborhood buildings to capture live pigeons and other birds for examination and testing.

A cop opened the van door and the men in the protective gear tossed the wrapped trap into the back. Birds screamed at the impact. The workers slammed the door closed, cutting off further complaint. The emphasis clearly was on speed—getting the trap off the sidewalk and into the van as quickly as possible—and not the well-being of the birds. Andy assumed this meant the birds were not long for this world. The van sped off with the two police cars as escort. He knew he could do nothing for the birds, but as a witness to their capture, Andy still felt guilty.

Cops removed the street barricades and urged the crowd to keep walking.

Andy couldn't get his legs to listen. The image of the birds locked in darkness, waiting for hands to grab them and pin their bodies to some metal table, was paralyzing. He remembered that sensation... hands squeezing...a dog snarling in the darkness...the back of a hand against his cheek...a bitter taste...

"Hey, Andy? You OK?" Kendall came up next to him.

It was enough to drag Andy back to the moment. "Yeah. Sure, Sergeant. Just sad, I guess. Those birds..."

"I know. I could tell you that they'll be tested and released but you'd know I was lying, right?"

Andy nodded.

Kendall looked up at the roof of the walk-up and the darkening sky. "It sounds horrible to say out loud, but thank God it's only pigeons."

Andy followed Kendall's upward gaze. He shook his head. "Why would we thank him for that?"

There was a long pause before Kendall answered in a voice thinned by worry. "Because there's always some other version of reality lurking around a corner that can put us in a much darker place. Get home safe, Andy," he said.

Andy knew that Kendall was probably right about that, but he was done with being thankful just because things were not quite as horrible as they might have been.

12

Kendall watched Andy continue down the street. *That's an odd one,* he thought.

The cop and the boy had had some difficult interactions when Kendall first came to the neighborhood. Andy bristled at anything even vaguely resembling the exercise of power and authority. They had managed to work things out after Andy realized that Kendall was not at all arbitrary and once they discovered their shared love of dogs. Still, Kendall always worried that Andy would cross paths with someone less willing to compromise and more intolerant of the kid's idiosyncrasies.

Kendall checked his watch. He was now officially off shift, but needed to stop by Sid's place before heading home. He was looking forward to the visit.

A well-stocked hardware store run by a proprietor knowledgeable about what is on the shelves can be critical to a city neighborhood, particularly if that proprietor is also an experienced locksmith. Riverside Hardware and Locks was precisely what a city hardware store should be. The aisles were cramped together to make more room for shelving. The shelves were overflowing with items organized so faithfully in accord with the rules of chaos, entropy, and inertia that only the proprietor could find anything, and this Sid Gold did happily for his customers with extraordinary speed and unfailing accuracy.

Kendall pushed the front door open and heard the bell above the door jingle. For some reason Kendall always found that little bell comforting—a gentle reminder of welcome. Sid came out from behind the counter and shook Kendall's big hand.

"Jim! So glad you came by."

"Thanks for helping me with this."

"Come," Sid said, and brought him to the counter. "I have it here." Sid took out a thick volume about the size of the phone book and opened it to a section near the back of glossy photos of girls' bicycles. "Deb will be ten, yes?"

Kendall felt uncomfortable looking at bikes for his daughter the same day a child in his neighborhood had died. There was something fate-tempting about it. But ten was a big birthday and he wanted to be sure they could get the bike in time. He had checked on Amazon, but quickly become overwhelmed with options and strangers' reviews. He didn't want to select a bike for his girl just because Ann in Idaho gave it five stars; he wanted someone he knew and trusted to help him pick. "Yeah. She's been begging for a big-girl bike, you know, with speeds and stuff...something that maybe can grow with her for a few years."

"No more bells or tassels, got it."

They slowly examined some of the bike photos and descriptions. Sid offered opinions and comparisons, but Kendall found it hard to concentrate.

"Do you want to do this another time?" Sid offered.

"No, why?"

"Because I just told you that this model comes in the form of a hippopotamus and you said, 'Fine.'"

"I'm sorry, Sid."

"You're worried?"

"Terrified, actually."

"Please don't take this the wrong way, but you would not be the man I know you to be if you weren't."

Kendall wanted to tell Sid that he was wrong, that Sergeant James Kendall of the New York City Police Department really was not that man. But Kendall, as always, remained silent because a knight could not show that kind of fallibility and remain respected.

Kendall nudged the catalog back toward Sid. "Which would you recommend?"

Sid pointed to a beautiful red five-speed in the middle of the page. "There are other bikes that are more expensive, but this one is well-made, dependable, and fun to ride. I buy them for my grandkids."

Kendall read the price and blanched. A cop's salary had its limitations.

Sid must have noticed. "Ignore that price. That's retail. You do not pay retail."

"I can't let you do that. I can't take a discount because I'm a cop."

Sid playfully punched Kendall in the arm. "Not because you're a cop, you goof. Because you're my neighbor."

"But—"

"Don't worry about me. I charge you a nice twenty percent markup on flashlights, batteries, and deadlocks, but I choose not to make a profit on a child's birthday present."

Ten minutes later Kendall left Sid's store a bit lighter for the conversation and grateful once again for the people who lived in the place he called home.

Because it was a school night and Deb was either already asleep or on her way, Kendall unlocked and opened the door to his apartment as quietly as he could. He ducked inside and passed the photos of his family in the hallway—of his wife and daughter, his mother-in-law in New

Jersey, and Phoenix both as a young German shepherd puppy and as an adult.

He found Ellen sitting at the kitchen table and gave her a kiss on the cheek. "Deb asleep?"

"Just. Rough evening."

"I'm sorry."

"Not your fault, hon. But you asked." She placed a plate of hot food and a can of ginger ale in front of him.

"What happened?"

"The department of ed is going to close the school till the weekend. Some kids from the school are sick."

Kendall pushed his plate away. "Anyone in Deb's class?"

"No. Not yet. But one of my fourth graders has been out with symptoms that sound too close for my comfort. All the kids were talking about the virus today. The teachers have been trying to keep everyone calm, but the department of health came to do some testing and scared the hell out of everyone."

"In hazmat?"

"Yes, but no masks, thank God. Deb asked me if I thought she would get sick." Ellen's voice cracked and Kendall reached for her hand.

"What did you say?"

"I said what a parent is supposed to say. I guess I wasn't all that convincing. Have you heard anything more?"

"No. The brass has been so tight-lipped. I did see some bird trapping on the way home, so I guess they're throwing a lot of resources at it. We should have some new information soon. In the meantime, we're supposed to reassure everyone."

"That's not good enough."

"What do you mean?"

"I'm going to take Deb to my mother's for a few days."

"You don't think that's a bit overreacting? It's only been a handful of kids out of how many? A few thousand living in Riverside?"

Ellen moved her hand away. "One of whom died."

"Unfortunately, kids die of the flu every year. Lots of kids, actually."

"Not like this, Jim. Not just in one neighborhood. Not in my school. You're not totally creeped out by this?"

"Yeah, sure I am."

"Then come with us. You've got loads of vacation and personal time due."

"I can't. I have a responsibility to—"

"Your wife and your daughter."

"And to this community that I serve."

"I know how you feel about your job, Jim. I love that about you, but you're not the mayor. You're just a cop. And when the shit hits the fan—and I believe it will—the brass and the mayor are not going to hesitate to throw people like you to the lions."

"I can't go. I need to face these people. I'm not going to run out on them."

"You really think they care?"

"Yeah. Actually, I think some do."

"When are you going to wise up and stop being so selfish?"

"How's that?"

"You wanted us to move to this neighborhood. We did. You wanted me to switch schools. I did. You wanted to go on the street instead of taking a desk sergeant job and expected me to hold my breath every time the damn phone rings when you're on the job. I do. Now I ask you for one thing to help give me peace of mind and you act like I'm asking the president to step down."

Like all married couples, Kendall and his wife knew how to argue, but this fight felt different to him. "What's with you?" he asked.

Ellen buried her face in her hands.

"What is it?" he repeated.

When his wife looked at him again, anguish had distorted her normally beautiful features. "I don't just teach these kids fractions and verbs. I escort these kids to the bathroom. I wipe the snot from their noses. I give them my lunch when they come to me hungry. I comfort them when they are scared, or at least I try. For seven hours every day, five days a week, I am their mother, teacher, and friend. And today... today I had to look into little faces terrified by this invisible monster called the Riverside Virus and answer all their questions about what it means to die."

Kendall took her in his arms because he didn't know what to say.

"Mommy? Are you OK?" Deb had stepped into the kitchen behind them.

"Of course, sweetie," Ellen said, and pulled away from her husband. "Some water just went down the wrong way."

Kendall held his arms open. "Come here, baby." Deb collapsed into him and he squeezed her until she giggled. "I would like the privilege of putting you back to bed, young lady."

Deb allowed her father to lead her out of the kitchen. When he looked back at his wife, she was cleaning off the kitchen table, but her eyes were lost in troubled thoughts he couldn't decipher.

13

Gabriel stood before the dusty Riverside Church sign with a box of tiny white plastic letters. It had started to rain, and Gabriel hoped there would be enough of a downpour to rinse the sign clean by morning. He stuck a plastic *D* on the sign and stepped back to review his work: "Isaiah 65:25: 'And the lion shall eat straw like the ox; and dust shall be the serpent's meat. They shall not hurt nor destroy in all my holy mountain, saith the Lord.'"

He thought it seemed appropriate for the day.

"Nice." Sid stepped behind him, an open umbrella in his hand. "But it would look better if the sign was about two feet larger. I'm thinking white backlighting, black block lettering. Size does matter, you know?"

"If people don't want to take the time to squint to get some meaning, well then screw them," Gabriel answered.

"Just let me show you some options—"

"I'm really not interested in a new sign, Sid."

For years Channa had tried to convince Gabriel that he should love the man behind the hardware store counter. Channa had made sure there were many opportunities for the two men to interact, including

Shabbat meals, casual dinner parties, and a weekly book club meeting at her store. Although she was one of the most perceptive people Gabriel had ever known, Channa had never discovered the truth behind the priest's ambient hostility toward her husband.

When Channa had succumbed to cancer a year ago, she had taken a significant part of both men with her. But it was what she had left behind that made dealing with Sid so difficult. Sid had become a widower, entitled to the sympathetic nods of friends and strangers alike. Sid had his memories of kisses, long evenings under the blankets, children—all those transformative elements of a married life that made two souls forever something greater by their combination. Gabriel, in stark contrast, had only his books, some photos, and a pathetic dream of a shameful future that had been impossible even when Channa was alive.

"I will drop the subject...for now," Sid agreed. "I'm heading over to the diner for a late dinner. Would you like to join me?"

Gabriel gave Sid the same answer he had given to the twenty previous offers. "Sorry. Can't tonight. Too much to do." Gabriel was getting tired of being made into the bad guy. He just wanted everyone to leave him alone.

Sid sighed at the rejection. "You know, Channa would have—"

"Channa's gone, Sidney," Gabriel snapped. He regretted the words as soon as he'd said them.

Sid chewed his lower lip as his eyes became wet. "Of this fact, Father, I assure you I am well aware." Sid turned away.

"Sid, wait! I'm sorry. That was—"

Sid ignored him and continued down the street.

"I'm sorry!" Gabriel called after him.

Sid either didn't hear him or didn't care.

Gabriel punched the church sign and all of his carefully placed lettering fell to the bottom except for one *T* and one *L*.

14

The rain was punishing by the time Sam and Beth left the diner. Neither carried an umbrella, although it was the type of city rain that quickly made such devices useless. Beth jumped on the subway to her mandatory AA meeting and Sam ran back to the shelter, where Nick and her contacts list waited.

Sam was at the reception desk working the phones even before she dried herself. She first called people she knew at the other animal shelters in Brooklyn, Queens, Staten Island, and the Bronx. They were all fourteen-day kill centers—"no exceptions." Then she tried the emergency numbers at the suburban shelters in Westchester, Nassau, Rockland, and Suffolk. The few that were no-kill were already overfilled and not accepting any transfers. Her contacts in the animal rescue world were hugely sympathetic about her situation but entirely unhelpful. Too many lost, abused, and abandoned dogs and too few willing and able hearts.

After ninety frustrating minutes on the phone, Sam lowered her head to the desktop. After ninety-five minutes she was banging her head on it to the refrain of "Stupid…stupid…stupid," while Nick looked on curiously. *Stupid* because somehow she had convinced herself that things were going to be OK when in reality she had known beyond any reasonable degree of doubt that things never turned out that way. *Stupid* because she had assumed that someone—at least just one person—would care as much about her dogs as she did. Worst of all, *stupid* because she had totally ignored the rule of "Sam's Razor"— when things go wrong, and they always do, animals are the first to take it in the neck.

She might have gone on smacking her head until she drew blood, but the loud knock on the front door startled her. Nick growled and took a protective position in front of the desk.

Sam checked her watch—9:35—and reached for the baseball bat leaning against the wall. At this hour and in this neighborhood, it could be the police looking for help with an injured stray, a junkie looking to score drugs, or just a drunk banging on the wrong door. She had dealt with all of those situations more than once.

Sam crept to the door with the bat in her hand. The banging became more insistent, almost panicked. She was a few seconds away from calling Kendall, but didn't want to appear like a wuss, so she slowly lifted the blinds covering the closest window for a peek.

A face suddenly pressed against the window, the features distorted by the glass and the rain. In her exhausted state, Sam thought of the last stupid scary movie she'd watched on Netflix. Her heart raced in the face of the obvious fight-or-flight scenario. Nick snarled and lunged forward.

"Dr. Lewis?" the deep voice called over the rain. "Can I come in, please?"

At least it was polite. "We're closed."

"Yeah, I can see that. And in thirty days I know you'll be closed for good."

That answer threw her. "Who are you?"

"I'm the bastard who's shutting you down. My name is Tom Walden. I'm the assistant deputy mayor." He held up his identification card to the window. "I just want to talk to you."

"That's why I have a lawyer." *Had a lawyer*, she mentally corrected herself.

"Yeah. We've done that. I was hoping we could maybe talk like rational people."

"This is still my place for thirty days."

"I'm asking, Dr. Lewis, not demanding. But you really don't have anything more to lose."

Sam figured he was right about that. "OK. But I've got a mean dog right next to me. He's very protective."

"I'm really wet and I actually like dogs. I'll take my chances."

Sam unlocked the door and let the man in. He shook his umbrella out onto the sidewalk and entered.

Tom Walden looked tall, wet, and very tired. He had a mop of black hair that hung damp in his eyes. Sam guessed he was a few years older than she was, but that was hard to tell between the dripping water and her seething anger.

Nick eyed him warily, but Tom immediately dropped to a knee and let the dog sniff him. "Who's this beautiful guy?"

"His name is Nick, and I'd be careful."

"Who's a good boy? Nicky's a good boy." Tom said these words with just the right tone and pitch so that Nick finally wagged his tail. Tom rewarded the dog with a rub on the ears and a scratch under his chin, all the while repeating, "Such a good boy." Nick glanced back at Sam for approval, but something about her demeanor must have translated into the word *traitor* in canine because Nick guiltily slunk back to her side.

Tom rose. "Well this is awkward, right?" There was a self-conscious boyishness to him. Sam assumed it was all an act and found it instantly irritating.

"What are you doing here, Mr. . . . ?"

"Walden. Tom Walden. I would offer you my hand, but I'm assuming you wouldn't take it."

"You would be correct, sir."

"Your dog seemed to be OK with me."

"My dog drinks from the toilet. We have different standards. Are you here to gloat? Is that what assistant deputy mayors do in their spare time these days?"

"Actually, no. They try to save the lives of little girls and boys."

"How do you do that? By shutting down shelters and killing old dogs?"

"This isn't about the shelter . . . at least not directly. I'm here because I need your help."

"You're joking, right?"

"I wish."

"This is absurd on so many levels." Sam made a point of looking around the room. "You have a camera hidden here somewhere? This video is going on the 'Practical Jokes in Seriously Poor Taste' blog?"

"No joke. Here's the deal. I'm just going to be straight with you."

Sam couldn't help rolling her eyes. "I have no doubt."

"The Riverside Virus is spreading. The CDC has hit a roadblock in its investigation and the state agencies are, well . . . not as far along as the mayor would like."

"You do realize that I am assuming everything you are telling me at this point is a lie, right?"

"A kid died from the virus. That's not a lie. Another kid probably won't make it through the night. Also not a lie. Four new cases reported. Not a lie."

When put that way, the virus was no longer abstract; Sam thought of dark dirt holes surrounded by families in unimaginable despair. "What do you want?"

"The city needs a consultant to work with us. Someone who can give us some independent advice about handling this situation without— how can I put this?—other agendas. We need someone of our own."

"Let the CDC do its job. I'm sure they have the best people on it."

"The fact is that the CDC *doesn't* have the best person to put on it," Tom said. "I'm here because the city needs you."

"Needs me? Me?" Sam scoffed. "Now I know you're full of shit. I'm just a vet. I'm not even a zoonotic virologist like—" The realization suddenly hit her. "You bastard!" Nick stood at her tone. Sam's entire body shook with rage. "The thirty-day notice...telling Bill he couldn't take my dogs? And now you just stroll in because you happen to need this favor?"

"It's not like that."

"Bill was right: this is personal, but it isn't about the appeal at all, is it? You set me up."

"You've got it wrong. The decision to close the shelter was made over a year ago. You brought the timing on yourself. And I had nothing to do with the decision about the transfer to the East Side shelter."

"Then why do you know about it?"

"I was briefed. That's all."

"So this is all a happy coincidence. Right? Go peddle your bullshit somewhere else, Walden. I'm not buying. You're just an extortionist."

"You don't need to believe me. Kids will still die whether you believe me or not. I've been to the hospital. I've seen the children... I've seen what the virus is doing...what it can do. We need your help and I've been sent here to get it."

Sam thought that Walden really could do the "genuine" thing well. But she had seen better performances. "I can't help you."

"He's one of the world's leading authorities on responding to zoonotic illness in urban environments. He was the leader in the Legionnaire's disease investigation. He is credited with preventing a SARS epidemic in this country. He has worked on the creation of innumerable vaccines for animal-borne illnesses. He—"

"I know exactly what he's done. I've lived through it."

"OK, so I get he wasn't Dad of the Year, but this is bigger than your family issues."

"You have no idea what you're talking about."

"You're right. I don't. All I know is that you two were—what's the polite word for it?—'estranged' at one point."

"So now you've been looking into my family? You really have no boundaries, do you?"

"Very few when it comes to saving kids."

"If you know so much, then you know you're talking to the wrong person. Why don't you just go and ask him? Call Cornell yourself."

Tom frowned at that answer. "He's not at Cornell anymore."

"You're wrong. He'd never leave Cornell. That place was his life and he's got nothing else now. He's just playing hard to get. Big egos. I'm sure you know how that is."

"He's not there anymore. Left. Gave up his tenure and left."

"He must be at some other vet school then. He didn't just disappear."

"Actually he did. He's completely off the grid. No schools, no publications, no active research grants. No one can find him. That's why I came to you. I thought you might at least know where he is."

"Not a clue. Of all people, why would you think I'd know?"

"Because you are still his only child. In my experience—"

"I don't really give a rat's ass about your experience, Walden."

"May I be blunt with you?"

"Is *blunt* different than *straight*?"

Tom ignored the jab. "It's just very important that I reach him and get him involved in this before . . . um . . . well, as soon as possible. If you help me secure his assistance, I can get you another thirty days on the lease. That will give you more time to find homes—"

"Thirty days is meaningless to the crowd I need to place."

"That's the best I can do. I don't have authority for anything more, and even that's pushing it."

"I said no. Your little setup isn't going to work. I'll find homes for my dogs. Are we done now?"

Tom took out a business card and placed it on the reception table.

"This has work and cell. Call me if you change your mind. Whatever you might think of me, I promise you I'm trying to do the best for those kids."

"I don't believe you even a little."

"Wow. Someone really must have done a number on you to allow you to believe I would lie about saving kids."

"I sorta find it hard to trust that someone who is so willing to kill a bunch of dogs for a little extra city revenue has such a golden heart."

"That's not—"

"But even if I did believe you, I couldn't help you. I didn't even know my father left Cornell. If you can't find him with your vast resources, I certainly can't. Now if you don't mind, I need to get back to doing what I can do to save my dogs in the limited time that I've still got."

Tom raised his hands in defeat and walked out of the shelter into the rain.

Wait! she wanted to yell as she watched him go. *Wait until I can find someone to tell me I'm making the right decision. Wait until I know for certain that I can't help those kids. Wait until the soundtrack kicks in and I can hear whether the music is sad or upbeat and full of promise. At least wait until I really know you are full of shit, Tom Walden, because the thought that you are telling me the truth is too overwhelming to bear.*

But she said none of these things and instead locked the door behind him.

Sam felt panic begin to swallow her anger. Too many living things were dependent upon the soundness of her decision-making and she knew that making choices had never been her strength.

Sam retreated to her office, pulled a large volume from her shelves, and dropped it onto her desk. She ran her finger over the gold lettering on the cover—*Studies in Zoonotic Pathogeneses*, by Daniel Lewis, DVM, MD.

Sam opened the book to an inscription inside the front cover, although she could recite the words from memory. "To my very best student. Love always, Dad."

She slammed the book closed and threw it against the wall, where it left a scar in the drywall before dropping to the floor.

Another scar. Sam almost laughed. Her father still excelled at making scars.

Sam had been only six, holding tightly to the bloody body of Hugo, her huge orange tabby, when she'd first learned that her father could perform magic.

As an only child, Sam had delighted in the company of her animals. Two dogs, four cats, a parrot, and three guinea pigs brought her full and fun days, so much so that she never really felt the absence of a connection her own age and species. Her animals, having grown up together, generally shared their time without serious conflict.

Her best days were filled with fancy tea parties, an animal at every place setting, discussing the serious matters of the moment—squirrels should not be chased, mice were friends, the dogs needed to respect the sanctity of the cats' food dishes and litter boxes, toys were for sharing. Sam felt safe in their company and proud to have been included among them. Hugo, the oldest and wisest of her animal friends, always sat on her right and stood guard over them all. When Sam slept she was surrounded by fur and the soothing sounds of canine snores and feline contentment.

During the day Hugo was as docile and comforting as a fluffy pillow, but at night he liked to prowl the woods around their house near Cornell. He would sometimes bring home a mouse or a mole from his nocturnal life and occasionally show up in the morning with a few scratches. But he always came back to take his place at the very top of Sam's pillow.

When he wasn't in Sam's bed that morning, she knew something was wrong. Sam ran out of the house and into the woods. She found him barely conscious by an old tree stump, his breathing shallow and blood leaking out of a gash in his abdomen. Sam scooped Hugo into her arms and yelled out for the one person she knew could help.

"Daddy!"

Sam's father, Daniel, came running out of the house in the goofy slippers she'd given him for Christmas, his bathrobe flapping behind him and half his face still covered in shaving cream. He gently took Hugo and quickly examined the wound.

"Fix him," Sam begged. "Please, Daddy."

Her father squeezed the big cat against his chest with one arm, oblivious to the blood seeping onto his robe, as he reached for Sam's hand with the other.

"Can you fix him?" Sam asked in a voice terrified of the wrong answer.

Her father looked upon his little girl's face and smiled. "Nothing bad is going to happen in our house," he said. "I promise."

Sam would learn much later in life that her father's words had been a lie—not only did bad things happen, he was the vehicle that had brought darkness to their house. But on that particular day, with that particular cat, he was true to his word. On that day his hands were touched by whatever force or energy allows a healer to cheat death. He was a magician. He was golden.

Hugo survived and the love Sam felt for her father that day lasted for a very long time.

Sam adored her "Dr. Daddy," and she watched closely in those early years as he treated Sam's animals. He could prolong life and comfort her creatures when they were in pain. That was the best kind of magic. She wanted to do that.

As a teen and through college, Sam began to see up close the characteristics that made Daniel Lewis a brilliant scientist: his tireless drive to find answers, his unwillingness to compromise, his ability to filter out all distractions, emotional and otherwise. She first emulated those characteristics and then took them on as her own as she followed his path to Cornell University College of Veterinary Medicine. While Daniel traveled the world looking for animal-related viruses to study and conquer, Sam volunteered her summers and holidays (at her father's suggestion, of course) at the animal hospital run by one of his well-known research colleagues—Jacqueline Morgan.

Sam's mother, Grace, carefully insulated Sam from any consequences resulting from Daniel's absences. If Sam noticed her mother's growing sadness, the daughter was too busy "succeeding" and trying to earn her father's approval to do anything about it.

The cracks began to appear in earnest in Sam's third year of vet school. Her father returned from some disease outbreak in Sierra Leone (or Liberia, or Haiti, or China) obsessed with finding what he called "the Bullet." Daniel theorized that it was possible to develop a single vaccine that could prevent the transmission to humans of all zoonotic viruses—Ebola, SARS, avian and swine flu, rabies, and hundreds of other diseases that come to us from our winged, furred, or scaled earth cohabitants. According to Dr. Lewis's research papers at the time, using the map of the human genome, it should be possible to take those genetic elements that define us as distinctly "human" and every other creature as something "other" and enhance them so that the viruses cannot take hold in the human body. "Exaggerate our inherent genetic differences to create a barrier to protect us," he was often quoted as saying. By doing so, Daniel Lewis hoped to save untold human lives, but also the lives of millions of animals killed every year through culls designed to reduce the spread of these very same viruses.

The quest for the Bullet vaccine became his singular reason for getting up in the morning on those nights he returned home from his very private office at all. It wasn't just that everything else became secondary; there was nothing else.

Years later Sam wondered why her father had become so obsessed, why unlocking the puzzle box of zoonotic disease transmission had grown into such an all-encompassing compulsion. She came to believe it hadn't just been the quest for fame (he was already famous by that point) or money (they always seemed to have plenty of that), or even his desire to save lives. He was just missing a critical piece in a way that Sam feared was genetic and patrilineal. While others might have tried to fill that void with drugs, violence, alcohol, sex, or personal codependency, Dad had chosen science, and the results had been just as destructive for him and his family.

Daniel Lewis missed birthdays, anniversaries, graduations, funerals, and every opportunity Sam offered him to show his approval if not love. Sam rationalized these repeated rejections through simple fantasy: her father was still "Dr. Daddy," the healer, prolonger of life, magician, and savior of animals. Grace's efforts to protect Sam from the truth about her father only deepened the delusion. Sam learned too late the true, steep price of that maternal shield.

Sam's vet school graduation was the last event she ever asked her father to attend. She was the class valedictorian and had worked hours on her speech to be delivered to the entire school and, more importantly, her father on graduation day. The speech was essentially a tribute to her father, whom she had not seen for months—about how he had instilled in Sam a deep and abiding respect for animals; how his work in zoonotic pathology had saved human and animal lives; and how he had demonstrated that you could live a life of both science and compassion. Daniel had promised to attend.

Sam began to cry when she saw the empty chair in the auditorium next to her mother. She made it through her speech, distracted, angry at her father's absence, and confused by some of the snickering at her comments.

As soon as graduation ended, Sam drove alone to Daniel's office— a place where she had never been invited. Security escorted her to a lab. She charged in, her speech in hand, ready to make him hear her words and prepared, finally, to accept his approval.

Sam stumbled at the vision before her. Twelve dogs stood in cages behind a tall man with gray hair and lifeless eyes. The dogs raised their heads to howl at her arrival, but no noise came from their open mouths. Their silence was monstrous, a distortion of nature itself.

Ignoring the man, Sam approached the dogs. She saw the fresh sutures across their larynxes, sealing the incisions that had severed their vocal cords. For a moment Sam was as mute as the dogs. Then the rage overtook her and she spun on the man. "You debarked dogs?" She was about to yell for her father but realized with a surge of revulsion so powerful she began to gag that she was staring at him.

Daniel initially looked annoyed at the interruption, but then his face softened. "Hello, Samantha. What are you doing here?"

"You debarked these dogs?" she asked again.

"Well, obviously," he said. "Otherwise we couldn't even hear ourselves think. Some of the protocols we employ in the Bullet vaccine research are of necessity somewhat invasive."

Sam shivered at that last word. She looked more closely at the dogs and noticed other surgical scars as well. "You're doing vivisection on dogs?"

Daniel turned annoyed again. "Dogs, cats, pigs, cows, among others. Why are you so surprised? You know full well the research I am leading."

"No!" Sam cried out, remembering Hugo. "You're a healer. You're a veterinarian. You do no harm. You took an oath." *You are magic*, she almost said. Her voice sounded embarrassingly childlike even to her own ears.

"Don't be such an idiot, Samantha. We're not at home anymore and you are not a child. These aren't your pets."

"But, Daddy—"

"I'm searching for something that can save millions. Of course animal experimentation is required. Now, what is it that brings you here?"

That was the instant when the illusion Sam had worked so hard to preserve fell around her. There was no longer any way to maintain it; and when it failed, it did so in a very big way, with questions she couldn't bring herself to answer: Was this the person she had always wanted to become? Had she wasted all those years seeking his approval while he was doing this? Had all the privileges of her life— the fine schools, the beautiful house growing up, the vet school she had just graduated from, the job with Morgan—been merely the fruits of this work?

Worst of all, Sam couldn't deny the small but persistent voice that told her she had known some version of the truth all along. Dr. Daddy, the kindly father who stayed up all night with her sick animals, the man who had saved Hugo and countless others, years earlier had been snuffed out by the search for the Bullet. It simply had been easier to believe her own bullshit and her mother's lies than to deal with the dissonant truth.

Sam knew that no one, other than perhaps the sociopaths of the world, simply woke up one morning and decided to become the type of human who severs canine vocal cords to stop the "distraction" of dogs howling in pain. It was always a series of incremental decisions that gradually led you further away from your own vision of your ideal self and your better angels—accommodations, rationalizations, compromises, greater ends overcoming more distasteful means. And Sam had been there all along throwing rose petals under her dad's feet.

She now understood why they had been snickering during her speech. They had always known the truth.

Sam threw her speech at Daniel and fled.

Those who deny the power of shame are neither students of history nor human nature. Sam had always planned to use her degree to help animals, but after that day she had a new purpose. She was no longer motivated by the desire to emulate her father or earn his approval. Instead she needed to wipe out the suffering her father had perpetrated in his quest. She needed to try to balance the ledger for her family. She needed to try to erase her shame.

Sam didn't speak to her father for six months. Because Daniel and Grace were a unit in Sam's mind, she included her mother in the freeze. Besides, Sam was pissed at her too and needed to review the record of personal history to determine her mother's culpability. Sam knew she couldn't do that with her mother's voice in her head. Grace's calls and e-mails went unanswered.

Late one night Sam's home phone rang. Her father's voice came on the machine. He sounded as if he had been crying. "Samantha, please, pick up the phone," he pleaded. Sam tried to ignore his tone. "It's your mother." Sam grabbed the receiver and learned that her mother had flipped the BMW. Grace Lewis had not survived. The autopsy revealed Grace had had a blood alcohol content of twice the legal limit.

Sam blamed Daniel for her mother's death and she took his stony silence as evidence of mutual recrimination. More shame. Sam buried her mother, Daniel Lewis buried his wife, and together, father and daughter buried any hope of reconciliation.

She had not spoken to her father in the two years since the funeral and believed that she could not start now and still hope to remain sane.

Sam ran out of her office and into the room where her dogs slept in their cages. She needed to get rid of the memory of her father, to remove the image of dogs who could howl only silently, to stop the sound of cruel sniggering.

She released Blinker and Scrabble first and, together with Nick, they escorted Sam around the room as she opened every other cage. Sam looked on with adoration as her dogs jumped one by one to the floor and barked, yipped, and howled with the joy of unexpected release. The room shook with their excitement. She took comfort in the noise.

The dogs soon surrounded Sam as she offered them words and caresses of gentle kindness. Then Sam dropped to the floor with them and, for a few precious moments, lost her shame and anger in wet noses, rough tongues, and soft fur.

15

Gabriel dreaded the nights. Darkness brought a deep sense of futility, confusion, and loneliness. He often spent the evening hours in the increasingly useless pursuit of introspection—what Channa had always referred to as "suicide on an installment plan"—until the sun rose again and illuminated the false promise of an even slightly more meaningful day. On some nights Gabriel became so frustrated that he abandoned his tiny apartment a few blocks away from the church. Then he wandered the streets of Riverside, invariably ending up at the church just as the first light of dawn brightened the stained glass windows.

This night, however, Gabriel sat quietly in the second-to-last pew. He stroked Molly and listened to the whimpering noises coming from Beth's slumbering form sprawled out in the next pew. He knew too well the sound of nightmares, but did not feel he had the privilege of waking her.

Before Gabriel could stop the cat, Molly leaped onto Beth's head. "What the hell?" Beth yelled as she bolted upright and pushed Molly to the floor. The cat hissed at her and sprang away, all hurt feline pride but otherwise unharmed.

Gabriel cleared his throat and Beth spun toward him with a

surprised gasp. The haunted look on Beth's face gave the priest pause. A mutual longing for a few minutes of peace made for strange but powerful connections in a lonely New York night.

"What?" she asked. "I got drool on my face?"

Gabriel shook his head.

"Sorry. I fell asleep," Beth admitted. "I'll go now. Exit the embarrassed lapsed Jew from the church. Cue the treacly piano music."

"Should I even ask?"

"What?"

"What you're doing here?"

"I wouldn't bother. I think you can find something better to do with your night."

"So you don't want to talk?" Gabriel asked.

"Nope. Not really."

Gabriel leaned back into the pew, stretched out his long legs, and clasped his hands behind his head. He was relieved he wouldn't be required to try to help someone with his increasingly limited skill set. It wasn't the trying that bothered him as much as the vague look of "that's it?" he would see on their faces—the obvious disappointment with the quantum of comfort he could provide. So why did he still feel the need to try? "You work at the shelter, right? I saw you walking one of the dogs this morning." He extended his hand and Beth shook it. "I'm Gabriel."

"Beth," she said. "Riverside's newest basket case."

"We do have our share. Would you like some tea? I can make some, if you'd like."

"Nah, don't put yourself out. I should get to my apartment."

"No bother. Back in a minute," he said, and darted out of the sanctuary.

Gabriel returned a few moments later with empty hands and a confused countenance. He stared at Beth as if she were an unknown intruder. Beth smiled at him and Gabriel's face slowly brightened in recognition. "Ah. Tea," he said, and left her again. This time he returned with two steaming mugs and handed one to Beth.

Beth sipped. "It's actually a pretty nice church," she said.

Gabriel sat next to her. "Thank you."

"The windows could use an upgrade, though," she said, pointing to the broken stained glass window. "What wonderful Bible story is that?"

"That was Abraham and Isaac on Mount Moriah."

"Old Testament? Something about a ram, right?"

"Sort of. Want to hear it?"

"Who doesn't love a good Bible story with their tea?"

Gabriel settled into the pew. "God tells Abraham to take his beloved only son, a teenager named Isaac, and offer him as a sacrifice. They start to head up this mountain, Moriah. Isaac knows that his father is preparing to make a sacrifice, but he doesn't know it's him— obviously. He also doesn't see any ram to put on the altar. Isaac at this point is getting a bit nervous. He asks his father, 'So where's the ram?' And Abraham says, 'God will provide a ram.' They get to the top of the mountain, but there is no ram. None. Nothing."

"Time to sip the coffee, Isaac."

"Right. By this time Isaac realizes he's pretty well screwed. Abraham, out of duty to, or his love or fear of, God, ties up his son who he loves more than anything else in the world, and prepares to slit his throat."

"Nice," Beth said.

"As Abraham lifts his knife to strike the sacrificial blow to kill his only child, God says, 'Lay not thine hand upon the lad, neither do anything unto him for now I know that thou believest in me, seeing thou hast not withheld thine only son from me.' And—drum roll please—a ram appears in the thicket for Abraham to offer as a sacrifice instead of his son. Another happy ending."

"Unless you're the ram," Beth snorted. "Yeah, I remember it now. In Hebrew school we were taught that God was testing Abraham's faith."

"Or perhaps the other way around. I wonder these days if maybe Abraham was testing God—how far would God let him go with it? Perhaps Abraham was calling God's bluff."

"Still, it's a crappy thing to do to a kid."

"Agreed. Bible stories are like Grimms' fairy tales when it comes to kids. Bad stuff always happens to them."

"So what happened to the window?"

"Some idiot who apparently felt the same way you do put a rock through it."

"Did you catch him?" Beth asked.

"Oh, I know who did it."

"Are you gonna get it repaired?"

"They wanted me to fix it, but then I couldn't be sure I wouldn't just break it again, so what was the point?"

Beth did a double take. "You? Why?"

"Because..." Gabriel closed his eyes to his truth. *Because the premise that a child must be threatened with harm to earn God's blessing is no longer acceptable to me; because that smug face cannot be the face of my God; because a rejecting and shaming God is a God of men created by men to serve the agendas of men; because I couldn't find any stained glass window maker who is able to capture the face of the God I want to see—the God of hope, of compassion, of acceptance.*

He couldn't give voice to any of the real reasons and didn't want to lie. He put a finger of silence to his lips and rose from the pew.

Gabriel disappeared behind a vestibule door and returned a few seconds later with a pillow, a sheet, and a blanket. He placed these on the pew next to Beth and dropped a hand onto her shoulder. "The third pew on the left," he said.

"What's that?"

"For some reason they made that pew wider than the others. I find I don't roll off so easy. Your nightmares won't find you here and mine are otherwise occupied. Get some rest."

Beth reached up and covered Gabriel's hand with her own.

16

Andy felt his breath come easier once he crossed the entrance into Central Park. This was always the way it was for him. The air suddenly became less dense, and somehow more satisfying. Time was different too, making each breath longer and deeper.

The nighttime pedestrians who lingered on the outskirts of the park with their dogs or cigarettes or worries of the day barely noticed him—another kid in a denim jacket with a large, worn backpack, shrouded in shadows. He quickly made it past the convention party construction site, now quiet but ominous in the darkness. The lone overnight security guard stationed in a booth near the fake Lincoln Memorial eyed Andy for a moment, but then returned to his iPhone.

The deeper into the park Andy traveled, the less noticeable he became. If he ever felt safe, it was here. He couldn't really explain that—didn't even want to try, for fear that understanding would cause it to unravel—but it was true. He could walk by the creepies and the preds without causing a glimmer of recognition or interest in their eyes. The only exception was the old black guy with the long coat. He always seemed to notice Andy, but only with a nod or a wave. There was no menace to that man, just presence.

Fifteen minutes in, Andy passed through a dense ring of *Ailanthus altissima*, improbably lush despite the tons of city concrete just beyond throwing distance. As Andy approached the rock formation hidden within these trees, he felt the sharp change in temperature. It was usually at least ten degrees cooler near the rock.

By any rational explanation, the cavern should not have been here. Some days Andy could almost swear that it wasn't. He would look for the thin crack in the rocks for an hour or more before he would finally find it and slide down into the space below. And if the cavern really was here, then by the sacred rules that govern all things in New York, it should have been vandalized or taken over by squatters or sealed up by the Parks Department as a hazard. Nevertheless, here it was, just as pristine as the first day he'd found it; the only squatters in it were the ones he always prayed he would find.

Andy took off his backpack, fished out his flashlight, and found the crevice without any trouble this time. He slid in feetfirst, holding the backpack over his head. The tunnel led him downward at a forty-five-degree angle for about fifteen feet and then dumped him into the empty cavern.

The cavern was tall enough for Andy to stand in, although he could actually touch the stone ceiling if he reached straight up and stood on his toes. The floor of the cavern also was stone, but it was dry and spread out before him for about three hundred feet.

Andy opened his backpack and heard the first stirrings of movement from the cave opening. He smiled at the sound. They'd probably been smelling him since the park entrance, but they wouldn't trust odors alone. "C'mon now," he called into the dark. "I don't have all night."

Andy sat and removed the contents of his backpack—first his violin case, then the cubes and slices of meat carefully wrapped in plastic and foil. The one he called Pacino, a big, brooding female pit bull with a scarred muzzle, came first. She tenderly took a cube of sirloin from Andy's open hand and then moved off. Penny came next, a copper-colored short-haired mutt of maybe fifteen pounds. Others followed—Onyx, Greybeard, Ginger, Shadow, Gold. They were each gentle with him, as if they recognized him as one of their own, and he had no doubt they would circle to defend him if it ever came to that.

Andy didn't know how many strays in total actually lived in the park or how many called the cavern their home. Different dogs showed up on different days. He had named nine of them, but assumed there were probably more who never came forward. He couldn't blame them given some of the scars he saw.

In minutes almost all the food was gone. Andy held back a single chunk of meat for the one who always arrived after the others had eaten. A warm current of air touched his cheeks and then she was there—a beautiful mix of husky, golden retriever, and shepherd, with doleful brown eyes and a badly damaged right ear. The ear had been torn or cut off so close to the dog's head that it was little more than a memory. She came to him and gently took the meat before settling beside Andy with a sigh.

Andy spent many nights in the cavern under the protection of the one-eared stray. He once had tried to take her out of the park, but that had proven impossible because she had turned into a screaming terror when Andy brought her near the park gate. That was the one and only time he tried. He understood the park was her home; Andy would need to come to her. And he did.

The one-eared girl had been his first find and she had eventually brought the others to him. These creatures were cautious and almost impossible to find against their will in the huge expanse of the park. To the outside world, they were all but invisible.

Growing up in the city, Andy had often heard about the legend of the Central Park Pack—that a group of stray dogs had formed a tight-knit unit around a leader and roamed Central Park subsisting on rats, squirrels, and pigeons. The lore was that they would come to the protection of people about to be assaulted or robbed in the park.

A few robbery victims swore that this was true, but those reports were always dismissed. No one had ever found conclusive evidence of a park pack, only the rare injured stray or stray sighting. In the way that New Yorkers celebrate the odd, the misunderstood, and the mysterious, the Central Park Pack had assumed a near-mythical status in the city—somewhere north of natural wildlife and just south of Sasquatch.

Andy didn't know if he had found some recent incarnation of the fabled park pack. He just knew that, as stated in the legend, it had saved him.

When all had eaten, Andy rose with his violin, rosined his bow, and began to play. The music he selected for the cave was always the same—the violin half of the concerto for violin and viola he had started writing but could never finish. Only one other human had heard the piece and Andy had promised himself that no one else ever would. He was afraid that what he had written might be beautiful and he didn't want to bring a thing of beauty into this world. He played now for only one reason. Even though he could perform only half of the notes, when they bounced back to him from the sides of the cavern, he imagined she was accompanying him. Then Andy's always-fragile shroud of time and memory parted. With the one-eared dog beside him, he allowed the individual threads of notes to entwine and become strings, and the strings to become rope.

The rope pulled him backward to Alexa. He was piking.

Their music had introduced them.

A special summer program at Juilliard for the college-bound musically gifted…a hot classroom…a pleated skirt…blue eyes narrowed in concentration…her fingers almost as long and agile as his…a shared glance and then a smile.

It was the warm glow of her tone on the viola and the power of his timbre on the violin during the Mendelssohn that actually brought

them together after class one evening. He had nothing except his violin and his scars. She had a family that wanted her to be something
unique and specific—Juilliard, Oberlin, summers split between the
Hamptons and music studies with the best of Europe.

The offer of coffee... that surprised first kiss, the clean, sweet taste
of her mouth... then the second... the smell of her hair, like sandal-
wood and fresh-cut grass.

One night led to seven more. Andy at first assumed it was a mistake
or that she would be gone as soon as she understood who he was, but
she remained. She asked him questions and he answered without lies.

Weeks later Alexa took Andy home to her parents' huge apartment
on Central Park West to show him off.

"Relax," she tried to convince him. A doorman... clean white
walls... oil paintings in the hallway of squiggles and lines... staring
at his battered shoes, waiting... judgmental frowns... "Beneath you,"
her father sneered.

They sent the boy away, disliking him instantly for everything he
didn't have. Alexa left with him.

The two met frequently after that night, but always within the shelter of the park. They weren't virgins when they met, but for all they
came to feel for each other, they might as well have been. There were
many secluded places in the park and Andy knew most of them, but
they discovered this rock formation and the hidden cavern together.
Here, under the beam of a powerful flashlight, they played for each
other and soon began composing their own concerto. Their fantasy
was that if they could complete the music and perform it for her parents, they could prove their bond was unique and worth protecting.

He and Alexa had once been inseparable.

He believed they still were.

*   *   *

At the middle of the adagio, Andy's bow clattered to the stone floor. The last echoes of rope thinned to strings, then to threads, and, finally, to the silence of his present. The composition remained incomplete, locked at the exact same measure. Andy had tried to finish it, but that had proven hopeless; even though he could see the entirety of his past, he could no longer envision a single note of his future.

Andy dropped to the ground, his back against the wall and his knees drawn to his chest. The one-eared dog joined him first, but the others quickly followed. They made a tight circle around him, paws and fur next to skin and hands.

Eased by the comfort of their touch, Andy soon fell asleep.

Book II

Hands

I

Sam woke to the sensation of the cold shelter floor pressed against her cheek and the sound of snoring. Although the left side of her body was completely and unpleasantly numb, she didn't feel her usual morning panic. Instead she inhaled the overwhelming scent of dog as she listened to the wall of heavy breathing and smiled.

No snickering. No afterimage of sutures sealing unforgivable incisions.

A dog's combined senses are about a thousand times more powerful than those of a human. A dog can hear a mouse tunneling under six inches of snow, smell the presence of another dog from a block away, and sense an owner's return from work minutes before the car appears in the driveway. Sam knew that for most dogs, particularly dogs of abandonment and abuse like her own crew, deep, paw-twitching slumber did not come easy. Trust was always a prerequisite—trust that violence would not visit; that a toy, bone, or blanket would not be stolen while unguarded; that a loved one would not vanish while eyes were closed. So Sam always experienced a little lift when Nick fell asleep in her presence, as if somehow she had been judged and deemed worthy.

That two dozen sleeping dogs were now following Nick's example, encircling Sam on the shelter floor, left her feeling both blessed and like a fraud. Very soon she would not be there to stop the violence, or protect the toys, bones, and blankets. Even if Sam could find another shelter to take all the dogs, it would not be *her* shelter. She would be gone to them and thus proven irredeemably undeserving of the trust these creatures had placed in her. One morning just thirty days from now, these dogs would open their eyes and learn that a loved one had indeed vanished.

Because Sam suffered from acute anthropomorphism, intense humanity, or a combination of both, she imagined that her dogs would wake that morning and pose silent questions to each other:

"Why are we here?"

"What is wrong?"

"What did we do?"

"Where are we going?"

"Where is she?"

"Why are we all alone?"

Sam heard these voices laden with shame and learned helplessness. They crescendoed in her ears, drowning out the comforting noises of sleep.

Nick woke and licked Sam's cheek. She lifted her head off the shelter floor with a groan and pushed herself into a sitting position. She managed to focus on the office clock. It was 6:03. *Another fun-filled Friday night*, she thought. "I'll give you a thousand dollars if you'll go out and get me a cup of coffee," she whispered to Nick. The dog stared back, his head at a tilt. "You're right," she said. "That was unfair... ten thousand dollars."

A few of the dogs began to stir at Sam's movement. The rest followed and the room soon filled with yawns, "downward dog" stretches, and playful biting. They all would need to go outside to pee before they ate breakfast, and it would be at least another hour before Greg showed up to help.

Sam led the dogs out the back of the shelter to the fenced-in yard she normally used only when a dog was too weak or sick to get to the park. The space was too small to allow for much play this morning, but it served her intended purpose. She made a mental note to hose it down later.

Sam was about to let the dogs back into the shelter to begin the breakfast process when she noticed that Blinker and Scrabble were watching her expectantly. Others soon joined them. That was when the truth hit her with a devastating clarity. Somewhere during the daily rituals of feeding, exercise, and elimination, somehow, by filling the interstices with affection, love, and kindness, her shelter dogs had become a pack and Sam not only was a member of this pack, she was their alpha.

She recalled the silent dogs in her father's lab and had a ridiculous idea. She raised her head to the sky. She thought of her mother and her mannequin-like appearance in the casket; Charlie and his look of defeat as he closed the door to their apartment for the last time; the panic in Little Bro's eyes; her father's cold stare; the little jelly bean canisters on the shelf of her office; the pendant around her neck.

Sam recalled all of these things, tilted her head back, and howled.

Scrabble joined in first, then Blinker, Nick, and Hips. Soon all the dogs were howling with her. Together they created a huge, beautiful, cacophonous mess.

Sam howled until her voice cracked. When she could howl no longer, the dogs gave her their voice.

By the time Greg, Luke, and Beth arrived at the shelter, Sam was already on the phone in her office. "Just one second," she said into the receiver, and grabbed a pen and scrap of paper off her desk. "I got it." She wrote down the information. "Any phone numbers?...Really?... Yes, it was hard for all of us...Thank you so much, Jonathon...And please give my best to Miriam and the girls...I hope soon...I certainly will tell him...Thanks again."

Sam disconnected the call and quickly dialed another number before she lost her nerve entirely.

Tom answered on the first ring. "Walden."

"I have an address," Sam said. "It will be about a three-hour drive."

"Dr. Lewis?"

"Pick me up outside the shelter. We'll take your car. The radio in mine is broken and I want to have something to fill the silence." Sam hung up without waiting for Tom to answer. Then she ran to the bathroom and threw up.

Beth bumped into her on the way out. "You don't look so good," Beth said.

"Stress," Sam shot back. "It's a killer."

"You just need to realize that today is the gift that makes tomorrow's post-traumatic stress possible."

"I'll keep that in mind."

"You want to grab a carrot stick or a head of iceberg lettuce for lunch? Maybe score some crack?"

"Yeah, would love to, but I can't. Gotta meet someone."

"Ah. Early date?"

"Hardly. I've got to go see a man I despise to convince him to help someone I don't trust."

"No one ever said you didn't know how to throw a fun party."

"Actually, that's precisely what they all say."

Sam found Greg and Luke and gave them instructions for the day that they didn't really need. She started for the front door and Nick followed.

"Sorry," she told her dog. "Not this time."

Nick whined and Sam almost changed her mind about bringing him, for the sake of her own distraction and comfort. She concluded it would be unfair to put Nick through six hours of driving in one day. "You'll have more fun here. I promise." She kissed Nick on his forehead and stepped out of the shelter onto the sidewalk.

In ten minutes a Ford sedan with city government plates pulled up next to her and Sam jumped in. Tom Walden had changed into a fresh shirt and suit, but that was the only thing about him that seemed fresh. He had the look of an all-nighter about him and the tight line of his mouth told Sam it had not been for fun.

"Are you OK to drive?" Sam asked.

"Yeah. I'm fine."

Tom drove slowly through the narrow cross streets of the Upper West Side as Sam silently looked out the window at an endless repeating pattern of Starbucks, Dunkin' Donuts, dry cleaners ("Tailor on Premises"), and small restaurants ("Happy Hour 5–7"). They passed several ambulances in active transport, with bubble lights and sirens on full. Sam wondered whether each contained a small child struggling for breath.

"So how'd you find him?" Tom finally asked.

"I called the dean of the vet school."

"Really? So did I."

"The dean isn't your godfather."

"Good point. Thanks for doing this."

"Just to be clear, I didn't do it for you. Whatever your real motives, maybe there is a chance to help these kids."

"But—"

"And you're giving me an extra thirty days, plus you will make sure that any of my dogs who are not placed at that time get transferred to Bill Ackerman's shelter."

"I can't make any promises beyond giving you the thirty days."

"You can, and you will, or this will be a short trip."

Tom's hands tightened on the steering wheel and his knuckles turned white. "OK. You have my word."

Sam took out her iPhone and held it in front of his face. "Now say it for the lawyers."

Tom took his eyes off the road long enough to glare at her. "Really? You're gonna tape me?"

"No offense, but I'm not really a trusting person."

"Fine. I, Tom Walden, assistant deputy mayor for the City of New York, do promise that if Dr. Samantha Lewis helps to secure the assistance of her father in this matter, she will receive an additional thirty days to vacate the premises currently occupied by her shelter and at the conclusion of that time, any dogs not placed will be turned over to the care of Bill Ackerman." Tom glared at her. "Satisfied?"

Sam turned the phone off and shoved it into her pocket. "Not nearly, but I guess it's the best I can do."

"Now that we're all official, should we at least try to call first to make sure he's there?"

"All Jonathon had is the address where they send the pension checks. They're still being cashed, so we can assume Dr. Daniel Lewis is alive. Jonathon and my father were no longer on speaking terms, so that's all we have."

"OK. I got it."

"I doubt it. You will never understand how many lives my father actually mangled."

"If he's anything like you, I think I'm starting to."

"You bought my cooperation, Walden, not the right to talk shit to me. So keep it to yourself." Sam turned on the radio and pushed the volume to loud. She closed her eyes and pretended to fall asleep. She pretended so hard that sleep slowly overtook her.

Before Sam gave in to the exhaustion, she had one last thought: *Panic 2; Numbness 1.*

2

A ndy was correct; Gabriel did not keep a television in the church, but he did use a computer. The priest sat before it now in his cramped office, searching through the "urgent adoption" Web pages of the city's dog shelters. On these pages Gabriel found the shelter dogs coming up on their compassion expiration dates. Without rescue, these dogs would face the city's euthanasia needle within seventy-two hours.

Gabriel studied hundreds of dog faces. Many were older, had been abandoned, or had been brought to a shelter because they had health problems that, although not terminal, were inconvenient or expensive to ameliorate. He saw the words *incontinent, cataracts, diabetes, flatulence,* and *difficulty with stairs* under many of the photos. The words were always easier to focus on than the faces. These were dogs who had once known the sweetness of homes and families—they had slept in warm beds next to the small feet of sleeping children, had eaten leisurely out of their very own food bowls, had gone through whole days without experiencing an odor that was unfamiliar, painful, or threatening—only to learn that their final house would be a small metal cage lost in a dark cloud of sharp noises and acrid, alien odors. The faces showed that these dogs had learned the truth about humanity. Ears back in submission, eyes downcast. They had given up.

But there were other, younger dogs who had not yet succumbed to the hopelessness of their situation. In their eyes Gabriel thought he saw confusion, doubt, and pain, but also a small remnant of forgiveness and, perhaps, hope. The demeanor of these faces most closely approximated what Gabriel observed on the face of the figure in the church sanctuary, the one on the suspended wooden cross. He scanned through several photos and found one face that gave him particular pause. Gabriel checked the anticipated euthanasia date—today—and grabbed his phone.

The animal shelter at Ninety-Second Street and First Avenue was the largest in the city. When animal control officers picked up strays or abused and abandoned dogs within the city, they typically ended up here. Notwithstanding the hundreds of dogs and cats housed within, the facility was clean, well-organized, and staffed by ultimately caring souls doing the best they could under the enormous physical and emotional weight of their task.

Gabriel presented himself to the young woman at the reception desk. He didn't identify himself as "Father," but his ever-present collar meant he didn't need to. The unfamiliar receptionist asked for his driver's license "for security" with an embarrassed smile.

"Of course," Gabriel responded.

In a few moments, a male Hispanic technician with the name Steve on his coveralls appeared, shook Gabriel's hand, and escorted him through a set of double doors that led to a large holding area lined with dog-filled cages. The area was twice as large as Sam's entire shelter, and every cage—over two hundred by Gabriel's guesstimate—was occupied. The dogs noticed the priest's entrance and clamored for his consideration.

"He's in cage 36-A," Steve said.

Gabriel focused his attention on the dog from the Web page and avoided looking into any of the other cages; it was the only way he could possibly accomplish his task. The desperate whining tugged at his conscience, but he knew that eye contact suggested the possibility of comfort and he had none to offer today except to the dog in cage 36-A.

Gabriel peered into the cage. A midsize but wiry black mutt—pit bull, black Lab, and maybe Rottweiler—stared back at him silently.

"You sure about this one, Father?" Steve asked.

"Yes."

Steve shrugged and opened the cage door. 36-A retreated to a corner of his enclosure and curled into a shaking ball. Gabriel produced a dog biscuit from his pocket and offered it to the dog, but 36-A only tried to get smaller.

"He bite anyone?" Gabriel asked.

"No way. The most he does is pee on himself when you get too close."

Gabriel slowly moved the biscuit forward into the cage. "You want this?" he asked gently. "Nothing to be afraid of here. Just a cookie." Gabriel inched his arm farther in and heard the hiss of urination. The pee passed through the grate and dappled the newspaper below.

"Maybe it would just be better—" Steve began.

"I'm not in any rush and you don't need to wait. Just leave me the leash."

Steve handed Gabriel a cheap plastic leash and left the room.

It took Gabriel five biscuits and forty-five minutes of coaxing, pleading, and cajoling, but it was worth it. 36-A emerged from his cage and allowed the priest to attach a leash to his collar. Gabriel led the dog through the double doors of the cage room. 36-A didn't look back. The remaining dogs made a final fevered plea for Gabriel, but the noise was cut short as the doors swung closed. Gabriel prayed for those left behind and for himself as well—that his condition would soon remove the memory of that sound of despair now echoing in his mind.

At the reception desk, the young woman gave Gabriel a form to sign and knelt before the dog to say goodbye. 36-A tried to hide behind Gabriel's legs, entangling the priest. Gabriel patiently freed his legs while offering soothing sounds as he signed the form. Then he led 36-A outside into the comparatively fresh air of a bright New York City morning.

Their first stop was the kosher-style deli on Lexington and Ninety-Fifth. Gabriel passed through the doorway and was hit with a wall of odors that transported him to the New York of his youth and his first congregation on Manhattan's Lower East Side. Corned beef, pastrami, salami, smoked fish, fresh bread. The priest had never lost his taste for the food. He would drag Channa out for the flavors once or twice a month and gladly pay the gastrointestinal debt that came due hours later.

The impact of the deli aromas on 36-A was likewise immediate. The dog whimpered, but his thin tail moved in an increasingly excited arc and he began to pant.

Gabriel waited his turn at the counter. It was still too early for the huge crowds that would begin to form an hour before lunchtime. One of the old countermen, in a food-stained apron, motioned for Gabriel to step away. "No dogs in the store," he warned.

An even older counterman whom Gabriel had never seen before jumped in. "I got this one, Max. It's OK." Max shrugged and took the next customer.

"How can I help you today, Father?" the second man asked.

Gabriel gave his order and the man had it packaged and ready in a few minutes. He handed the bag to Gabriel.

"What do I owe you?" Gabriel asked.

The man looked from Gabriel to 36-A, and then back to Gabriel. Gabriel felt a sudden chill under his knowing gaze. The man shook his head. "Nothing."

"Please," Gabriel said. "Let me pay for it."

"Even a *prost ben-odem* can recognize the *malakim* when he sees one. It is the least I can do." The man walked away without waiting for further discussion. Confused, Gabriel took his package and his dog and headed toward the park.

3

Not a growl. Not a whimper. Not a whine.

An endless row of terrified caged dogs, fresh sutures across their throats, raised their heads as one. They opened their mouths to howl in protest against their circumstance, but they made no sound.

"Dr. Lewis?" The voice touched her through the heavy blanket of sleep and denial. "Samantha?" The same voice, a little louder this time. Maybe a bit irritated, but Sam didn't care about that. What she cared about was that the voice wouldn't go away and she didn't want to be conscious. Consciousness meant knowledge—cold, painful, obdurate knowledge—and facing the fact that her past and present failures were merging into a single shit show. But it was no use. She was waking now and sliding slowly from the cages of her dreams into the thick walls that molded her life.

She opened her eyes just as their car passed the Latham, New York, town limits sign. "Damn. I'd hoped it was all a bad dream," she said.

"Then next time, can you dream someplace a little closer to the city?"

Sam glanced over and saw the exhaustion in Tom's face. She almost felt a little guilty about sleeping the whole ride, but then reminded herself that this was the jerk shutting her down. She noticed the beat-up Timex on Tom's right wrist—4:05. That couldn't be right. "What time is it?"

Tom looked down at his left wrist, where he wore one of those multifunction runner's watches. "Almost eleven."

"Your other watch is wrong," Sam said.

"That's the time in Tokyo."

"No, it's not."

"Right, it's not. Do you know what you're going to say to your father?"

She knew precisely what she was going to say. Nothing. "I can get you through the door, but then it's up to you."

"He's your father. I'm sure he's going to want to hear from you."

"He *was* my father. Just like I *was* the operator of a no-kill animal shelter in Manhattan. It is a curious historical fact, nothing more at this point. Trust me on this, Walden. If you want his help, you should nod politely to me once in a while, but don't invite me to open my mouth."

"OK. I guess you know how to handle him best, but can you do me one small favor? Can you stop calling me Walden?"

"What should I call you?"

"How about Tom?"

Sam nodded. "No."

Tom sighed and reached across Sam into the glove compartment.

"Going for your gun?" Sam asked.

Tom ignored her and grabbed a bottle of Advil. He popped the lid with his teeth, fished out three tablets, and tossed them in his mouth. Sam took the bottle and returned it to the glove compartment. "Thanks," he said.

She dropped the bottle on top of a photo of an adorable seven-year-old boy. She thought the kid looked like the guy behind the wheel, with a chunk of someone very pretty thrown in. Walden wasn't wearing a ring, but Sam knew that didn't mean much these days.

After a few more minutes of silence, the lady from Tom's nav system instructed him to make a few lefts and then a right. Sam anxiously watched the number of "miles to destination" dwindle and the "ETA" get closer until Tom pulled the car into a hidden driveway and up to a modest house. The nav lady announced, "You have arrived!" in the voice of a proud parent.

Although the front door was open, that was the only evidence of life on the property. Tom hopped out, but Sam was slow to join. The stillness of the bucolic setting was so disorienting compared to the vibrancy of the city and the shelter that she coughed just to make some noise. Together they walked up three cracked slate steps to the front doorway.

Tom rapped on the open door.

"Yes?" a voice called from inside the house.

Sam gasped. Some part of her had really believed he wouldn't be here, or that he would be dead, or that a comet would hit Walden's car before they pulled up the driveway.

"Dr. Lewis?" Tom called into the hallway.

"Hold on a moment," the voice called back.

When Sam heard the footsteps, she spun toward the car, calculating if she still had time to make a dash for it. Tom must have sensed what she was thinking, because he reached for her arm—not as a sign of affection or support, but to keep her in place. Sam managed to free her bicep from Tom's grip, but by then it was too late for escape. Besides, she remembered that Tom held the car keys.

A face appeared at the door.

Sam took a step backward, this time not to run, but out of shock. She had thrown her father out of her life while he was still in the beginning stages of grief and denial. Since that time, Daniel Lewis's demons had feasted well on whatever makes one human. Sharp edges and cold gray hollows had replaced any flesh that had once been soft and warm. His gray hair had turned a sickly translucent white. Always slight but fit, Daniel was now specter-thin and frail, as if the slightest breeze might take him and spin him into cold, dry dust.

Sam nearly fell off the top step, but Tom steadied her and his touch brought her back. "Dad, this is Mr. Walden…" Sam fought hard to keep her voice from breaking.

"Sam?" was all Daniel Lewis could manage before his dry lips began to quiver. "Are you all right? Why are you…?"

"Mr. Walden has something…there is something…he needs you to…" Sam couldn't finish. Her body began to shake.

Tom stepped forward, his hand outstretched. "Dr. Lewis, I'm Tom Walden, assistant deputy mayor for New York City. I was hoping I could ask you a few questions about your work."

Daniel shook Tom's hand in a trance, all the while staring at Sam. "I'd forgotten how much you look like her. For a moment I thought…" He snapped back into focus. "Please, come inside."

Sam hesitated.

"Sam, please," her father urged. "You came all this way. One cup of coffee together won't deprive you of your right to hate me. I promise."

That was true, Sam knew. But she worried about how long she'd be able to look into that ghostly face and not feel even an ounce of compassion. She squeezed her eyes shut and allowed Tom to bring her into the house.

Daniel Lewis offered Sam and Tom a seat on a small couch in what passed for a living room, and excused himself.

Once they were alone, Tom asked, "Are you OK?"

"Really?" Sam snarled. "You're gonna ask that? I should've demanded more to suffer through this."

"Well, we're here now…"

"Yeah, no shit. By the way, my feelings toward you are not really improving."

Daniel returned with three mugs of coffee, a glass of milk, and a box of sugar on a plate. If he was going for pathetic, Sam thought he had succeeded. He handed out the mugs and then took a seat across from her.

"Thank you, sir," Tom said. "I appreciate you meeting with me. I would have called but we can't seem to find a working phone number..."

Sam tried to ignore this intolerable chatter and surveyed the room. Her father's house looked as if he'd furnished it straight out of a cheap rental catalog. No item revealed any history of the occupant. Sam wondered what he had done with all the once-beloved odds and ends from the house of her childhood—the ceramic candy dish she'd made in sixth grade, the painting of wolves howling at the desert moon they'd bought on a vacation in Arizona, the Lalique cat Sam had given her parents on their twenty-fifth anniversary, all her school awards, her mother's...

Too much...she felt herself starting to topple into the pit and willed herself back to Tom's voice and the conversation.

"...hear about the Riverside Virus?" he was saying.

"What about it?"

"We could really use your help."

"I'm no longer with the school, Mr. Walden."

"I know, but..."

"There are many people who are more capable," Daniel said.

"We don't think so."

Daniel turned to Sam. "We?" Sam heard the hint of hope in his voice.

"The mayor and her executive staff," Tom clarified. "You've done more work than almost anyone in transmission of zoonotic viruses and nontraditional sources of contagion in urban environments."

"You're talking history, Mr...."

"Walden. You've also had the most experience on the ground researching certain Lyssaviruses."

Sam did a double take at that last word. "Lyssaviruses? You didn't mention that, Walden."

"Yes," Daniel added. "That's a fairly specific inquiry. Perhaps you would like to stop playing games?"

"Well, um, maybe...," Tom fumfered.

"You guys never change," Daniel scolded. "I've dealt with you government types my whole professional life. You always think you can get away with half answers. Many people have died as a result of that arrogance."

Tom ran his hands through his hair, the portrait of someone struggling with a decision beyond his authority. "I guess it really doesn't matter," Tom said. "It will all be public soon anyway. The brain biopsy of the child that died came back this morning. It is a preliminary positive for a Lyssavirus."

"Which one?" Daniel asked.

"Rabies."

"Hold on," Sam snapped. "Rabies? You guys all said it was avian. Birds don't even carry rabies."

"The bird vector hypothesis apparently was incorrect," Tom offered meekly.

"Ya think?" Sam scoffed. "And how many birds did you kill before you figured this out?"

Tom put his palms out defensively. "You're using the word *you* pretty broadly. I'm not running this show."

"What type of animal bit the child?" Daniel asked.

"There was no bite," Tom answered.

"That can't be," Sam challenged. "There are only two known means of rabies transmission—a bite from a rabid mammal—which birds are not, just by the way—and transmission of blood or saliva from a rabid animal through an open wound. That's textbook."

"Yeah, well, the textbook is a little light on this one," Tom replied. "No bite marks, no open wounds, no swelling or even redness. The boy's skin was totally and completely intact. Not even a hangnail."

"Then the poor child must've swallowed infected saliva, or it came in through the nasal passage," Daniel offered. "That's extremely rare, but possible. What species variant?"

"Non-variant," Tom said.

Daniel shook his head. "Someone has made an error," Daniel insisted. "All rabies virus contains the genetic marker that tells you the source of the rabies—canine, raccoon, skunk, fox, whatever. We always know."

Tom shrugged. "So I've heard. Maybe someone at CDC made a mistake, but they can't find the variant marker. And here's the other problem: we haven't found any rabid animals at any point of contact with this child. The kid never left Manhattan."

"There've been cases of rabies in the city and the surrounding counties," Sam countered.

"Yes," Tom responded. "But the incidence is low and the number of confirmed cases of animal-to-human rabies transmission is far lower than that."

"What about that rabid raccoon they found near the convention stage in the park?" Sam asked.

"We've confirmed the kid wasn't in the park for at least ten days," Tom answered. "I'm told that's the incubation period for rabies."

"Were his symptoms even consistent with rabies?" Daniel asked.

"In very general terms, yes. Initial flu-like symptoms progressing to partial paralysis, painful swallowing, hallucinations, organ failure. He was heavily sedated when he passed."

"What about the other sick kids?" Sam shot back. "They all just suddenly contracted rabies too? You're not making any sense."

"The other children have similar symptoms and are getting progressively worse. But as you know, there's no single definitive test for rabies in a living human victim. People generally have issues when you try to take even little pieces of their brains. The tests they've been able to conduct came back inconclusive. All the sick kids are being given rabies vaccine on the possibility that somehow they've been infected."

"That won't work," Daniel cut in. "The vaccine is ineffective once someone is symptomatic."

"Yes, that we know," Tom said. "Unfortunately."

Daniel rose on creaky knees. "What you are suggesting, Mr. Walden, is some type of aerosolized transmission of rabies virus from an animal carrying the virus but showing no symptoms. That is extremely difficult to believe."

"More so than Ebola in Manhattan?" Tom challenged.

"This would be far beyond what anyone has actually seen to date in the field."

"That's why I'm darkening your door, sir. The mayor would like you to join the city as a consultant to help manage the problem."

"Have you considered the possibility that this may be a man-made problem?" Daniel asked.

"You mean like weaponized rabies?"

"Something like that, yes."

"We've been told no one has that, not even us," Tom said. "Do you know something I don't?"

"No," Daniel said. Sam found the denial less than convincing.

"We've been assured that this is a naturally occurring phenomenon."

"That's very comforting," Sam said, her voice filled with sarcasm. "I mean, given that you all were sure yesterday this was from pigeons."

Tom ignored her. "Can we count on your help to manage this situation, sir?"

Daniel returned to his seat. "If what you're saying is to be believed, there isn't much to manage."

"I don't understand," Tom said.

"You have one of the deadliest zoonotic viruses known to humanity—almost always one hundred percent fatal—being transmitted from an unknown and possibly asymptomatic source in an as-yet-unknown manner. The only thing you've got going for you is that it appears to be a fairly localized transmission. That is typical for rabies because infected animals are unable to travel far."

"So what would you recommend?" Tom asked.

"The only thing we know. A QCK campaign."

"What's KCQ?" Tom asked.

"QCK," Sam corrected him.

"Quarantine, cull, and kill," Daniel said. "The government-imposed veterinarian response to every zoonotic-based epidemic since the microbe was discovered. Find the animal source and remove it and every animal the infected source has contacted. Separate the sick animals from the healthy, move the sick someplace else, euthanize them, and pray it stops the spread."

Tom rubbed his eyes as he shook his head. "But at this point, the rabies could be from any mammal, right? So we can't even start to isolate."

"The source animal cannot stay hidden forever. It will show up," Daniel answered.

"We can't wait. We need to do something now."

"This virus is not concerned with your need for expedience, Mr. Walden," Daniel said. "If you really must do something now you can put a big fence around Riverside and explain to the nice people why you've trapped them on the wrong side with a deadly virus. Or you can start rounding up every raccoon, mouse, rat, dog, cat, squirrel, and chipmunk in the area, although I'm guessing that despite your best efforts you'll probably miss a few."

"There must be another strategy."

"As I said at the beginning, I have no doubt at this point in my life that you can find smarter people with better ideas. Assuming, that is, you are telling the truth about all this. What does the CDC suggest?"

Tom suddenly found his shoes particularly interesting. "The CDC is a political agency. It is more concerned with a politically acceptable solution."

"In other words," Daniel said, "you've been shut out. That's really why you're here, isn't it? The CDC isn't talking to you. Which senator on the CDC funding committee did you piss off?"

"I really can't answer that, sir."

"Then you should take your secrets elsewhere," Daniel said.

Sam saw the conversation was about to crash and burn. That wouldn't help any kids or her dogs. "What about the Bullet, Dad?" She looked into her father's face for any hint of a reaction. She'd forgotten what it was like to be on the other end of those probing eyes. Sam instantly felt as if she were back in his office that day she had graduated from vet school.

No, she told herself. *They are just eyes; they can't hurt me anymore.* Besides, the giant countdown clock in the sky demanded more hours. "I mean, if some good can come of all that history, now would be the time," she said.

"I had assumed you knew," Daniel answered.

Sam shook her head.

"I did complete the Bullet research."

"And?" Sam probed.

"I made a remarkable discovery. Unfortunately it was the wrong one. The deeper I got, the more I found that the similarities between humans and the rest of the animal kingdom dwarf the dissimilarities. Genetically we are too close to birds, pigs, rats, and chimps to be able to manufacture a genetic transmission barrier. Given time, the virus always finds a way to cross. Always."

"Cross-species transference?" Sam offered. "You were never able to solve for it?"

Her father nodded. "We are not different enough to matter."

Tom jumped in. "Can someone please tell me what the hell you're talking about and whether it can help us stop a zoonotic virus?"

"You are asking the wrong question, Mr. Walden," Daniel responded. "What I discovered is that there really are no zoonotic viruses; there are only viruses. At the genetic level of a virus, when you look into the electron microscope, we are all one species. The virus knows what we refuse to acknowledge—we are all the same in the most material ways; we are all just life. And humans are not even that special—an asymmetrical off-the-rack mammal from the same mud pit as all other forms of life."

Sam leaned back in her seat. "So that's why you quit," she concluded.

"Not exactly," Daniel said. "First I tried to warn them about what was coming. I spoke to the National Academy, the Conference of Virologists, and a dozen other groups. I explained that we can no longer pretend that the divide between us and them is so huge or even relevant and we are running out of time."

"Time for what?" Tom asked.

"We've already dodged so many bullets. These so-called animal viruses are mutating and jumping over to humans at an alarming rate. Some threshold has been broken. The swine flu that recently hit us? The vaccine was bullshit—every competent immunologist knows that. The only reason it didn't kill a hundred thousand in this country is because for some reason the virus mutated left instead of right. Stupid luck. Remember the outbreak of SARS in Asia? If that had crossed to the US, who knows how many hundreds of thousands would have died before it mutated into something benign? And then there's H5N1. Avian. Bird flu. Deadly. We have H7N9 coming over from the poultry markets in China—uniquely adapted to kill humans. And now, of course, Ebola that started in bats in a single cave in Africa. So many near misses. But I promise you, those are all the common cold compared to the big one that's coming."

"Can we stay on message here, Dr. Lewis?" Tom interjected.

"This is the message," Daniel snapped. "No one wants to consider that these animals are so closely related to us that our very own actions toward them are the reason we're getting sick. The diseases we are giving to these animals through our own agricultural practices and food production are returning to us. Everything follows something that came before."

"So what are we supposed to do?" Tom asked.

"You are not listening. Unless we change things dramatically very soon, all we can do is wait for the next mega-virus to hit. Until then, we quarantine, we cull, and we kill."

Daniel crossed the room, opened a credenza, and returned with a large three-ring binder. He placed the binder in Tom's lap.

Tom opened the cover and he and Sam looked down into the photographic horror of a large bulldozer pushing hundreds of pig carcasses into a huge pit. The next photo was similar, except the carcasses were sheep. Another photo showed a chicken cull—humanoid figures in hazmat suits shoveling thousands of chickens into a giant furnace. Many of the chickens were still alive.

"The threat of rabies in particular has triggered massive culls of dogs on the most tenuous of justifications." Daniel flipped the page for them.

Of all the images, Sam knew this one would remain in her memory forever.

"Hanzhong Province, China, 2009," Daniel said. "Thirty-seven thousand healthy dogs killed in a failed attempt to stop the spread of rabies." The carnage in the photograph was overwhelming. Sam felt the bile rising to her throat and tried to breathe through her nose. "I was there for this one. The stench of dead dog bodies was overwhelming. The police pulled healthy dogs from the arms of screaming children and shot them in the head. Would you like to see the pictures from the dog cull in Kakinada?" Daniel asked. "I was there too."

"No," Tom said quickly. "I think you've made your point. But this is New York, not China."

"Panic feels the same all over the world," Daniel said. "The specific language we use to describe that feeling doesn't matter. You think we're such better people? That chicken cull I showed you? Iowa. The pig incineration? Georgia. What happened to the hundreds of pigeons you trapped? This," Daniel said, pointing to the binder, "is all we know to do. It is as far as we've come. The children must be the priority. As soon as they have sufficient justification—a symptomatic animal, a higher mortality rate…" Daniel turned to Sam. "Would you tell him, please? You of all people know that I'm right."

"Can you give us a moment, Walden?" Sam asked.

"But—" he protested, then caught Sam's eye. She nodded at him. "I guess I could use some air," Tom said.

Sam waited until she heard the front door slam. She had not been alone with her father for over two years and now his proximity was crushing. "Why didn't you tell me, Dad?" Sam asked. "Why didn't you tell me about your research?"

"I tried, but you weren't picking up the phone. If—"

"I had pretty good reason."

"I don't blame you…it's just that…would it matter if I said that I am sorry? Would that make you any less angry?"

Sam had no context for dealing with the weakened being before her. Numbness dulled her thoughts. She glanced at the floor, then out the window. Anywhere but at her father. "I don't know what I would do with that apology now." Her voice sounded cold, even to herself, and she hated that.

Daniel stared at her, waiting.

"Look, Dad, if you think this ends in a big hug while Mom's smiling ghost looks on and Leonard Cohen sings 'Hallelujah' on the soundtrack, it's not gonna happen. I'm not that person anymore. I can't be. Whether that's because of you, or Mom, or it's just who I was destined to become, I don't have those instruments of compassion anymore. I can't stop seeing those dogs you debarked."

"What dogs?" Daniel asked.

"You don't even remember?" Sam's anger flared at the thought that such a pivotal moment in her life had gone unnoticed by the man before her. "Of course you don't. Why would I think otherwise? Look, I didn't come here for the family reunion. I came because I want you to help that jerk out there so he can maybe save those kids and I can get what I need."

"Please, Samantha, don't ask me to get involved with this campaign. He's obviously lying about this whole thing or at the very least he is ignorant about his mission. They want me to try and find the reservoir animal so they can start a cull. I'm sure of that. And not because it is the best option or even because they believe it will work, but because it is all they know. Perhaps that is the correct answer this time, but I've already done too much harm for one lifetime. I can't be responsible for one more death. I will do anything else you ask, but not that."

"Tell me something, Dad. Why did you leave the world? Was it that you failed with the Bullet or was it Mom?"

"Does the answer matter so much?"

"It does to me."

"I think you already know."

The Bullet, Sam concluded at first. But then she looked in her father's eyes again. She no longer saw pride or ego. Instead she saw her own reflection. At that moment Sam understood; he hadn't left because of the Bullet or because of the loss of his wife. He'd left because with Grace's death, Daniel had lost any hope of connection with the only living person who knew him as father and husband, just as she had lost the identity called *daughter*. Daniel was adrift and alone. She knew what that felt like. With that realization, Sam decided it would be inhuman to try to force him to help, particularly when she too questioned Walden's veracity and motives.

"Just my luck," Sam said. "Dr. Daniel Lewis picks now to find his conscience. Better late than never, I guess." Her voice was not unkind. "I'll let Walden know. We can leave you alone now."

"Do you think I might be able to see you again?"

Sam shrugged. "I feel like someone with twelve legs trying to cross a minefield," she said. "Too many memories."

"Without memory there's no history. Without history there's no context. Without context there is no meaning."

"Who said that?"

"My wife." Daniel must have seen the look of surprise on Sam's face. "She may not have shown it all the time, but notwithstanding the fact that she stayed with me, your mother was one of the most intelligent people I ever knew."

"I don't suppose she gave you any advice for making the meaning less painful?"

"Not one that didn't involve a bottle."

Sam let herself out the front door without looking back.

4

At 10:46 a.m., after Beth had spent an hour playing with Hips, she exited the number four subway at the last stop, joined by twenty other pilgrims. Together, but without saying a word to each other, they walked to the ornate gated entrance that had been unlocked and opened precisely a minute earlier. The operators of Woodlawn Cemetery well understood that the living had no patience for delays caused by the dead.

Andy watched as Beth strode through the entrance and started on the winding path through the graveyard. He didn't make a habit of following people; he recognized he was weird, but tried to draw the line at that sort of weird. It was just that the night had been particularly bad — the "filled with memory" kind of bad—and there was something he needed to know. He had long ago lost the type of coping mechanisms that would allow him to put off his quest for an answer for a more convenient time. So he'd blown off his morning classes and followed her.

Beth paused at an angry gray headstone.

John "Johnny" Miller
1996–2013
Beloved Son and Brother
Why?

She dropped to the ground before the marker, bowed her head, and closed her eyes. To Andy's amazement, Beth began to chant in a low but sweet voice: "*Shema Yisrael, Adonai Eloheinu, Adonai Echad—*"

Andy knew it would be offensive to remain hidden any longer. He cleared his throat.

Beth's eyes flashed open and she spun toward the sound, her face bright red. "What are you doing here?" she demanded.

"I, um...followed you."

"I can see that, but why?"

Andy was surprised at how angry she sounded. He should've anticipated that. *Stupid boy*, he chided himself, and lowered his eyes. "I had a question."

"And it couldn't wait?"

Andy shrugged. "Not too good at that."

"Don't lurk," Beth scolded. "Come and sit down like a normal person."

Andy was grateful for the invitation and complied. "What were those words you were singing?"

"It's a Hebrew prayer called the *Shema*."

"You know Hebrew?"

"Some. Less and less every day. You said you wanted to ask me something?"

Andy tried to compose his thoughts into language that would make sense to someone outside his head. "Dr. Sam told me you tried to help Little Bro."

"Who?"

"The dog I brought in yesterday. You were there when he died." Andy's demeanor transformed despite his efforts at control. His current expression was more appropriate for the terminally ill, the lonely elderly, or parents who had thrown dirt on the coffin of a child; it had no place on the face of someone so young and luminous. "What happened?"

Beth stared at her fingers. "You should speak to Sam."

"She left before I could see her. I just want...please?" he asked again, this time just short of begging.

"There was so much going on, an awful lot of blood...honestly, I didn't even know he was dead. Sam had to tell me. He was alive one minute and the next he was gone. It happened so fast."

"Do you think he felt any pain?" Andy asked. What he really wanted to know was more elemental and selfish and likely unanswerable— *would it have made any difference if I had been there?*

"I don't think so. He was pretty well out of it. Drugged up. I think whatever that dog was seeing in the end wasn't in that room."

The silence dragged on between them as Andy processed that answer. It sounded true to him. In the small voice of a child, Andy asked, "Does that prayer bring comfort?"

"Depends...I guess."

"Can you teach it to me?"

Beth slowly enunciated each syllable of the prayer and waited as Andy repeated her words. He quickly memorized the prayer and recited it by himself to the stone.

"Thank you," Beth said once he had finished.

"Who is he?" Andy asked timidly.

"Someone who once came to me for help."

"And?"

"And, what?"

"And you don't want to talk about it. I get it." Andy rose to his feet and examined the other stones nearby—first the ones to the left and then those to the right. Most looked abandoned. "What a mess." He began pulling some of the dead weeds and clearing the old scrub from those plots in the worst condition.

Beth watched him for a moment and then joined in. They tugged at the dead plants with determination and ferocity, as if clearing away the decay might mean something to those beneath their feet.

"Why don't people come to take care of their own?" Andy asked as he yanked at a thorny weed.

"Too hard, I guess," Beth said, grabbing another handful of dried brush. "It's one thing to remember the face or voice of a dead loved one, but another to know you're standing on their actual body. Your mind can't pretend that they weren't real or deny that they're really gone forever. You're only separated by six feet of dirt, but you could dig to infinity and never get back what you lost. So we avoid. The dead always seem to make ghosts of the living."

"Why do they hold such power? I mean, whether it's their memory, or fighting against their memory, they're always there. Sometimes even more than when they really were standing beside you."

"I think you need to find someone a bit better at living than the humiliated and humbled recovering drug addict sitting before this gravestone to answer that one."

Dirt and scratches soon covered their hands, but, working together, Beth and Andy cleared out the entire area.

They stood back and took in the results of their effort. Andy read part of an inscription. "'Rachel Stoner. Born 1987. Died 2001. Nevermore in my arms. Forever in my heart.'" He moved to another stone. "'Isaac Janson. Born 1990. Died 2003. My son.'"

Hot, silent tears spilled down Andy's cheeks, but he kept moving from stone to stone, a bit manic, reading aloud as he went. "'James Pelra. Born 1993. Died 2007. Safe in the hands of God now'... 'Mandy Brown. Born 1994, died 2006. I will always remember you.'"

"Jesus. They're all kids," Beth said. "I never noticed. So many children. That's so sad."

"No, no. Not sad," Andy said, smiling through his tears. "Don't you see? Johnny's not alone. These children are not alone. None of them! They will all grow old together for eternity. They'll always have each other. They've found a family again." Andy stopped at the last headstone in the row. "'Abraham Sauls, 1998 to 2014.'" The rest of the words were in Hebrew. "What's this one say?"

Beth studied the inscription carefully. "'*Lefanim tziporim afot letoch chalunot.*' In English, 'Because sometimes little birds fly into windows.'"

"I don't understand."

"I think someone meant it as an answer to the question on Johnny's stone. It's an idiom—roughly it means 'shit happens.'" Beth shrugged. "That's not a very comforting view of the universe, is it?"

"I don't know." Andy dried his eyes with his denim sleeve. "Maybe it actually is. If things happen for no reason at all, maybe the moment is really all you ever have."

Beth studied Andy's face for a long minute, her head cocked to one side, deciding something. "Can you find a small stone for me?" she asked finally.

Andy searched the ground for a few seconds, picked up a stone, rejected it, then picked up another. He showed the stone to Beth. "Good," she said. "Now put it on top of Johnny's gravestone."

Andy complied, but looked at Beth quizzically. "What's it mean?"

"It means that he's not forgotten. That someone was here and cared."

Andy selected another rock, and then another. Soon his hands were full. He placed a stone on each of the nearby grave markers.

When he was done, Andy wiped his hands on his jeans. The sleeve of his jacket pushed up on his arm, revealing markings on skin. Four vertical lines that ran deep into the tissue.

Beth couldn't take her eyes away and Andy made no effort to hide the cuts. "My old professor used to tell us that horizontal lacerations are a cry for help; vertical cuts are a plea for an ending," Beth said. "You really meant business, didn't you?"

"I did, yeah."

"You must have been in a lot of pain."

Andy nodded. "Taking control hurts. But there are all different kinds of pain."

"You done with that option?"

"Yes."

"Good."

Andy appreciated the absence of judgment and interrogation. Still, this was much more than he usually shared and he felt embarrassed at his disclosure. "I've got to get to class."

"I'll ride with you?"

Andy nodded. Together they left the dead of Woodlawn and walked back to join the living on the number four subway.

5

They had been driving for almost an hour in complete silence. Sam was so jittery that this time she couldn't even pretend to be asleep. She was certain that Tom had started to say something several times.

They passed a sign for a full service rest stop and Tom hit his blinker.

"I need coffee," he said.

He pulled off the ramp and into a crowded parking lot.

"You want anything?" Tom asked.

"I'll use the bathroom," Sam said.

They entered the building together, passing a "Liberty, New York, Welcomes You!" souvenir shop. While Sam found the bathroom, Tom stopped at a Top Hat Donuts counter and joined a long line of customers.

Tom was still on the line when Sam found him. "What's the holdup?" she asked.

She glanced at the counter and saw the problem. There was only one employee, a teenager with a name tag reading "Jimmy." As Jimmy moved behind the counter to fill orders, Sam noticed that he dragged his left leg while his left arm hung useless at his side.

"Just busy," Tom said.

"They could've given the kid some help," Sam said.

"If they need to hire a second, then Jimmy probably wouldn't have a job."

The line, although moving now, was becoming increasingly restless. A few customers grumbled audibly. Jimmy must have heard them, because he started sweating.

Tom cleared his throat and said loud enough so the rest of the line would hear him, "You know how it is. People are very accommodating about disabilities—until it delays their lattes. Then all bets are off. Another proud human history moment."

The comment shut everyone up.

By the time Tom and Sam arrived at the counter, Jimmy was shaking. "Just take a breath," Tom said. "Ignore the assholes. You're doing fine."

"I heard what you said in the line. Thanks," Jimmy said.

"I admire your courage," Tom responded.

"You know, I see these people walk in and out of here every day. They open the door without thinking which arm they need to use. They aren't afraid of those four front steps. People take so much for granted."

"But hopefully you remind them."

Jimmy poured Tom's coffee and handed it over. "On the house, sir."

Tom pulled out a twenty and, when Jimmy was turned away, shoved it into the tip jar.

"Can you grab us a seat?" Tom asked Sam. "I need to get something from the shop."

Tom found Sam at a table three minutes later. He was carrying a small plastic bag from the souvenir shop. "You mind if we sit for a minute before we get back in the car?" he asked.

Sam shrugged. "You're the one with the public health emergency," she said coldly.

"Did I do something wrong?"

"I really don't like to be manipulated."

"I don't understand."

"That whole thing with Jimmy. You did that to show me what a good person you are, right?"

Tom stared at her. "For you? Really? Man, you are one self-involved human being." He shook his head in a manner that Sam took as pitying. Tom took a small snow globe out of the plastic bag and set it on the table between them. A tiny sign inside the globe read: "Thank You for Visiting the Liberty Rest Stop, Liberty, New York." "I pick one of these up for my son whenever I'm in a new city. He collects them."

"The boy in the glove compartment?"

"Yeah," Tom said.

"Cute kid."

"Thanks."

"I'm guessing the looks came from your wife."

"Yes. Ex-wife. He had encephalitis when he was four. It left him with some gross motor deficits. His left arm is pretty much just for show."

Sam felt her cheeks blush in shame. "I'm sorry."

"It could have been a lot worse, so he was fortunate. But on the other hand, I got to explain to him why he can't play basketball and football like his friends and probably never will. So I'm a little sensitive when it comes to disabled kids. And just for your own information, I know exactly what it is like to spend night after night in a hospital with a sick kid wondering if they will ever recover."

"Just so you know, I'm feeling pretty small now."

Tom nodded. "I bet. Let's get going."

On the way to the car, Tom kept pressing the heels of his hands to the sides of his head.

"Headache still there?"

"Yeah."

"I'll drive."

"I've imposed enough. I can do it."

"Not looking like you do. This is self-interest. I want to make it back alive."

Tom tossed Sam the keys.

Once they were settled back in the silent car and driving, Sam couldn't escape her own self-judgment. "Does apologizing for the comment a second time make it any better?"

Tom appeared to think about that. "Don't feel too bad. I haven't exactly been a paragon of virtue with you."

"So my dad was right? You are lying?"

"Not exactly."

"Do tell, Walden." After a few minutes of silence, Sam said, "I'm growing old here."

"I'm just trying to think of how to begin. Do you follow politics at all?"

"Not at all."

"How can you live in this city and not follow politics?"

"I assume all people in politics are lying to me about something."

Tom shook his head. "Such a cynic. The truth is most people in politics are lying about something, but not everyone and not about everything."

"Great. I feel very comforted. So assume I know nothing."

"OK. The governor of New York is trying to be the president."

"Yeah, that I know. He went through that whole weight-loss surgery procedure and all."

"The governor and the mayor of New York City are not pals. My boss, the mayor, is extremely stubborn and opinionated. But she is also very loyal and, actually, one of the most honest politicians you will ever meet."

"And I'm sure if she were a conniving, malicious liar, you would tell me."

"Absolutely. Despite the fact that the governor and the mayor belong to the same political party, the mayor has refused to come out in support of the governor for president. She's actually been very negative about him and what he's not done for the city."

"Yeah. I think I read that."

"See? You do know. The governor will get the nomination without question, but he's worried about losing New York in the general election polling. And there are those who believe if he cannot carry his own state, he shouldn't lead the nation. So the governor wants a huge New York show when he gets the nomination."

"I saw the party preparations in the park. Very lovely."

"He will not tolerate anything that might interfere with his New York coronation. That would be hugely embarrassing in his own backyard, so to speak, and set precisely the wrong tone leading up to the general election."

"And a rabies outbreak without an identified source sets the wrong tone."

"Right. And the other thing that sets the wrong tone is the mayor seizing control of the situation and forcing the governor to take a backseat. At the very first sign that the mayor is vulnerable—God forbid a bunch more kids get sick, or another one of them dies, or there's a public disturbance that attracts media attention—the governor will step in and take control and try to make the mayor look like a bumbler. If that happens, all bets are off. He's not a subtle guy."

"But what does the governor really have the power to do?"

"A lot. It is a health crisis. There's precedent for this. You remember the surprise Ebola quarantine for health care workers even though they tested negative?"

"Yeah, I get it. The governor gets to look all presidential doing the white knight thing and at the same time he makes the one who didn't endorse him look like an idiot who can't be trusted."

"Yep."

"What does the CDC really say about the virus?"

Tom shrugged. "Your father was right about that. We've been shut out on the granular, 'let's sit around a table and be honest' stuff."

"Why?"

"Dunno."

"That sounds like bullshit."

"It's not. We assume the governor's office told them to. He wants control of the flow of information. It all goes through him. The governor is very likely the next president of the United States. No one is anxious to piss him off. They're not about to violate the law by withholding information from me, but they're not leaping for the phone on the first ring either."

"So what are you going to do now?"

"Not sure. Having your father on our team would've helped our credibility."

"I did try."

"I know. And I'm sorry it was painful. Maybe I should've handled it differently. Just been direct with him from the start. I'm not good with father chats that don't take place through Plexiglas."

"How's that?"

"My dad. You know who that is, right?"

Sam shook her head.

"Really? Walden is my mother's maiden name. My dad's last name was Shroeder."

Sam thought it was familiar but couldn't place it.

"Shroeder? You really don't know? Ponzi scheme? Multibillion-dollar fraud? Stealing people's pensions? Sentenced to twenty-five years in prison?"

Sam took her eyes off the road long enough to take in Tom's features again. Now she could see the resemblance. "Holy shit," she said. "You're that Shroeder's son?"

"Dear old dad. I thought you knew. It's not like it's a secret."

"Except for the name change."

"OK, so I've still got a little shame thing going on. That, and the death threats and hate mail started becoming a little tedious."

"I read a *New York Times Magazine* story about you a few years back."

"Ah, yes. 'The Sins of the Father.' Lovely piece, except for the part that suggested I'm a liar."

Sam remembered now. His father had been convicted a decade ago. Tom had been forced to leave Harvard Business School after the trial. There was always a cloud about what the son knew, although he repeatedly protested his innocence. Tom eventually finished his degree at City College and claimed he went into government and public service to try to make up for his father's misdeeds.

"Wow," was all Sam could manage. "Your dad really ruined your life."

"For a while. But I decided that my father's choices didn't need to be mine. I try to own my life."

"And how's that working for you?"

"Pretty good, I guess. Except for the headaches. But I do think it made me stronger when I needed to be there for my own son." Tom yawned. "Anything else you want to know?"

"Actually, yeah. What's with the two watches?"

Tom threw her that boyish grin and for some reason this time Sam didn't find it nearly as irritating. "A birthday present from my kid. It stopped working two days after he gave it to me. I wear it because it reminds me."

"Of him?" Sam asked.

"No. I don't need to be reminded of that. I wear it because it reminds me of who he expects me to be."

Sam liked that answer. Maybe he wasn't completely full of crap. "My mother once told me that I couldn't trust a man with two watches because he never really knows the correct time. Sound right to you, Walden?" *Will you be able to tell me the correct time when I need it, Assistant Deputy Mayor Walden? Can I trust you?* Sam wondered.

Silence.

"Walden?" Sam repeated.

She glanced over. Tom's head was tilted back on the rest and his breathing was slow and deep. He had fallen asleep. Sam decided that probably was best for the both of them.

* * *

Tom finally awoke as Sam double-parked in front of the shelter.

"Crap. I'm sorry," he said as he stretched. "That was really selfish of me."

"No worries. It was the most pleasant time I've actually spent with you," Sam replied, but her tone was more teasing than unkind.

"Did I do anything stupid in my sleep?"

"More than you'll ever know. So what about the shelter?"

"You probably think you earned your part of the deal."

"Yes, I do think that."

"I guess that's fair."

Sam exhaled in relief. "An additional thirty days?"

"Yes. See? I'm not horrible. Just a weak-minded civil servant."

"And they can go to Ackerman if I can't place them?"

"Yeah, I guess. I'll need to smooth over whatever feathers you seem to have ruffled, but I should be able to do that. I'd like to be able to give you more time, but Morgan is pushing really hard."

Sam bristled at the name. "Morgan? What the hell does she have to do with my shelter?"

"You don't know that either? Lady, you need to get out more. She put an above-market bid on your place and is racing to get to contract."

"Why? What does she want with my shelter?"

"She says she wants to turn it into a lab annex. But honestly, I think it has more to do with the fact that she wants to be the one to put your lights out. She's not very nice."

"I noticed." Sam switched off the engine and handed Tom the keys. After she got out, Tom slid over to the driver's side and started the car. "Good luck with the dogs," he said.

"You'll let me know if there's a problem I might need to know about?"

"If I can," he said.

Sam knew this was only a partial answer, but it was an honest one. "OK. Thanks, Tom."

Tom's eyebrows lifted a bit. "Tom?"

"That is your name, isn't it?"

Tom smiled as he drove away from the curb.

6

Under a large oak in the shadow of the convention party stage, Gabriel sat a few feet away from 36-A, half a dozen paper-wrapped packages of deli meat in his lap. The priest opened the first package and a cloud of garlic, black pepper, and roasted meat enveloped them. "Pastrami," Gabriel said, and removed a thin slice of the meat and held it in his open palm. 36-A crept forward and, with his eyes on Gabriel the entire time, took the slice and retreated. The dog's touch was gentle—more lips and tongue than teeth. It was easy to see the dog's appreciation of the flavor; he immediately returned to Gabriel's hand, his tail moving in broad circles. Gabriel laughed and offered 36-A another piece.

"Your tail's about to come unscrewed, friend," he said.

Gabriel introduced the dog to the other meats, careful to make sure that 36-A didn't overdo it. The distance of the dog's retreat gradually shortened so that by the time Gabriel opened the final package, 36-A was pressed against the priest's thigh. Gabriel pulled the copy of *Old Possum's Book of Practical Cats* from his jacket and began reading to 36-A aloud about "Gus: The Theatre Cat."

Curious visitors stopped to speak with the priest and admire the dog. During the first of these visits 36-A dropped to the ground and peed on himself. Three visitors later, the dog allowed himself to be touched. On the fifth visit, 36-A initiated the contact, approaching the stranger with tail in full motion, requesting attention.

Gabriel couldn't help but marvel at the incredible resiliency of this creature. 36-A's true personality was resurfacing—or perhaps even showing itself for the first time—and all that the dog had required was a small space free from the threat of harm.

Gabriel quickly cleaned up their trash and brought 36-A across the park. During their walk the dog tried to look at everything at once—a black squirrel that crossed their path and chattered angrily at the pair; a plastic bag floating before them on a gentle breeze; an ice cream vendor shouting his flavors of the day; a group of friends playing with a Frisbee.

And, of course, there were all the dogs. 36-A had met others of his kind at the shelter, but they had been nothing like this. These animals had an infectious excitement and confidence about them. They came up to 36-A, hopping from side to side one moment and then frozen, butts shoved high in the air, the next. 36-A either had forgotten the canine language of an invitation to play or had never known it. After the first few failed efforts, however, the dog got the idea. He looked longingly at Gabriel. The priest knew he might spend the rest of the day chasing the dog down through the park, but he couldn't bring himself to say no. Gabriel let him off the lead. 36-A ran, tumbled, jumped, and yipped among his playmates without a shred of self-consciousness. Every few minutes the dog looked up to make certain Gabriel was still nearby.

After about thirty minutes, Gabriel knew it was time to move on. He whistled and 36-A quickly returned to his side. The priest experienced a tiny bloom of pride; he had sent out a message and it had been received and understood. They had begun the process of creating their own language based on mutual trust. As Gabriel led 36-A out of the park to the huge pet store on Columbus Avenue, he found it hard to keep from grinning.

Inside the store Gabriel directed 36-A to the long row of stuffed dog toys. Fuzzy stuffed animals (sheep and cows apparently were the big sellers), humans (the mailman and the veterinarian were popular), and common objects (bones, of course, and fire hydrants) in different shapes, sizes, and colors spread out before them.

The dog looked around uncertainly. "Pick one," Gabriel said kindly. 36-A stood transfixed. "Go on. It's OK." Gabriel grabbed the first toy he saw—a fuzzy basketball—and squeezed it near 36-A. The toy gave out a noise somewhere between a dry wheeze and a squeak. 36-A winced and backed away. "Not your style. Got it."

Gabriel walked the dog up one side of the aisle and down the other. 36-A showed momentary interest in a few of the toys but ultimately rejected them. After ten minutes the dog paused before a bin of fuzzy green turtle plushies with large, kind brown eyes and broad smiles. The dog gingerly picked one of these out of the bin and stared at Gabriel with the toy dangling from his mouth.

"You're sure?" Gabriel asked.

36-A sat on his haunches, the turtle secure in his jaws.

"Done," Gabriel said. He steered 36-A to the row of registers at the front of the store and paid. Once they stepped outside, the dog pranced for a beat or two.

As the pair walked the streets of the Upper West Side, 36-A carried the turtle in his mouth with his head high, eyes wide open and bright, proudly displaying his new toy to every passerby.

Gabriel's knees throbbed in earnest, but 36-A looked so happy showing off his turtle toy that the priest didn't have the heart to take him off the streets. Instead he offered up a silent benediction to lost youth and Advil and kept walking.

At 105th Street, Gabriel stumbled and nearly fell. He caught himself just in time. Once he regained his physical balance, he forgot where he was and how he had come to be walking with a dog he didn't recognize.

A name came to him in the fog of his disorientation. *Atlas.* He recalled a dog named Atlas. Was this Atlas?

Gabriel's head filled with different voices. Men, women, and children competed in the same limited space for his attention.

"Forgive me, Father, for I have sinned..."

"I smacked the kid...yeah, hard. He deserved it..."

"My wife knows about the affair; she said she would kill herself if it didn't stop, but I love her..."

"...four weeks since my last confession..."

His vision blurred under the weight of the burdens others had thrust upon him and of snippets of old sermons long devoid of meaning.

"...if they won't give me a bonus, I figured I would take one..."

"We read now from Psalm 137:8: 'O daughter of Babylon, you devastated one, how blessed will be the one who repays you with the recompense with which you have repaid us. How blessed will be the one who seizes and dashes your little ones against the rock...'"

"He's married, but he says he is leaving her for me..."

"I worry where we will get the money..."

"...dashes your little ones against the rock..."

"I called him a faggot and then threw him out of the house..."

"Because his damn dog bit me, that's why..."

"...and the lion shall eat straw like the ox...They shall not hurt or destroy in all my holy mountain..."

"...dashes your little ones against the rock..."

Men, women, children. Which voice was his? Which memories were his own? Gabriel smacked the sides of his head to clear the voices.

A woman on the street bumped into Gabriel's hip. "I'm sorry, Father," she said. She smiled at him and then vanished into the moving crowd of pedestrians. The woman was familiar—not an exact match by any means, but close enough to force Gabriel to catch his breath.

Channa?

The narrators in Gabriel's head stilled, but before reason took over, the dog tethered to his wrist jerked him forward after the woman. The dog dodged bodies from both directions, tugging the bewildered priest in his wake.

The woman disappeared around a corner. The dog pursued and the leash slipped out of the priest's hand. "Atlas!" Gabriel called. Gabriel lost sight of the dog at the bend. "Atlas, come back." Gabriel charged after the dog.

When Gabriel turned the corner, he found the dog in the arms of a boy with green eyes and a strange aliform protrusion jutting from his back. Gabriel blinked hard twice and recognized the odd appendage as an ordinary backpack with an instrument case pushing out of the top.

"Hello, Father," the boy said, petting the dog in his arms. "Who's this?"

"Atlas," Gabriel answered. "I think his name is Atlas."

The boy paled at the name. "Is that a joke?"

"No, son." Gabriel gazed at the boy. A warm sensation spread through his chest, like a sip of Scotch during Advent. "Do I know you?"

"Christ." The boy led Gabriel by the arm to an empty stoop and urged him to sit down. He placed the dog in the priest's lap. "I'm Andy, Father. You know me. And that isn't Atlas."

"I'm sorry. I know that name…I know it is a dog's name, but I can't place it. Where is Atlas?"

"Atlas is dead. Don't you remember?"

"Tell me."

Andy shook his head. "Don't ask me to do that."

"Tell me, please," Gabriel begged. "I can't make any of the voices match."

Andy stared down at his dirty sneakers. "OK, Father," he said.

Andy inhaled deeply and closed his eyes.

"An eleven-year-old boy runs away from his fourth foster home. He runs because he can and because he knows no one will look too hard for him. He finds a German shepherd mutt on the streets. The boy calls the dog Atlas because the dog lifted the boy's world.

"The boy gets stuffed into a new home and his shrink convinces his new foster parents to allow him to keep the dog. The shrink believes that Atlas gives the boy a sense of stability. Stability... the boy doesn't even understand the concept because he has never experienced it; he just knows that the dog had been one of the few living things in his life he could count on.

"The new fosters actually seem OK, but the boy's new foster uncle is a different creature entirely. The boy sees the looks his foster uncle gives him. These are leering, predator glances that, even at the age of eleven, the boy has learned to recognize and fear.

"When the door to the boy's bedroom creaks open one night during his third week in the house, Atlas is instantly alert. The uncle grabs Atlas by the collar and locks him in the boy's closet. Then the uncle turns on the boy: 'You say anything about this, I'll kill your dog.' The boy would sacrifice anything for the dog, even himself. The boy feels the uncle's hard, calloused hands under the blanket pulling on his pajama bottoms. Groping and desperate hands. Punishing and controlling hands. The boy whimpers. The uncle smacks him across the mouth. 'Shut up, you little punk.'

"The closet door must've been broken or something because one second the boy squeezes his eyes shut as the uncle rolls him on his stomach and the next Atlas is on the uncle, ripping into the flesh of his forearm. The uncle screams, but Atlas will not let go. The boy wills Atlas to rip and tear.

"And he does.

"Lights snap on, the uncle screaming, blood seeping through fingers, a kick to Atlas's ribs. 'Remember what I told you,' the uncle hisses through pained gasps.

"The uncle tells the foster father that he was just coming in to check on the boy when the dog attacked without reason or provocation. The boy tries to come to the dog's defense and, notwithstanding the warning, explains what actually happened in that bedroom.

"But no one believes the boy. He has been known to lie."

Gabriel squeezed his eyes closed against the flood of images the boy's voice brought to life. When that didn't work, he wrapped himself in his arms and began to rock in place.

"The foster father and the uncle insist that Atlas is a dangerous dog and must be euthanized. They bring the boy to the animal control office with them. The boy keeps waiting for someone or something to intervene and save the dog. He had seen enough television and movies to know that horrible events like this only happen to horrible people and he is not horrible. The dog will be saved; the uncle will be punished. The boy is so sure of the happy ending that he doesn't even think to say goodbye. Instead the boy and the dog share a last confused and frightened glance as the tech takes the dog to a back room.

"Atlas dies from the needle. The earth drops. When the dog does not return from the back room, the boy's understanding of defender and victim becomes hopelessly muddled. Heroes die. And they die at the hands of creatures you wouldn't even honor with your spit.

"The boy cuts himself that night…deep, vertical cuts. Irrevocable cuts."

Gabriel felt the boy's hands on his cheeks, lifting his face. "Now open your eyes, Father. Look at me."

Gabriel could not resist the boy's command.

"That was where you found me," Andy continued. "At the hospital. You showed me a glimmer of the possibility of peace through my shadows. You believed me and offered me the beginnings of a life in a new foster home. You had the foster uncle arrested and prosecuted."

Gabriel knew the face before him. The murk and confusion receded. "Andy?" he asked tentatively.

Andy nodded. "That's how you know the name Atlas, Father. You shared that burden with me."

"I'm so sorry. I should never have asked you to remember. Forgive my selfishness. I didn't—"

Andy shook his head. "There is nothing to forgive. The memories of Atlas and everything after are always with me. But that day in that hospital room? I had nothing left. You walked in and you were the face of God for me, Father. Not hope exactly, but something other than despair—and that was what I needed."

Andy kissed Gabriel lightly on the forehead and then whispered in his ear. "Whatever other memories are taken from you, you can never forget that."

7

Sam knew she was struggling.
Seriously struggling.

That knowledge didn't help her, though. Neither did the passage of hours following the meeting with her father. So many feelings competed for dominance in her raw psyche that she had been fairly close to catatonic.

Greg, Luke, and Beth each had peppered her with questions about the trip, but Sam found her own words sluggish and imprecise. She'd asked them for a little time and space as she retreated to her office, and they'd begrudgingly complied.

Until now.

"Hey, Dr. Angry, it's Beth," Beth called through the door. "I thought maybe if you weren't getting laid in there we could grab a nonalcoholic beverage and a plate of fries and chat. No pressure... sorry, did I say that 'getting laid' thing out loud? I meant to say 'reading the Bible.'"

Inside her office Sam actually laughed. She took that as a divine sign and opened the door.

"Boundaries aren't a real big thing for you, are they?" Sam asked.

"Actually," Beth said, "I find the whole 'coloring within the lines' thing a bit confusing." Sam stepped aside and let Beth enter. "You seem distressed," Beth said.

"Really? What gave it away?"

"You look like me immediately before or immediately after a binge."

"Thank you."

"So what happened?"

"I don't want to get into it."

"I completely understand. No problem." Beth said, but made no attempt to leave the office. "So how's dear old Dad?"

"Who told you?"

"I don't kiss and tell. Think of me as sort of a fat Hannibal Lecter. I can extract information in all sorts of subtle ways, Clarice." Beth dropped into a bad Anthony Hopkins imitation. "Do you still hear the fava beans screaming?" She licked her lips and made a sucking sound.

"I mean it. I don't want to talk about it."

"Got it. I really came in to talk about myself anyway. Tell me, do you think I should go blond?" Beth asked as she pretended to show off her dark and stringy strands with a model's pretentiousness. "I think it would brighten my whole face."

"Not sure you want to put more light on that face."

"Ouch, but good. That was good. Express your feelings, sister. Let it out."

"You are so incredibly annoying sometimes."

"I get worse the better you know me."

"I'm not looking forward to it. What are you really trying to do here?"

Beth appeared to think about the question for a moment. "I think—and I'm not sure, so don't hold me to this—that I may be trying to show you that I sort of care. Is that right?"

"Why are you asking me?"

"Because I thought you might be a little more facile in knowing what better people are supposed to do in these kinds of situations. You know, the caring thing."

That answer took Sam back a step. "So you don't know either?"

Beth shook her head. "Not a clue. All I know is you start caring about a crippled dog and maybe a troubled kid and the next thing you know, it all goes to hell. Honestly, when I think about it, the caring actually felt pretty good. Not OxyContin good, but…" She shrugged.

Beth seemed to be waiting for Sam to volunteer something, but the truth was that Sam didn't know how to respond. The space between numbness and panic was narrow and not well trod when it came to her dealings with humans.

"OK," Beth said into the growing silence. "So I'm gonna leave you alone now, since it's clear I have no idea what I'm doing."

"Hold up a second. I need to speak to you about business."

"What? Did I screw something up again?"

"Yes. Apparently your life up until now."

"Nice."

Sam opened the middle drawer of her desk and removed something small. She tossed it to Beth, who caught it in one hand.

Beth stared at the key.

"It's heavier than you think," Sam said.

"You sure you really want me to have this? All joking aside, it's not like I've done a lot to earn your trust at this point, and you do have quite a few drugs around here."

"We've got to start sometime, right? Everyone who works here gets a key—for emergencies, if you want to check on Hips in the middle of the night, or even just to get out of your own apartment or head. And I really don't think you'll screw me."

"No, I won't," Beth said softly, holding the key in her palm.

"Don't make such a big deal about it. It's not like we're engaged or anything. Besides, the narcotics cabinet has a separate lock."

Greg entered without knocking. "Sorry to interrupt this women's empowerment minute, but I need you." Sam knew that tone. Her internal alarm pinged. They followed Greg to reception.

Tom waited for her with a sheaf of papers in his hand and two men in white protective lab coats stenciled with "NYC Department of Health Technician."

Her internal alarm roared.

"What are you doing here, Walden?" Sam demanded.

"I'm sorry," Tom said. "It's official business." He handed the papers over. "These are notices issued by the city department of health to take blood and saliva samples from every dog in the shelter."

"What the hell for?" Sam was so angry with herself for even thinking that she might trust him.

"A moment alone in your office?" Tom asked. Sam didn't move. "Please?" Tom added.

Sam led the way and Tom closed the door. "Your father was correct. The source didn't stay hidden. We found it."

"What is it?"

"A dog."

"More bullshit? There hasn't been a confirmed case of canine-variant rabies in Manhattan for decades."

"Well, there's one now. The dog lived in an apartment next to one of the sick kids. According to the records, the dog had already been vaccinated."

"Sometimes a vaccine wears off or is defective. The dog must have been scratched or bitten by a primary rabid animal."

"Sam, listen to me, it was a little terrier owned by a retired teacher. We're talking about the canine equivalent of a car driven by a little old lady only to church on Sundays. And she made sure that the dog got a rabies vaccine booster every year even though the dog never left the apartment off a leash. There's no connection that we can find to any rabid animal unless the rabies somehow became aerosolized."

"My father said that's not possible."

"No, actually he said it's beyond what we have seen. And look around. Your father's not here."

"That's not my fault."

"I never said it's your fault. Stop making this all about you. The reality is that we've lost control of the situation. We're assuming the source of the virus in this case is canine and so is the governor."

"What does that mean?"

"Every dog in the same building is being confiscated and quarantined. They will be monitored and if there is any sign of the virus, they will need to be euthanized to confirm or exclude the existence of rabies. Every dog that was living in the household of one of the sick kids has already been tested and conclusively ruled negative."

"Hold on. How'd you do that? There's no conclusive test for a living animal." Then she realized the real meaning of Tom's statement. "Shit! You killed them?"

"Those dogs had to be euthanized. There was no choice. We're talking about the potential for carrier-type aerosolized rabies. We couldn't take the risk those dogs were shedding virus throughout the city."

Sam felt like her whole body was vibrating. She paced the small office. "Those poor kids. They're going to wake up and find out that they were responsible for killing their own dogs."

"*If*, Sam. If they wake up."

"But why test my dogs?"

"Because they're in the geographic zone."

"And because you can, right? Because they're just strays to you and I take your money so I can't say no. Because you need to announce that you're doing something even if it's nothing." Tom didn't answer. "And when those preliminary tests come back negative, will you be coming back to take them away and open them up just so you can—what was your phrase? 'Conclusively rule them negative'? Because you're scared? Because you can? Because you don't know what else to do?"

"I don't have any good answers. I think it's a continuum based on proximity to the sick kids. The nearer a dog has been to one of those children or to another sick dog, the greater the need to rule out that individual vector with certainty. Right now we're going to settle for a good exam of your dogs and blood work to look for any sign of systemic infection."

"I can hear the *but* at the end of that sentence, Tom."

"Good. Because there are a lot of contingencies. I'm trying to be honest with you. I can't make long-term promises. And the news doesn't get better. The governor will be imposing a fourteen-day canine quarantine under his state health emergency authority. No dogs will be allowed out of the Riverside area radius. If a dog has been infected with rabies, it should show within the quarantine period."

"But that means my dogs won't have access to Central Park."

"You and everyone else. I'm sorry."

"What about Riverside Park?"

Tom shook his head.

"And it's just a coincidence that the convention and the Central Park event will be over by the time the quarantine ends?"

"Of course it's not a coincidence. You can't have rabid dogs running through the governor's big party in the park. For him that would be a crisis of biblical proportions."

"A political crisis, you mean."

"Any crisis at this point in the election cycle is a political crisis."

"How can this quarantine possibly be enforced?" Sam asked.

"NYPD cops with guns and National Guard with bigger guns moved over from the WTC site, Penn Station, and Grand Central Terminal. It's not like you're stopping people—just the dogs."

"You say that as if it will be easy. What if someone with their dog challenges the quarantine?"

"No one will. But if they are stupid enough to try, the dog will be restrained—one way or another."

"So why are you telling me all this?" Sam realized that Tom could have just insisted that she comply with the testing order with no questions answered.

"Actually, I'm not really sure." Sam saw the confusion in his face and almost believed him.

Almost. "I think people like you always have an angle, Tom," she said. "Whether you know it or not."

Tom shrugged. "I guess I'm looking for an ally."

"You're talking to the wrong person if you want me to help you destroy these animals. I know these kids are very sick, and maybe there's a right choice here, but honestly I don't think you even have any idea what the hell you're doing. Any of you. You're just grasping at the next politically expedient thing. This is what panic looks like. First it was pigeons. And if the next thing just happens to be dogs, then look out Rover."

"What if you could help save the dogs?"

"I don't do the what-if thing anymore. It hasn't exactly worked out for me."

Tom rubbed his neck. Sam got the sense he wanted to kick something across the room. "Was there ever a time when you trusted anyone?"

"Sure," Sam said. "It was about the same time that someone proved worthy of my trust. I think I was maybe six years old."

Howls from beyond the door interrupted them. Then a shout: "Don't touch my dogs!"

Sam ran out of the office toward the familiar voice.

8

Andy had a troubled relationship with help, so he rarely asked for it. He believed that those who claimed they had much to teach often also felt that they had much to prove. That was a particularly bad combination in his history. And many who offered help were simultaneously reaching for something else—pajama bottoms, a wallet, or some type of psychological income drawn from another's bank account.

Still, there were a few people Andy had learned to trust. Unfortunately Gabriel—the person he now needed to help—had been first among them.

Was it a stroke? Alzheimer's? A brain tumor? Whatever it was, Andy knew it wasn't good. But once Gabriel recovered, he had turned away all of Andy's inquiries with an "I'm fine," and "Don't worry about me." Andy had used those phrases enough in his own life to know they were bullshit. Worse, the priest insisted on being by himself, and then made Andy promise not to tell anyone. He felt awful about breaking that promise, but telling Sam wasn't really like telling anyone. She was one of the other people on his "can be trusted" shortlist.

When Andy entered Finally Home looking for Sam, he immediately knew something was amiss. He followed the sound of angry voices and barking to the cage room, where he found Greg and Luke in a standoff with two guys in white jackets. Andy didn't like lab coats, and from the agitated state of the dogs in the cages, they didn't either. Andy's presence made the dogs even more excited: he heard Hips and a few of the other dogs whimper. For Andy, that sound—the admission of complete and utter powerlessness—was a forceful trigger of shameful memories devoid of mercy.

"...until Dr. Lewis gives the OK," Greg was saying, hands on his hips.

"We're on a clock here, sir. We have orders to start the exams," one of the lab techs countered. Andy thought the guy looked like a very tall version of the character Beaker from *The Muppet Show*. Beaker carried an insulated lab cooler. The other tech stood by a large metal suitcase on wheels.

"What the hell is going on?" Andy demanded.

"You really shouldn't be here, kid," Beaker answered.

Beaker's patronizing tone pushed Andy a bit further along his well-worn path to conflict.

Greg must have sensed the energy Andy brought into the room. "We got this, Andy," he said.

Andy wouldn't be put off. "Got what?"

"They're here to take some blood from the dogs," Luke said. "Everything's OK. We're just waiting for Dr. Sam."

Beaker took a step forward. "We'll just start some of the paperwork then."

Andy grabbed Beaker's arm. "We said wait!"

"No, Andy," Luke warned.

Beaker spun on Andy. "You are interfering with a city employee in the performance of official duties. If you don't let go, I will have you charged. That goes for all of you."

Andy felt himself slipping. He could actually see himself from a few feet away squeezing this asshole's bicep. This wasn't piking. Andy knew this sensation, although it had been years since he had experienced an episode. The doctors had called it a dissociative reaction. He heard himself shout, "Don't touch my dogs!" He felt more than saw Luke trying to remove his hand from Beaker's arm, but the grip was too strong. Andy couldn't get his mind to connect with his own hand.

"Let him go, Andy." Sam's calm but firm voice brought him back into his body with a nauseating rush of vertigo. He released Beaker and the tech scurried away, rubbing his arm.

"You OK?" another man standing with Sam by the doorway asked Beaker.

The tech nodded slowly. "This jerk assaulted me. They won't let us near the dogs."

"You need to let us do this," the man told Sam. "It gets ugly quick if you don't."

"It already has," Beaker added.

Andy knew he should just keep his mouth closed at this point, but he couldn't. That whimper echoed in his head. "You can't let them. They want to—" Andy started. Sam shut him down with a glare.

"How about a little compromise, Walden?" Sam offered the man. "You let me take the blood and saliva under your supervision, and you forget about my young and overzealous colleague over here."

Walden looked at Beaker, who shrugged in an "I guess it's the best we're going to do" way.

"OK," Walden said. "But your overzealous colleague needs to make himself scarce."

Sam signaled Andy to leave the room with a nod of her head. Andy complied, but his clenched fists and low growl on the way out left no doubt that he was extremely unhappy with the order.

9

Kendall kept the phone pressed to his ear, hoping for an answer. It had been a strange and challenging day so far—even by city measures—and he just needed to hear her voice.

"Hello?" Ellen finally answered.

Kendall was so relieved that he couldn't form a sentence.

"Jim? Is that you?"

"Yeah...sorry, hon. Bad connection. I just wanted to make sure you and Deb got there OK."

"Actually, we just got in. Traffic out of the city was insane. It seems that a lot of folks had the same idea." Ellen's tone was matter-of-fact. Kendall recognized it as the one she often used with her students.

"Is everything OK?"

Silence.

"Is Deb all right?" he pushed.

"What exactly do you want me to say, Jim?"

"The truth."

"She's scared."

"But you're out of the city now."

"You're a cop. You know damn well fear doesn't work that way. It isn't tied to a zip code. She knows something bad is going on. School is closed…kids are sick…we're here in New Jersey and you're not with us."

"But—"

"You asked, so I'm telling you how it is. That's Deb. Should I even bother to tell you how scared I am? Deb was plugged into her iTunes so I had the news on for the drive. You know what I heard?"

Kendall didn't respond. He already knew the answer.

"I heard what sounded like an awful lot of bullshit. No one has any confidence that they have a handle on this. The CDC is just ducking and weaving. They're still at the 'Is it bigger than a breadbox?' questions. Do they think people won't notice? Well, I've been looking around…people are noticing and they are just as scared as me. This virus is spreading and you've decided to stay at ground zero. Now they have set this perimeter without any explanation as to why they think it is a good idea."

"It is just a temporary solution."

"Really? And who was the genius who thought it was a good idea to literally draw a line in the concrete between those who are safe and those who aren't? That line is going to be a physical flash point. Tell me I'm wrong, Sergeant Kendall."

This wasn't good. Ellen called him that only when she was good and pissed. But he knew he had made the right decision. Ellen needed to make some effort to at least try to understand that. "No," he said. "You're not wrong and that is precisely why I asked for perimeter duty, so I can—"

"You what?"

"I asked to be assigned to supervise the perimeter. I need to be there."

Kendall heard Ellen blow out a lungful of disappointment. "You win, Jim. I give up. You go do your knight thing. I need to get Deb settled. You can call her later."

"Don't hang—"

Kendall heard the line click dead and resisted the urge to throw the phone.

Of course he had requested perimeter duty. If someone was going to tell his people that they couldn't take their dogs with them when they went out into the city at large, he wanted to be that someone. Judgment was critical because words were the only tool he had in his arsenal. The precinct captain had been very clear about their instructions at the emergency meeting: those on perimeter patrol were to advise and, if absolutely necessary, detain and call for backup. "No firearm will leave the holster and no baton will leave the belt," the captain had said. "Any use of force in the absence of a direct and serious threat to your physical person will result in charges."

A few of the knuckleheads in the room had barked and howled in the usual attempt to bring levity to an uncertain situation. But then the captain stepped off the podium and walked among them—something that had never happened during Kendall's time in the precinct. "I can't begin to tell you how much this situation frightens me," he said quietly, so that everyone in the room had to strain to hear him.

Thinking about it now, Kendall realized the captain had sounded a lot like Ellen.

"We've all done perimeter duty before, Cap. What's the big deal?" one cop said.

"This isn't like keeping a bunch of drunken New Year's Eve revelers from pissing on the sidewalk, or moving people away from the mayor's car," he said. "You're going to be telling people who want to leave the area for an hour or a day or even a week that they can't take their animals with them. You ever done that before, Wilson?"

The cop looked at the ground. "No, sir, I haven't."

"And you're going to be telling people who want to cross the barrier into the quarantine area with their dogs that it is a one-way trip because some piss-head politico or scientist said so."

"But everyone is gonna understand. They've seen the news," Wilson said hopefully.

"Three more kids hospitalized in the last hour," the captain answered. "Two more moved to ICU and not expected to make it through the day. No answers about what this thing is or why it hit here. If I was living in Riverside and had kids, I wouldn't trust anything I hear at this point. And guess what?" the captain continued. "You've got nothing better to tell them other than 'go/no go.' I hate that I've got to put you all in that situation. But that's all I've got to work with today. And all you've got to work with today is your training, experience, and professionalism."

"Captain?" Kendall raised his hand. "Why is the governor bringing over the Guard?"

"I don't have an answer for you that is explainable by anything other than one word," the captain replied. "Politics." He spit out the word like it was pus from a tooth infection.

After the meeting, the morning had compressed into a blur of kinetic energy. With a speed learned from numerous anti-terrorism exercises, the NYPD used its familiar blue-and-white sawhorses to establish a perimeter around the city blocks that comprised the Riverside neighborhood. The eastern perimeter ran on Broadway between 103rd and 108th, and Riverside Drive was the western border. Central Park lay four blocks east of the perimeter—an inviting but for now off-limits 843-acre playground of woods, bike paths, and hidden places. Kendall thought that the whole setup looked like a bizarre Macy's Thanksgiving Day Parade route except that the pattern was roughly square, there were no floats or ginormous balloons, and no one was laughing.

All vehicular traffic out of the perimeter was funneled through a barricade at 106th street and Broadway. The police searched all cars and trucks crossing the perimeter to ensure that no one was trying to take a Riverside dog out of the area.

Kendall and his men had explained, joked, smiled, and nodded, and in the end, no one traveling on foot or by auto had made a serious challenge. That was the value of experience and familiarity. His shoulders had even begun to unknot.

Then the National Guard had arrived, and the tenor of the exercise changed. The lieutenant in charge of the Guard unit, a career pro named McGreary, seemed competent and friendly enough, but most of his "men" were just kids in their early twenties. They had little or no history dealing with real New Yorkers, and the automatic weapons these soldiers carried, while intimidating, were a poor substitute for judgment. Kendall felt as if he had been holding his breath since the Guard arrived. He had thought talking to Ellen might make him feel better. Hopefully, that was his one bad idea for the day.

Kendall put his phone in his pocket and watched a heavyset man in his fifties exit a BMW sedan waiting in line for clearance at 106th. Although Kendall didn't recognize the man, he could tell from the way he held himself that an attitude was coming. Kendall wasn't wrong.

The big man reached the front of the line, where two of Kendall's cops waited. "I've been waiting for twenty-five minutes," he told them. "I need to get to my office."

"We understand, sir," a young cop named Tully answered respectfully. "We apologize for the inconvenience, but we need to search the cars. We will get you out as soon as we can."

"That's not good enough," BMW shot back.

Kendall's cops were prepared to ignore him under the heading of typical NYC self-important bullshit. Kendall's standing advice to his cops about blowhards, even before the quarantine, was to let them blow. But one of the soldiers, a big kid—no more than twenty-one or -two—with "OWENS" stenciled on his uniform, walked over to the man. "Please return to your vehicle, sir."

"Look," BMW said, "I don't even own a fucking dog. This is bullshit."

"Return to your car," Owens ordered in clipped speech.

"Who the hell do you think you guys are?" BMW challenged. "You don't tell me what to do. This is the United fucking States of America! My taxes gave you a job, you ungrateful, unemployable bastard."

Owens adjusted the shoulder strap on his M4. "Sir," Owens said, straightening to his full six feet three inches, "this is your last warning. Return to your car."

Kendall looked for Lieutenant McGreary but couldn't find him. Crap. He didn't want to get into a turf war with the Guards, but he couldn't let this escalate either.

BMW took a step back, apparently suddenly aware of the gravity of his situation; he turned and walked to his car as quickly as he could without breaking into a run. Owens followed and leaned into the passenger side window until he was directly in the driver's face. "You're going to insult me for doing my duty? You really have no idea what a bad idea that is, sir. No idea."

"OK, I think that's enough," Kendall said from a step behind.

"Just a friendly conversation, that's all, Officer," Owens said.

"Let it go," Kendall answered. "We don't need that shit here."

Owens stepped away from the car smiling while the terrified man quickly rolled up the window and moved up the line.

Breathe, Kendall reminded himself. *Just breathe.*

10

Gabriel slowly made his way back toward the Ninety-Second Street shelter with 36-A. The priest was in no rush; he knew what awaited his return. Besides, the dog insisted on showing the toy turtle he still carried in his mouth to almost everyone they passed.

Lost within his thoughts, Gabriel was not surprised to find Channa suddenly walking beside him.

"I see you're no longer playing hard to get," Gabriel said bitterly.

"I didn't go anywhere. You were the one who got a bit distracted. Now you feel bad about putting the poor boy through those memories and you're taking it out on me."

"You have a point," Gabriel answered. "I'm also not looking forward to bringing the dog back."

"That's a choice, you know? You don't have to do that. You could give him many more days."

"But then who would be there for the others?"

"Ah, I see," Channa said, her hands folded behind her back in a professorial pose. Gabriel got the sense she was making fun of him. "So you are of the view that the Lord God, Ruler of the Universe, would rather you take a thousand different dogs and give them one good day instead of offering one dog a thousand good days?"

"Yes, I am. And stop being so condescending."

"What makes you believe this? Is this a New Testament or an Old Testament thing?"

"Stop."

"Isn't it better to offer a loving home to one than a glimpse of love to many? Don't you think that by raising them up for only a few hours, you make their return to the cage all the more cruel?"

"I want as many of them as possible to feel kindness—just simple damn kindness—before the end."

"And is that to feed their souls? Or yours?"

"Why are you doing this to me, Channa? Why now?"

"You don't really believe this is coming from me, do you? You know exactly what I am, so stop your whining."

"We could have had this oh-so-meaningful discussion five years ago when I still had a thousand good days to offer a dog like this... when you were still alive. But now? They don't take dogs at the home for demented priests. He appears to have made the choice for me. Let Him grant me a few more years with my mind intact and then we can talk about such niceties as personal philosophy and redemption."

Channa shrugged. "Perhaps He will provide a ram."

Gabriel and 36-A arrived at the Ninety-Second Street shelter entrance. When he took in his reflection in the glass door, he saw only himself and the dog. "Coward," he said, and pushed the door open.

The dog Gabriel brought into the shelter was an entirely different dog from the one he had lured out of a cage that morning. After only a moment's hesitation, this dog pranced from person to person in the waiting room, tail in full wag, the stuffed turtle secure in his mouth. The dog barked playfully at a few of the familiar staff.

36-A obviously had no idea why he was back at the shelter or what was coming, but Gabriel could tell that the staff knew. No one would meet Gabriel's eye. They probably had held out hope that the priest would keep the dog. Now they looked upon his return as just one more confirmation that even the best people—those who are supposed to be the most virtuous—would disappoint them. Gabriel felt their judgment. He wanted to explain his motives, but realized that they probably didn't care at this point; a dead dog was still a dead dog, regardless of the justification.

Steve, the tech, greeted Gabriel with a perfunctory handshake and quickly escorted the priest and 36-A to an exam room where an elderly male veterinarian waited. "You'll stay through it?" Steve asked.

Gabriel nodded. Steve started to close the door. "One moment, please," Gabriel said. He walked 36-A back into the waiting area and scanned the large space, searching. He saw nothing out of the ordinary...nothing that offered any hope.

They returned to the exam room and, without further comment, Gabriel lifted the dog onto the bare metal table. 36-A didn't struggle and instead rubbed his stuffed turtle against the priest's hand. Gabriel knew then that he had earned the dog's trust and he hated himself for it.

The vet produced a small vial of clear liquid and a syringe. He filled the syringe and inserted the needle in 36-A's hindquarters. "It's going to be all right," the vet told the dog kindly. To Gabriel he said, "The shot is just to keep him calm while we insert the IV."

"I know," Gabriel said.

"Father Gabriel has been through this before," Steve explained.

"I'm sorry," the vet said. "It never gets easier. I wish we could keep them all."

Gabriel just wanted it to be over. This one made him feel particularly shameful. He wondered if feeling this bad could actually be the result of doing something righteous. Perhaps it was the progression of his own disease, but Gabriel suddenly felt the weight of every soul he had witnessed in transition pressing on his chest. He made the mistake of glancing into the face of 36-A. The dog looked at him with such open affection that Gabriel's stomach contorted into an excruciating cramp. Then the sedative hit. The priest thought he saw doubt cloud the dog's eyes for the first time. Gabriel placed his hands on the dog's muzzle. "I'm sorry," he whispered. 36-A's eyes slowly closed against the world. The turtle dropped from the dog's mouth and landed on the floor with a soft bump.

Gabriel leaned over and kissed the dog's head. He felt his clerical collar bite into his neck so hard that he gasped.

Steve took out an IV pack. "Are you ready?" he asked Gabriel.

How many times had he been asked that question? How many dogs had passed under his hands on this or a similar cold metal table?

Gabriel willed the exam room door to open, hoping for someone or something to interrupt this sacrifice. Nothing came forward. Rage-fueled tears blurred his vision. Gabriel swayed unsteadily, the memory of prior euthanasias forming a stinging afterimage on his retinas. He recalled other dog toys—pink tennis balls, plush footballs, plastic chewing rings—dropping lifeless and abandoned onto other floors. "Where is Your ram?" he whispered.

The vet inserted the needle into 36-A's forepaw.

"No!" Gabriel shouted. Steve and the vet froze in shocked surprise.

"What is it?" Steve asked.

"There's been a change in plans," the priest said, wiping his eyes. "This one is coming home with me . . . if that's OK."

Steve grinned, his face filled with relief. "Is it OK? That's the best damn news I've had all week."

The vet removed the needle and wrapped bandage tape around the dot of blood already forming on 36-A's forepaw. "He'll be a bit groggy for a little while." When the vet turned to him, Gabriel could see that he was crying. "Thank you for sparing me this one, Father," the vet said, and quickly left the room.

"Each one hurts," Steve offered by way of explanation. "Let me get the adoption forms."

Steve returned a few minutes later and Gabriel completed the paperwork. By that time 36-A was on his feet, although a bit unsteady.

"What are you going to call him?" Steve asked.

Gabriel and the dog exchanged a glance. "Eliot," Gabriel answered. "After my favorite poet."

"I think that suits him," Steve said. The tech escorted the priest and his new dog to the entrance. "So I guess we won't be seeing you anymore for the others?"

Gabriel had been trying to answer that very question himself. There were still so many faces behind cages looking for a single instance of kindness. Should they all die alone? How could that possibly be His purpose when the priest still had days of breath left?

"I'll be back next week," Gabriel said. "For as long as I can still find this place, I'll be back."

11

Kendall had phoned Sam to let her know that he was stationed at the 106th Street vehicle bottleneck if she needed him. At her first break, she picked up an extra cup of coffee and looked for him there.

In the post-9/11 world of New York City, soldiers were not an alien presence. They usually stood silent guard at the main commutation areas: Grand Central Terminal, the Port Authority, and Penn Station. But, except in the immediate aftermath of the Towers and a handful of other situations, the military never actually patrolled the streets; that was Kendall's job. So seeing them at the perimeter was not just odd; it was dissonant and, for Sam at least, frightening.

A line of cars waited for inspection at traffic cones marking the perimeter. Two National Guardsmen in army fatigues and carrying M4s watched as a pair of city cops in street blues searched cars under a large white sign with red lettering that commanded, "No Canines Beyond This Point Under Any Circumstances. No Exceptions."

No one appeared happy to be working together. Kendall had warned her that there was a jurisdictional tug-of-war in play between the cops, under the authority of the mayor, and the Guard, under the authority of the governor. "When the elephants fight," he had said, "the mice get crushed."

She found Kendall standing nearby and offered him the coffee.

"So are we at war?" she asked.

The somber and vexed look on Kendall's face told Sam more about the situation than she really wanted to know. "Define war." He took a sip from the cup. "Thanks for this, but you probably shouldn't be here right now. I'm not loving some of these kids." He indicated the Guard with a lift of his head.

"Please tell me they trained for this."

"As much as you can train a twenty-one-year-old boy. Their CO, McGreary, is pretty solid, but he can't be everywhere and I think these other guys have seen too many movies."

A horn blared. The line of cars waiting to exit across the perimeter remained dead still behind the head car as the cops argued with the driver.

"What the hell now?" Kendall asked no one, and jogged over.

A familiar woman stepped out of the driver's door. Sam recognized her as the usually pleasant history teacher at the nearby intermediate school. Sam had spent last Christmas Eve with the woman, her twelve-year-old daughter, and their beagle Monster after the dog ate a string of Christmas lights—one of those desperate knocks on the shelter door. Because of that prior history, Sam felt privileged to ignore Kendall's advice and joined him at the car.

Sam peeked through the passenger window. The daughter sat in the backseat squeezing Monster into her chest. The only time the daughter loosened her grip on the dog was to wipe away the tears rolling down her cheeks.

"Dr. Lewis! Thank God," the woman said, and grabbed Sam's arm like a bad swimmer going under for the last time.

"What's going on, Joan?" Sam asked, but she'd already guessed the answer.

"I need to get Sarah out of here before this virus or whatever spreads. We're going to stay with her father for a while in Jersey. But they're telling me"—Joan pointed to an officer with the name tag "Tully"—"that I can't take Monster with me."

"I'm afraid that's right," Kendall said with a sympathetic nod.

"Why?"

"I explained this to her," Tully said. "She won't listen." Kendall warned him off with a wave of his hand.

"You didn't explain. No one has. I've been watching the news. The CDC doesn't actually know anything. If they did, they would have made some sort of statement. They're just guessing. First it was birds, now it's dogs, will it be cats tomorrow? This is ridiculous."

"I'm sorry, ma'am, but—"

"What am I supposed to do?" Joan challenged. "Leave Monster in the apartment to starve while we ride away?"

"Isn't there someone else you can leave him with?" Kendall asked.

"Everyone I know is trying to do the same thing. If they're not leaving today, then tomorrow or the next day."

"This should all be over soon. Maybe it would be best if you just turned around and went home," Kendall offered.

"Do you have kids?" Joan asked.

"Yes, as a matter of fact I do," Kendall said.

"Do they live in Riverside?"

Kendall didn't answer.

Joan took his silence for a no. "Lucky you. If they did, you wouldn't even suggest that. Kids are dying from this thing and you all just expect people to hang around?"

"The virus isn't transmitted that way. They need to come into contact with a rabid animal," Kendall argued.

"You don't really know that, do you? And you're telling me to play Russian roulette with my child while yours is safe in his bed? How dare you tell me how to protect my child!"

"Now hold on—" Kendall began.

"No! You hold on. You're not giving me any choice," Joan said, near tears. "Do you have any idea what it's like to have no option?"

"As a matter of fact, I sure do," Kendall said.

"He's just trying to help," Sam said. "Don't take it out on him." Sam leaned into the car window again. Sarah and Monster were both trembling. "Don't worry," she told the girl. "It'll be OK." Sarah nodded but seemed far from convinced.

Sam turned back to Joan and Kendall. "Maybe I have an idea."

"I'm all ears," Kendall said.

"You need to trust me, Joan. Turn the car around and meet me at the shelter."

"But—" Joan protested.

"I said you'll need to trust me."

Ten minutes later Sam led Joan, Sarah, and Monster through the front door of Finally Home. The girl was still crying. "It's OK now," Sam told her. A phrase from another lifetime popped into Sam's head and she voiced it: "Nothing bad is going to happen in our house."

Sam was a little shocked to see that the phrase still held some magic; Sarah smiled at her for the first time.

Luke and Greg joined the group at reception and Sam introduced them. "Can you bring Sarah and Monster into the back and find a comfortable place for him? He may be with us for a little while." Luke led the family to the back room.

"Can I speak to you for a minute?" Greg asked, and pulled her into a corner. Sam didn't miss the fact that he was using his "Daddy voice." She knew a reprimand was coming and she was not disappointed.

"You want to let me in on what's going on here?"

Sam explained the situation at the perimeter.

"Your lease specifically prohibits boarding. Morgan will make sure that this is the final nail."

"We're a little beyond worrying about my lease at this point, don't you think? I'm done here, Greg. Might as well blaze out. Morgan isn't taking anyone in and Sarah's got no one else."

"Yeah, I get it, but you could also lose your shelter license and you won't be able to get that back for anyplace else. And you're probably gonna end up bringing those fools in the lab coats right back to our door. That puts our own dogs in the cross hairs."

"I know, but—"

"Another kid died," he said.

"I know."

"This whole situation will get worse. And when it does, others will come to you as a safe haven."

"Maybe. I'm not sure that's a bad thing."

"You've got no guarantee that you'll be able to protect any of these dogs."

"Yeah, I know, but—"

"But what, Sam?" he snapped.

"But it's the right thing to do."

"When did that ever really matter when it comes to strays?"

"Maybe it should start, OK?"

Greg raised his hands in exasperated capitulation and turned away.

12

The pain shooting through Gabriel's knees from years spent kneeling in prayer would not let him delay his return to the church any longer. He didn't know precisely why he dreaded bringing Eliot across the perimeter into the quarantine zone, he knew only that he did. Steve had offered to board the dog until the quarantine was over, but Gabriel had nixed that idea. The truth was that he couldn't stand the thought of Eliot returned to a cage at this point; the dog would believe the priest had found him unworthy and Gabriel could not be responsible for inflicting that pain on a creature who had done nothing to lose God's light.

As Gabriel crossed over to 106th, he saw the barricades and then the sign: "DO NOT BRING YOUR DOG ACROSS THIS BARRIER. IF YOU DO, YOUR DOG WILL NOT BE PERMITTED TO LEAVE THE AREA UNTIL FURTHER NOTICE. THERE WILL BE NO EXCEPTIONS."

"Not a lot of gray in that," Gabriel told Eliot. When he glanced down, the dog was looking right back at him, wagging his tail and waiting for their next shared experience. The dog's trust left Gabriel a little frightened, but there was another feeling alongside that that

Gabriel at first didn't recognize. It had been so long. Then he knew: the emotion was excitement.

Gabriel searched for a familiar face at the perimeter and found one in Sergeant Kendall. Kendall smiled at him from behind a police sawhorse.

"Hello, Father. And who is this?" Eliot wagged his tail at the attention and lifted the stuffed turtle for Kendall's admiration.

"I'm going to try to foster him for a little while. Keep my cat company."

Kendall's smile faded quickly. "Wish it was another cat. Not a great time to be bringing new dogs into Riverside."

"So I've heard."

"I'm sorry, Father, but once he is in, he'll be stuck in here for two weeks. I don't have the authority to make exceptions."

"I understand."

"You sure you want to bring him through?"

"I'm afraid his urgent circumstances didn't permit another choice."

Kendall pulled the barricade back. "Then welcome to the fun side of the island, sir."

Gabriel closed his eyes and stepped across the line. Kendall pushed the sawhorse back in place behind them. Gabriel imagined he heard a click and a dead bolt sliding closed.

"You got a minute, Father?" Kendall asked.

"Of course."

Kendall brought Gabriel and Eliot over to an older man in army fatigues with a silver bar on each shoulder. "Father Gabriel, this is the officer in charge of the National Guard contingent, Lieutenant Ray McGreary." The lieutenant extended his hand and Gabriel shook it. "Father Gabriel knows a lot of the people in the neighborhood. I figured you might want his number just in case you come across a situation and I'm not around."

"Very much obliged, Father," McGreary said. "I hope you don't mind if I call on you."

"Not at all. I don't know how helpful I can be, but of course I'm happy to try. Any problems so far?"

"Not really," McGreary answered. "Seems like a good bunch of folks, although it doesn't feel like anyone is too happy to have us. A lot different from the feeling we get when we walk through Grand Central Station."

Gabriel noticed a young soldier with the name Owens on his uniform hovering nearby. Owens glowered at Kendall and finally moved off. Gabriel had seen that kind of stare-down before—part dominance display, part territory marking, part insecurity. It was the kind of look you never wanted to see on someone carrying a gun.

"Just nerves, Lieutenant," Gabriel said. "In Grand Central you're stopping terrorists. Here you're telling New Yorkers they can't do something that they've been doing every day, because of a force of nature they can't see. That's a hard thing for people to take in the best of circumstances."

McGreary's cell phone chirped and he grabbed it. "McGreary here … Where? … OK, I'll check it out." McGreary shook his head as he replaced his phone. "You know what a Shiba Inu is, Kendall?"

"Nope," Kendall answered.

"Well, someone on 104th insists that, whatever they are, they're not subject to the quarantine."

Kendall turned to Gabriel. "Catch up with you later?" Gabriel watched Kendall and McGreary move away, already lost in conversation.

Gabriel debated whether to attempt to introduce himself to the other members of the Guard at the 106th perimeter, but they all seemed disinterested or, in the case of Owens, hostile. Fourteen days was a long time. Gabriel figured there would be opportunity enough for pleasantries.

As the priest walked Eliot toward the church, he noticed the back of Andy's head and familiar backpack half a block ahead. Gabriel shouted for him, eager to share the news of Eliot. The boy must not have heard because he continued on, head bent forward in concentration, hands opening and closing to an unknown rhythm or memory.

13

Andy met Sid and his new dog, Louis, at the entrance to Tessie's Bagel Nosh on 104th. The boy and the hardware store owner often met on the bench outside to grab a bagel, drink coffee, and discuss their shared love of classical music. Andy had asked for the meeting today because he thought that, since Sam was unavailable, Sid might be a safe place to raise his concerns about Gabriel. He was pleased that Louis was with them—dogs were always a welcome addition for Andy.

Sid directed Louis to the bench. "Sit," Sid commanded. Louis whined and tugged at his leash. "S-s-s-i-i-i-t-t-t." Sid repeated the word slowly so that it lasted a full ten seconds. Louis wagged his tail, and for just an instant acted as if he might comply. Then a plastic bag blew past and Louis tried to catch it.

"I think you'll need to work on that one," Andy offered. "His ADHD may actually be worse than mine."

Sid looped the leash through the slats of the bench and tied a knot. "Be a good boy and we'll get you a little something." He patted Louis on the head and, together with Andy, walked into the store.

Five minutes later—about when Louis's limited patience expired— a young woman left the shop and rubbed the bored puppy's head. The attention had the same effect as tying a rope around Louis's neck and tugging him down the street.

As the woman walked away, Louis tried to follow. He strained at the leash until he pulled his head through the collar. Finally free, he bolted after the woman.

A few people on the sidewalk noticed the puppy and smiled down at him—a brief respite from the worries of their day. No one associated Louis with the virus or the quarantine; he looked too healthy, too young, and, ultimately, too cute to be carrying a deadly disease. One man tried to grab him, breaking the dog's eye contact with his woman. Louis darted away and the man soon gave up. But by then the woman was gone. The dog spun in a tight circle of confusion and whimpered.

A block behind Louis, Sid and Andy emerged from Tessie's, with Sid trying to manage two messy bagels and a large cup of coffee. "Look, Louie, turkey for—" Sid stopped when he saw the empty leash. "Louis?" Sid called. They searched the area around the bench, but found nothing.

Andy stopped an old woman walking past. "Did you see a puppy?" She shook her head. He repeated the same question to three other pedestrians with the same result.

Sid dropped the bagels on the bench. "I'll go back to my store," he told Andy in growing panic. "It's the one place he knows so maybe he went there."

"I'll keep searching around here."

Once Sid departed, Andy's mind began traveling its overworked path to the worst possible outcomes. One jumped out above all the rest. Of course Louis would not just return to Sid's hardware store. That would happen in a world of love and light—a world where innocent creatures were not destroyed. Andy knew too well that this was not his world.

Andy ran toward the perimeter.

For Andy the act of running was transforming. That sensation—legs and arms pumping, warm city air flooding his lungs, salty sweat beading on his upper lip—brought him back to the many times when he was either running to or away from something. Most often it was running away. Behind him trailed an endless line of foster parents (some who'd tried and some who hadn't), foster brothers and sisters (some of whom he'd loved, but most of whom he'd feared), teachers and school psychologists (who'd come the closest to reaching him, but too often were crushed under the weight of overwhelming caseloads and stifling bureaucracy), and bullies of various ages (whom he could usually outrun but never fully escape).

And ahead of him? Only the knowledge that *innocence* was a synonym for *weakness* and that all promises matured into lies.

"Don't ever look for me in the park at night," he had told Alexa.

"Why?"

No answer. He had his reasons... unpleasant things he had seen in his life, people capable of perpetrating incredible cruelty, all replayed in the shadows of the park. "I will always meet you at the entrance," he said. "If I'm not there, go home. Promise."

She must have seen the love and concern in his face. "OK," she said, and kissed him. "I promise."

Her parents had learned about their park meetings. They had Andy picked up on various bullshit charges. He tried to explain that he needed to meet her, but no one would listen. They threw him back into the juvie system—a bare room behind a cold metal door—to await his disapproving caseworker. Judge Allerton sorted everything out and arranged for Andy's release, but that took until dawn. Andy ran toward Alexa and the park that morning as fast as he could. He was not fast enough.

This time would be different, he told himself. This time he would get there before the shadows. This time he would not be too late.

Andy tried to lock out every memory and focus on that one thought—pick the right street and get there in time.

In less than three minutes, Andy had Louis in his sights. But that was three minutes too long. The dog was a hundred feet away and trotting directly at the perimeter. Andy thought he might have the angle to intercept, but it was going to be close.

"Louis!" Andy called out as his long legs motored and he closed in.

Sixty feet now, but Louis showed no sign of stopping. Andy pushed harder, his quads burning as he closed the gap.

Louis was ten feet away, but picking up speed.

Andy was down to no choice. He went airborne, his arms stretched out to their full length, his body cutting a sharp line through the air. He timed it perfectly, like something out of a football highlight film.

Andy landed hard on his chest with an *umpf*, his wind gone. His fingers—strengthened from years on the violin—quickly tightened around the dog's middle. Louis strained for a moment against the contact and then relaxed in Andy's hands.

But the shadows were unyielding. In the next moment, Andy was on the ground staring at his empty hands. Louis had slipped free and was running again at full speed toward the perimeter.

Andy scrambled to get to his feet. He knew he would be too late once again—this time by seconds. With no ally in the twenty feet between Louis and the perimeter, the entire street was about to witness in vivid, bloody color the reality of the new quarantine.

Andy could only look on in horror as a hulking blond soldier dropped to one knee no more than ten feet in front of Louis and slipped a black baton from his belt. The soldier raised the baton an inch above his shoulder.

"No!" Andy screamed.

Louis was less than three feet from the perimeter, oblivious to the threat. The pedestrian traffic froze in place, watching the inevitable. Andy braced himself for the blow as the soldier swung the club down.

14

Kendall threw his right shoulder into Owens's chest. The blow lifted Owens off the ground. They rolled on the sidewalk and came to a stop with Owens on his back and Kendall straddling him. Kendall's face was inches from Owens's eyeballs. "This is New York, you dickhead!" Kendall screamed. "We don't club puppies in New York!"

Kendall heard the telltale mechanical clicks before he finished his sentence. He looked up and saw that four Guards had surrounded him, their automatic rifles pointed at his head.

"I'm NYPD," Kendall shouted. He raised his hands while sitting on Owens's chest.

"We so don't care," one of the other soldiers said. "Get off him."

Kendall struggled to obey, his arms lifted uselessly in the air and the rifles aimed at his skull. Kendall saw Andy step forward and quickly waved him away. A crowd began to gather around them and the Guard urged it back. In the commotion Louis retreated unharmed from the perimeter and Andy was able to scoop him up.

One of the soldiers noticed. "Sit tight, kid," he ordered. Andy reluctantly complied.

Owens staggered to his feet, pulled his handgun from its holster, and pointed it at Kendall's head. The crowd gasped almost as one, but Kendall didn't even blink. "Get that gun out of my face," Kendall snarled. "Or I will shove it up your ass."

McGreary arrived panting. "What the hell is going on?" he yelled. "I'm away for one goddamn minute! Stand down, soldiers, and secure those weapons. And move this crowd back."

The soldiers with the M4s surrounding Kendall immediately complied with McGreary's order and lowered their rifles. Owens, however, seemed to be thinking it over.

"I said stand down, Owens, you big idiot," McGreary hissed. "You can comply with that order or finish your tour in cuffs. Your choice."

Owens finally holstered his weapon. "Sir, yes sir," he said through clenched teeth. "He attacked me," he added, and then turned to Kendall. "Asswipe!"

"Enough!" McGreary yelled.

Owens walked off, rubbing the back of his head. The other soldiers tried to keep the crowd moving.

Kendall stepped up to McGreary. "That jerk pointed his firearm at me on a public street, Lieutenant. He shouldn't have a gun."

"I have this situation now, Sergeant," McGreary said wearily.

"Well, I don't want him on my street. Get him off it or I will."

"Look, here's the deal," McGreary said. "You could drive a large truck between where you're now standing and the end of your jurisdiction. You've assaulted a member of the New York National Guard in the performance of his lawful duties."

"Lawful duties? He was about to club a puppy on a pedestrian-filled New York City street for no reason other than—"

"Other than he was following his orders."

"What the hell are you talking about? Killing puppies? You got orders to do that?"

"This isn't some game we're playing here, Kendall," McGreary snapped. He glanced at the crowd and dropped his voice. "We have orders to secure the perimeter with force. No dog crosses out of the quarantine area. Period. No exceptions. You want to know what that really means? Talk to your commanding officer or someone with clearance."

"But…" Kendall sputtered.

McGreary's demeanor softened. "I know you're doing your job, Jim. Guess what? Me too. I didn't ask for this assignment and God knows I don't want it. But I don't get to choose my wars or where I fight them. Let's just get through this."

"War? There's no war."

McGreary turned to Andy. "Is that the canine in question?"

Andy didn't answer.

"That's him," the Guard nearest Andy volunteered.

"Did he actually cross the perimeter at any point, Private Bryce?" McGreary asked.

The Guard shrugged. "Don't think so."

"It's not brain surgery, Bryce. Those barricades are the perimeter, did the dog cross it or not?"

"There was a lot going on, Loot," Bryce responded.

"He didn't cross it," Kendall said.

"Give me the dog, son," McGreary ordered.

Andy shook his head. "This can't end that way."

"Come on, kid," McGreary said. "Don't make a scene. Just give him to me."

"What are you going to do with him?" Kendall asked.

"Turn him over to the lab coats. Those are my instructions."

The crowd was getting sticky again, some slowing down while others stopped altogether.

Sid reached the perimeter sucking wind. "What's happening," he gasped.

"Everything's OK," Kendall said. He knew he needed an exit strategy that would protect the dog and that McGreary could accept.

"We're just going to take him to Dr. Lewis to make sure he's OK."
He turned to McGreary, hoping the lieutenant understood that bad
things happened in crowds and this was neither the time nor the place
for an aggressive move.

"She's a vet?" McGreary asked.

Kendall nodded. "She's just a few blocks away, within the
perimeter."

"Please," Sid added. "Let us take him."

McGreary looked like he was doing some calculations in his head.
"OK. Makes sense to me," he said. "Bryce, you go with them to make
sure the dog is OK and report back." McGreary moved Kendall two
steps farther away and spoke in a whisper. "I'm giving you this one
because you say the dog didn't cross over. I'm trusting you. Don't
prove me wrong."

"I won't," Kendall said.

"And please, for both our sakes, stay away from Owens until I can
get him transferred out of here."

15

In the relative quiet of Sam's exam room, Sid held Louis on his lap while Sam completed her examination. Sid's hands trembled so badly that she took them in her own. "It's OK now," Sam told him, trying to convince herself of the same thing.

A tear rolled down Sid's cheek and he wiped it away with a meaty paw. "I was so scared. I thought that was going to be it. Thank God for Jim and Andy. I was so stupid leaving Louis tied to the bench with all this going on."

"Louis is fine." Sam rubbed the dog's ears as if that would prove the truth of her statement.

"But for how long? You didn't see the look on their faces. There's something else going on here."

Her father's words about the inevitability of a QCK campaign echoed in Sam's ears. "Let's not panic yet," she said.

"I just don't want to sit around waiting for the day they decide to start knocking on doors. But there's no place to go either. I feel so helpless." Sid rose from the chair holding Louis to his chest. "What would you do if they ever came for Nick or your other dogs?"

Sam allowed herself to think about the reality behind the question.

Could it really happen here? In vet school one of her professors had made her class memorize a quote from William Ralph Inge: "We have enslaved the rest of the animal creation, and have treated our distant cousins in fur and feathers so badly that beyond doubt, if they were able to formulate a religion, they would depict the Devil in human form."

She fought against Inge's image of damnation every day, and it really was a fight because complacency was so much easier. How many others were prepared to fight? Certainly not her father. Why would she expect the governor or the mayor to be any different?

And what if they did come through that door?

Sam wore the answer to Sid's question on her face.

"Just promise me that you'll take Louis with you," Sid said.

"If it ever comes to that then Louis will be right beside me, Nick, and all the others."

She realized it was a silly thing to say even before the words came out of her mouth. As if she really could save these dogs when she didn't even have the first idea of the cause or the epidemiology of the virus. As if she was going to take on the governor and the Guard with her volunteers and little stethoscope. As if she even mattered.

"I want you to keep Louis here with you," Sid said.

"But Sid—"

"You can say he's under your care."

"I don't think they're gonna give a damn what I say."

"Please. Perhaps it will buy him some time when the knock comes."

Because Sam knew she had no better answer for him, she nodded. She escorted Sid to reception and left him with a hug and a kiss, after which he looked a bit better.

Back in her office, Sam stared at a favorite photo of her mother, taken during a rare mother-daughter weekend a year before her death. They had been hiking in the snowy Vermont woods. Her mom looked youthful, confident, and fit, so vivid.

"I could really use some advice, Mom."

"Trust yourself," her mom would always say. But now it was too easy for Sam to see where her own decisions had taken her. Charlie? Gone. Shelter? Gone. Sanctuary? Gone. Dad? Gone. Mom?

Gone.

"I'm not smart enough to figure this out," Sam told the photo.

Nick nudged the door open, lay down at her feet, and broke her spiral of self-doubt. "Why are you so tired?" Sam knelt and carefully examined Nick's eyes. She had a fleeting horrible thought, but then shoved it out of her mind. It's not possible, she decided; the universe just isn't that cruel.

She buzzed Greg on the intercom. "Did Nick's blood work get faxed over?"

"Yep."

"Any problems?"

"And I'm just keeping that information from you?"

"Just checking. Don't be mean. My inner child is suffering enough today."

"His blood was perfect like all the rest."

That was a profound relief. "Well, you sure as shit tired him out today."

"I do have that effect on men."

"Can you take him back to my apartment? I want to give him a break."

"That I can do."

Nick was fine. Of course he was. She knew that. But she also knew that she had lied to Tom. She did do the what-if thing—so often, in fact, that she was surprised she got any sleep at all.

What if Nick wasn't fine?

What if Sam had been a member of one of those families with a dog that needed to leave the quarantine?

What if soldiers started to knock on doors because people panicked?

What if another dog challenged the perimeter?

Sam knew that she could try to wait it out, play the odds, and see if someone would attempt to do something to her or the creatures she cared about. Or she could try to do something now.

Trust yourself.

With a final glance at her mother's photo, Sam fished the business card out of her pocket. She dialed his number and paced until he picked up.

"Walden," he said.

Sam explained her plan.

"I don't know about this," he said finally. "You have no idea the crap that's going on. The situation is deteriorating and the governor isn't helping. Now there've been multiple reports of a pack of strays in the park exhibiting suspicious behavior."

"You guys do know the park pack thing is all an urban myth, right?" Sam said.

"It's impossible to tell what's real and what's just mass hysteria at this point. Maybe there is a pack of strays. We know there have been rabid raccoons in the park. Perhaps the strays could be infected."

"But none of those raccoons have ever transmitted to dogs. There's some species transmission barrier going on there."

"Maybe the barrier is broken now for some reason. I don't know. I'm waiting for people to start showing up at Bellevue claiming they've got puppies growing inside them."

"You said you wanted an ally. I'm giving you a way to avoid trouble at the perimeter and a more aggressive response from others. But for this to work, I need the mayor's commitment that the dogs who come in will be safe. No visits from your lab brigade. I will draw bloods and turn them over to your folks; the dogs here are under my care. Otherwise people won't trust this. And I want your commitment, Tom, that I can believe her."

"Am I talking into a microphone again?"

"No. I now know about something better."

"What?"

"Your broken watch."

"I should've never told you about that…What if a dog shows signs?"

"You'll be the first to know."

"You'll need to give those animals up. No fight."

"I know and I will."

"So you're saying I'm supposed to trust you?"

"Think of it as a two-way street."

"But you don't have a broken watch," Tom said.

"You visited the shelter, Tom. You know I'm surrounded by them."

"OK, I'll speak to the mayor. But this isn't a halfway thing, Sam. *Old Yeller* didn't exactly have a happy ending. You can't just change your mind once the shit hits the fan. Even if it gets painful."

"I know. Don't worry about me. I can do painful."

16

The approach of another evening found Gabriel again in his sanctuary. This time, however, the room did not feel so dark, the ornamentation was not as overwhelming, and the wooden crucifix did not seem so high above his head. He didn't even pay attention to the broken window.

Gabriel sat cross-legged before the chancel with Eliot on one side of him and Molly on the other. The first few interactions between cat and dog had been less than successful. When Molly initially saw the dog, she glared at Gabriel as if he were an unfaithful husband bringing his mistress to Thanksgiving. Eliot, for his part, could not have been more excited. He must have known a friendly cat in the past because he barreled into Molly, oblivious to her claws and temperament. Molly whacked him on the nose a few times, even drawing a bit of blood, but Eliot was undeterred in his affection. Gabriel would have felt bad for the dog, but the mutt seemed to be having such a good time.

This was now the second hour and Eliot was beginning to wear Molly down. The cat allowed him to get within six inches before hissing and turning around to show the dog her rear end. Gabriel thought of the song one of his younger congregants sang—"Talk to my butt 'cause my hand's too busy and my face ain't got nothing to say"—and laughed.

"I haven't heard that sound in this room for quite some time, Gabe." Channa stood next to him.

"What can I say? You were right after all. As usual."

Channa reached down and rubbed Eliot's head. "I wish you could see the world as he does," she said.

"And what would I see?"

"You would see the entirety of his *were*. To know things even though he can't recall precisely how or when he had learned them. No memory as you conceptualize it."

"You mean instinct."

"No." Channa shook her head. "I mean grace. He knows that what he smells can be trusted more than what he sees and what he hears. He knows that people lie through their appearance and their speech— a bright child with beautiful clothes, blue eyes, blond curls, and a sweet voice can deliver a mean kick or offer spiked water, while an old man whose only possessions are his half-rotted teeth and an impossibly worn shirt can offer warmth and comfort. He knows to walk away if the child smells wrong, no matter what the child looks like or says. If the man smells kind, then his filth and grime are illusory and the gibberish he speaks is no more dangerous than the thunder the dog often hears over his head on August evenings. That type of knowing is not instinct. It comes from his connection to the Divine."

"And is there a message for me in that?"

"Memory and knowing are so different. Give up on memory, Gabriel. You will not have it. But you will still have knowing."

"Will I still know divisiveness? Will I continue to know hurtfulness and malevolence? Will those persist as the gifts of my own connection to the Divine?"

"Yes," Channa said, her voice low with regret.

"Then you can tell Him to keep his damn knowing."

"Gabriel?"

A hand pulled at him. "Gabriel? Are you all right?" The priest knew this was not Channa's voice. "Gabe?"

Sid stood beside him. "Of course I'm all right," Gabriel snapped, and glanced around. Molly was long gone, but Eliot was now asleep in his lap. How long had it been this time, the priest wondered.

Sid's face dropped into his view. "No, you're not. You were just sitting there. Staring off. I've been calling your name."

"What are you doing here, anyway?"

"What? A Jew can't go into a church?"

"You know what I mean."

"You need to see a doctor, Gabe."

"Don't change the subject."

"What subject is more important than your health?"

"I can think of a few. Besides, I've been to a doctor. Several, in fact. The church has a marvelous medical plan."

"And?"

"And I smoked cigarettes and drank Scotch every day for forty years. I'm in perfect health for a hundred-and-twenty-year-old." Gabriel moved Eliot off his legs (the dog didn't even stir), and rose from the floor.

"Let me help you at least."

Gabriel ignored the plea. "Are you going to tell me why you're really here or not?"

"I came to tell you about what happened with Louis and to see your new dog."

"Andy told me about Louis. Tying him to a bench? Not your brightest move, Sid."

"Thank you for your comforting words, Father." Sid closely examined the priest's face. "You have no idea how bad you actually look."

"I wasn't really asking for your opinion."

"Maybe you should. You know, even a blind pig finds an acorn once in a while."

"Meaning?"

"I know I can't hold a candle to Channa when it comes to being insightful, but sometimes relief comes simply from knowing there's an interested ear—regardless of what the head attached to the ear actually understands. She valued your friendship and I really would like to honor that, but you just keep on pushing me away."

"And what if I have? I'm old. I don't want to make friends anymore."

"Are you so sure there is nothing left to be learned?" Sid put out his hand. "Whatever else you've got going on, just allow me the privilege of being your friend."

Gabriel thought of Eliot. There was more to learn. But he was so weary. "I don't think I still know how to do that—if ever I did."

Sid pushed his hand out farther. "You do know. I saw it between you and Channa...when I wasn't blinded by my jealousy."

"You? Were jealous of me?" Gabriel grinned like a high school boy who learns for the first time that a girl thinks he's cute.

"Don't get smug about it," Sid said. "But Channa always said if you weren't a priest you would've given me a run for my money." Sid nodded to his still-outstretched hand. "You do know how to do this, Gabriel."

The priest felt something shift within him, or, more accurately, return to a space long since vacant. Was it that simple? he wondered. Just knowing that someone had once loved you back? That you had been worthy of the affection of someone you thought was more than worthy? Perhaps it wouldn't be sufficient for tomorrow or the day after, but for today, it was enough to allow him to see the way forward.

Gabriel took Sid's hand in his own. "Fair warning, though," Gabriel said. "I can be a miserable bastard sometimes."

Sid laughed. "I've actually heard that about you. Now tell me about this new dog."

17

Sam was sitting in her office attempting to make it through a mound of neglected paperwork when her cell phone pinged with an incoming text message. The caller showed up as anonymous. "Terms are accepted. Mayor to announce in 30 minutes. Get prepared. Will be a 4-hour open window for drop off. Best we could get the gov to agree to. Supplies coming. Thank you. Broken Watch."

Sam summoned Greg, Luke, Andy, and Beth into the break room and explained the development. She expected a hundred questions, but instead faced a stunned silence.

"I want you to know that this was my decision and I own it. I thought it was the best way to try to save some dogs. But I know you guys didn't sign up for this. I don't know what we're dealing with or whether any dogs we'll take in have the virus or even whether the virus can be transmitted. As a precaution, I am going to ask each of you to take a rabies vaccine. I've already had mine. It's not as bad as it used to be. If you can't stay, I totally understand and you'll always be welcomed back when this is over. I won't think any less of you. But I need to know who is staying and who's going and I need to have your decision now."

Beth raised her hand. "So are you saying that I'm free to go?" she asked.

Sam tried hard to swallow her disappointment. *Shame on me for believing people can change,* she told herself. "Yes," Sam answered. "This wasn't part of the deal. You can go and I will recommend to Judge Allerton that you be released from any further service."

"Good," Beth said as she lifted herself off a chair. "Can we order some pizza? The threat of a biological disaster always makes me hungry."

If the pope had suddenly appeared in the room with sunglasses and a Mohawk, he would not have received more openmouthed stares.

"But...," Sam stammered.

"Look, I just wanted to have a choice again," Beth said. "Now I do."

Sam found her voice after a minute. "I don't know what to say."

Beth rolled her eyes, uncomfortable with the positive attention. "Just say half green peppers and half onions."

Sam turned to Greg. "How many more dogs do you think we can handle here?"

Greg, maybe for the first time ever, was at a loss for words. "I don't...I..."

"Just give me your best guess."

"Maybe eighty? If we had extra help and we used the basement."

"I was thinking ninety, but maybe that's pushing it."

Greg shook his head. "But we don't have any equipment or supplies for that many."

At that moment Kendall entered the room, carrying an armful of blankets. "Hey," he called out. "I need a hand unloading the truck."

They all followed Kendall outside to a New York City police truck parked in front of the shelter. The truck was loaded with kennel crates, mats, towels, a stack of fifty-pound bags of dog food, and metal bowls. Two Guards in a Jeep on the opposite side of the street paused to watch

Kendall lift a kennel off the police truck, but they made no move to help him.

"Is this all for us?" Sam asked.

"Yeah," Kendall said. "A gift from Her Honor, the mayor."

Sid stepped out from around the police truck wearing his ancient tool belt. "We're going to need to do a bit of reorganizing," he said. "How's the basement?"

"It's the same as always," Sam responded. "Just spiders and storage."

"Then I'll start there," he said, moving past her and into the shelter.

"I'll go help him," Luke said.

"Me too," Andy added.

"But I don't like spiders," Beth volunteered.

"Don't worry. These are city spiders," Andy told her. "I'll give them a dollar and they'll leave you alone."

"My hero," Beth said, and followed them inside.

Sam listened to these diverse humans join together to come to the aid of dogs they had never met and took it as compelling evidence that she had made the right decision.

18

Andy stared at a tower of empty litter boxes stacked against the rear wall of the shelter exercise room. "This is it," he said.

"Is there like a magic word?" Beth asked.

"Yeah," Luke said. "The word is *push hard.*"

"That's actually two words," Andy teased. Despite everything going on outside the shelter and his inability thus far to grab Sam's attention to share his concerns regarding Gabriel, Andy was excited to be included in Sam's plan. With his present fully occupied, there was less space for his past to screw with his head. He also didn't mind the quiet and dim dustiness of the basement; it reminded him of the stacks in the New York Public Library, where he had often found safety in years past. Nothing bad had ever happened to him in a library.

Luke and Andy pushed the boxes aside, revealing the door. Beth tried the knob. Locked. Luke produced a key and opened the door. He flipped on the light switch at the top of the stairs and they all made their way down the dozen steps to the basement. They stepped over a few rolled-up carpets, stacks of old newspapers, and broken furniture.

"It's really not all that bad," Beth said. She reached down and picked up a few pieces of what appeared to be large chocolate sprinkles covering the floor. She showed them to Luke. "What's with these?"

"Mouse pellets," he answered.

"She even feeds the mice?" Beth asked. "How sad, in a Cinderella kind of way."

"Not pellets as in food," Andy said. "Pellets as in shit."

Beth dropped the pellets and began to gag.

"Actually," Sid said as he picked a few off the ground, "from the size of them, I'd say rats, not mice. May need to deal with that."

Beth moaned. "I'm gonna die from the Hantavirus in the middle of Manhattan."

Luke handed her a broom and a dustpan. "Sweep first; die later."

Andy pushed a decrepit bookcase away from a wall, exposing an equally old and unused door.

"Creepy," Beth said. She used her broom to swipe some cobwebs from the doorframe.

"Any idea what's behind it?" Andy asked.

"With my luck," Beth said, "it's probably an ancient burial crypt haunted by the malevolent ghosts of kosher deli countermen."

Sid pulled the handle, but the door wouldn't move.

"Anyone got a key?" Andy asked.

Luke shook his head. "As far as I know, it hasn't been opened since we've been here."

"Who needs keys," Sid said. He took a small leather case from his pocket and, using some tiny tools, picked the lock in fifteen seconds.

"Impressive," Andy said. "We could've made a great B&E team, Sid."

Beth took a step back. "This is the part where some monster leaps out and eats the fat girl, isn't it?"

Andy pulled the door. It screamed on old hinges as it slowly opened.

"Here it comes," Beth said, and dropped down behind him.

The group stared straight into the gaping maw of…

Another door.

This one must have been locked from the other side because they saw neither a lock nor a doorknob. Andy pushed on the door but it didn't move.

Beth brushed the dust from her hands. "So much for that."

"We can probably break it open," Andy offered.

"Why would we?" Beth protested. "Locked doors are usually locked for a reason."

"Where's your sense of adventure?" Andy asked.

Beth shook her head. "Those very same words have started every great journey toward a painful and humiliating end."

19

"Need help up here!" Sam yelled down from the top of the stairs.

The crew from the basement joined Sam in reception just in time to see the first dogs enter the shelter—a Havanese with her elderly woman, a pug with a father and daughter, a Pomeranian with a woman about Sam's age, and a black Lab pulling a man in his twenties.

With the arrival of the dogs, Sam could no longer deny that this really was happening. She tried to channel all her emotions—exhaustion, fear, anger, and a half dozen others—into controlling the situation in the hope this would delay the brewing panic: "Luke, start taking the histories. I want to know as much about these animals as we can. Andy, you're in charge of crates and blankets. Let's start up here first until we know what we've got in the basement. Beth, you've got supplies—bowls, food, newspaper. Greg, you're in charge of every-thing. I want to start exams as soon as the dogs are settled."

By the end of the first hour, the shelter had received thirty-three dogs. By the end of the second, the total was fifty-one and more were coming.

The humans doing the drop-offs all looked grim, steeling themselves for a separation of uncertain duration and consequence. They were choosing a path before someone else chose for them and that was both empowering and terrifying. Some brought their dogs because children lived in their homes or down the hall. Others brought their dogs because they were taking their children out of the zone until the virus was resolved. And still others brought their dogs to the shelter because of swirling rumors that any dog not in an official shelter would eventually be confiscated and that Sam's shelter was going to be the only game in town. Nothing brings out New Yorkers in droves like the phrase *space is limited*.

The dogs Sam examined showed no obvious signs of disease, only heartbreak. It always came down to this—pleading, confused, and imploring eyes watching as their human companions backed away. Dogs lunged after their departing owners, whimpering and looking for anything familiar. No amount of soothing words could convince them that their new cages were only temporary. Owners lingered in the reception area, trying to catch glimpses of their beloved creatures after Sam or her staff took them into the back. Some owners brought their children to say goodbye, and these partings were the worst of all—neither child nor animal understood the why of what was happening, only that it was and it hurt.

The shelter crew worked nonstop taking histories, performing exams, giving the dogs whatever limited exercise they could manage within the confines of the building and small yard, and cleaning cages. The last was a Sisyphean task; there was always more shit and pee to clean.

During the course of the day, Sam learned that six of the dogs were refusing to eat the food provided. This by itself wasn't unusual given the dramatic and traumatic change they had just experienced in their lives. But when Sam checked on them, she noticed they were also listless—what she called logy.

In an abundance of caution, Sam moved these six into a small room on the second floor of the shelter. Sam knew there wasn't enough distance between these dogs and the others for much hope of true isolation, but it was the best she could manage under the circumstances. Just like the humans living in Riverside right now, the dogs were all in this together—whatever "this" turned out to be.

Sam was halfway up the steps to the isolation room when she heard someone call her name. She turned to see Tom charging after her. Sam prayed that no one had mentioned the isolation room in his presence.

Tom smiled. That was a good sign. She brought him to her office and closed the door. "What are you doing here, Tom?"

"I thought I'd stop by to see how it was going," he said.

"You really didn't need to. I would've called if there was an issue."

"Yeah, well..."

"You're checking up on me?"

"Let's just say my motives are mixed. My ass is on the line with this too. So when the mayor asks, I want to be able to give her a little more detail about what I got her into."

"The detail is that we're going crazy, but so far we've been able to manage. Tell her that I've got a good crew."

"They certainly seem loyal to you."

"If you believe in the same things, loyalty comes easy."

"So nothing suspicious?"

"The whole damn thing is suspicious, Walden."

"You know what I mean."

"No signs of sickness. I told you that you'd be my first call. You're getting copies of the lab work anyway, so it's not like I'm going to be able to hide it from you."

"I didn't think you would. I was kind of hoping that you would start to see we're sort of on the same team...at least I'm trying to meet you partway there."

"I'm sorry. I'm just tired and really stressed."

"I understand. Is there anything you need? Anything I can do for you?"

"You can tell me what you're hearing and make it good news."

"The Guard is getting jittery. The governor is insisting that we take a very close look at the park based on rumor. And the CDC is being as tight-lipped as ever."

"So basically you've got nothing."

"I got nothing. Now you know why I'm so darn happy. But at least I've got nothing to hide."

"I'm counting on that."

"I know."

"I've got to get back." Sam quickly escorted Tom out of her office and to the shelter's front door. If he believed he was being given the bum's rush, Tom kept it to himself. "Keep the lines open," she told him.

"You too," Tom said just before Sam closed the door on him.

20

Gabriel visited the shelter to see if he could offer any help and perhaps even some comfort. What he saw left him speechless at first.

The dogs and their humans had formed three rows in front of a
long folding table. Riverside's canine population was as varied as the
humans who lived there. The larger dogs were on leashes, some with
muzzles. Because these were city dogs, they generally were used to
people and other dogs, so there were few fights and nothing that drew
blood. The smaller dogs, the noisiest of the group by far, stayed in carriers, crates, or cardboard boxes of wildly differing quality and cost.

Gabriel saw that helplessness and fear were great equalizers:
investment bankers stood in line behind teachers, construction workers, housekeepers, and the chronically unemployed. Dogs with pedi-
gree papers and breeder certificates waited in line next to mutts, and
all seemed keenly aware that their humans were stressed and, in some
cases, close to panic. The humans left behind the usual city-dweller
practice of avoiding eye contact with strangers. Now they not only
shared glances and understanding nods, but also sentences—short to
be sure, but entire sentences—of compassion and support.

Amid the confusion and anxiety, Gabriel also observed instances
of dignity, grace, and empathy:

An African-American Vietnam War veteran in full dress uniform patiently waited in line with his cane and white-muzzled German shepherd. When it was his turn at the table, he filled out the required paperwork, gently patted the dog on the head, and handed him over to Luke. The veteran must have recognized Luke's military tattoos: he snapped a crisp salute and Luke returned it with equal respect. Then the veteran spun on his heel, straightened his uniform jacket, and, with tears streaming down his cheeks, limped out of the room.

A few moments later, a woman in her thirties held tightly to her Pomeranian with one arm and her eleven-year-old son with the other. She told her son that he needed to be brave and that everything would be OK. When they got up to the table and it was time to hand the dog to Greg, Gabriel saw that she was literally unable to unfold her arm and release the dog. "Pommie was a gift from my late husband," she told Greg.

The son gently reached into the crook of his mother's arm and, asking the dog and his mother to be brave, passed their dog over.

An elderly couple held hands as they waited in line with their golden retriever. They made an effort to smile encouragement at everyone around them. When they got to the table, they completed the paperwork together and passed the golden over to Beth, their hands entwined through the leash handle. The man smiled. "Please take good care of her."

"We will," Beth said.

"You see, we never were able to have human children," the wife added.

Gabriel looked on as Beth purposely dropped a pen under the table so she would have an excuse to bend down and quickly wipe her eyes.

Throughout this tide of drop-offs, Gabriel shook hands, hugged, and led prayers for safety, health, and peace. He would've thought that the partings, continually repeated, would become indistinguishable. But like dreams and lies, each one was different, as unique as the dog being transferred and the family it had lived with. The only constant was fear.

"Look into their faces," Channa had told him. "Bear witness."

Gabriel honored Channa's request for as long as he could, but in the third hour he succumbed to the swirl of emotions surrounding him. Gabriel ran back to the quiet of his sanctuary and the comforting embrace of Eliot and Molly moments before he collapsed into an exhausted heap.

He dreamed of cold steel tables and piles of dead dogs.

21

Sam was almost an hour late for her hourly check of the dogs in isolation, but she finally made it up the stairs. As soon as she opened the door, the stench nearly overwhelmed her. She recognized the odor in an instant. The dogs were still at her approach, which was even more frightening because it brought her back to another room with silent dogs in rows of cages. But no one had severed these dogs' vocal cords. The silence here meant only one thing.

Sam peered into the nearest cage, dreading what she anticipated. She wasn't wrong. "Greeeeeg!"

He ran up the stairs in seconds and charged into the room. He took one look at the dogs. "Christ! What the hell happened?"

Bloodstained diarrhea was splattered across three of the cages.

"We need to start IV fluids now!" Sam ordered. "Get Luke and the others."

"On it." Greg ran out of the room.

"Don't you die on me," she told the dogs.

Working together in the tiny room, Sam and her team ran IV lines, started the dogs on a powerful antibiotic in case the cause was bacterial, took new blood and fecal samples, and cleaned the dogs and the cages. Greg, Luke, and Beth all helped. Sam had never been more grateful for her staff. They were tireless and worked without complaint in the face of a biological foe they couldn't see or understand.

When they had finished, Sam sent everyone except Greg out with instructions to check on the dogs in the basement and to process the few additional dogs waiting for intake.

Once they were alone, Greg eyed the row of hanging IV bags. "We're going to need to let the CDC know about this," he said. When Sam didn't respond, he added, "Aren't we?"

"We don't even know if this illness is related," Sam answered. "There is no stage of rabies with these symptoms, and none of the rabies symptoms are present in any of these dogs. Plus, all these dogs were vaccinated, according to the records."

"But you said the rabid dog they found was also vaccinated."

"That was one very rare instance where the vaccine didn't take. You think the vaccines for all these dogs just failed?"

"Hey, I'm not the one living the 'this is all a coincidence' fantasy."

Sam shook her head. "These people trusted us with their animals. If we turn them over to the CDC, what are the chances they'll ever see them again?"

"But if they're contagious...?" Greg let the question hang.

"I know," Sam replied. "But they're just as contained here as they'd be anywhere else."

"And I'm assuming you don't want to send out the new samples for testing because it will alert the city and the CDC."

"Right, we will need to use our own equipment."

"We're talking about the same 'equipment'? Our high school–level microscope and a box of chem strips?"

"Better than nothing. They're good enough for basic blood and fecal smears."

"If you say so. What about telling your new best friend Walden?"

"Same answer." Sam shook her head. "Then he will just report them."

She recalled Tom's words about the proximity continuum. How close were these sick dogs to ground zero? Pretty damn close, she concluded. Their heads would be off and their brains biopsied two hours after she made the call. Then they would seize every dog at the shelter, and then each one in the neighborhood—including her own. The continuum would demand their lives, just as it had those of the pigeons. When it came to animals, those in charge had a "shoot first, ask questions later" mentality that resulted in unacceptably high body counts.

Greg examined Sam's face until she was forced to look away. "Did I miss a conversation somewhere?" he asked. "You know? The one where you tell me what the hell is really going on here?"

"We just need a little time."

"Who says?"

"My conscience."

"Time for what, exactly?"

"A better option. The moment I turn these dogs over, that'll be the precise excuse they need to begin a cull—whether this is related or not. I'm just not ready to do that yet." Sam didn't need Greg's agreement, but she wanted it.

"This is a huge risk you're taking, hon."

"I know. All I can tell you is that something isn't right. The mayor and Walden know it too, but they may not be able to do anything about it. Maybe I can."

Greg shrugged his acceptance. "I never figured you for the 'pray for miracles' type, Sam."

"I'm trying to learn to trust."

"You picked a fine time to start. It's your call and I'm with you, but may I remind you that one of the kids with the virus in ICU is sixteen."

"I know."

Beth walked in on them. "You wanted me?"

Sam tossed Beth the keys to her apartment. "I need you to check on Nick. He hasn't been out and I can't leave these guys. Take Andy with you. Get him out of here for a bit. I may need your help with him on something when you get back."

"OK. Can I go through your unmentionables while I'm there?"

Sam couldn't muster the energy for even a mildly hostile verbal response, but the look she gave Beth was enough to send her quickly on her way.

Twenty minutes later Greg ran into isolation and handed Sam the phone. "It's Beth," he said.

"What now?"

"She don't sound right."

Sam tore off her rubber gloves and grabbed the phone. "C'mon, Beth," she barked in the receiver. "I don't have time for games."

"Get over here."

"What's wrong?"

"Just get over here." Beth's voice broke. "Now, OK? It's Nick."

Sam ran.

22

Sam banged open her apartment door and nearly tripped over Beth sitting cross-legged on the floor. Beth cradled Nick's head in her lap and rocked back and forth. She was sobbing so hard she couldn't speak.

Sam saw the pool of bloody diarrhea on the floor at the same time that she smelled it, and dropped to her knees next to Beth. "Let me see him," Sam said. She willed herself into vet mode. She had no choice; otherwise she would melt into an emotional puddle right next to Beth, and Nick needed a vet, not a mourner—at least for now.

Sam felt Nick's abdomen and he whimpered. Then she checked his gumline—gray and sticky. His whole body radiated heat. "I'm so sorry I left you alone," Sam whispered. "I can't believe this all happened so quickly."

Andy came in from the bedroom carrying a stack of towels.

"Did you touch him at all?" Sam demanded.

"No. Beth wouldn't let me go near him. She told me to leave, but I wouldn't."

"OK," Sam said. "We need to get him to the shelter."

Beth turned her ghostly-white face to Sam. "When I walked in, I thought he was dead. When I found Johnny...after he called me...

the smell...I can't..." Beth wiped her nose with her sleeve. "His bowels had opened..." Beth's voice trailed off.

Sam pointed to Andy. "I need you to get downstairs."

"No. I can help."

"You can't help here. Keep watch downstairs and let me know if you see any Guards or cops. Call me on my cell immediately if you do." Andy hesitated. "Please," she said. Andy finally nodded and ran out.

Nick was too weak to walk. Sam called Greg and when he arrived, he helped carry Nick down the stairs in a sheet. After Andy gave them the all clear, they moved Nick into the back of Greg's waiting car.

Sam sent Andy and Beth on ahead to the shelter on foot while she sat in the back of the car with Nick's head in her lap. Thank God they wouldn't need to cross the perimeter, she thought.

At the shelter Greg and Sam quickly carried Nick inside without meeting any Guards. They brought him directly to the isolation room and immediately ran an IV bag into his right leg. Beth hovered and tried to be helpful, but Sam wanted to stand vigil over her dog alone and be something other than a vet. She directed Greg and Beth to other tasks, but Beth wouldn't leave her side.

Sam checked the other dogs in isolation; they were no worse, which at least was something. Still, Sam knew she couldn't just continue to push fluids indefinitely. She understood that she needed help, but if she told Tom, then the dogs—including her Nicky—would become some political football between the mayor and the governor. And then what? The QCK campaign would move forward under its gathering momentum. Yes, she would tell Tom. Just not yet. Not until she found at least one thread to follow, not before...

Beth broke into her thoughts. "Will he be OK?" Sam noticed that Beth was still unsteady and ghoulishly pale.

"I don't know yet," she said. "Back there at my apartment, when you talked about that boy, Johnny...I didn't know you were the one who found him."

Beth pushed the tips of her fingers through Nick's cage and, in a fleeting moment of macropsia, Sam couldn't tell where the cage ended and where freedom began—if it ever did.

"He called me," Beth said, her voice filled with shame. "Said he needed to talk. I missed the call. The service didn't send it. Or they did, and I just didn't pay attention. I don't really know anymore. I got the second message, though. He said he would be waiting in my office. And he was. I had these beautiful antique wooden beams in my office. He brought his own rope." Beth tried to reach Nick's fur, but couldn't get close. "And no, I don't know why or even if there is a why. I'd like to believe there was one and I just didn't figure it out in time, but I'm no longer sure of that."

Sam stared into Nick's cage, afraid to look Beth in the face. "I identified my mom's body at the morgue. I knew the why—my mom's BAC was over twice the legal limit when she flipped the car. I think I even know the why behind the why. Knowing the reason doesn't change anything. At least it didn't for me."

"That can't be true."

"How's that?"

"If it didn't matter, you wouldn't hate him so much. And even a disgraced rube like me can see what that anger has cost you. The truth is, when you cut through all the bullshit, we are all only the product of what someone else did to us or didn't do to us." Beth shrugged. "I'm too old for this heart-wrenching shit. I liked me better when I was self-medicating."

"You don't really mean that."

Beth thought for a moment. "No, I don't, but oh how much easier it was." She walked out of the room, leaving Sam alone to ponder the cages.

Sam dug out her cell phone, scrolled through the directory, and located the number she needed. She pressed "Talk" and waited for the phone to ring on the other side.

"Hi Jonathon, it's Samantha again. I need a really big favor. I need you to get a note to my father."

23

Sam dreaded this meeting, but it had to be done and, unfortunately, she was the one who had to do it.

She called Andy into her office. "I know there was something you wanted to talk to me about," she said. "But there's something I need to get out first. You've been absolutely terrific... I couldn't ask for a more dedicated worker."

Andy nodded. "Thanks."

"I'm sorry, Andy, but you can't stay here tonight."

Andy's head snapped backward as if she'd slapped him. "What?"

"We have sick dogs now. You're too young. It would be irresponsible to let you stay."

"The sick dogs have nothing to do with the virus hurting the kids."

"We can't be sure of that."

"You don't believe the two are related. Otherwise you'd be turning those dogs over, wouldn't you?"

"That decision is a lot more complicated."

"And even if the two are related, I'm nineteen, not a kid!"

"We don't know anything about this virus except that it affects younger people. That means you."

"But—"

"A sixteen-year-old kid is in intensive care. I'm not taking a chance on a few years' difference."

"It's my choice. I control my own life now."

"No. Actually, this time you can't. Your presence here is my responsibility and my decision."

"Don't do this to me."

"Andy, right now this shelter is like one big cage, a dangerous one. And I'm trying to keep you safe by taking you out of it."

Andy shook his head in a way that struck Sam as both knowing and very sad. "I don't think you know a lot about cages, Dr. Sam."

He sounded so young and hurt that Sam's resolve momentarily wavered. Then she remembered the video on the news of the ambulance pulling up to Riverside Hospital and the young girl on the stretcher with the bag valve mask over her face. "I promise, as soon as we get through this, you'll be back. It'll probably only be a day or two. Besides, Sid will need someone to cover the store while he's working on stuff here. It would be a big help."

Andy charged out of the office without another word.

After a few minutes, Beth knocked and entered. "What'd you say to the kid?" she asked. "He tore out of here like you just told him Santa was dead."

"I told him he needed to stay away until we figured this virus thing out. He's too young."

"Yeah," Beth said. "I was actually wondering when you'd realize that."

"I'm slow, but I eventually get there. You think he'll be OK?"

"I'm like the last person you'd want to offer an opinion on that."

"Can you just check up on him? Try to be an ear for him?"

Beth was already shaking her head before Sam finished the question. "We discussed this, remember? Dead kid? Suicide? In my office? Swinging like a pendulum?"

"Please? He seems to like you for some bizarre reason."

"You hear that sound?" Beth asked.

"What sound?"

"The sound of me banging my head against the wall until the brains spill out of my skull."

"So that's a yes?"

24

Andy entered the park more hurt and angry than he could remember. His mind raced with questions. How could Dr. Sam do this? Didn't she understand what they all meant to him? And if she understood, how could she do this knowing how important it was for him to be a part of something bigger than the jagged confines of his history?

Screw them, he decided. If they didn't want him, he knew another family that welcomed him no questions asked.

Andy left the main path and crossed into the familiar area of the park—his place—so blinded by rage that he didn't notice the object until he almost tripped on it. Once he saw it, though, he knew precisely what it was—a heavy wire mesh cage three feet long, two feet high, eighteen inches wide, and open on one side, with an irresistible ball of chopped sirloin in the center. Andy had seen smaller versions of these "humane" traps for raccoons and skunks. The trap was pressure-triggered. The animal, in this case clearly a dog, would enter the cage to get the bait and then, when the animal stepped on a metal panel on the floor, a spring-loaded door would snap shut, trapping the creature. The bait, Andy knew, was often laced with a tranquilizer so the trapped animal wouldn't struggle in the cage.

At least it wasn't one of those claw traps Andy had seen in PETA ads and the Humane Society magazine at the shelter. The images of foxes and coyotes caught in the grip of those traps, gnawing off their own limbs to get away, was something Andy knew he could never unsee. He'd once read an article claiming that trapped animals engaged in this self-mutilating behavior because the prospect of freedom was so near and the instrumentality to achieve it so much in their own control. Andy wasn't so sure. He believed from his own personal experience that the answer often was a great deal simpler: sometimes a part of you hurt so much that you would do anything to excise it even if the short-term consequence was more pain. You didn't destroy your own flesh for freedom, he knew; you did it to be free from the pain—two very different motives.

Although it lacked the outright cruelty of a claw trap, Andy understood the device before him now wasn't exactly "humane" either. An animal suddenly locked in a box so small it couldn't turn around? Waiting in terror for the unknown thing that would come for it? Andy knew exactly what that felt like too, and the feeling was anything but caring and compassionate.

But Andy was also smart enough about the world to realize that the assessment of "humaneness" wasn't that straightforward. There was always the issue of context. Always. And context required asking and answering two questions: what was the purpose and what was the alternative?

He checked the tag affixed to the cage with a heavy wire: "Property of the City of New York Department of Parks and Recreation. Anyone tampering with this equipment will be prosecuted. Conviction may result in fine or imprisonment."

Were they trapping the strays to protect them from the virus or because they thought they were the cause? Or was there a different reason entirely? So many questions and, Andy realized, too much he didn't know. He believed the one-eared dog was way too smart to get trapped by such a crude device, but he wasn't so sure about the rest of the pack. Perhaps he had even made things worse by feeding them and making them less fearful of human contact.

With that concern in mind, Andy took a long stick and pressed hard on the floor of the trap, depressing the trigger. The door swung shut, locking the bait inside. The very act of springing the trap made him feel better about what had happened at the shelter.

Andy spent most of the night scouring the park for other traps. He found twenty and triggered them all, rendering them useless.

He was lucky. He got caught only once. The old black man in the long coat surprised him at trap number fifteen. The guy didn't even try to stop him, just said, "I'm not your problem and I won't tell, but are you sure you know what you're doing?"

Andy ignored him and moved on to the next trap.

Much later that evening, in the cavern, with the one-eared stray snuggled up next to him, Andy dozed with the self-satisfied expression of someone who believed he had accomplished real change.

He was about to drop off into deep sleep when a sensation of wrongness jerked him awake. He had missed something important. Some connection struggled to break the surface of his consciousness. Although he was exhausted, Andy stayed awake another hour trying to figure out what was gnawing at him. He finally fell into a fitful sleep no closer to his answer.

25

By the time Sam had ordered in pizza, the number of drop-offs had finally slowed to a trickle and ended at eighty-seven. Two of the new ones seemed to have the vague lethargy that foreshadowed bad things, so she moved these into the dwindling space of the isolation room.

Dwindling. It was a word that captured so much about their situation—time, resources, and, now that Sam had learned from the dean that her father was missing again and not even aware of her plea for help, hope. She would need to tell Tom about the sick dogs, she decided . . . and then convinced herself that a few more hours of delay would be excusable.

When the pizza finally arrived, the shelter crew all took a needed break and gathered around the staff room table, numbly chewing slices while watching the local news report that there was no progress in halting the virus or isolating the vector.

"This sucks." Greg finally broke the silence. He tossed pieces of his crust to a few dogs sitting at his feet.

"Let's take a step back," Sam said. "What do we know?"

"We know this sucks," Greg repeated.

"Something slightly more constructive?" Sam pressed.

"We've got sick dogs and dogs that show no signs of infection," Luke offered.

"And," Beth added, "we've got humans that have come into contact with the sick dogs, with no signs of infection. At least not yet."

"What do we know about the dogs that are sick?" Sam asked, and passed around a stack of patient folders. They each reviewed a file, although they already knew the limited contents.

"Bloody diarrhea," Sid said, reading from his file.

"Abdominal tenderness," Luke added.

"Dehydration," Beth chimed in.

"Yeah, but the second two symptoms are probably the result of the first," Greg said.

"Right." Sam nodded. "There's also a fever, but we know there are no signs of parasites and our initial blood slides showed nothing out of the ordinary under the microscope."

"What do we know about the dogs themselves?" Greg asked.

"Not a lot, except for Nick," Luke responded, looking through the file folders.

"Nick was a park stray before he found me," Sam responded. "So nothing useful in the history there. What about the others? Who's their vet? Maybe those offices have some helpful background."

They all looked through their files.

"Morgan for mine," Luke said.

"Morgan," Sid said, reading from his.

Greg scanned his intake interview notes. "According to what they told us, except for Nick, the eight sick dogs had Morgan as their primary vet."

"But that sort of makes sense," Sam said. "She's the only local practice. Most people don't travel too far for their routine vet care. Plus she's got the lab."

"So that's a dead end," Greg said. "Morgan's not going to turn over her files to you."

"Maybe I can have Walden call her on the authority of the mayor. We were promised city hall support." Sam checked her watch. Morgan was probably gone by now anyway. "Greg, are you still friendly with that tech over there?"

"Petra? Yeah, I guess."

"See if you can reach him. He's at least reasonable. Tell him to expect a call from downtown, but don't tell him any of the dogs are sick."

Greg gave Sam his "How stupid do you think I am?" look and left the room.

Beth cleared her throat. "Isn't it a bit... I don't know... fantasy to expect that we're going to be able to figure out something that the CDC with all its resources can't understand?"

"My father worked with the CDC," Sam said. "He was never a fan. They have some great people, but it's a bureaucracy with lots of protocols. They don't move fast."

"And we have one thing the CDC doesn't," Luke said. "We have the dogs."

"Exactly," Sam concurred. At least for the next few hours. After that, Sam figured all bets were off.

Greg returned to the room rubbing his chin. "No answer at Morgan's either on the phone or from the service."

"Someone must be there," Sam said. "At least a tech for the overnight. Probably just not picking up the phone with everything going on. Can you go over and take a look?"

Greg returned fifteen minutes later. "Locked up tight."

"What do you mean?" Sam asked.

"Lights out, nobody home," he answered. "No signs of life at all."

Sam shook her head. "That can't be. What about her staff? Her clients? She's a twenty-four-hour operation."

"Not today," Greg said. "I called Petra on his cell. He told me that all the staff got an e-mail that the practice would be closed for the duration of the quarantine, and they would be on paid leave. Petra said that Morgan's just sitting at her big old house in Bedford watching *Ellen* while you do the city's crap work."

"But what about the animals Morgan had in-house when it happened?" Sam asked.

"Petra said Morgan sent the surgicals to the Animal Medical

Center across town before the wall came down, and the rest went home or were transferred."

"This still doesn't make any sense," Sam complained.

"You're not thinking like Morgan," Beth offered. "I know her type. Shit, I am her type. She doesn't want to get involved, doesn't want to get pressed into doing service for the city for free, and doesn't want to stay in the infection zone."

"Yeah, I guess, maybe," Sam said, far from convinced. "I guess we—"

The pounding on the front door stopped her.

"Another drop-off?" Greg asked.

"Not likely," Sam said. The drop-off window had closed and the Guard had taken to turning people away.

"Probably more press then," Luke said. "I'll get it."

Sam was already on her feet. "Finish your pizza. I'm not hungry anyway." She left them and opened the front door, still thinking about Morgan.

In the next instant, every thought flew out of her head as she struggled to process the fact that her father was standing before her.

Daniel attempted to smile, but Sam could see the pain behind it. "I wanted you to know...you deserve to know that I lied to you," he said. "I do remember the faces of those dogs I mutilated...I actually see them all the time...they stare out at me from the cages. But those aren't the worst of the images. I know those are memories and beyond any power to repair. It's the ones with you—the dreams I have where you are locked away alone in a cage of my construction—that are the most painful to bear. Those gut me because I know they are both true and told in real time."

Sam's first instinct was to say something hurtful. But her fear and need for help in this moment were greater than her urge to cause pain.

She stepped aside and allowed Daniel to cross the threshold into the shelter.

26

Sam and her father examined a male bull terrier, one of the new deliveries to the isolation room. They were making such an extraordinary effort to avoid any subject that might call for anything other than a clinical response that their conversation sounded like something out of a vet school lab practical. Sam's emotional guard—well trained to protect her around anything to do with her father—was up so high at this point that she couldn't see where it ended.

Daniel's expert hands felt the dog's abdomen. The dog winced and snarled. "Tenderness," he said.

"Same as the others," Sam replied.

He pulled down the dog's lower lip and touched his gums. "Dehydration."

"Same as the others."

He checked the dog's chart. "Fever."

"Same as the others."

Daniel slid his hands along the dog's spine. "Lipoma on the left side. Do any of the other dogs have it?"

"Not that I noticed. But my hands have been pretty full."

"I'm not judging, just asking. How many dogs have you seen since the virus was first reported?" he asked.

"I'll need to check the records. We have over eighty new ones with us now, so maybe another twenty-five on top of that. A hundred and ten would be a good guess."

"And these were the only ones that were symptomatic, of all the ones you saw?"

"Yes."

"Show me the dogs that have been in the isolation room the longest."

Sam led her father to the cages.

"How do they seem as compared to when they first came in?" he questioned. "Any worse?"

"No. Actually a bit brighter. The blood in the diarrhea appears to be resolving."

"What are they on?"

"Flagyl."

"You didn't keep a comparison group?"

"No."

"Then I guess we don't know if that worked or they're just getting better on their own."

"I was trying to cure them, Dad, not test a hypothesis," she snapped.

"Asking. Not judging," Daniel repeated. "It is odd, though."

"What?"

Daniel turned to his daughter. "All of it, actually. The fact that the disease is self-limiting, that more dogs are not ill despite the close proximity, the sudden onset, the absence of an obvious vector. This is atypical for contagion. I'll need to review all the lab results."

"Be my guest."

"And I'd also like to run some additional tests—a few pathogen screens we developed at Cornell for emerging viruses. What kind of equipment do you have in your lab? I'll need to recalibrate."

"My lab?" Sam laughed at him. "You're not in Cornell anymore, Toto."

"You need to send everything out?" Daniel asked. "How do you function?"

Sam despised that all-too-familiar tone. "You're forgetting that I run a shelter. All I've got is a crappy little microscope set up to do fecals and basic blood smears, chem strips, and an old X-ray machine."

"This won't be enough."

"I know, Dad. That's why I was seconds away from calling the CDC."

"Really?"

"This is way out of my league. I don't want to do anything that might make more kids sick."

"But this," Daniel said, pointing to the cages, "obviously isn't rabies. I can tell you that without running a single test." Daniel took a bowl of water and placed it before the dog he had been examining. The dog took several laps and then rested his head near the bowl. "No hydrophobia, no evidence of painful swallowing."

"Then how do we explain this otherwise impossible coincidence?"

"I don't know yet. But if you want all the dogs in this shelter kept alive, I would delay that call to Atlanta and get us some access to appropriate equipment."

Sid jumped into the room, his shirt soaking wet. "We need more towels," he said.

"What happened now?" Sam asked.

"A little problem with a water pipe in the basement. I'm taking care of it."

"There's a box of rags in the storage area in the back," Sam said. Armed with that information, Sid jumped back out.

"What equipment specifically?" Sam asked her father.

"Cellular-level magnification, gas chromatography."

"That's all? Well, I'll just pull all that out of my ass."

He waved the comment away. "So where can we go?"

"What about Cornell?"

"Too far," he said. "And given how I left things, it's not like I can just waltz in there and borrow a million-dollar machine."

Sid entered again. "Sorry. I checked. No rags there."

"Hold on a sec," she told Sid, and turned back to her father. "Even if I convinced the dean, I guess he'd need to tell the CDC what we're doing."

"And that would be the end of this little project," Daniel confirmed. "How about someplace else in the city?"

Sid raised his hand like a schoolboy asking to go to the bathroom. "Excuse me, but I could really use those towels."

"Morgan's place is the only one I know with that level of equipment and she's not about to let us use it," Sam said.

Sid tried to interrupt. "Samantha?"

"What if I ask her?" Daniel suggested. "Tell her it's an emergency?"

"Are you kidding? There's only one person she hates more than me—and I'm looking at him. What the hell did you really do to her anyway?"

"I tried to help her. She didn't see it that way."

"You do have an odd effect on people."

Daniel shrugged. "You asked. What did you do to her?"

"I wasted years of her precious training when I declined her offer of employment after Mom died. Oh, and then I started giving away free vet care to her clients."

Daniel nodded. "That would do it. So she's off the list."

"The only way would be to get the mayor to order it and Morgan would just get her lawyers to stop us. And we'd still need to disclose to the mayor what we're doing. That's a dead end. You'll need to find another way."

"Samantha...," Sid tried again.

"In a minute, Sid!"

"There is no other way," Daniel argued. "You said I can't go to the city. We certainly can't go to the CDC. And if they find out that the dogs are ill, regardless of whether it's related, they'll start the cull and these dogs—including Nick—will be on the first truck out, euthanized and on a necropsy table an hour later."

"But Samantha...," Sid interrupted.

"I know, Sid, I know! The towels!"

"No, no," Sid started, the excitement making his voice squeak. "I think I can get you in."

"What?" Daniel and Sam asked at the same time.

"Morgan's place. I can get you in. I've done work there. I know her security system."

It took a moment for Sam to get her mind around Sid's proposal. "You'd risk that?" Sam asked finally.

"For you, Samantha? The world."

"But if she finds us in there..." She didn't finish.

"There is no 'us,'" her father said. "Only me. If I get caught, you had nothing to do with this."

"I'm already in this. Don't start trying to protect me now. Besides, you're going to need another pair of hands."

"No," Daniel said. "If you get involved in this, it will destroy everything for you. You'll have no future. I won't allow that."

She moved to within an inch of her father's face. "I'm in," she said. "They're my dogs. You owe me this." At this truth Daniel's shoulders slumped forward in defeat. "I'll let the others know," Sam said. "You start drawing new bloods."

27

Carrying a small Coleman-like cooler in each hand, Sam and her father peered into the dark of the evening from the sidewalk in front of Morgan's hospital. They served both as lookouts and as a human screen for Sid, who, standing behind them, examined the alarm control panel adjacent to Morgan's front door. The panel, about the size of a paperback novel, with two LEDs on the front that blinked like angry red eyes, had an alphanumeric keypad and a swipe groove for a key card.

Sid scratched his head, a concerned look on his face.

"You really know how to disarm that?" Sam asked.

"I think so." Sid did not express the confidence Sam had been expecting.

"Can we get on with it then?" Daniel hissed.

"I'm thinking," Sid answered, but made no move toward the panel.

Daniel shifted nervously on his feet. "Well, if you're thinking it looks perfectly natural for us to be on the street carrying lab coolers in the middle of the night, I'm going to disagree."

"Leave him alone, Dad," Sam cut in. "He's thinking." Then her nerves kicked in. "How much longer, Sidney?"

Sid took a key card from his pocket, wiped the metallic strip against his hand, and slid it through the swipe strip. The LED continued to blink.

Sam glanced behind her. "Is it supposed to do that?"

"No. Actually, the light should turn green."

"What happens if it doesn't?" Daniel asked.

Sid checked his watch. "My guess is that the cops will be here in under two minutes, so listen for sirens."

The alarm box beeped sharply. This time Sam and her father both spun around to stare. Sid shrugged. "I maybe would get ready to run," he said sheepishly.

After what seemed like an eternity, the LED finally turned green and the three of them exhaled in relief. "I guess it still works," Sid said. "Now for the code."

"What code?" Sam asked.

"I have thirty seconds to punch in Morgan's specific password or the alarm will trigger. So count out."

"One Mississippi, two Mississippi," Sam began. "What's her passcode, four Mississippi, five Mississippi—"

"I dunno," Sid said.

"What!" Daniel exploded.

"Eight Mississippi, nine Mississippi..."

"It's a personal password. She never told me," Sid explained. "I was taking it one step at a time."

"Are you joking?" Daniel spit. "What the hell are we supposed to do?"

Sam tried to concentrate on her count, rhythmically calling out the numbers, but her heart was already skipping beats. "Twelve Mississippi, thirteen Mississippi, I can't believe you don't know it Mississippi, fifteen Mississippi. We are so fucked Mississippi...seventeen Mississippi..."

"I originally put in a skeleton key password, just in case she ever got locked out," Sid said, rubbing his generous chin.

"...nineteen Mississippi, twenty Mississippi..."

"Hopefully, she never reprogrammed the override." Sid began punching letters into the keypad—"*C-H-A*—" He spoke the letters out loud as he keyed them in.

"...twenty-two Mississippi, twenty-three Mississippi..."

"For Christ's sake, type faster," Daniel spluttered.

"*N-N-A*. There, that's it," Sid said.

Nothing happened.

"...twenty-six Mississippi, twenty-seven Mississippi—"

"I don't understand!" Sid declared.

"...twenty-nine Mississippi—" Sam's voice quivered in panic.

"Wait! That's right!" Sid said to himself, and punched in an *H*.

The bolt of the door slid open with a reassuring click. Sid smacked his forehead. "I forgot that the skeleton key is always a seven-symbol password. So I needed to add an *H* to the end of Channa's name to make it fit."

"That's really nice," Daniel snarled. "But can we get the hell off the street now?"

They moved inside and quickly shut the door behind them.

Even in the dim emergency lighting, Sam could see the stainless steel polished to a high sheen that served as a proxy for professionalism and a poor substitute for empathy. She always felt like a contaminated swab in an otherwise sterile surgical field in Morgan's hospital. "She keeps the heavy-duty lab stuff on the floor below us," Sam said.

Daniel and Sid followed her to a door that led to the staircase off one of the corridors. The door had the same type of alarm box as the entrance.

"I don't remember seeing that before," Sam said, pointing to the alarm.

"I put it in a few months ago," Sid said. "Morgan told me she wanted to protect her more expensive equipment."

"Trusting fellow, isn't she?" Daniel said.

Sid took another key card out of his pocket and passed it through the box. Once the light on the box turned green, he entered the skeleton key passcode. The door snapped open, revealing a short flight of stairs.

Sam reached to flip on the light switch at the top of the stairway.

"Don't!" Sid yelled. He was too late. Bright lights illuminated the stairs and then the floor below. "Does the phrase *breaking and entering* mean anything to you, dear?" Sid asked.

"Relax. There are no windows downstairs," Sam told him confidently. "No one can see the lights."

"I actually was worried about an auxiliary alarm system integrated into the light function."

Sam stopped mid-step. "A what?"

"A remote alarm that gets triggered when the light switch is activated."

"Is there one?" Daniel asked.

"I didn't put one in," Sid said. "Didn't think of it. But I'm not the only locksmith in New York, you know?"

"How do we find out?" Sam asked.

Sid turned his head in every direction and listened. "There would be some signal—a beep or chirp—to give you a chance to deactivate. I don't hear anything. And the light switch looks pretty low-grade— not strong enough to carry an alarm current." Sid shrugged and led them down the stairs.

The sublevel of Morgan's animal hospital was huge and loaded with high-tech medical and computer equipment. "Jesus, you weren't joking, Samantha," Daniel said. "This is some serious stuff."

Sam was just as shocked. "This wasn't here when I used to work with her. Most of this tech looks brand-new."

Daniel ran his hand over a particularly large and intimidating machine. "It would have to be. This Voss gas hematology machine was just being tested when I left Cornell."

"Where would she get the money?" Sam asked, furious at all the times Morgan had accused her of cutting into the profitability of her practice.

"Perhaps she invested wisely," Sid offered.

"Well, it's ours for the night," Daniel said. "Let's fire this stuff up and get to work." He rubbed his hands together like a little kid with his first radio-controlled toy.

Sam studied the digital controllers on the daunting machine. "You know how to use this?"

"A little," Daniel answered. "But luckily"—he grabbed a thick black binder from a spot next to the machine and showed it to her—"it comes with instructions." He pushed a red button on the computer console attached to the machine and it whirred to life. "This'll take a few minutes to boot up."

"What's it do, exactly?" Sid asked, peering over their shoulders.

"In about ninety minutes, it will kick out a detailed chemical analysis breakdown of a blood, urine, or fecal sample, tell us what's in there that shouldn't be and what should be there that isn't." Daniel dropped a pair of reading glasses on the bridge of his nose and, within moments, was lost in the manual, oblivious to everyone and everything except the workings of the machine slowly awakening in front of him.

"Like on *CSI?*" Sid asked.

That got only a "Hmmm" from Daniel.

Sam knew that response. Her father's all-encompassing concentration was what had made him such a brilliant scientist—and, as he got more successful, an increasingly crappy father. His enthusiasm for "solving the puzzle," as he often called his work, was mutually exclusive with those characteristics that most people looked for in their fellow humans—like warmth, compassion, empathy, and self-awareness.

"Can I help you?" Sam asked. Daniel's response from behind the binder was unintelligible, but she took it as a "Not yet."

Sam found a computer monitor and keyboard across the room and powered them on. She figured that as long as they were here in violation of many laws, she would also pull the medical records on the dogs in isolation in the hope that there might be something useful in the treatment histories.

In a few seconds the screen kicked into the Veterinary Office Practice Management Software program that Morgan and most other large veterinary practices used. VOPMS was a menu-driven program that allowed the treating vet instant access to any patient's medical history. Morgan, not surprisingly, had the version of the system that also auto-billed for each service administered and then robocalled the client every ten days in the sinful event the client had left the office with a balance due.

Sam clicked on the section of the screen for patient medical records and then double-clicked on the "Browse by name" section. She typed in the name of one of the dogs. The screen told her, "No records found." She tried another name and got the same answer.

"What the hell?" she muttered, and pulled out the list of owners of the dogs in isolation. Sam typed in the first name—"No records found." Then the second name—"No records found." She went down the list one by one and typed in the name of every owner. For each name she received the same smug answer from the computer monitor: "No records found."

She thought over the animals she knew and typed in "Monster"— "No records found."

Sam eventually guessed the terminal wasn't connected to the master system, so she moved to another terminal. She received identical answers.

She tried a third terminal with the same inexplicable results—no records of any dog.

Finally Sam tried the terminal upstairs in the reception area. That terminal reported the same three impossible words: "No records found."

She returned to the basement scratching her head and found Sid reading a book entitled *Canine Anatomy Studies*.

"Fascinating stuff," he said. "I never realized how closely the heart resembles your average, bottom-of-the-market lock tumbler system."

"Some hearts are less complicated than others," Sam said with a nod toward her father. "How much do you know about computers?"

"I can turn them on, but that's about it," Sid said.

Sam phoned Luke at the shelter. He was their resident computer geek.

"How do you feel about a little breaking and entering?" Sam asked.

Luke had a deeply rooted moral code. The problem, Sam had learned, was that his code actually had little to do with the law. She was counting on that now. "I need your help with a computer problem."

"Sure." Luke sounded oddly happy with the request. "Give me two minutes to pull my thumb drives together."

"The alarm is still off. We're in the basement," she told him, and then hung up.

Less than five minutes later, Sam heard soft footsteps on the floor above. She hoped Luke would be able to make sense of this.

"Right. Checking it out now," the voice upstairs said.

Sam knew that voice and it didn't belong to Luke.

Sid, Daniel, and Sam shared a look of "the thing is coming for us and we can't get away" panic. They couldn't hide under a desk, turn off the lights, or fade into the walls. They were nailed.

Kendall reached the bottom step, still talking into his cell phone. He scanned the room, taking it all in. Sam could tell that he was as shocked to see them as they were to be seen. "Hold on, Cap. Need to check something out," Kendall said into the phone while staring at Sam. She met his eyes and slowly shook her head.

"No," Kendall spoke into the phone. "All fine here. Must be a short in the auxiliary alarm. I'll let Morgan know everything is OK so she can go back to bed." Kendall turned around and headed back up the stairs without a further glance at the intruders.

When Kendall reached the top, they all started breathing again. "Just be sure to turn off the lights and lock up when you leave," Kendall called down the steps. He closed the basement door without waiting for an answer.

A few seconds later, Sam heard the front door close. She turned to Sid. "Auxiliary alarm?"

He shrugged. "Not mine. I guess she didn't trust my work."

Before Sam could say another word, Luke bounded down the stairs like a puppy freed from a kennel. This time Daniel didn't even bother to look up from his binder.

"What've you got?" Luke asked.

"I'm trying to retrieve the medical records of the dogs that came to us through Morgan. No matter what I do, the system tells me there are no records."

Luke sat at the nearest terminal, removed a thumb drive from a chain around his neck, and shoved it into the USB port on the terminal. The screen went blank and then returned with a blinking A:/ prompt. He made a few keystrokes and a wash of information poured onto the screen almost too fast to follow. "Well, that's a problem," he said, and tugged on his ponytail.

"What?" Sam asked.

"All the data on the main drive has been dumped and scrunched."

"Dumped?"

"Yeah, backed up onto a portable flash drive and then—"

"Deleted?"

"No, not just deleted. Deleted you can find. Deleted material stays on the hard drive and can be reconstructed. This drive was scrunched—a specific program was used to shred the data on the hard drive to prevent it from being reconstructed."

"Seems like a lot of effort to go through," Sam said.

Luke shook his head. "Not really. You can download a program off the Internet for twenty bucks, load it onto your machine, and it will do it automatically. Maybe she had a problem with security and liked to keep her records mobile."

"Or maybe she was trying to hide something from her staff," Sam suggested.

"There's that too."

"But you're sure it's all gone?" Sam found it difficult to believe Morgan would just delete her files. She had always seemed so anal.

"Pretty much. Let me see something." Luke took another thumb drive off his chain and swapped it with the one in the USB port. "Depending on what program she used, I might be able to…" Luke watched the data load on the screen. "There it is." He hit a few buttons and the printer attached to the computer spit out three sheets. "I can tell you the file names that were downloaded onto the flash drive. This is the most recent activity." Luke handed Sam the sheets.

"Thanks, but I need the records themselves. The names won't help."

"Sorry. Best I can do. There might be other scraps buried here and there on the system, but not the whole records and probably obscured by gibberish. You'd need a real computer forensics guy to figure that out."

"Thanks for trying," Sam said, both confused and disappointed.

Luke rose from the chair. "I better get back before Greg kills someone. Things are a bit tense at the moment. I'll keep thinking, though." Luke jogged up the stairs.

Sam flipped through the sheets from Luke. Sure enough, many of the file names matched the last names of the dogs now in her care. "Weird," she mumbled. She was just about to give up when she noticed a record name on the final page.

Nick.

No last name. Certainly a coincidence, but…

"Luke!" Sam waved him back down and showed him the page. "Can you see if you can find any other references to the name Nick on the system? Anything, anywhere, OK?"

Luke was already at the terminal, his fingers flying across the keys.

Sam paced, trying to make sense of this latest development. In five minutes four sheets of paper shot out of the printer. "There were only two other hits," Luke said. Sam grabbed the papers. The first three pages appeared to be a duplicate of the prior printout except that all of the file names were followed by "-cvtp." The last page was covered with binary code gibberish. Totally meaningless, except—

There, in the middle of the page, squeezed among all the zeros and ones, Sam saw two words that made the room spin: *Nick Lewis.*

"That can't be," she said. "Wait a minute. Could this be an old record, like from when I worked here?"

Luke shook his head. "These are the most recent activity entries. That's why I can still get them. Two weeks old maybe, and that's probably tops."

"But why does she have a record of my dog?"

"Only Morgan can tell you that."

Sam called Sid over. "Can you go back to the shelter with Luke and give Greg a hand?"

"Of course," Sid said, and followed Luke up the stairs.

Sam grabbed her cell phone and dialed Greg. She could hear the barking and whining of a roomful of dogs behind him as soon as he picked up. "Sending you back some help. Is everyone stable?" she asked.

"So far. What did you find?"

"Trying to figure something out. Has Nick been at Morgan's in the last week?"

"Nope. Why?"

"This is really important. Think!" Sam hoped the urgency in her voice got through to him.

"OK, OK." Greg was silent for a long minute. "Wait. Yeah. I had to return some of her mail we got by accident. You know how she gets about—"

"Was he ever out of your sight?"

"I'm thinking... maybe... wait. Morgan said she wanted to talk to me. Some bullshit about warning me not to provide veterinarian services at the shelter. I left Nick in reception for a few minutes—didn't want any more trouble between them. But he was right where I left him when I got back. Now tell me why?"

"I'll explain later," Sam said, and hung up on him.

In the cold confines of Morgan's basement, Sam stared at the list of files in her hand and struggled to pull the jagged pieces together. The problem was that the pieces made no sense. She began to get the feeling that everything was tilting out of control and downward.

"Samantha!" Daniel shouted from the other end of the room. She found him bent over the eyepieces of a stereomicroscope. "I need you to look at something," he said.

"From the blood analysis?"

"No. The first samples are still cooking. But while I was waiting, I figured I'd take a look at some of the fecal samples using Morgan's high-mag microscope."

Sam peered into the tubes. "What am I looking at?" She saw what appeared to be a tiny jumble of elongated translucent capsules. "What are those? Parasites?" she asked.

"I don't think so."

"Then what?"

"Not certain. I've never seen it in a canine sample before."

"But you have seen it before?"

"I think so," he said, and looked into the scope again.

"Can we stop playing twenty questions, Dad? I'm having a bad day. What the hell is it?"

"Cholera. I think it's cholera."

Sam stared at him as if he'd lost his mind. "Dogs don't get cholera."

"True. Generally not. Unless they ingest a massive amount of infected material or are immune-compromised."

"There's no cholera here. Those kids at Riverside have rabies symptoms, not vomiting and diarrhea. And anyway, cholera is bacterial, not viral. You must be wrong."

"Maybe, but I don't think so."

"Whose sample is this anyway?"

Daniel checked his notes. Sam witnessed the very rare event of his scientific confusion. "It's Nick's," he said.

"What?" Sam grabbed the notes from his hand and confirmed the name. "Now I know this is FUBAR. My dog eats organic dog food at fifty dollars a bag. There's no way he picked up a casual case of cholera in New York City."

"Then I can't explain how. There's a dip test that can confirm this, but..."

"But we can't get it without disclosing why."

"And turning the dogs over to the CDC," Daniel said.

"And assuming it is cholera?"

"We're doing everything correctly. Fluids, antibiotics, careful disposal of contaminated feces, and lots of bleach in the infected areas. This also may explain why the dogs seem to be doing better. With appropriate palliative care to minimize dehydration and antibiotics, cholera usually isn't fatal."

"What about the other samples?"

"I'm working on it."

Sam remembered the papers in her hand. "Do the letters *CVTP* mean anything to you?"

"No. Why?"

She explained the deletion of the records and the reference to Nick on Morgan's computer.

"You don't think this is coincidence?" Daniel asked.

"No. And you don't either," she said.

"But where's the connection? As you said, these kids certainly don't have cholera."

"There may be no connection to these kids at all," Sam said. "That's the point. The dogs are being blamed for an illness that has nothing to do with them—"

"Then how do you explain the dog with the positive rabies test?"

Sam couldn't. Not yet. "One thing I do know, though, is that Morgan has a medical record for my dog and I'm going to find out why."

"So you think Morgan's just going to sit down and tell you her life story?"

"No," Sam said, deflated and suddenly exhausted. She'd been so caught up in the prospect of actually being able to do something that she'd forgotten what a bitch Morgan could be. "I'll need to persuade her."

"With what? Your righteous indignation?"

"Not helpful, Dad."

Her father nodded. "You're right. That wasn't." He pinched his nose between his thumb and his first finger—the image of the contemplative professor. "Try this. Tell her I have a complete set of her Ramses data. If that doesn't motivate her, nothing will."

"What's Ramses?"

Daniel shook his head. "She'll know."

"Why won't you tell me?"

Daniel was silent for a moment and then answered in one word. "Shame."

Sam knew her father well enough to know that he wouldn't change his mind at this point. "Do you have a cell phone?"

Daniel shook his head.

Sam took out her cell phone and put it in her father's hand. "In case I need to reach you. I'll borrow one from the staff and call you with the number."

"Are you going to tell anyone at CDC or city health about these smears?"

"Sure," she answered. "As soon as you tell me you're one hundred percent certain and we figure out what they'll do with the information." *And*, she thought, *right after I convince myself that Tom really can be trusted.*

Sam was already on the stairs before her father could respond.

28

Back in the shelter, amid the barks, yelps, and yowls coming from all directions, Sam explained her plan to Greg, Luke, Beth, and Sid. They each asked to go with her and she refused them all with, "I need your hands here." No one was happy with Sam's answer, but each accepted it because it was true.

"I do need to borrow a cell phone," Sam said.

Beth placed her iPhone in Sam's hands. "Too much of a distraction anyway."

At the shelter entrance, Sam looked at each of them in turn, suddenly feeling very alone. "I'll be back as soon as I can." They all nodded back. There was nothing more to say.

Sam opened the door and was about to step out into the cold night when Beth suddenly appeared beside her.

"What are you doing?" Sam asked.

"I'm going with you."

"We went through this already. It's more important that you help out here."

"Let's be honest. I'm the least valuable assistant you've got."

"You're supposed to check on Andy."

"I already spoke to him. Twice, actually. He's pissed, but in my professional opinion—or what's left of it—pissed for him is good. Luke's taking him out for an early breakfast later. Andy likes the crazy old man."

Sam shook her head. "I don't know what, if anything, is really going on with Morgan and these dogs, but I do know that getting her to talk to me won't be pretty."

"I'm good in a fight, actually. You'd be surprised."

"I appreciate this, really, but—"

"I made a promise, Mr. Frodo...a promise. 'Don't you leave her, Beth.' And I don't mean to...I don't mean to."

"What the hell was that?"

Beth shrugged. "*Fellowship of the Ring*. Seemed appropriate."

"You are so weird," Sam said. She closed the shelter door behind them, grateful that Beth wouldn't take no for an answer. "The car's in the garage across the street. I'll drive."

Book III

Between, Among, Within

I

Andy woke to the darkness of the predawn hours and watched as the one-eared stray paced near the front of the cavern. He sensed that something was happening in the park—something bad.

In his experience, good had to be cajoled and, sometimes, even forcibly dragged into the vacuum created by apathy and indecision. Bad, in contrast, was an opportunist. Bad didn't require pushing or prodding forward; it continued under the force of its own dark inertia, always and without exception expanding to fill all the cracks.

Andy heard voices. Two men at least. Sounds traveled in strange and unpredictable patterns in the cavern. He crawled up to the entrance and peeked out of the cave opening. He saw the flashlight beams of two men in canvas jumpsuits.

"This one's been sprung too," the taller man said, shining a light into the trap. "Bait's not touched."

"That makes seven," his companion said, checking his clipboard in the light of the beam. "Someone's screwing with us."

"Yup. So what now?"

"Enough OT to pay for my kid's summer camp. There have been too many reports of dogs acting strangely in the park for this to just go away."

"That's bullshit, though. A mutt vomits and now everyone thinks it's rabies?"

"There's a name for that. They call it *rabies hysteria*."

"I call it, 'The governor doesn't want to screw up his party.'"

"Either way, the park will be closed to all dogs at some point today. Then we go tree by tree, rock by damn rock. The Guard delivers the Q sign to any unattended dogs."

"The what?"

The other stuck his tongue out of the side of his mouth, tilted his head, and closed his eyes. "Q sign. The big sleep."

"What a waste."

"My conscience is clear." He kicked the sprung trap. "Thanks to whatever group did this, there's no alternative."

With an agonizing jerk, Andy realized what had been nagging at him since the night before. Humanity was always determined by context and alternative. The context was sick and dying kids. And the alternative? He had taken that from them. His well-intended actions in reality had been naïve and juvenile. He had signed death warrants and now they would come for his only remaining family.

Andy pounded his forehead with the heel of his hand as he mouthed the word *stupid*. The violence of his movements must have surprised and alarmed the dog. She tried to lick his face, but Andy's punishing hand did not stop.

2

It was nearing dawn by the time Sam and Beth arrived in Bedford, the heart of horse country north of New York City.

They passed mansions, rolling lawns, and huge horse paddocks almost as soon as they turned off the highway. Morgan's place was at the end of a winding road, opposite the entrance of a large horse farm. A Mercedes-Benz convertible stood guard in Morgan's immense circular driveway. *Sid was correct*, Sam thought; *Morgan must have invested well.*

Sam pulled into the driveway and was out of the car and pounding on the front door before Beth had unbuckled her seat belt. Morgan opened the door just as Beth joined her.

Despite the early hour, Morgan was already dressed—definitely not from Kmart, Sam noticed—with her hair pulled tight into a perfectly severe bun.

"What the hell are you doing here?" Morgan challenged.

"I came for some answers," Sam said.

"I don't know what your questions are and I really don't care. Now please go away before I call the police." Morgan attempted to close the door. Sam put her foot in the entrance to stop her, but Morgan still pushed.

"Hey, cut the crap!" Beth bellowed and slammed the door with her shoulder. Morgan stumbled backward and almost fell. The door swung open and Beth stepped in. "I told you I was good in a fight," she whispered to Sam.

Morgan recovered quickly and walked to the phone on the hall table. "I'm calling the police."

"That's fine," Sam said, hands on her hips. "We'll wait. My father sends his regards, by the way. He says to tell you that he has a complete set of the Ramses data." Morgan snapped to attention at the name. Sam saw the opening and pushed. "I told him I didn't know what that meant, but he said that you would. Do you?"

"He's bluffing." Morgan picked up the phone and began to dial, keeping one eye on Sam.

Sam pretended to take in the expensive artwork in the hallway as she spoke. "Maybe. I don't know him well enough anymore to tell. But if you think he wouldn't disclose something because it will also implicate him, I can tell you one thing: he is a man who feels he has absolutely nothing left to lose. You ever have that feeling? Really unpleasant. And if he thinks he can bring you down with him in the process, my money's on him."

Morgan's face clouded over and Sam knew she'd gotten to her. Morgan slowly lowered the phone into its cradle. "Fine," she said. "I can always call the police later."

Beth leaned close to Sam's ear. "That was pretty good," she whispered.

"What do you want?" Morgan demanded.

During the ride up from the city, Sam had worked through how she'd play this. If she revealed what she knew about the records, she would disclose the office break-in. Morgan could get the cops back on the phone and in a few minutes her father would be in cuffs no matter what Kendall tried to do to protect him. She was much less worried about the prospect of a criminal record than about the police stopping her father before he had any answers. End of game.

But Sam had also realized she needed to see Morgan's face when she asked her the question. That could tell her so much. And if Morgan really was hiding something, would she risk calling the cops to her office? Maybe, Sam realized. This was the problem when you dealt with people who had always gotten their own way—they never saw failure as a real possibility. For Sam, however, failure was a frequent visitor and she had learned to expect it.

Sam thought about her mom and her oft-repeated admonition to trust her own judgment. She stepped in close to Morgan so she could get a straight-on look at the older woman's face. "Why do you have a medical record for my dog?"

It was present only for maybe a breath. Morgan was very very good at this. But it was there—a moment when her entire demeanor shouted one word unequivocally.

Caught.

Then it was gone and all Morgan's facial muscles relaxed into the arrogant expression Sam knew so well. "I have no idea what you're talking about."

"Really? My dog, Nick, you remember him? He's quite ill at the moment. You have a recent record of treatment for him. I want to know why."

"You tell me. You're the one making up records. So what does it say?"

"You know damn well all your records were deleted. I have proof of a record, but not the narrative."

"Deleted? Clearly whatever criminal you hired to hack into my records system is lying to you to earn his fee. There is no record and was no record because there was no treatment. Perhaps you should get your money back from the hacker. Unless he is implementing your wish to frame me for something."

"Did I mention the Ramses data set?"

"You did. That worked to keep this matter private. It does not require that I make up facts to support a record of treatment that I never had. Your father can wipe his ass with the Ramses documents if he thinks otherwise."

So that was it, Sam realized. Whatever was going on, Morgan would risk an awful lot to keep it secret. She could do nothing more here.

Sam took Beth by the elbow and headed to the front door. "See ya around, Morgan." At the door Sam turned back to her. "So I guess there's no point in asking you what *CVTP* means either? It's on the same record."

There it was again—that flicker of panicked guilt. But Morgan caught herself even more quickly this time.

"No idea," she said. "Have you tried Google?"

"I'll do that. Good luck with that whole Ramses data set thing. I hope whatever my father does with it is not too embarrassing for you."

"Get out!" Morgan yelled. "Get the hell out of my house!"

It was the only time Sam could recall Morgan's losing it. She smiled at that thought and banged open the front door.

3

Look into their faces.

Gabriel woke with Channa's admonishing voice in his ears. At some point during the long evening, he had fallen asleep on a sanctuary pew with Christ staring down at him, Eliot stretched out at his feet, and Molly dozing on his head.

He knew what Channa would have expected and the prospect terrified him.

Still, he couldn't get the voice out of his head. It repeated mantralike as he fed Molly and Eliot and then walked the dog along the streets of Riverside. It mocked him while he tried to cobble together a sermon. It shamed him while he swept the sanctuary floor and organized the symbols of his office.

"Damn you, Channa."

Gabriel determined that it was useless to try to do anything else in this state. He locked the church door and began walking to clear his mind.

Fifteen minutes later the priest looked up and realized he was standing before the entrance of the one place he had avoided since Channa's death—Riverside Hospital. He showed his clergy identification to the security guard before he could change his mind, and entered the lobby.

The hospital had the same smell that he remembered from his numerous visits with Channa. He wondered if they would ever develop an antiseptic powerful enough to overcome the odor of fear, desperation, and guilt. He took the elevator to the third floor—pediatrics.

The elevator doors opened into the waiting area. Here parents and siblings sought cold refuge from the monotonous clicks of IV drips, the smell of puke, and the feel of hot skin. They always came here when they could no longer keep up the pretense of strength, when they couldn't bring themselves to utter another "Everything is going to be fine" or "When you get out this time we will go on that trip..." This was the truth room, where doctors came to speak to mothers and fathers in hushed tones about red blood counts, liver function, and kidney failure. This was where parents spoke to each other about the most insignificant things because the past was too painful and the future nonexistent. Here brothers and sisters wept silently behind old issues of *Sports Illustrated* and *People* magazine.

Fifteen pairs of eyes rose to follow the priest when he stepped out of the elevator. Strangers were a distraction, and any break from the tedium of waiting that didn't cause pain was welcome. But priests were different. With the exception of the maternity floor, in the hospital the presence of a priest meant death was near, that science had failed and faith would now take center stage.

Gabriel tried to smile encouragement at a few of the faces, but he soon gave up and stared at his shoes. He turned right and read off the room numbers to himself without thinking.

He peered through a patient's window and his heart raced. For just a moment, he saw Channa in the bed, propped up on pillows with the ever-present IV attached to her arm. He saw Sid and Channa's sister sitting on either side of their beloved wife and sibling. Sid held a damp cloth to Channa's head and her sister held the vomit basin. Channa waved to him from the window, beckoning him to join them, but he couldn't bring himself to enter. Channa nodded her forgiveness.

Gabriel blinked hard and then felt the ground beneath him begin to tip. He leaned against the window to steady himself. When he made contact with the glass, a young mother and father dressed in isolation garb looked up from their ministration to their son. They were surprised at first, but surprise quickly turned to horror, as if he were the Reaper, scythe pulled back and ready to swing. Gabriel tried to mouth an apology through the glass, to explain that he wasn't there for last rites, but that only made the situation worse.

He backed away as quickly as he could, but every window brought him fundamentally similar scenes of suffering, of mothers and fathers looking down upon the still bodies of their young sons and daughters. Gabriel could hear their despairing questions whispered in Channa's voice: "What is wrong?" "What did we do?" "Will you leave us?" "How can we make you stay?"

He also saw the children, enslaved by the virus ravaging their bodies. He knew they were listening to these questions, just as surely as he knew they could not answer them. Instead Gabriel heard them ask questions of their own in Channa's exhausted voice: "Why are we here?" "Why is my family crying?" "Why are you leaving me?"

All these questions. They drowned Gabriel's spirit. Once that vessel proved too small, they echoed across the hospital hallways and elevator shafts in a fruitless search for an understanding ear until, finding none, they dissipated with agonizing slowness.

Gabriel knew he should not have come. He staggered to the elevator and just made it through the hospital exit as he dropped to his knees. When he lifted his head, the hospital was gone and all he saw was thick gray smoke billowing against him. His breath came in ragged, gasping wheezes.

This is hell, he thought. I have arrived in my hell.

He struggled to his feet and then on through the strangling smoke. One step...another. The priest kept moving forward, oblivious to any other pedestrian. He stumbled twice, but did not fall.

After several minutes the smoke dissipated and his church rose before him. Gabriel made it to his office, where Eliot and Molly waited, and he collapsed into his chair.

He didn't know how long he had been out before the persistent tapping on his shoulder woke him. He wanted to sleep for days.

"Father!"

Gabriel opened one eye and Andy appeared before him. The boy looked awful—dirt-encrusted fingernails, hollow eyes, three days of blond stubble.

"I'm sorry, but I really need your help, Father," Andy said.

Andy's plea brought the priest to his feet.

4

Beth stretched and yawned loudly once they got back into the car. "Well that went well, don't you think?" she asked. "Would I be correct in concluding she doesn't like us?"

Sam couldn't answer. Her head was pounding. She made it down Morgan's driveway just as her adrenaline ran out. The delayed exhaustion hit her hard, blurring her vision.

Sam drove across the street and into the entrance of the horse farm. She parked behind a stand of trees, believing this was as far as she could safely drive until the booming in her head subsided.

"Why're we stopping?" Beth asked, and turned to Sam. "Wow, you look like crap."

A look in the rearview mirror confirmed Beth's opinion. Her skin was ugly-pale with dark rings under her eyes. When she was in vet school and had been on call for forty-eight hours, her classmates used to call the look "zombie chic" and laugh. Now it wasn't funny. Nothing was funny. "Just give me a minute before we head back," Sam said.

"Sure thing. Want me to drive?"

Sam glanced in the mirror again. This time she noticed something in addition to her sickly reflection. She could see Morgan's house through the trees. Morgan stepped out of her front door with a lab sample cooler in each hand, looked around to confirm that no one was watching, and dropped the coolers into the back of the Benz. She ran back to the house, returned with two storage boxes, and dropped these into the car next to the coolers. Then Morgan jumped behind the wheel and started the car.

"Holy shit," Sam mumbled, her headache and fatigue forgotten for the moment.

"What?" Beth asked.

"She spooked."

"Morgan?" Beth strained to see the house beyond the trees. "Maybe she's going to get the newspaper or ran out of toilet paper or something."

"Maybe," Sam offered. But she didn't think so... not with those coolers. Sam pulled the car deeper into the horse farm to hide it from the road. In a few moments, the Benz shot out of the driveway and turned onto the street. Sam waited for a few cars to pass as a buffer and pulled out. "You got anyplace you need to be? Parole officer meeting or something you can't miss?" Sam asked.

"Does my answer matter?"

"No."

"I figured. By the way, the word you're looking for, dear, is *apophenia*."

"What's that?" Sam asked.

"That is the experience of seeing false connections in random events."

"This isn't random."

"That's exactly what Russell Crowe's character says in *A Beautiful Mind* before he goes totally bonkers."

"Shhhh."

"I just don't want you to be disappointed when she stops at the mini-mart for some Charmin," Beth said.

"Quiet. I'm concentrating."

"Haven't you ever followed someone before?" Beth asked.

"Of course not."

"Not even a creepy boyfriend to see what he does when he goes out carrying a paper bag stuffed with women's underwear?"

Sam broke her gaze with the road long enough to throw Beth a quizzical stare.

"Don't judge," Beth said. "I was young...OK, so I was thirty. But I was a young thirty."

"You really are a disturbed person," Sam said.

"Have I not been telling you this?"

They followed Morgan as she got onto the state highway going north. "So much for your toilet paper hypothesis," Sam said.

"She's probably going to a Costco. Must be a sale on multi-roll packages."

5

Andy felt like a stranger as Gabriel led him into the shelter reception area. He had known rejection before, but this was different. The power of rejection came from the importance of the person delivering it and the unexpectedness of the act. Andy's dismissal from the shelter had been a complete surprise from one of the few people he trusted. Sam's words had left Andy reeling; returning to the shelter now rubbed that wound raw. He shifted from one foot to the other with the nervous distraction of a drug addict on a low.

"Try to calm down," Gabriel said. "We'll figure this out."

Andy wanted to believe the priest's words, but his history left him with little reason for optimism. "Trying," he said.

Luke spotted them. "Hey, Andy. I'm sorry, but you know you can't be here."

"I know," Andy said. "But it's important."

Gabriel stepped forward. "Can you tell Samantha that we need to speak with her?"

Greg joined them. "Sam's not here."

"When is she due back?"

"We don't know," Greg answered.

"Did she leave someone in charge?" Gabriel asked.

"Lucky me." Greg pointed to himself. "What's up?"

Gabriel ran his hands through his hair and then blew out a chestful of air. "We have a problem."

"Can't really take on one more problem, Father," Greg said. "Can we deal with this later?"

Gabriel shook his head. "I'm afraid—"

Andy broke in. "They're going to kill the park strays. All of them."

"Start at the beginning," Gabriel suggested.

Andy told them about the strays and the plan to kill them all. He left out the part about the cave and the one-eared dog, though; he knew his story was a hard enough sell as it was.

"You're talking about the park pack? Come on now, Andy," Greg said. "You know that's just an urban myth."

"It's not. I've seen them," Andy answered. "Often."

"Maybe you saw a few dogs off-leash traveling together...," Greg offered.

"No!" Andy shot back. "I know what I saw. There are at least ten and they're not just off-leash. They have structure. They're a pack. They have an alpha."

"OK, let's say that's right," Greg said in an obvious effort to placate the boy. "Let's pretend there is a park pack and that they may get destroyed in this campaign. What do you want me to do about it? No one's asking my opinion about right versus wrong these days."

"I want you to help save them."

"In case you haven't noticed," Greg said with a sweep of his arm, "we're pretty tied up here with our own mess."

"I know, but—"

"Even if we were able to catch them—"

"We can. They'll come to me—"

"We can't bring them here because we'd need to cross the perimeter. I'm pretty sure the Guard would take an interest in a priest and a kid walking a pack of strays that you say they are actually trying to kill into the quarantine zone, don't you?"

"I can figure out a way," Andy said.

"And what if they're sick? Isn't that the reason you say the Guard has orders to kill them in the first place?"

"They're not sick. These dogs have eaten out of my hands and they are fine. So am I."

"Then why does the Guard have orders to kill them?"

"You know why! The Guard has orders to kill them just because people are scared and there's no one to speak for them...except me. They're only strays, so who cares? Strays just like—"

"You'll bring the Guard right through our door, Andy. We can't have that and I can't take the risk, not while I'm protecting all of the dogs here."

"But there must be some way," Gabriel insisted.

"We can't," Greg snapped. "I'm responsible for the shelter right now. I'm sorry."

"I did this!" Andy shouted. "These dogs are going to die because I messed with those traps. I need your help. Dr. Sam would never let these dogs be murdered."

"You don't know that," Greg pushed back. "Not with so much at stake."

"Yeah, I do," Andy said.

"Can I speak to you in private?" Gabriel asked Greg. Greg rolled his eyes, but followed the priest to the back.

6

As soon as they were alone, Greg's frustration poured out. "No disrespect here, Father, but what the hell were you thinking? The park pack? Really?"

"The boy believes what he believes."

"Yeah, but that doesn't mean we all need to follow him down the rabbit hole. There's already some seriously confusing shit going on."

Gabriel almost said, "Spend a day in my head." Instead he said, "I'm not prepared to dismiss what Andy believes. I would give him the benefit of my doubts."

"I don't have that luxury. I got a hundred lives depending on my doubts."

"We're the only real human family that kid has left. You can see how important this is to him...how important it is that we trust him. This is what families do for each other. I don't want to even think about what might happen if he is abandoned again." That was a low blow, and Gabriel knew it. He would repent for it later...if he remembered. "Why don't we ask Sam?"

"Tried that. The knucklehead gave her phone to her father. She's got Beth's phone and we don't have that number."

"Her father? He's here? But they haven't spoken in years."

"Yeah, I know. Long story. Like I said, seriously confusing shit."

"I think Luke believes Andy. I'm sure he would help."

"And that's supposed to encourage me? Luke is still trying to find heaven through a computer program. You're all nuts."

"We know what Sam would do, don't we?" Nick had once been a stray, as had so many others who now were neighborhood family dogs. "Sam would at least try to figure out a way and go down swinging."

Greg shut his eyes for a long moment. "I'm really not happy with you right now." When he opened them, he said, "OK, no promises. You two figure out a plan. If I think it can work without bringing the walls down on us, we can give it a try. If not, then you're gonna need to drop this."

"Thank you," Gabriel said.

"You know you'll need at least another pair of hands to have any shot, right?"

"I have a pair in mind."

"Was afraid of that. And when this is all over, you, me, and Sam are going to need to talk about the boy. We're not doing him any favors pretending he's OK."

Gabriel nodded. He knew that Greg was right, but he also knew that youthful faith was a delicate thing and did not respond well to the blunt and inelegant fingers of those probing for reason.

An hour later Gabriel and Eliot stood alone in the middle aisle of the church nave. The priest tossed a small stone in the air, measuring its weight as he stared at the intact section of the stained glass window of Abraham and Isaac. He was about to take aim when Sid entered and took a seat in one of the nearby pews. Eliot trotted over and gave Sid a warm greeting of wet licks on his hand.

"I got your message," Sid said.

"And your thoughts?"

"Rounding up living creatures and shooting them because we're afraid? What do you think?"

"There will be issues. Lots of issues. Our neighborhood may never recover if we are wrong."

"No doubt. But there always are issues," Sid answered.

"All the more reason to tread carefully," Gabriel cautioned. "You don't have to."

"Actually, I think I do."

"How's that?"

"You know what Channa would say: 'Good thoughts are nice, but love requires action. You need to just do.'"

"You sound like a Jewish Nike commercial," Gabriel said.

"You got a plan?"

"Not even a glimmer."

"The others?" Sid asked.

Gabriel shook his head.

"Well then, I can see why you're so enthusiastic. Let's get some paper and pens."

"Why?" Gabriel asked.

"A map," Sid said. "All good plans start with a map."

With one final glance at the broken image of Abraham, Gabriel slipped the stone into his pocket and mumbled an Our Father.

"A prayer for our success?" Sid asked.

"No. For different cells when we get popped."

7

After an hour tailing Morgan, Sam came upon the rolling pastures of Dutchess County, New York, farmland.

"Maybe we should just turn around," Beth said.

"No," Sam shot back.

"Thank you for being so reasonable. Has it occurred to you that maybe she's driving to a vivisection conference in Canada?"

"No."

"What can I do to get you to move past monosyllabic answers?"

"I'm concentrating. This isn't easy." Sam stayed a quarter mile behind Morgan, keeping a few cars between them, making sure she didn't turn off at an exit. The whole following thing had made her head hurt again.

"I've got to pee," Beth declared.

Sam glanced at her. "Are you kidding me?"

"You may have the bladder of a camel, but I don't. Too much Tab before we left."

"You're gonna need to hold it."

"I have been."

"Hold it more."

"I can't."

Sam reached into the backseat and pulled out a thin blue pad of gauze and cloth.

"What's this?"

"A puppy wee-wee pad."

"What am I supposed to do with it?"

"Try not to splatter," Sam told her.

"Oh," Beth said at the realization. "Gross. No fucking way."

"I can't stop. We'll lose her."

"Why don't I just hang my ass out the window?"

"You can do that too."

Beth began to unbuckle her pants.

"Wait," Sam stopped her. Morgan had turned on her blinker.

The Benz pulled off at the exit marked "Annandale-on-Hudson" and then took a two-lane road for another two miles. Sam shadowed.

Morgan turned into a narrow, winding road that ran up the side of a wooded hill. Sam gave her a three-minute lead and then followed.

After a mile at a forty-five-degree incline, the road crested.

Sam gasped. "Holy shit!"

Below them, separated by a large metal gate and completely hidden from the road, a hundred acres of valley pasture supported a large barn and dozens of cows grazing peacefully on huge wheels of hay. It appeared to be a typical dairy farm—except for the two-story, five-thousand-square-foot glass-metal-and-concrete structure rising up from the middle. The building looked as if someone had accidentally Photoshopped it into this pastoral setting from an industrial park. Morgan's car sat at the entrance.

Only one sign was visible in the entire complex: a large "Private Property—Keep Out. No Trespassing" command in angry red letters against a black background posted on the gate. Sam slowly drove toward it.

"Do you think the sign is ambiguous?" Beth asked.

"Quiet."

A keypad and tiny speaker stood guard on a metal pole adjacent to the gate. The speaker squawked and a pleasant male voice came on. "Can I help you?"

Sam powered down her window. She noticed a small camera lens above the keypad. "I think I'm lost," she lied to the box.

"No problem, ma'am. What address were you looking for?"

Crap. Good question, she thought. "What address is this?"

"What address were you seeking, ma'am?"

"Main Street," Beth blurted out. Sam punched her in the thigh. "What?" Beth whispered. "Every town has a Main Street. That's why it's called Main Street."

"Sorry," the voice said. "I'm not familiar with that one."

"That's OK," Sam said. "I'll find it."

"Have a good day," the cheerful voice replied.

"This is a beautiful place," she told the box. "Can you tell me what facility this is?"

The box was silent.

"Hello?"

Again, no response.

Sam turned the car around and headed down the road that served as the driveway. She stopped where the driveway met the main road and turned on Beth. "Main Street?"

"I didn't see you come up with a better idea. And I still have to pee," Beth said. "It's becoming an urgent matter."

A UPS truck came into view down the road. Sam flicked on her hazards, jumped out, and flagged it down.

"Problem?" the driver asked.

"I'm sorry," Sam said. "But we're lost. Can you tell me what address this is?"

"One-twenty Willoughby," he said.

"Is there a bathroom somewhere nearby?" Beth called over from the car.

"Over in town. There's an info center on Grand Street with a bathroom. About five miles. Turn left out of the service road. Not much between here and there, though."

"Grand Street," Beth muttered. "That was gonna be my second choice."

"Do you know what this place is?" Sam asked, pointing up the hill and trying to sound as innocent as possible. "It's really beautiful, but they weren't too nice."

"When I was growing up around here, it used to be the Malone Dairy Farm. Now I think it's part of some company called VetMed Biologics or something like that. Never been allowed past the gate myself, even for deliveries, so I don't think they'll let you use the bathroom. There's always the woods, though."

Sam thanked the driver for the information and he drove off. She jumped back into her seat. "You heard the man," she said, and pointed out the window. "There's the woods."

"In the interest of fairness and full disclosure," Beth said, "I'm not sure I can limit it to just a number one at this point. Happens when I get over-stimulated."

Sam reached into the backseat for a roll of paper towels.

Beth grabbed the roll. "You always come prepared, don't you?"

"Life of a vet."

"I may be a few minutes."

"You'll want to go pretty far in for humanity's sake."

Beth left the car. "You got anything to read?"

"Just go!"

Beth ran—or what counted for running in Beth's world—into the woods. Sam grabbed Beth's phone and dialed her own cell number.

"Where the hell are you?" her father barked before she got to *hello*. "Everyone is trying to find you."

"Why didn't someone call me?" Sam complained.

"Perhaps you should've thought of that before taking the one cell phone with the unknown number."

"Damn. Didn't think about that. Did you find something?"

"Pieces. I can't connect them yet. But there's an issue."

Sam's stomach dropped. "Are they coming for my dogs?"

"Not yet. I couldn't understand Greg completely, but it has something to do with some trouble with your friend Andy."

"I'll call them."

"Did you speak to Morgan?" Daniel asked.

"Yeah, but she wasn't talking. So we followed her."

"To where?"

"Dutchess County."

"What the hell for?"

Sam wasn't in the mood for parental judgment. "Because that's where she was going."

"Well, stop playing games and get back here as soon as you can."

"Listen, where do I know the name VetMed Biologics from?"

Daniel was silent for almost a full minute.

"Dad?" Sam asked. "You there?"

"You don't know the name," he said. His voice suddenly sounded somber and far away.

"But you do, don't you?"

"I did. That entity no longer exists," he said defensively.

"It does."

"How do you know?"

"I'm looking at it. That's where we followed Morgan to."

Sam heard something on the phone that sounded like a cross between a gasp and a moan. Her father had never made either sound before and it made Sam's heart jump. "She wouldn't," he finally said.

"Dad, you're talking to yourself again."

"VetMed was a major funding source for my Bullet research. They're a big player in agricultural vaccines for diseases prevalent in factory-farmed food animals."

"But you were working on a human vaccine. I had always assumed your money came from the human vaccine industry."

"It's economics. Human vaccine development is now highly regulated. Farm animal vaccine development is not. It is within the jurisdiction of the—"

"The USDA," Sam answered.

"Correct."

"Let me guess: the USDA is still underfunded and under the thumb of the huge agribusiness legislative lobby?"

"We count on that. You have maximum flexibility to develop the vaccines on the agricultural side of the equation and then move it over toward human development. By that point you have already, how can I put this, exceeded the envelope of what might be acceptable on the human side."

"But if you were testing vaccines on animals for zoonotic illnesses, and if your theory of cross-species transference is true, then—"

"Correct. Whatever you do to the animal, you eventually do to us. It is only a question of opportunity and time."

"What's the relationship to the cholera?"

"Ramses, I think. One of the most promising areas of agricultural animal vaccines is experimental adjuvants—something added to a vaccine to accelerate the immune response to the vaccination, usually to aid adsorption or to inflame the immune system. They're sort of vaccine turbochargers, and—"

"I know what a vaccine adjuvant is, Dad. I went to vet school too."

"Right, sorry. What you may not know, however, is that adjuvants are now a huge business in agriculture. Because they reduce the amount of vaccine required per dose, and the number of doses given per animal. If they can use adjuvants to make each dose more powerful, and can therefore use fewer doses per animal, then they can cover far more animals with the same amount of vaccine. It means more individual doses available for mass vaccination campaigns. Coincidentally, this is exactly the goal of government and the pharmaceutical companies who stand to make millions from their vaccines—if they can deliver them. The problem is the more dilute the vaccine, the more powerful and toxic the adjuvant must be to stimulate the immune response. VetMed started looking into some very toxic areas."

"What areas?"

"Bacterial toxins."

"Like cholera?"

"It was one of several on the list."

"That's insane!"

"Actually, not insane at all. Just dangerous. There were a number of studies that demonstrated the efficacy of cholera toxin as an experimental adjuvant for oral inoculation in pigs and cows. The good part is that it is highly toxic and triggers a strong mucosal immunity response in amounts that should not cause harm to the host. The bad part is that it is—"

"—Fucking cholera, Dad!"

"Well, yes, there is that. And the proposed delivery mechanism required more than a little. Add that to the fact that you don't really want to be in the business of manufacturing cholera toxin, and you get the picture."

"How deep were you in this shit?"

"Not too far. Even I have my own limited standards. But Morgan said yes to the research."

"Why am I not surprised?"

"She completed a study in which she concluded that bacterial toxin was an effective and safe adjuvant for a number of food animal vaccines. I had my doubts, so I paid off one of her assistants to get me the data sets."

"Why?"

"I could tell you that I was on a crusade to protect us all from dangerous bacterial adjuvants, but the reality is that if she succeeded and I was wrong, I wanted in on it."

"Oh," Sam said as she fought the memory of her snickering classmates.

"Yes, I know," her father said. "Another proud moment in your family history. But I wasn't wrong in my assumption. Morgan had falsified the data. I called her on it and obtained certain promises from her in exchange for keeping my discovery quiet."

"You blackmailed her?"

"A little."

"But you didn't stop her."

"I thought I did, but then the accident happened and..." Their shared loss hung in the momentary silence between them.

"So why does my dog have cholera?"

"I don't know, but it is hard to believe that is coincidence, given where you are standing and Ramses."

"And what about rabies?"

"That one makes no sense. There's no crosswalk between these dogs with cholera and canine rabies that I can find."

"Are you telling me the truth?"

"About this? Yes. Ramses had nothing to do with rabies. No one is seriously researching rabies vaccination anymore because there's no money in it. Rabies is all pets and wildlife, not livestock. The current vaccination protocols are long established and working fine."

"What are you saying, Dad?"

"Maybe Riverside really does have a naturally occurring canine rabies crisis on its hands. There are reports of another rabid dog—this time in Central Park. People are being warned away."

"But if that's the case—"

"Then many dogs in Riverside are as good as dead. They've already established the quarantine. The next step will be a cull."

"There must be a connection. What are we missing?"

"I need to make some calls," Daniel said. "In the meantime, don't do anything stupid."

Yeah, right, Sam thought as she ended the call.

Beth emerged from the woods with a satisfied smile and a quarter of the roll of paper towels. "Look at me," she called, and did a quick pose with the paper towels. "I'm finally at one with nature."

"Get in the car."

Beth hopped in. "What'd I do now?"

Sam hit the accelerator and shot out of the driveway so fast her wheels squealed.

Beth stared at her. "You gonna talk to me, Thelma, or do I just have to guess where the cliff is?"

Sam drove for about a hundred yards, turned off onto a dirt path that looked as if it had once served as a horse trail, and cut the engine. "You stay here," she said.

"Come again?"

"Stay put. I'm going back to the facility."

"I think they were pretty clear they didn't want to see you."

"That's why you need to stay here. With your record you can't afford to be picked up for trespassing."

"Do you have any idea what you're doing at this point?"

"Honestly? No, except Morgan can be in there right now destroying more files and data that we need unless I can stop her."

"Then I'm coming with you."

"Not an option this time. I'm sorry, hon."

Beth covered her head with her arms.

"What the hell are you doing?" Sam asked.

"This is the point where you knock me unconscious for my own good so I don't follow you."

8

Luke drove his daughter's small truck with "Heaven Scent Florist and Nursery—Nothing Else in Brooklyn Smells This Good!" signage to the park entrance at 108th Street. He cut the engine and jumped out of the cab. Gabriel and Andy, his backpack stuffed with his violin case and packages of meat, followed.

Gabriel read one of the postings that had been plastered every few feet on the stone wall encircling the park. Considering the bold black letters, the devil-red background, and the overuse of exclamation points, there could be no question that someone wanted the message to be noticed and obeyed.

Gabriel called Luke and Andy over to look:

WARNING!
HEALTH EMERGENCY! HAZARDOUS AREA!

The park will be closed to all dogs at 5:00 p.m. until further notice. No parking or unattended vehicles on this block after 5:00 p.m. Violators will be towed and fined. Absolutely no exceptions! Hazardous poisoned bait in use. Any dog found

in the park after 5:00 p.m. will be subject to quarantine. Entry
into the park after 5:00 p.m. will be deemed unconditional
consent to search by proper authorities.

By order of the state Department of Environmental Protection and the Governor of the state of New York.

In the face of the severity of the posting, Gabriel thought their plan
was absurdly simple—find any strays, get them in the truck, and then
drive them through the perimeter and to the shelter. They needed to
do all this before the DEP closed the park and began its search-and-
contain operation.

Gabriel pointed a thumb at the poster and spoke to Luke. "Looks
like we only have an hour before we become the newest guests on
America's Most Wanted. Your daughter's name is on the truck registra-
tion so you'll need to stay with the truck in case someone comes."

"Right," Luke answered. "But how're you going to get them all
without me?"

Gabriel turned to Andy: "So you think ten, right?"

"I've only seen ten," Andy said. "I don't know how many there
really are."

"It's gonna be hard enough to get the ten," Gabriel said.

"But—" Andy started to protest.

"We'll take as many as we can," Gabriel agreed to avoid an argument. "But we need to get started now or else it won't matter."

Andy was already moving before Gabriel had finished his sentence.

"Call me on the cell when you're on the way out," Luke said.
Gabriel nodded and jogged after the boy.

Once Gabriel caught up, he asked, "How're we going to find
them?"

"Just stay behind me."

As they walked through the north end of the park, Gabriel noticed
joggers, cyclists, walkers, Rollerbladers, people just sitting on the grass,

and several dogs attached to their owners by leash, but that was all. Not even an untended pile of shit, he thought. "Any ideas?"

"They've gotten really good at hiding," Andy answered innocently. "A few more feet."

Andy brought them to a stop and pointed to a copse of trees surrounding a large rock outcropping.

Although the trees were thick in some places, Gabriel could see through them to the rock formation. There were no dogs anywhere.

"Wait here," Andy said.

With a growing unease Gabriel watched Andy walk to the trees. Had he already failed this boy in the one way that mattered? Could it be that Andy's historical demons had caused him to create this fantasy about a Central Park Pack? If that was the case, the challenge would be to convince Andy to rejoin reality without inviting some type of psychotic break. Gabriel knew that his own current condition left him too weak to accomplish that task.

These thoughts dissipated in an instant when the boy moved into the trees and suddenly was gone. Not just obscured by branches and leaves, but vanished. "Holy crap," Gabriel muttered. He recalled the boy's words about the dogs: "They've gotten really good at hiding."

"Yeah, no kidding," he said.

Gabriel sensed a tingle at the base of his neck just as a slight wind picked up. A cold breeze passed across his brow although the air was hot and the trees were still. He felt refreshed, as if he had just showered and stepped into a soft, thick robe. The smell of wet snow, incongruous in the heat, filled his nose and mouth. Time fell away. It could have been two minutes or two hours before Gabriel heard Andy's faraway voice on the breeze. "Coming out now."

"From where?" Gabriel whispered.

The priest got his answer when Andy led nine dogs out between tree trunks that suddenly seemed massive, verdant, and primordial.

The dogs looked about as dissimilar as nine dogs could be in size, hair color, hair length, age, and breed. There were recognizable pieces of Lab, golden, beagle, pit bull, Saint Bernard, Scottie, Westie, shepherd, husky, border collie, and maybe a half dozen other breeds. They had at least one thing in common, though. Excited by Andy's proximity, they jumped, ran, and played with each other and the boy as if they were puppies, even though their physical characteristics suggested they were all older.

"These can't be strays," Gabriel said when he finally found his words. "They're too healthy, too well behaved. They belong to someone."

"Not *to*," Andy said. "*With*. They belong with me." His tone left no room for debate.

"What is this place exactly?" Gabriel asked.

Andy smiled at the question. "Just a safe place in a big city park."

Gabriel was about to press further, but concluded that this was one of those times when greater inspection would not bring enlightenment. "Is this everyone?"

"There's one more I need to find. She's not here."

"Let's get these in the truck and we can come back for her." Andy hesitated at the suggestion. "We can't risk leaving these nine, can we?" Gabriel pressed.

Andy reluctantly nodded his agreement.

Gabriel looped slipknot leashes on the dogs, not because he needed to, but because the farther the dogs moved from the particular spot in the park where Andy had found them, the more attention they would attract. Even with the leashes and even though they still had a good thirty minutes before the deadline, something about the connection between the boy and the dogs invited stares. The fact that a tall man wearing a priest collar walked among them didn't help mute their conspicuousness. Gabriel mentally ran through a list of explanations in case someone stopped them. None sounded plausible and he couldn't even be sure he would be able to articulate them if pushed.

But no one even stepped into their path. When Gabriel glanced at Andy, he began to understand why. The boy was so confident in his task, so certain that this was where he needed to be, even the priest felt sheltered in his presence.

They made it to the truck without incident. But by the time they got the dogs settled in, they had only fifteen minutes before the Guard arrived and the efforts to cleanse the park of all canine life commenced in earnest.

"I've got to go back," Andy declared.

"We're cutting this too close," Gabriel said.

"You can go," Andy answered. "I need to find her."

"But you'll never get her out of the park, and if you do, the Guard won't let you get to the shelter at this point. I don't think you under-stand how serious this has become."

"I'm going," Andy said with finality.

"I'll go back with you," Gabriel offered. "We've got a better shot with two people." That wasn't Gabriel's true reason for his offer; the priest had a bad feeling about leaving the boy alone in the park that he could not attribute solely to the Guards' activities.

"You can't," Luke said. "You need to stay in the back and keep the dogs quiet while I drive. It's the only way or we'll never make it past the perimeter." Luke turned to Andy. "I'll come back for you. I'll find out which side the surveillance is thinnest and wait for you there. Call me when you're ready."

"I don't like this at all," Gabriel warned. "If the boy gets caught…"

"I won't," Andy said as he removed his backpack. He took out sev-eral ziplock bags stuffed with cuts of raw meat and handed them to Gabriel. "Take it. It'll keep them busy during the ride."

Gabriel climbed into the back of the truck just as a van from the state's Department of Environmental Protection pulled up to the curb one block south of them. Two men in blue vinyl hazmat suits jumped out and opened the rear doors. Rows of orange canisters marked with a black skull and crossbones and labeled "HAZARD" and "POISON" stared out. A flatbed truck pulled up carrying blue-and-white police sawhorse barricades. Two cable news vans followed.

If Gabriel had retained any lingering doubts that this was for real—that there would be loss of life—those doubts abandoned him here.

"If you're gonna go in," Gabriel told Andy, "you better do it now."

Andy gave them a thumbs-up. "Thanks for trusting me," he said. "Means a lot."

"I always trust you, son," Gabriel said. "I just don't understand you. Now go."

Andy left them at a jog in the direction of the Lake.

9

Sam and Beth scrambled through the woods, racing back toward the facility.

"You realize how many ticks are probably latching onto us as we speak?" Beth asked. "I can feel the Lyme disease coursing through my bloodstream. I'll need to start myself on doxycycline when we get back. Oh, wait, I can't write scripts anymore."

"You know, I think you're right," Sam whispered. "I should've knocked you out in the car. Are you trying to get us caught?"

"Perhaps if you told me the plan, dear?"

"I told you already. I just want to see if we can get a closer look at the facility without going through the front door."

"That's not really a plan, is it? Besides, didn't you see that fence? Don't you think it goes around the whole place?"

"I don't know. That's what I want to see. Now keep quiet, we're getting close to the back."

Sam stood in the shelter of the trees and looked out onto a small field. One hundred yards farther on, an eight-foot-high chain link fence protected the entire rear of the facility. Beth stepped beside her. "What do you know?" she said, wheezing. "A fence."

"Shhh. Do you see any surveillance cameras?"

Beth shook her head.

"Me neither, but we're pretty far away."

Another field an acre in size lay between the fence and the rear of the facility. This field had been further divided by chain link into several large sections. Each section included a long wooden structure. What were those? Sam wondered. Chicken coops? No. She could not fool herself and simply turn away. She knew what they were.

Dog kennels.

Sam left the cover of the trees and stepped out into the open field.

Beth grabbed for her. "What the hell are you doing? You're not wearing your invisibility cloak."

Sam kept walking forward. She needed to know.

"And they say my judgment is impaired," Beth muttered, and went after her.

Sam broke into a run and didn't stop until she met the fence. The dogs jumped out of their shelters to greet her. Twenty-five dogs—mostly beagles and beagle mixes—leaped against the fence. They lifted their heads to howl and bark at their surprise visitor but the result was a cacophony of silence.

Sam saw the scars on their mutilated throats. Such cruelty no longer surprised her—she had actually seen worse on some of the dogs at her own shelter—but familiarity didn't make the discovery any less horrifying. She laced her fingers through the chain links partly to offer the victims some painless human contact and partly to hold herself up, because she felt her legs turning rubbery.

Beth reached the fence. "Are you crazy?" she asked breathlessly. "We need to get out of here before the dogs...wait...Why aren't they barking?"

Sam didn't answer. She had already returned in her mind to her father's office on the day of her graduation. She knew that those particular dogs were long gone from this earth, but she also knew with equal certainty that these dogs were the current consequence of that same unbroken line of humanity gone wrong. The Devil in human form. Sam had no doubt that somewhere William Ralph Inge was nodding knowingly.

Sam had never tried to save her father's dogs. That failure haunted her. This time she swore it would be different.

"Christ," Beth said when she saw the scars. "That is seriously fucked up. But we've got to get out of here." She attempted to tug Sam back toward the woods.

Sam wouldn't move. "I'm going in."

"OK, but let's go back and at least think of a plan."

"No more plans, Beth. I'm going over the fence."

Beth eyed the chain link fence and shook her head. "Do you have any idea how much I weigh? What in our brief relationship together makes you think I can physically accomplish that?"

"You can't come with me."

"Would you stop with that already? I've got a plan. Trust me." Beth again pulled Sam and this time she gave in.

"What's the plan?" Sam asked as she followed.

"I'll create a distraction. I'm good at distractions."

IO

Gabriel stood in the back of the florist truck trying to control the strays with a combination of meat from Andy's pack and pleading. A terrier type ran through the legs of three large dogs on one side of the truck while a shepherd mix howled on the other. A Labrador-something left a steaming pile in the middle of the floor and Gabriel was trying to clean it up as best as he could with paper towels and one hand while holding the phone in the other.

Noise control was going to be the key. Luke had padded the walls of the truck with gym mats borrowed from the preschool next to his daughter's flower shop. When they had tested the mats earlier, the padding had seemed generally effective in keeping the noise inside the truck. The problem, however, was that the padding kept the noise inside the truck. Gabriel's head was already pounding and the truck was still at the curb.

Gabriel dialed his phone. "We're ready to move. You ready for us?"

Greg answered at the shelter. "We'll be waiting."

Luke slid open the small divider between the truck cab and the back. "You set back there?" he asked.

"Just waiting for a confirmed all clear from Sid," Gabriel said.

"I just spoke to him three minutes ago. We're good."

"Let's wait a sec. I don't want to drive right into something."

"Starting to get hot out here. We're out of time. I'm pulling out," Luke told him. "You better hold on to something." Without waiting for further protest from Gabriel, Luke pulled away from the sidewalk.

The dogs in the back initially quieted at the truck's movement, but once the truck picked up speed, the dogs lost their momentary restraint and began to bark and howl as the truck headed toward the perimeter and the shelter.

Gabriel dialed again and reached Sid, stationed at a traffic light post three blocks from the shelter.

"I'm checking in," Gabriel said.

"You already did."

"I'm doing it again. Any sign of the Guard?"

"And I'm just keeping it from you?"

"Don't be a smartass, Sidney."

"The militia seems to be preoccupied at the perimeter for the moment."

"That could change, and anything coming to the shelter from the perimeter would need to pass your way."

"I know. Trust me: you'll be the first to know if it does."

"Don't get distracted."

"I won't if you stop calling me. Are you ready?"

"I doubt it," Gabriel said, and signed off.

Gabriel jammed his cell phone into his pocket, put out a hand against the wall to steady himself, and turned to face the dogs. "Work with me." As if in response, a black Lab mix jumped on Gabriel and pushed him to the floor, where he narrowly missed the pile of shit.

"So did you ever hear the one about the rabbi, the priest, and the dog?"

Gabriel looked up from the floor and saw Channa leaning casually against the side of the truck, suppressing a laugh.

"Not yet. Do I need to?" he asked, slowly rising to his feet.

"You might find it of interest given your present state of mind."

"Then by all means."

"So this priest and this rabbi die and go to heaven."

"Funny so far."

Channa ignored him. "They're waiting in line at the pearly gates to speak with God. But there's a dog ahead of them. God appears and says to the three of them, 'Tell me what you've done to make me smile.' The priest says—"

"Of course the priest speaks first—"

"Do you want to hear it or not?"

"Sorry, go ahead," Gabriel said.

"So the priest says, 'I have been true to Your spirit and sought to bring comfort to everyone I met.'"

"And the rabbi?"

"I was getting to that. The rabbi says, 'I have been true to Your heart and sought to carry out Your will on earth.' God smiles at them and moves aside to let the three of them pass. Once they cross over, the priest says, 'Excuse me, Heavenly Father, but what did the dog say in answer to your question?' And God says in surprise, 'I thought you were speaking for him.' So the rabbi says, 'Excuse me, Heavenly Father, but if You thought we were speaking on behalf of the dog, why did You just let us through?' And God says, getting annoyed now, 'I told you, I thought you were speaking for him.'"

"Thank you for the inspiration, dear," Gabriel said. "But I would have preferred a cigarette and two fingers of Scotch."

Gabriel reached down to remove one of the dogs humping his leg. When he glanced up, Channa was gone, as he'd expected.

Gabriel felt the truck begin to slow and then music blasted all other thoughts out of his head.

Luke was implementing his plan.

They had confirmed through about seven prior test runs that the

Guard was not checking vehicles entering the perimeter for dogs. Still, the line into the quarantine area was slow because of all the rubbernecking. This was where the dog noise could hurt them the most. The gym mats were useful, but they couldn't take any chances. Luke had promised that he had a plan. "In Jimi we trust," he'd said.

Gabriel now understood what he had meant.

A block before the perimeter, Luke opened the windows of the truck cab, put his Jimi Hendrix *Electric Ladyland* CD into the truck's player, found the fifteenth track—"All Along the Watchtower"—and turned the volume to the max. Jimi's guitar and ghostly voice reverberated off the surrounding buildings.

"Hey!" Gabriel heard one Guard shout above the music. "Do we all need to hear that crap?"

Luke added his own surprisingly melodious voice to Jimi's. They picked up speed again as Luke continued singing with the CD.

They were free of the perimeter. Or more accurately, Gabriel thought, they were now trapped inside it.

II

W ait here." The big man with the crew cut and reflective aviator shades shook his head disapprovingly as he closed the heavy metal door on his exit.

Sam quickly scanned the room. It looked like a break room or perhaps a presentation room—a long metal table, a few uncomfortable chairs, a projection screen at the front of the room, and a podium. There were no computers and, more importantly, no phones.

"East Harlem," Sam said.

"What?" Beth asked.

"That was Judge Allerton's other option for you. I could've let you serve your sentence working with the crack addicts, hookers, and pimps in East Harlem. But no, I had to try to do the right thing."

"Don't get all bitchy," Beth protested. "It wasn't my fault. Did you really think there wouldn't be security?"

"You said you had a plan. That you would create a distraction," Sam insisted.

"I did create a distraction," Beth shot back.

"Asking Crew Cut out there about his feelings toward his mother is not a distraction."

"It is where I come from. A man's relationship with his mother is one of the most powerful and complicated influences on his life."

"Just stop talking," Sam snapped.

That worked for a second. Then Beth said, "What do you think Morgan is really up to?"

"I don't know. Whatever it is, we're losing time to figure out if it's got anything to do with what's going on in Manhattan." *And*, she thought, *to figure out if we have any chance of stopping the cull*.

"Don't worry. I'm sure the cops will be here pretty soon. Crew Cut mentioned criminal trespass. I wonder what class of felony that is. Well, at least you'll get to see how the other half lives."

"Could you be any less helpful?"

"The day is still young," Beth said.

Sam tried the door handle and then shoved the door hard with her shoulder. It didn't move.

"Is it locked?" Beth asked.

Sam rubbed her shoulder in an attempt to restore feeling. "Gee, you think so?"

"I never said I was good at this spy business. When I hear the word *commando* I think of going out without underwear, not breaking into some research facility."

"You know what I like about you, Beth?"

"No, what?"

"It isn't a quiz. I thought maybe you'd know."

"See? The fat girl is always the first one attacked."

Sam sat down across from Beth and upended her bag on the table. Beth looked at her quizzically. "You're cleaning out your purse?"

"I'm trying to see what kind of resources we have. They took the phone, but they didn't look too hard, so maybe…" Sam looked through the contents with an expanding feeling of helplessness—a few Tampax, tissues, gum, car keys, a wallet, and some loose cash. Nothing doing. She returned the items to her bag. "You have anything?"

Beth reached into her pocket and pulled out a few singles, a pack of gum, and an empty Tic Tac container. She reached into her other pocket. "Hold on. I think I've got something." She pulled out some paper clips and proudly showed them to Sam.

"OK, MacGyver, what do you think you're gonna do with those?"

"Just observe and learn." Beth straightened two paper clips as she moved to the door. She inserted one into the lock and then the second. Sam watched closely as Beth confidently jiggled and rotated the clips. "The key to picking a lock like this…," Beth said smugly.

"Is getting a locksmith?"

"No. Is that you must…ow! Ow! Ow!" Beth whipped her hand back and inspected the drop of blood on her finger where the paper clip had poked her. "I'm bleeding." She ran over to Sam and displayed the tiny speck of blood.

"Just come clean, Beth. You were sent here to destroy my mind, weren't you?"

"Hey, did I mention that I'm bleeding here?"

Crew Cut returned with a large file folder and a legal pad.

"So nice to see you again," Beth said.

"You can make this easier on all of us if you would answer a few questions before the police arrive."

"And where are our friendly police officers?" Sam said. "I've got a few things I'd like to tell them about the way we've been treated."

Crew Cut smiled. It wasn't pleasant. "You know how it is. We're a pretty small town. Our police need to cover a good deal of ground. It may be a little while before they can get here. No rush, now that you are secure."

That didn't sound right to Sam. The cops should have already been here. Unless…Sam looked over to Beth and guessed that she was having the same thought.

"And how can we be helpful?" Beth asked.

"Why were you trying to enter this facility?"

"We told you. We were just looking for a bathroom," Sam said.

"Cut the crap," Crew Cut demanded. "Who are you working for?"

"Really?" Beth chuckled into her hand.

"Something funny?" Crew Cut asked.

"I just thought I'd go my entire life without hearing someone actually use that phrase for real." Beth eyed her interrogator. "Where were you trained? *Dragnet*?"

"You're not helping, Beth," Sam complained.

"Agri-Vet?" Crew Cut volunteered. "It's them, right? When will you people learn? There's a reason they're called trade secrets, you know?"

So Crew Cut either had not spoken with Morgan yet or Morgan was pretending she didn't know them. "I guess we should tell him the truth before this gets out of hand," Sam suggested.

"Your call, sweetie," Beth answered.

"OK, look, we're actually investigative reporters," Sam said.

"Pulitzer Prize–winning, by the way," Beth added.

"We work for the *New York Times*."

"Have you heard of them?" Beth asked.

Sam took the ball back from Beth and ran with it. "We're investigating Morgan. We know the kind of shit you've been doing here. Cholera toxin is the least of it. My editors will have this place swarming with lawyers any minute if you don't let us go. And of course I'll need the correct spelling of your name for the story."

Crew Cut leaned into Sam's face. "You're investigative reporters like I'm a ballerina."

"I've been wondering," Beth said. "How is it that you learn to dance on pointe?"

"You won't think this is so funny when you're in the backseat of a squad car."

Sam ignored the threat. "Tell Morgan we'll only speak directly to her. Otherwise we'll just wait for the cops."

I 2

Andy arrived at the spot on the edge of the Lake that he thought of as "theirs"—the place that had first heard their music.

It was deserted. He tried to choke down his panic. This was his one shot to find her. If he had guessed wrong, he wouldn't be able to double back. There was no time. They'd both be done.

Andy pulled his violin case from his backpack and quickly removed the instrument and his bow. His first notes were horribly off, hesitant and jumbled. He was too nervous, although he never became nervous when he played.

He counted to three in his head, closed his eyes, and then moved the bow across the violin once more. This time the sound was different—long, sinuous tones eventually gave birth to a fast-moving melody that surged skyward out of his violin. Andy knew this was a beautiful refrain. It had to be, because this was their composition. Whenever he played this part of the piece, he thought for some reason of angels having sex.

Andy opened his eyes and she was there, sitting on her haunches staring into the growing darkness on the water. He stopped playing and the dog turned to look at him. There was something so lost and sorrowful in the dog's expression that Andy almost dropped to his knees as he remembered.

Alexa had made it to the Lake that night, more than halfway to their cavern. But so had someone else. Blood from two stab wounds to her chest…her gray face…her right ear gone—torn or bitten off… ripping off his shirt and stuffing it into her ugly wounds…seeing all the blood that had already left her body seeping into the ground.

"Don't leave me," he whispered into the disfigured ear.

That was where the police found them. Andy screamed when they took her body out of the park. Only her bloodstain remained.

It took two months before he had the courage to enter the park again and three before he could walk past the Lake to the rock formation. When he finally entered the cavern, the stray was waiting. He saw the missing ear. That was all he needed to know.

His shrink, the one Judge Allerton made him see, called it necroanthropomorphism—projecting the characteristics of a dead human on a living animal. It was a big name to try to convince him that he'd lost it. But Andy wasn't convinced. Instead he learned not to talk about her. Not even with Father Gabriel, who might have understood that the death thing wasn't nearly as linear as everyone thought.

Andy could never bring himself to name the one-eared stray. He felt she already had a name.

"C'mon, girl. Time to get out of here," he called to the dog. She turned her gaze back to the surface of the Lake, searching.

Andy stowed his violin and took a few steps forward. The dog whined but didn't move. She allowed Andy to rub her head and then take a leash and loop it around her neck.

Andy needed to tug hard to get her moving.

"It's not safe here anymore. You can stay with me now," he told her.

He tugged again and this time, her tail down and ears flat, the dog surrendered and slowly followed him.

They made it twenty-five feet before they ran into their first patrol—three men in blue vinyl biohazard suits, each carrying one of the ominous black-and-red canisters Andy had observed in the DEP van.

Andy quickly pulled the dog behind some trees, held his breath, and waited for them to pass. As they moved away, he heard one of the men say, "Hell, Pete. I didn't take this job to kill dogs."

"They aren't dogs anymore, remember?" the other said. "These are 'biological pathogen vectors.'"

Once their voices moved off and the trail was clear, Andy stepped out again.

"What the hell you doing, kid?" The voice came from behind him.

Andy spun around expecting to see more DEP insignias, or cops, or maybe even Guardsmen. Instead he came face-to-face with the old black man in the long coat. "The park's been closed now to dogs. You can't be wandering all around with her," he said, pointing to the dog. "Especially not her. They get their hands on her and…well, that changes everything."

"She's my dog. I'm taking her home."

"Don't play me, kid. I'm like the last friend you got right now. You won't make it out."

"I'll be fine. Don't worry about me."

"I've always worried about you, Andy."

Andy startled. None of this felt right. "How'd you know my name?"

The black man smiled, showing his stained brown teeth for just a moment. "We all know you. Just like we know she's not your dog."

We? Andy stepped away, suddenly frightened.

The man grabbed Andy's arm more quickly and with more power than Andy would've thought possible. The one-eared dog growled, but the man silenced her with a glance and turned to Andy. "She can't go with you, you know?" The dog nuzzled up to Andy and the affection between them was unmistakable. Even the old man lost his words for a moment. "Look, it ain't nothing on you, Andy. But she can't go beyond the wall. That's not her place anymore. She's given enough."

"Get your hand off me," Andy demanded, but there was no force behind it.

The man nodded and released the boy. "No harm intended. Just trying to save you some ache. She doesn't end here...but she does for you. You and I can't change that."

"I've got no idea what you're talking about."

"I think you do. But whether you do now or you don't, you will in a bit."

The black man moved off as silently as he'd arrived.

13

Luke pulled the truck up to the front of the shelter next to Greg. The dogs, excited by the sudden absence of forward motion, barked and howled, but the sound was low and muffled on the street.

Luke jumped out of the cabin. "We'd better get the dogs inside before the noise attracts attention."

"Where's the boy?" Greg asked.

"He's coming."

"Don't like that answer," Greg said as he followed Luke to the back of the truck. Luke unlatched the rear door and yanked upward on the handle. The door lifted a few inches and sniffing snouts began to materialize in the gap. "You got them?" Greg asked through the space.

"Yeah." Gabriel was exhausted and couldn't muster enough energy to hide it. "I really need to get out of here. I don't even think I like dogs anymore."

"You'll be out in a second," Luke promised.

Greg opened the truck door all the way and jumped inside. The dogs eyed him for a guarded moment, but judged quickly and approved. "I'll take them down from here, Father." Feeling guilty but relieved, Gabriel handed over the leashes.

As Gabriel climbed down from the truck, he saw it and almost let out an expletive.

Luke followed his stare. "How the hell did that get here?"

A Guard Jeep pulled up across the street in front of the corner deli and double-parked. If the driver turned their way, he would be able to see directly into the back of the truck.

"Not enough time to get everyone inside," Greg said. "Close us up." Greg pulled the dogs farther into the truck and Luke slammed the door down.

The lone Jeep occupant reviewed some papers on the front seat.

"I'm gonna hurt Sid," Gabriel hissed.

As if the utterance of his name had summoned his form, Sid strolled into view wearing the self-assured look of someone who had completed a difficult task beyond all expectations. "Everything OK?" he asked as he arrived at the truck.

"Not so much," Gabriel said through clenched teeth, and nodded to the Jeep.

Sid stumbled and almost fell. "That's the guy who tried to kill Louis at the perimeter. Owens. How the hell did he get here?"

"You tell me," Gabriel snarled. "He passed you."

"Not possible!" Sid argued.

"You're right, Sid. The Virgin Mary just dropped him down from the heavens. There's only one way here—and it was through you. How could you miss a military Jeep?"

"Let's not panic," Luke said. "He's only on a break from the perimeter...going to get a sandwich or coffee or something. We just need to keep everyone calm until he leaves." Luke stepped on the rear truck bumper and leaned over to pretend to tie a shoe. "Hang in there, Greg," he told the door.

Several dogs whined in response.

"How am I going to keep them quiet?" Greg asked.

"Do magic tricks," Gabriel said. "Give them your leg to hump. It did wonders for me."

Owens left his Jeep and started up the steps to the deli. He was almost in the store, but then stopped. Gabriel saw it as if in slow motion—the train starting to break from the tracks, the building of momentum sending the line of cars in a way that is at once terribly wrong and inevitable. Owens turned toward their truck.

Gabriel put a hand on Luke's shoulder. "You and Sid get inside. I'll deal with him."

Luke nodded and then he and Sid were gone.

Owens crossed the street toward Gabriel. "Everything OK here, Father?"

"Certainly," Gabriel said.

"This truck with the shelter?"

"No, it's a flower delivery for us. We have a wedding scheduled for later."

"You want me to have the guys help unload?" Owens asked.

"No, no," Gabriel said too quickly. "Not necessary at all. You've got more important things to do."

"Actually"—Owens leaned in as if he was sharing a secret—"we're bored out of our freaking minds. It would be fun for me and the guys to do something useful." Owens reached for the truck door.

Gabriel grabbed Owens's hand in both of his and gave it a vigorous shake. "Really, thank you so much," Gabriel said, still shaking the hand. "But it's an insurance coverage issue." Gabriel led Owens away from the truck.

"OK. If you say so," Owens said. But Gabriel knew that tone. He'd heard it often enough when he tried to give comfort to someone who had suffered an inexplicable loss—when he tried to tell them about "God's greater plan." That tone was one of pure, unadulterated disbelief. Owens was calling bullshit. Perhaps he would leave the shelter alone for now, but he'd let his CO know that some weird shit was going on. He'd be back.

Owens was three steps away from the truck and headed back

toward the deli when a noise from inside the truck stopped him in mid-stride. Owens turned to Gabriel, one eyebrow raised.

Another sound—like nails scratching against metal.

Owens returned to the truck. "Didn't I just see this truck outside the park?"

"Not this truck," Gabriel said.

"Are you sure?"

Gabriel nodded.

Owens rapped the side of the truck hard with his hand. The truck barked, woofed, yapped, and howled for thirty seconds until Greg somehow managed to quiet the dogs. By then it was far too late.

"Doesn't sound much like flowers," Owens said. He stared at Gabriel for an explanation, but the priest gave him back a blank "I didn't hear anything" look.

Two pedestrians paused to watch the scene from a few feet away.

"Please open the truck, Father," Owens asked quietly.

"That's not really necessary," Gabriel said.

"I think it is." Owens took a position at the rear truck door. "I don't know what game you all think you're playing, but we have a serious health situation. So stop screwing around and open the truck, or I'll do it myself."

"This is on you then, son," Gabriel said in his most stern confessional voice, and close enough to the truck door for Greg to hear him. "You can still just cross the street, get your coffee, and let this one go. I swear to you on all that is holy that we're doing the right thing here and you'll regret this decision."

For the first time, Owens seemed unsure of himself. "Stand away from the truck. I need to report this."

Gabriel sighed with paternal disappointment and moved to the side. "Then I cannot help you," he said.

Owens grabbed his phone and dialed. "Yeah, this is Owens. I'm in front of that animal shelter. I could use another pair of hands for something." He listened for a moment, eyes to the ground. "I know it's off our list...No. I don't think so. No...I believe they're transporting dogs *into* the quarantine area, not out of it," he whispered. "No, I don't know for sure. I did not have visual confirmation, but I sure as hell heard it...That's what I need the hands for."

The two pedestrians grew to four and then six. They stood close to Owens and it was clear he didn't want the company. "Keep moving," Owens told them, but they ignored him. Owens spun away from them and spoke into the phone again, his voice edgy and anxious. "Then don't bother McGreary with this, but could you just send someone, please? This doesn't feel right."

While Owens had his back turned, Gabriel quickly undid the latch and swung the truck door upward.

The overwhelming frustration of dogs locked in a space too small for too long exploded all over Private Owens. The first dog out of the truck—a large shepherd/Lab/Doberman combo—hit Owens square in the back before the soldier realized what was happening. The force knocked him to the ground and his phone skittered three feet away.

Owens rolled onto his back just as a second dog—an improbable combination of pit bull and Saint Bernard—jumped out and landed on his chest. In moments the remaining dogs, excited to be free from the confines of the truck, jumped out.

Greg grabbed all the dogs and led them into the shelter before Owens could clear his head enough to realize what was happening.

"Are you OK, son?" Gabriel called to Owens.

Owens scrambled to his feet, pulled out his gun, and held it pointing down at his side. "Don't move, Father." Owens looked more confused than angry as he wiped a thin line of blood from his nose. The pedestrians crowded around him and his eyes darted from face to face like a cornered animal's. "Stand back!" he yelled at them.

"I'm sorry to do that," Gabriel told Owens calmly. "But there was life in there. I had no choice."

Gabriel backed up toward the shelter. Owens raised the gun, pointing it at Gabriel's forehead. "Don't move."

"Can't do that. They need me in there more than you need me out here." He took another step backward.

"Hey, what the hell?" one of the bystanders called.

A second Guard Jeep, with its sirens blaring, cut the corner hard two blocks down and drove at them. Gabriel glanced at it and then ignored it as best he could. With the sirens came three more pedestrians.

"I'll make this easy," Gabriel said. "I'm going to turn around and walk into that shelter. For what it's worth, I promise that there are no weapons in there. Just life. You do what you need to." Gabriel turned.

Owens steadied his pistol with his empty hand.

Bystanders shouted in anger, panic, and outright disbelief: "He's a priest!"

"Let him go."

"Lord, no!"

Owens looked around and slowly lowered his gun. The bystanders—now a crowd—cheered.

Greg held open the shelter door and Gabriel dashed inside just as the second Jeep screeched to a stop between Owens and the crowd. Four Guards, all privates like Owens, jumped out.

"What the hell's going on?" asked one of the soldiers, a kid with impossibly orange hair.

"Some crazy priest just locked a bunch of dogs inside the shelter," Owens said.

"You're kidding, right? Sounds like the opening line to a bad joke," one of the other soldiers said.

"Do I look like I'm kidding, asshole?"

"Wait a sec," Orange Hair said. "That truck was just at the park. You're saying it had dogs? Like dogs from the park?"

"How the hell should I know?" Owens complained. "All I know is they attacked me and then ran inside."

The crowd swelled to fifteen. One teenager yelled, "Leave the shelter alone!"

His friend, another teen, joined in. "Looks like someone's finally standing up to you."

"I said stand back." Owens made a move to push them away.

"Or what?" the first teenager challenged. "You gonna shoot me?"

The kid's friend stepped up beside him. "And me too?"

Several people had their phones out, recording the scene.

A Guard from the second Jeep grabbed his cell phone. "I'm gonna call Command for help." He dialed. "Captain McGreary, sorry to disturb your meeting, sir, but I think we have a situation... The shelter... Yes, we know it was removed from the patrol list, but I think it just got back on."

14

After thirty minutes the door to the security room opened. "It was incredibly stupid of you to follow me," Morgan said as she entered. "This is criminal trespass. I will have your license for this at the very least, Samantha. And your friend over here can say good-bye to probation."

Beth shrugged her "I'm not impressed" shrug. "Easy come, easy go."

Despite Morgan's strong words, Sam could see that she had shaken Morgan's usual confidence. Something else was going on and Sam knew she had precious little time to find out what it was. "We don't want to bother you, Jacqueline. We'll just wait for the police to arrive," Sam said with a sudden interest in her fingernails. "It is taking the police an awful long time to get here, though. Are you sure you dialed the correct number?"

"Yeah," Beth added. "Do you have a deck of cards or something? Perhaps a checkerboard while we wait?"

"Actually," Sam jumped in, "a pen and paper would be great. I want to be sure that I can collect all of my thoughts for my statement to the police. How do you spell *adjuvant*, by the way?"

The effect of that word on Morgan was immediate and apparent: she squeezed the bridge of her nose, clenched her jaw, and twisted her perfect hair.

"You've been continuing the Ramses study all along, haven't you?" Sam pressed.

"I see your father is still telling you tales and you're still believing them like a little girl."

"Perhaps, Jackie—"

"Don't call me that!"

"Look, we know about the cholera toxin adjuvant," Sam bluffed.

"I don't care what you think you know. Cholera toxin as an adjuvant is no longer that novel. Your father has been away from the science world for too long."

"But I didn't authorize you to use a cholera adjuvant–based vaccine on my dog and I'm sure the others who brought their dogs to you didn't either."

"I did no such thing."

"*CVTP*—the indication after all of those names. At first I couldn't place it, but *VTP* sounded familiar. Then I remembered—it's the acronym for *vaccine trial protocol*. The *C* is for *cholera*, right? Sounds like you're the one about to lose her license."

"You're just guessing now. Why would I use dogs in my own practice? As you've already seen, I have unlimited access to all the research subjects I need."

Samantha knew Morgan had a point. Why would Morgan test on her own patients? It made no sense. But she also felt that Morgan was trying to figure out how much Sam already knew—what Sam could tell the cops and maybe others. Sam needed to keep Morgan talking. If Sam could keep Morgan worried and interested, there was a chance she might slip. At least Sam could buy some time and prevent Morgan from destroying files until...until when, exactly? There was no cavalry waiting to swoop in from over the hill. But Morgan didn't know that.

Sam glanced at her watch conspicuously. "Oh, yes, we saw those poor creatures," Sam said. "Tell me, did you do those alterations yourself? Looks like your handiwork."

"Actually, I order them that way now. It keeps the noise level down, and silent dogs do not attract attention."

"Attention from whom?" Beth asked. "You're like in the middle of nowhere. Can you even get Tab here?"

Beth was right. The VetMed facility was isolated. There was no one to complain about the noise unless you included the deer, raccoons, and opossums living in the forest. The chain link fencing would prevent those creatures from mixing with the dogs in any event.

The middle of nowhere . . . isolated.

Morgan stared at Sam with an "Is that the best you've got?" smugness. "Well, it was really lovely chatting with you girls," Morgan said as she rose. "But I've got work to do and I know you want to get ready to speak to the police about . . . well . . . I guess about nothing, really, except your crime." Morgan smiled at them, newly confident that Sam could do nothing to hurt her.

Morgan opened the door to the room, ready to seal them again in their isolation.

Sam thought back to the isolation room at the shelter and prayed that Nick and the dogs were still recovering. Hopefully, the sick dogs had not given the illness to the other dogs or Luke or Greg. Because cholera was zoonotic, there was the risk of . . .

"Cross-species transference," Sam said.

Morgan turned back from the door. "What?"

"I said, 'Cross-species transference.' That was why you were running tests on the dogs in the city. You needed dogs that were in circulation in an urban environment to prove you had solved the problem of the transference—the same problem my father has been trying to answer all these years. The dogs here were too isolated to provide an effective test group."

Sam heard sirens. She had to work fast. From the look on her face, Morgan heard them too.

"That's just silly, Samantha. No one would believe that I, of all people, would risk that."

Sam nodded. "Probably not without some proof."

"And that is?"

"Records, of course."

"What records? There are no records of any of this in my possession or, as you say, at my office."

"True. But VetMed has records too."

"Oh, good point," Beth added.

Morgan laughed out loud. "And many, many lawyers. The chances of them offering anyone access to their files is precisely zero."

"Not if they think you are the source of their problems." Sam listened to the sirens. They were very close now. "You hear that?"

"Yes. The police are coming to take you away."

Sam shook her head. "Nope. That's the sound of the VetMed bus about to back over you once I explain to them what you've done."

"Thump, thump goes the big bus," Beth said, and winked at Morgan. "Isn't that a song?"

Morgan made a show of stretching her fingers. "If you'll both excuse me now, I have some files to—"

"Delete?" Sam offered. The sirens had reached their loudest, and stopped abruptly.

"No," Morgan said with a tight smile. "Don't be so paranoid. The word is *reorganize*." Morgan closed the door on them.

Beth turned to Sam. "That stuff about VetMed actually sounded good. Do we have a prayer of making that happen?"

Sam shook her head. "Not even a little."

"Thought so. Look, I will totally understand if you want to have separate trials."

15

Andy's progress out of the park was slow both because he was careful to avoid the numerous DEP work crews now taking over the area and because the one-eared dog fought against him the entire way. No amount of cajoling or begging moved her faster. Every time she pulled against her leash to go back—whether to the Lake or the cavern, he couldn't say—Andy's heart broke a little bit more. The old man's words didn't help his state of mind either.

Andy's sense of despair increased with every step and, because it was so familiar, it threatened to suck him back into the river of his past. If he gave in to that history, he knew he would never get the dog out of the park alive. The fight required all his concentration and it was exhausting.

His phone rang and he jumped at the noise before he answered it.

"You got her?" Luke asked.

"Yeah. Where should I meet you?"

"Well, we've got a little problem over at the shelter. Our truck is stuck here. The shelter is being watched."

"Watched how?"

"Like 'waiting for the invasion' kind of watched. It appears they actually found a rabid dog in the park."

"I haven't seen anything like that, and I've covered a lot of ground."

"True or not, that seems to be the justification they're using. They know we brought your dogs in from the park."

"But how?"

"Long story. But now they want those dogs for testing and they want all the other dogs in the shelter as well because of the risk of contagion."

"So Greg was right. I did bring this all down on us."

"Don't give up yet. Nobody's going to do anything right now. We're trying to reach Sam."

"She didn't come back yet?"

"No."

Andy felt his heart begin to race. "What should I do? I'm trapped." He thought of the image of the fox in the claw trap gnawing off its own foot and shuddered.

"If you can get her out of the park, take her to your place or mine. We can reconnect after. But listen—all the park entrances are blocked off now. You'll need to take her over the wall."

"Isn't the Guard patrolling all the walls?"

"I seriously doubt it. Remember, the Guard is looking for strays, not *Stalag 17* escapes."

"What?"

"Never mind. You're too young. Can you lift her?"

"Yeah, but which direction?"

"I'd try north first. You get her over the wall there and you'll be above the perimeter. The dark will help cover you. Stay off the paths and keep moving."

Andy hung up, swallowed his panic, and started north.

16

Kendall looked upon the scene in front of the shelter and tried to hold on to a positive thought. It didn't work.

He had arrived at the shelter ten minutes after Lieutenant McGreary brought twenty more Guards and just before the reporters stationed at Riverside Hospital relocated their live feed satellite trucks. By that time the crowd outside the shelter had expanded to eighty.

McGreary had called the NYPD for a truckload of blue-and-white barricades to keep the growing crowd away from the shelter entrance. The NYPD was being inexplicably slow to respond, so McGreary was forced to do it the old-fashioned way—with soldiers spaced every three feet facing the crowd. The crowd didn't like that and began calling the soldiers names. The news outlets caught it all and the coverage was drawing even more people to the street.

Kendall watched and listened as the reporters began interviewing people who knew Sam, or at least those who claimed they did. Some in the crowd told stories of how she'd saved their dog or cat or bird in the middle of the night, but others appeared quiet and afraid. Kendall guessed that many more spectators had grown distrustful or angry in the vacuum created by the CDC's opaque reports and the governor's condescending statements. If that confluence of forces wasn't a perfect storm for conflict, Kendall knew it was pretty close.

Kendall's phone rang, and his wife's name appeared on the screen. He answered.

"Is it as bad as it looks on the television?" Ellen asked. Kendall could hear her worry through the phone and it made him feel guilty. He hadn't had time to watch what the news was reporting, but if it was anything close to what he was looking at in real time, he could imagine.

"I'm sure they're making it seem worse than it is. It's a fluid situation, honey. But people are going to be reasonable," he said.

"Reasonable?" she said skeptically. "CNN is now reporting that an anonymous source within the CDC is claiming the entire canine link is bullshit and that's why the CDC still hasn't made any statement to support or justify the quarantine."

"You know what I told you about anonymous sources."

"Except this time it makes perfect sense. Why hasn't the CDC made any real statement? And where are all the sick dogs if it is true?"

Kendall had no answer.

"And the governor's press conference was a joke," Ellen continued. "Not one fact. You can call New Yorkers a lot of things and get away with it, but we aren't stupid. Now he's moving beyond a quarantine and trying to take these dogs. Have you ever seen a New Yorker give up anything they love without a fight? What on God's green earth makes you think people are going to be reasonable when they haven't been given reasons?"

"Because we've been through so much worse."

"But then we were all on the same side. Did you know someone has already set up a 'Free Dr. Sam's Dogs' Facebook page? I just checked and it had over thirty-five thousand followers. Some knucklehead blogged that this whole thing is a conspiracy, that the Riverside Virus is the result of the army's chemical biological warfare program and that the army is now coming to destroy the evidence."

"There are always crazies, Ellen."

"The link to the blog post has already been re-tweeted over twenty-five thousand times. And he just uploaded it in the last hour. Sure, it is crazy talk, but it is only fighting against silence."

Kendall sighed. "It's like a digital game of telephone. Rumor becomes news, news becomes truth."

"And you're in the middle of the fallout. Have you spoken to Sam?" Ellen asked.

"She's still MIA, but the shelter just released a statement saying that because the dogs were entrusted to them by the mayor, only the mayor has the authority to force their surrender."

"She's not going to do that, is she?"

Kendall glanced around to make sure no one was near. "No," he said quietly. "But I'll be fine. I promise."

"You are still a terrible liar," Ellen said.

"Yeah, well..." Kendall caught sight of the expected NYPD truck carrying five of his cops and the familiar blue-and-white sawhorses. The truck drove slowly through the crowd and parked in front of the shelter. A tactical police van followed.

"I know you're worried. Maybe you shouldn't watch it. Go for a run or something," Kendall offered hopefully.

"You're joking, right?"

He wasn't, but even with only a second of retrospection, he realized it had been a stupid thing to say. Still, he decided it was probably better than explaining the truth about to unfold.

"You know I love you, right?" Ellen said.

"I do. I love you too."

"About what I said to you before I left..."

"It's OK. Forget it."

"I can't. I just wanted you to know that if anyone is smart enough and brave enough to figure a way through this, I believe it is you. I guess that's the way it is supposed to be...why you need to be there. I'm proud of my husband."

Kendall didn't know what to say. Relief brought him close to tears. "I...I..."

"Go do your job. Do it for us. We want to come home."

Ellen spared him further broken sentences and disconnected.

Lifted by his wife's confidence, Kendall walked to the NYPD truck and McGreary met him there. "About time those barricades got here," McGreary said.

Kendall shrugged. "Bureaucracy. You know how it is. Can you guys give us a hand off-loading these?"

McGreary directed three Guards to join the five cops in the back of the truck and help remove the barricades. Kendall was relieved to see that Owens was not in the mix.

The cops and the Guards quickly piled the barricades on the sidewalk in front of the shelter. "We got it from here, gents," Kendall told the soldiers.

Kendall and his men began setting up the barricades on the street, lining them up very close to the shelter. As a result, the barricades separated the Guard from the shelter.

Kendall gave the police van a thumbs-up. The doors opened and a ten-officer tactical unit jumped out. This was the same type of unit that patrolled Grand Central, Penn Station, and the 9/11 Memorial. The officers were armored and armed with automatic assault rifles, and distinguishable from the Guard only by the color of their uniforms (all black) and the insignia on their jackets. The tactical unit quickly took positions behind the barricades.

McGreary came over shaking his head. "We don't need tactical," he told Kendall, keeping his voice low because of the row of video cameras pointed at them. "And you're not giving us enough room. We're all gonna be wedged up against the shelter."

"Who's *we*?" Kendall said.

An angry red vein pulsed in McGreary's neck. "What the hell is going on here, Sergeant?"

"Actually, you can congratulate me. I just received a provisional promotion from the mayor herself about thirty minutes ago. It's Captain Kendall now, which—no disrespect, Lieutenant—makes me the most senior command officer on site at the moment in this joint operation."

"Except my chain of command reports directly to the governor," McGreary protested.

"Yup." Kendall pulled out a folded sheet of paper. "That reminds me. I've been authorized to give you this."

McGreary grabbed the paper and read it. "I don't understand this," he said. Owens took a position behind McGreary, using the opportunity to scowl at Kendall, but McGreary directed him back.

"It's a mayoral executive order," Kendall said. "Number 107."

"No shit. I can read that part."

"By order of the mayor of the City of New York, the NYPD has been given authority to protect city property from all forms of trespass during the health emergency. I emphasize the phrase *all forms.*"

"You're telling me that we can't go into the shelter?"

"Um-hmm."

"And that you're authorized to use force to prevent our entry?"

"That's what I'm saying."

"If I remember my history correctly, they call this treason, don't they?"

"You know, Lieutenant, I asked that very same question. But it turns out that the city acting through the mayor has the right to protect its property against trespass through its executive command—that's me, by the way—absent a specific order from a higher level of government. You have a specific order from the governor or the president of the United States directing you to occupy this building?"

"Nope. Sure don't."

"Then I don't think we have a conflict."

"And when I get my direct order?"

"Until then, sir. Until then."

McGreary saluted Kendall and gave him a thin, almost amused smile. He stepped away to confer with his men by their Jeeps.

Kendall knew that by the time they had finished their conversation, every news outlet had received a press release from the mayor about the executive order, explaining that the shelter was under the mayor's protection until further notice. Although the press release didn't say so expressly (because it didn't need to), it certainly left the reader with the impression that the governor's action in the face of the CDC's silence might be politically motivated. The news outlets immediately ran with the story, and more people from the neighborhood and beyond came to support the shelter.

For the moment the shelter and the dogs within it were safe.

17

Morgan was gone less than ten minutes before Crew Cut led two New York State police troopers into their room.

"Is this them?" one of the troopers asked.

"Yes," Crew Cut answered.

Crap, Sam almost said aloud. The appearance of the state police instead of the local cops was a bad sign that someone was taking this very seriously. Sam quickly ran through the story in her mind, how this was Morgan's experiment gone wrong, and how she was trying to find evidence to save thousands of dogs. But it all sounded implausible, even to herself.

The officer approached her. Sam waited for the order to present her wrists for cuffs like in the movies. This would be a first for her. She stared at the officer, silently promising herself that she would not be intimidated.

The officer tried to stare her down. Sam was about to cave when he winked at her. "Jim Kendall sends his regards."

"Kendall?"

"Yeah. He mentioned something about having your back."

Beth laughed out loud.

"I don't understand," Sam said. The swelling *whoop* of helicopter blades shut down the possibility of further discussion.

"I sure hope those are the good guys," Beth said.

Moments later Daniel banged open the door and Tom stepped in behind him. "Are you OK?" Daniel asked his daughter.

Sam struggled to process these developments. There was a perplexing "then she fell out of bed and woke up" feel to everything now. "Yeah, I guess so," she said. "What are you doing here, Dad?"

"You were right," Daniel said. "There was a connection. I made a few calls to some old CDC contacts and, after a few threats, convinced them to recheck the necropsies. Both of the rabid dogs also had evidence of cholera in their stomach contents and the mucous linings of the intestines. They're repeating the other necropsies now for any evidence of cholera."

"Wait a minute. So the rabies was related to the cholera vaccine? She was using rabies as an adjuvant too?"

Daniel shook his head. "The rabies *was* the vaccine. The cholera toxin was being used as the adjuvant to allow the rabies vaccine to be administered orally—through some kind of special bait."

Tom broke in, but when he spoke he was looking directly at Crew Cut. "We were able to put some heat on VetMed. They became very cooperative once we started tossing around phrases like *murder indictment.*"

"Slow down," Sam said. "I don't understand."

"We're still filling in the pieces," Daniel said. "We know that Vet-Med was developing a recombinant DNA vaccine for rabies. It was designed to be added to a bait with the adjuvant. Once consumed by an infected animal, the vaccine swaps a portion of the DNA of the rabies virus with something totally harmless."

"You're making that up, right?" Beth asked.

"Not at all," Daniel answered. "It's called a chimera vaccine. We already developed one for dengue fever and West Nile. We had experimented with one for rabies for a few years because it had the potential to cure an already symptomatic animal."

"So it could cure animals that already have rabies?" Sam asked.

"It's supposed to. That's why it is valuable. It isn't just a prophylactic like the other vaccine."

"But how did it end up in New York City?" Beth asked.

"The convention," Tom answered. "The vaccine was intended to be used in advance of the convention event in the park to deal with the threat of rabid raccoons, dogs, squirrels, and rats. It seems you can't run the risk that a rabid animal will run up and bite some of the presidential nominee's biggest donors at his own party."

"According to VetMed," Daniel continued, "the vaccine needed additional testing before it was ready to be used in an urban environment. They contracted with Dr. Morgan to study and provide evidence that there was no cross-species transference."

"The same problem you couldn't overcome with the Bullet," Sam said.

Daniel nodded. "After they found the rabid raccoon at the Central Park work site, Morgan must have run out of time; she gave the new vaccine to dogs in her practice—"

"And Nick," Sam added.

"It provided Morgan with the perfect opportunity for regular observation in an urban area."

"Excuse me," Beth cut in. "But isn't this all a little...I don't know...'mad scientist' stuff? You really think Morgan was flying the freak flag that high?"

"You're ignoring the context," Daniel said. "This isn't about crazy or evil. This is about the seduction of the science—the drive to solve the puzzle before someone else does. Morgan comes from the loosely regulated world of agricultural pharmacology like me. Our limits are largely self-imposed. Cows do not complain and they don't report. If you believe this is the first time there's been testing without knowledge or consent, then I envy your inexperience. And here Morgan actually believed she had solved the challenge and that the vaccine was completely safe."

"But it wasn't," Sam confirmed.

"No. Like me, she really had not solved the transference problem."

"Whatever we do to them—"

"—We are really doing to us," Daniel completed her sentence. "The cholera toxin in the bait or something about the virus caused systemic colitis, and the inflammation must have interfered with the vaccine process. The body couldn't properly respond to the vaccine. The dogs given the vaccine passed live rabies virus in their feces. The kids picked it up through contact and ingested it somehow—fingers in their mouths, picking their noses, who knows. But that's why the virus was localized in Riverside. The vaccinated dogs all stayed in the area."

"So that's how the kids got rabies?" Beth asked.

"Yeah," Sam said. "We gave it to them."

"And VetMed is putting it all on Morgan," Tom added.

"So the bus actually did pass through," Beth said. "I wanna see the tire tracks on Morgan's ass."

"But why don't the children also have cholera?" Sam challenged.

"I assume that it didn't pass through in its virulent form," Daniel said. "The dogs' natural antibodies had already attacked the cholera bacteria. That's why the dogs were sick. The body did its job in killing that organism off. The rabies, on the other hand, passed through undetected by the body because of the DNA swap."

"Except two dogs did get rabies," Sam reminded him.

Daniel rubbed his chin. "I wonder if that was also because of the interaction with the adjuvant or something else. After all, Morgan was screwing around with a living organism's entire immune response in the face of two particularly virulent pathogens. And that's probably why only kids got sick—they have less-developed immune systems."

"And they're not so good with the handwashing thing," Beth added. "Trust me."

"Where's Morgan now?" Sam asked.

"Not far," Crew Cut said. "The CDC is on its way here. The guys from Atlanta want to interview her. The police are here to make sure she stays put."

"Did she destroy any more documentation?" Sam asked.

"No," Crew Cut said. "We shut her out once I got the call and before she could do any damage."

"We need to see her files immediately. There must be other dogs she injected that are not at the shelter. They'll need to be identified, located, and quarantined ASAP," Daniel directed.

"Of course," Crew Cut said.

"So you turned out to be a good guy?" Beth asked Crew Cut.

"Just trying to do my job."

"Sorry about that stuff I said about your mother," Beth responded.

Crew Cut rolled his eyes and left the room.

Daniel pulled Sam to a quiet corner. "If I'm correct about this, the dogs that received the cholera-based vaccine may very well still have rabies in their system. I don't know how long the virus can survive in an asymptomatic state. They may have been turned into some type of carriers."

"But then how can we save them?"

"We may not be able to, although the fact that they show no signs of rabies and that no other dogs at the shelter have shown symptoms is promising. We won't know more until we start reviewing the data. We need to find some proof that the CDC will accept."

"Does Tom know about the sick dogs?"

"I had to tell him, but I think he had already figured that out himself—as others will soon enough."

Tom cut in. "I just got word that there's something going on at the shelter. The governor has made a demand for your dogs. The mayor is trying to resolve it, but..." Tom shook his head. "We need to get down there ASAP to have any chance."

"I will stay and work through the VetMed data," Daniel said. "There must be something helpful." He followed Crew Cut out of the room.

"Where do you want me?" Beth asked.

"There's only room for two and the pilot in the bird," Tom answered. "I'll tell the pilot to get ready." He left them.

"Can you stay with my father for now?" Sam asked. "Help him with these files?"

"That I can do," Beth said. "I wonder if I can find some Tab up here."

"You know, you *are* pretty good in a fight. Not sure I could've stopped Morgan without you. Thank you."

Beth shrugged. "It was a lot more fun than the meeting I blew off with my parole officer . . . which you may get a call about, by the way."

Five minutes later Sam and Tom were ready to walk out the door. Daniel was already buried in the test data. As Sam passed him, Daniel held out her phone. "Don't forget this." Sam took it from his hands. "I know it means less than nothing," Daniel said. "But I couldn't be prouder of you."

Sam realized that this probably was as far as her father would ever be able to go—powerful emotions always encased within the protection of cold, hard data points. Yes, that was living of a sort, all filtered through the safety of control and, because of that predictability, somehow less valuable. But that was *his* choice, the product of a lifetime of *his* experiences. Like Tom, she was not her father and she wasn't obligated to repeat her father's life. She refused to be only the product of what someone else had done to her. She had choices, and whether to keep her anger or not was a decision she could own.

"I wouldn't say 'less than nothing,' Dad." Sam offered her father a small smile. "Figure this one out. Save my dogs."

18

Andy was exhausted, his nerves fried, when they finally reached the north wall. He stared at the seven-foot-high stone barrier and wanted to cry.

Tears...darkness...an empty room...rough hands. He knew he was falling backward into a dark and hostile place.

Andy bit into the web of his hand. That brought him forward—at least for now. He shook off his despair and took the eighty-pound dog in both arms. He lifted her toward the wall, holding the dog as if making an offering to some stone god.

That was when the first convulsion hit. The dog's paws trembled and she jerked her head backward in a gruesome spasm. Andy fought to keep hold of her, but her suffering was far too strong. He lowered her to the ground before she tumbled there.

The dog tried to crawl away from the wall as if her very proximity to the stone was painful...as if what existed beyond the wall of the park was too vast and too broken to allow her survival...as if the old man of the park had spoken the truth.

Andy tried to soothe her, but he could not find those words. Instead he said, "I'm gonna take a look around." He climbed the wall, cutting his fingertips on the jagged stones. From the top he had a clear view of Central Park North and even Central Park West to his left. He was shocked to see that Central Park North was free of Guards and work crews. Luke had been right, north was the best direction—but if he couldn't get the dog out, what was the point?

Andy turned back to the dog to get a sense of how hard the carry would be.

She was gone.

He jumped down from the wall, bewildered and ready to search the park for her. They had been so close to freedom—just one damn wall.

As soon as his feet hit the ground, the dog was there again in exactly the same spot where he'd left her moments before. Andy tried to convince himself that the top of the wall or his fatigue had obscured his view. He climbed the wall once more and looked for the dog from that vantage point. Again the dog was gone, and again she reappeared on the ground as soon as Andy touched down inside the park.

Twice was enough. Andy knelt down beside the dog and swallowed hard. Their eyes locked—hers wide with fear and his searching for understanding. In that moment he had his answer.

Andy lifted the dog and carried her away from the stone, back toward the center of the park. When he reached a stand of trees about a hundred feet from the wall, the dog jumped down from his arms without any sign of tremor. She trotted a few paces ahead and dropped to the ground, head on her paws.

Andy tried to determine his next move—or whether he even had one. He didn't hear the DEP crew until they were already too close to avoid. The dog was up in an instant. To Andy's shock she ran toward the four men in their protective gear, not away from them. Andy scrambled to catch her, but he was too late.

She leaped directly at the man in the middle of the group with the word "CHIEF" stenciled on his biohazard suit. She was two feet above the ground and headed straight for the man's chest. Andy wanted to shut his eyes against the impact, but something kept them open, some need to bear witness.

The dog crashed into the man at full speed...or she should have. Instead she passed through him as if he were merely a reflection of a man. From where Andy stood, he couldn't tell which presence gave way—whether the dog somehow ceased to be flesh, blood, and bone, or the man for that one moment gave up his corporeality in deference to the dog's desperation to get away. However it happened, the dog landed behind the crew with a graceful step. With one last, sad glance at Andy, she disappeared into the trees.

Andy finally realized his painful personal truth: if ever he had actually seen this creature, he would never do so again. The words of the old man—a being no doubt as real as the dog—echoed in his ears. "She doesn't end here...but she does for you."

That was when Andy's world, and everything real or not real that kept him even slightly tethered to it, unknotted.

The chief stepped forward, oblivious to what had just happened. "Kid, you OK?"

Andy struggled to find a word while he held back tears. "Fine," he managed to get out.

"Not a great time to be in the park, you know?" the chief said. "We need to lay some nasty shit down."

"Leaving now."

"You see any strays around here?" the chief asked with that resigned and weary "I already know the answer is no, but got to ask anyway" tone.

"Nope," Andy said as he raised his face to the sky. "I thought that was all just an urban myth."

"Starting to look that way."

Andy stumbled off to the park entrance, his head on fire with a rage nineteen years in the making. That rage, born when he lost his parents, had matured in toxic and abusive foster homes that left him both damaged and with ridiculously few tools to make his own way in the world. It had ebbed when he met Alexa, and gushed again when he lost her. Now, without the one-eared dog that maybe wasn't ever anything except his hope and his need, Andy's fury was self-sustaining, with one external focal point. The only thing he had left.

The bastards would not get his dogs.

They would need to kill him first.

19

"Have you ever flown in a helicopter?" the pilot asked. Sam shook her head.

The pilot went through some basic instructions about safety and then started the engine. The noise from the rotating blades became a physical presence; it shook Sam's entire body.

"You guys OK?" the pilot shouted over the noise. He caught Sam's eyes in his rear mirror. "You look a little green."

"Long few days," she answered.

"You're not gonna hurl, are you, miss?"

"No guarantees," she said.

"We'll have you on the ground before you know it. No worries."

They lifted off and Sam tried to focus on something other than her propensity to vomit in new and stressful situations. There were few options available. As they flew over the facility, she could see the police cars with their bubble lights flashing below. It would be a miracle if Beth and her dad avoided arrest, and she probably could include herself in that sentence as well.

"They'll be fine," Tom said. "The police know the score. Kendall and the police commissioner spoke to them."

"Beth has a record and she isn't the most stable person on the planet."

"As long as she doesn't hit anyone, they'll leave her alone... probably."

Sam started a sentence a few times before she got the whole thing out. "Thank you for coming up here."

"You're welcome. It probably would've been better if you had told me a few of these things along the way." Sam thought Tom sounded more hurt than angry. "You know? The small stuff like the sick dogs in the shelter, the cholera toxin adjuvant?"

OK, maybe a little angry. "I'm sorry. But I had no reason to trust you with something like that."

"But what—"

"And if I had told you about the dogs? What would you have done? Your job, right?" Sam pointed to the broken watch on his wrist. It was suddenly important to her that Tom understand her reasons. "For you that would have been the right thing to do. But it wasn't my right thing."

"Maybe. But maybe it's more complicated than that. Maybe loyalty has something to do with it too. Maybe I also make decisions because I care about someone. Maybe if..." Tom stopped himself.

Sam suddenly had that "uh-oh" feeling she usually experienced in awkward personal situations. "What are you...?"

Tom waved the question away before Sam could finish. "Whatever your reasons, it may not change the outcome for those dogs now. It's become politics."

"It always was. Who gave the directive to eradicate rabies from Central Park in time for the convention? That wasn't a public health decision."

"No, it wasn't. And that's all the more reason why the governor and his people won't back down now."

"And what about your boss?"

"She'll try to do the right thing … until she can't. She won't give up the dogs unless there's no choice and she definitely won't want to give them over to the governor so he can pretend he was right all along."

"So right result but for the wrong reason?"

"At the moment I'll take that over a wrong result. Wouldn't you?" Tom tapped the pilot on the shoulder. "Where are we putting down? The heliport on the West Side Highway?"

The pilot shook his head. "They just called in a change. My instructions are to touch down in Central Park—near the Great Lawn. The NYPD will meet you there. Stuff is happening."

"You think there's any chance this turns out OK?" Sam asked Tom. He didn't answer.

20

The plan to protect the dogs in the shelter worked perfectly—for precisely thirty-three minutes. That was the amount of time it took for a black FBI sedan with bubble lights flashing to arrive on-site with an order signed by the governor.

McGreary approached the police barricade and signaled to the NYPD officers on the other side of his intention to cross. Kendall nodded his permission.

"I think this is specific enough," McGreary said, and handed Kendall the order.

Kendall read it carefully, although he had already guessed the contents. The order authorized the National Guard to "take all steps necessary or appropriate to protect the lives and health of the citizens of the State of New York pursuant to the New York and federal Constitutions by immediately confiscating all dogs currently domiciled at Finally Home Animal Shelter. This supersedes any contrary order."

When Kendall was finished, he studied McGreary's face and, for the first time, saw fear there. Kendall understood why.

If Kendall refused the order, as absurd as it sounded, McGreary's men would be forced to remove him, his heavily armed men, and the occupants of the shelter before a hostile crowd chanting for (depending on which voice you listened to) more information, the protection of the dogs, or the governor's head. The street would soon devolve into a scene out of a third-world country, with the local police on one side and the army on the other. Kendall trusted his men to keep their weapons secured and locked, but what about these Guards? Would they be able to tell friend from foe? They had no contextual experience for this. And what about that nut Owens?

Kendall didn't see an exit strategy that could accomplish everyone's goals, and this left him profoundly frightened. How the hell had things gotten this far? He glanced at the NYPD tactical van as if that vehicle might be able to provide some answers.

After a few seconds, the side door of the van slid open. A diminutive silver-haired woman stepped out to surprised cheers from the crowd. Kendall met her.

"May I see that paper?" she asked.

"Of course, Madam Mayor," Kendall said as he handed it to her. The mayor reviewed the document silently. McGreary joined them.

"I see the governor has left us no choice," the mayor said.

"That's the way I see it, ma'am," McGreary said.

"Very well. But this is still my shelter," she said. "I will advise them to open the doors."

Kendall and three of his men began clearing a path for the mayor through the crowd. Kendall could feel the heat coming off some of the impromptu protestors. Somewhere along the way this had become bigger than some stray dogs in a shelter...bigger even than this virus of unknown origin, and certainly bigger than the politics of the convention. The street outside the shelter had become a microcosm for the city's current emotional state—one of fear, distrust, powerlessness, and cynicism.

As the mayor, Kendall, and McGreary approached the barricades, some of the Guards stationed near the shelter began to push forward, clearing the path from the other direction. Although the crowd was unruly, it obeyed the line of brusque soldiers with automatic rifles.

All except one.

Andy.

Kendall didn't know how or when Andy had gotten there, but he couldn't miss the look of anguish and pain in his young face. In that instant Kendall knew this was someone beyond caring about soldiers' orders and automatic rifles. He also knew that this was how innocent people got killed.

The Guards moved or pushed the crowd to the sidewalk in front of the church or onto the opposite side of the street. Andy stood alone in front of the barricade before the shelter.

A soldier walked over to deal with him.

"Oh, holy shit," Kendall spit. He sprinted toward the shelter, leaving the mayor and McGreary openmouthed and staring at his back.

The soldier was Owens.

21

Andy was disappointed that the others had given in so easily. Disappointed, but not surprised. Everyone has a threshold. It all comes back to context and alternative. Clearly they had much more in their lives to protect and so the cost of their dissonance was that much higher. In contrast, whatever Andy cared about now was in that shelter.

"You need to move down the steps." Andy recognized the prick talking to him. It was that soldier, Owens, from the perimeter.

Andy was too angry to speak in any way that wasn't primal...in any manner that would make sense. He just shook his head.

"Now don't make this a YouTube moment, kid," Owens said. "Just move along like all the other idiots."

Andy felt his reserve breaking. "Screw you."

"What'd you say, freak?" Owens's tone was all challenge as he grabbed Andy's arm.

That was the line. "DON'T-TOUCH-ME!" Andy brought his fist up in a powerful uppercut under Owens's chin.

Kendall caught Andy's fist a millisecond before it connected.

"Get off me," Andy protested. He struggled against Kendall, but the cop was too powerful. "You can't let them take the dogs."

"Stop it, Andy," Kendall commanded. "You're gonna get yourself killed."

"I don't care," Andy shot back.

"But I do," Kendall answered.

The mayor reached them. "And so do I," she said.

"They're going to kill my dogs." Andy tried to push Kendall away.

"Listen to me," Kendall whispered in his ear. "Those dogs have only one shot out of here alive and you're looking at her. Let her do this."

"I'm not going to abandon them," Andy snapped.

"No one said you had to, son," the mayor said. "You can still make your voice heard and I hope you will. Just do it from over there where you'll be safe. Don't give them a reason."

"But I—"

Kendall cut him off. "All martyrs are dead, Andy. These dogs need you alive. There's no one else."

Something in Kendall's voice reached Andy. He studied the Guards surrounding them and knew Kendall was telling the truth. Andy moved down the stairs and away from the shelter entrance with the rest of the crowd.

Owens followed. "Hey, kid!" Andy spun to face him, bristling.

"Get back here now, Owens!" McGreary yelled.

Owens appeared torn between compliance and violence.

"Aww, listen, his master's voice," Andy taunted.

"Another time, OK? I'll be waiting," Owens said, and turned away.

Andy lost interest in Owens and focused on the mayor. She stood alone behind the barricades in front of the shelter door with the governor's order in her hands. She eyed the crowd that filled the street and raised her hands for silence.

"What does the paper say?" Andy called out. The question was echoed by others standing near him.

"It says," the mayor began in a surprisingly loud voice, "that by order of the governor, we must turn over the dogs in this city shelter."

Instantly shouts, expletives, and general dissent ran through the crowd as cameras flashed.

The mayor waited for the crowd to quiet. "Yes, it reeks of politics, and yes, the governor will have to answer to you come November. But for now we must comply with his directive."

"My dogs are in there!" a woman yelled in a panicked voice.

"Ours too," a man shouted. "We brought him here to be safe! We were told he'd be safe!"

There were more shouts.

"I know how you feel," the mayor said, looking directly at the line of video cameras. "Decisions being made for you with little or no explanation and without so much as an ounce of compassion about how we live in this city." The mayor's voice cracked with emotion. "But the reality is that this is now the best way to resolve this situation without loss of life and I ask for your continued patience and cooperation. We will get to the bottom of this very soon. Until that time, I ask you to trust me. I promise I will not betray that trust."

The mayor turned from the crowd and knocked on the shelter door. She waited but got no answer. "This is the mayor of the City of New York. Please open the door," she shouted.

Again no answer.

"If you open this door, I promise that no harm will come to you."

Andy and the rest of the crowd waited in silent anticipation.

22

Kendall and McGreary joined the mayor at the shelter door. Kendall had a bad feeling as he watched the door swing open. The lights were on, but the reception room was empty.

"Hello?" the mayor called out. No response, only a disconcerting stillness underneath the hum of the fluorescent lights. "You know these people," she told Kendall. "Go in and find out what's going on. They need to understand that I can only protect them if they cooperate."

"Whoa. Hold up," McGreary said. "This is my jurisdiction now. I make those decisions."

The mayor spun on him. "Do you want to resolve this without a fight or not? If you want to show me what big balls you have, I'll borrow a microscope. But I promise I will make this such an embarrassment for your superiors that you will be confined to base for the rest of your life." The mayor finished the sentence with a nod toward the television cameras.

"What about if just the two of us go in?" Kendall offered, pointing to McGreary.

"Fine. But you will not go in with your guns drawn," the mayor ordered. "They're only armed with dog bones and bags of kibble."

"Agreed," McGreary said. "But one attempt to resist and all bets are off." McGreary held the door open for Kendall and they stepped inside.

Kendall thought the quiet was disorienting at first. Then it was frightening. He had stopped in the shelter almost every workday for years now and he knew it as a place of near-constant activity and noise. But now the shelter seemed lifeless.

"Hello? It's Kendall," he called out, really just to hear something in the stillness. The absence of response—not a bark or a growl, not to mention a human voice—the wrongness of the silence, made him shudder.

McGreary looked to him for an explanation, but Kendall couldn't offer one. They moved quickly to the upper floor and entered the room that had served as the isolation room. Empty.

"Is there a basement?" McGreary asked.

Kendall nodded and led the way to the door that opened onto the stairwell. The door was closed, but unlocked. Kendall pulled it open. "Hello," he called down the stairs to the lights below. "It's me, Kendall of the NYPD. You're gonna need to come out of there now."

No answer.

Kendall took the stairs slowly with McGreary right behind. He knew the basement was empty long before they reached the bottom floor. The cages Kendall had helped move down here were gone. Large plastic bags filled to overflowing with soiled newspapers, disposable kennel pads, empty bags of dog food, and red barrels marked for "Sharps Disposal" had taken their place. The room smelled of disinfectant and, underneath that, urine and feces.

McGreary turned on Kendall. "If you know something about this bullshit, you'd better tell me now before someone gets hurt."

"I don't know crap."

"And if you did, you'd tell me?"

"Look, Lieutenant, the last thing I want is for one of your Jeep jockeys to get surprised by someone hiding behind a corner, OK?"

McGreary's radio phone squeaked. "All OK in there, sir?"

He grabbed the phone. "There's no one here."

"Excuse me, sir?" The radio crackled.

"You heard me. No one home."

"Sorry, sir. That's really not possible. We saw them go in. We've been monitoring the rear exit from the start. No one came out."

"Then I—" McGreary loped across the room to a large set of metal shelves. "Stand by," he said.

A square rust mark on the floor appeared to match the footprint of the shelving unit, but the mark was four feet from where the shelves now stood. McGreary gave the unit a tug and managed to move it five inches—enough to see the door behind it. McGreary pulled the unit the rest of the way, uncovering the entire doorframe. A rope tied to the back of the shelving unit ran under the door. "What's this?" he asked.

Kendall shrugged.

McGreary yanked on the rope and it came free from under the door. "Looks like they went through and then pulled these shelves behind them." He tried the door handle. Unlocked. His hand dropped to his gun.

"Stay cool," Kendall warned.

McGreary opened the door, revealing the inner door. Someone had taped a handwritten note to that second door: "You are looking at the property of the Catholic Church. Do not even think about entering. Signed, GOD."

Kendall barely suppressed a smile.

McGreary noticed. "You think this is funny?"

"Well, actually—"

McGreary gripped his phone so hard that his knuckles turned white. "They're in the church."

"Repeat that, sir?" the phone squawked.

"There's a damn connecting door in the basement. They're all in the church."

After a confused pause, the voice on the phone asked, "What are your orders?"

"Damned if I know," McGreary said. "Heading out to you now."

23

While Sid, Greg, and Luke worked tirelessly in the church basement to set up crates and ensure that the dogs were clean and comfortable, Gabriel and Eliot became the de facto guardians of the church sanctuary. This was where they had placed the nine dogs from the shelter isolation room. These dogs, recovering but still weak from their battle with illness, lay silently in their crates under the tortured stained glass eye of Isaac and the wooden image of Christ on his cross.

Greg had earlier moved their IV lines from one front paw to the other to keep the lines from occluding, but he hadn't had time for the usual niceties of cleaning and wrapping the old IV port sites. Gabriel had offered to do that for the dogs and this was what occupied him now.

He took a bottle of sterile saline solution, a box of cotton swabs, and a roll of paper towels from the supply box they had brought over from the shelter, and sat cross-legged before the first crate.

Nick lay curled up on his side, completely exhausted, but he thumped his tail when he saw the priest. Gabriel unlatched the crate and Nick immediately stretched out his long frame and yawned. Gabriel rested his hand lightly on Nick's head and he thumped his tail even harder.

"Now, let's see that paw." Gabriel reached for Nick's foreleg and gently pulled it forward.

Working as carefully as he could, Gabriel cleaned the affected area with saline and a cotton swab. Nick was forgiving but Gabriel could see by the way the dog winced that the site of the old port was sore. "I have an idea," he said. "It works for my knees."

Gabriel rose and grabbed the nearest substitute washbasin he could find—the large ciborium on the altar. He filled it with warm water from the bathroom behind the dais and brought the bowl to Nick. Gabriel delicately placed the dog's wounded paw into the warm water. Nick dropped his head in Gabriel's lap, closed his eyes, and sighed.

As Gabriel stroked Nick's head, a deep sense of peace came over the priest. It had been so long absent that at first Gabriel couldn't identify the feeling. Then he noticed the worn wooden image of the crucified Jesus looking down on them and understood. He desperately wanted to say something to that figure—that sometimes, maybe only twice in a lifetime, it is all laid out before you; discrete pieces of a life that have no business even being in the same area code meet and join to create something so much more powerful than their parts; worlds open and the divine spirit becomes not only real, but tangible and measurable; that in this moment Gabriel loved his God at least as much as he had ever loved another human being; that without the love he now felt there could be nothing else. And he knew—with a degree of moral certainty that came only from years of hopeless searching in all the wrong places—that he was loved as deeply right back.

Gabriel wiped his eyes and moved on to the spent dog in the next crate.

He was cleaning the paw of the last dog in the sanctuary when Sid found him. Gabriel sensed Sid's presence but addressed him without turning around. "I have a very aggressive form of Alzheimer's," the priest said. "Within six months on the outside, I will lose most of my ability to speak. I will not be able to recognize you or anyone else. I will shit and pee myself and need to be cleaned by someone else. I will not be able to read the word of God or the Sunday comics. I will again become a baby, except in the body of a man. Then I will become only an empty vessel in human form. After that I will lose the ability to swallow. I signed the paperwork to decline a feeding tube."

Sid placed his hand on Gabriel's shoulder. "How long have you known?"

Gabriel rose. "A month. This may sound ironic, but I don't believe in miracles. Or, even if they do exist, that I'm worthy of one. I've prayed every day since I found out that God would take me into His house before another sunrise. But I guess sometimes God's greatest gift to us is an unanswered prayer. Everything follows something that came before, doesn't it? If He had taken me, these creatures would not have found sanctuary, even if it is perhaps just for a day. Eliot would have been dead on some cold metal table, and you, my friend"—Gabriel turned to face Sid—"would have been denied the opportunity to pull my head out of my ass."

"Is there nothing I can do for you?"

"Oh, on the contrary. I intend to extract a promise from you."

"Of course."

"But you don't even know what it is. You're supposed to make this hard. I had it all planned out."

"You are a good man. You would not impose an unreasonable burden."

"I want you to take Eliot and Molly when the time comes."

"It would be my honor."

Gabriel sighed as the weight lifted from his chest. "There is one other thing." Gabriel struggled for words, but they would not come. The request was too large, the language required to frame it too alien to a Roman Catholic priest.

Sid appeared to think for a moment and then nodded. "Make sure she is happy, Gabe."

Sid's blessing made Gabriel's knees weak. He desperately wanted to switch subjects before he became a blubbering mess. "So," he said, "did you hear the one about the priest, the locksmith, and the sick dogs all locked in a church?"

"What sick dogs?" Sid asked, pointing.

Gabriel followed the direction of Sid's finger.

Each dog that Gabriel had cleansed and bathed—each of the nine that had been sick and in isolation at the shelter—now stood alert and renewed, waiting for freedom.

24

By the time McGreary and Kendall stepped back onto the street, CNN had already sent a "Breaking News" e-mail blast that the dogs were now being given "sanctuary" inside Riverside Church. The video cameras jockeyed over new positions for the best live images of the top human interest story of the day.

McGreary returned to his troops while Kendall spoke to the mayor. "I'm going to assume you didn't know about any of this," the mayor warned Kendall.

"Of course not," he said, but there was a smirk in his voice. "The Guard doesn't have jurisdiction over the church, does it?"

"No. The order was specific as to location. Plus the church is neither city nor state property."

"Clever. What do you think they'll do now?" Kendall asked.

"I guess they could ask God, but in the meantime I'm sure the governor is calling the head of the diocese. I just hope Tom and Dr. Lewis get me some news I can share before that happens."

McGreary approached them a few minutes later with a look of weariness—the demeanor worn by a professional who knows that an ending will be bad, that he will be an instrument in that ending, and that he is powerless to alter it. "I just wanted to advise you as a courtesy that we will be setting and enforcing an armed perimeter around the church."

Kendall looked to the church entrance and pushed down the urge to vomit. Many of the bystanders had already gathered on the sidewalk in front of the church and started an impromptu protest facing the news cameras. Some had locked arms while others carried signs, hastily made with cardboard and paint conveniently stacked outside Sid's shop, that read "Free Our Dogs" and "Tell the Truth!" They chanted, "Sanctuary!"

Andy led them, his fists pumping above his head.

"People will get hurt," the mayor said.

"I've got no choice," McGreary replied.

But the mayor wouldn't be put off. "Of course you have a choice. You've already screwed this up and made—"

"Me?" McGreary shouted back at her. "I'm not the one who—"

"Look at this!" the mayor said, pointing to the crowd. "The Keystone Cops could've handled this better."

"With all due respect, Madam Mayor," McGreary said with an obvious effort at control, "screw you!"

"Perfect," she said. "You really have to love the subtlety of the armed forces. Tell me something, Lieutenant. When they gave you your rules of engagement for this little exercise, which part said, 'Trap an old priest and a hundred dogs in a church in front of network television on the eve of the presidential convention'?"

Kendall turned to McGreary. "Let me try to talk to the priest. I know him. Maybe I can convince them to come out."

McGreary was already shaking his head before Kendall finished. "This is not a negotiation."

"The way I see it," Kendall countered, "my offer has no downside and lots of upside. At least it may help get those folks off the front steps."

Three minutes later Kendall had made his way through the mass of people standing before the church. He banged on the door to the narthex. Gabriel opened it a crack. The crowd glimpsed the priest's face and cheered.

"What do you want?" Gabriel asked.

"We need to talk."

"So talk."

"C'mon, Father. Let me in. I may be the only thing standing between you and a canister of tear gas at this point." Gabriel opened the door a few inches wider and Kendall darted in.

Kendall scanned the sanctuary, took in the caged dogs and the odor of antiseptic, urine, and feces. "Wow," was all he could manage.

"What? You've never seen the inside of a church before?" Gabriel brought Kendall into his office.

"Have you heard from Sam?" Kendall asked.

"Not since they got into the helicopter. You?"

Kendall shook his big head.

"So where does that leave us?

Kendall shrugged. "Dangerous ground, I guess."

"If you're here to try to convince me to give up the dogs, forget it."

"Give up the dogs," Kendall said.

"Forget it."

"OK. I can say I tried. On to Plan B. Get me a sheet of paper and a pen," Kendall said.

"You gonna write me a love note?"

"No, you're going to write one."

"Say again?"

"You need to give me a demand that I can deliver to the Guard and the mayor."

"You're acting like I have a hostage."

"You do. A peaceful end to this circus."

"How bad is it out there?"

"Let me put it this way: if Al Pacino showed up, they'd be yelling, 'Attica! Attica!' You own that, at least for now. Or they think you do. So give me a demand."

25

Sam forced herself to look up from her clenched hands and noticed that the sky outside the window had turned a sickly gray.

"We're being given instructions to put down," the pilot called back to Sam and Tom.

Sam risked a peek at the ground. "That isn't New York City."

"No. Still seventy-five miles away."

"What's up?" Tom asked.

"A line of thunderclouds straight ahead. Always a problem in September. But you'll need to drive from there. State cops will meet you."

"Damn," Tom said. "What about going around?"

The pilot shook his head. "The line goes all the way to Connecticut."

Sam felt a vibration in her pocket and it took a moment for her to realize that it was her phone. She pressed the phone hard to her ear, but it was still nearly impossible to hear the voice on the other end over the propeller blades.

"...rabies virus used for the vaccine is self-limiting."

"Dad? I can barely hear you!"

"...important! Listen, the VetMed documentation...the dogs that received the original vaccine are no longer shedding the virus. The virus is out of their systems and the immunity..." Daniel's voice faded into static.

"Say again, Dad."

"I said that the sick dogs at the shelter should have developed a blood serum immunity to the rabies virus. That part of the vaccine actually worked. The immunity they've developed may be critical to figuring out an antiviral to reverse the effects in the infected children."

"Do you have proof?"

"...working on it. The serum is..." More crackling.

"What?"

"...you need to save those dogs. We need those antibodies from live animals. I'm trying to get through to the CDC now, but you must tell the mayor. We need those dogs alive."

"No one's gonna believe us without proof," Sam said.

"Be persuasive!"

An explosion of thunder rattled the helicopter and Sam's connection went dead.

"What?" Tom asked as soon as Sam lowered her phone.

Sam ignored him and called to the pilot, "Is there any way you can take us straight through the storm?"

"In an emergency I might be able to get permission."

"Get it. Please. We have an emergency."

"OK," the pilot said. "But I hope you both brought a change of underwear."

She turned to Tom. "You need to get the mayor on the phone. Now!"

26

Kendall ran back to McGreary and the mayor, carrying Gabriel's demand note. "What's this?" McGreary asked.

"A demand. But it's short. They just want to speak to the mayor."

"I'm not agreeing to that," McGreary said. "No way. I can't guarantee her safety."

"It's actually a good idea," the mayor said. "I'll go."

"I'll be with her at all times," Kendall volunteered.

"I don't care," McGreary shot back. "No."

Kendall wouldn't give up. "She might be able to defuse this. Let the priest save face. At least it would be helpful in getting the crowds to back off from the church without a riot."

McGreary shook his head. "But I can't—"

"You need to learn to interpret and improvise, Lieutenant," the mayor cut in. "Take a look over there." The mayor pointed to a group of reporters across the street standing beside a CNN satellite feed truck. She removed her cell phone and selected a number from her speed dial. A second later one of the reporters reached into his pocket, removed his ringing phone, and answered it. Kendall heard the reporter say, "Hello," on the mayor's phone right before she terminated the call. He assumed McGreary heard it as well.

"I have thirty others on speed dial," she told McGreary. "You may want to remind your superiors of that."

McGreary muttered one word—"Politicians"—and rolled his eyes. "I've gotta make a call to clear this." He jogged over to the Jeeps for some privacy.

The mayor didn't wait. She passed through the crowd as Kendall and some other cops cleared her way. She ran to the church with Kendall beside her.

Gabriel was waiting and he escorted them in stone-faced silence to his office. At the door the mayor turned to Kendall. "Can you give us a few moments, Jim?"

"I promised I wouldn't leave you," Kendall answered.

"It's quite all right," the mayor said. "I'll be safe."

"It's not really you I'm worried about," Kendall said.

The mayor nodded at Gabriel. "I promise I won't do physical violence to this person." Kendall left them and closed the door.

27

Once they were alone, the mayor and Gabriel stared at each other for a long, guarded moment. Then the mayor took a step forward and hugged the priest tightly.

"I'm so sorry I got you into this, Gabe," she said.

Gabriel returned the embrace. "You do keep life interesting, Sandi. If only it kept us young."

"When I asked you to take the dogs, I didn't really expect—"

Gabriel pulled back and looked down at her—he had a good foot in height on her. "You didn't expect only because you didn't let yourself think about what would happen. You ignore fundamental rules of causality. Everything follows what came before."

The mayor smiled. "You've been saying that to me for years."

"And here we are again. How, may I ask, does this little excursion end? An act of God, perhaps?"

The mayor slumped down into an offered chair. Molly came out of her hiding place and jumped into the mayor's lap as if they were old friends. Eliot came over next. "Who's this? One of the shelter dogs?" The mayor reached down and rubbed his head. Eliot stretched and returned to Gabriel's feet.

"No. Actually an impulse acquisition that was probably the best decision of my later years."

"Ah. We're never too old to have a happy childhood." The mayor stroked the cat absently while she spoke. "According to Daniel Lewis, the dogs are no longer contagious."

"Even I could have told you that."

"And he believes they may be important to figuring out a way to save the sick children."

"That's very good news."

"Yes, but we need someone to believe us. Dr. Lewis is trying to convince the CDC as we speak. There are some countervailing influences and they don't like being wrong on a good day. But if he can get the CDC on our side, maybe we can convince the governor to back down. Then we can hold the press conference on the church steps and still pull out a Pixar ending."

"When was the last time this governor backed down?"

"Including this time? Never."

"And what are the contingencies if he does not?"

"Then we're looking at the potential for violence and I can't let that happen. I won't. I would need to turn over the dogs first and hope they stay alive until I have more proof."

"So this may all be for nothing?"

The mayor smiled, but only for a moment. "I actually think it's going to work out."

"Why would it? It never has in the past."

"I need you to hold the line for a little longer. This will all be over soon."

"That's what I'm afraid of."

"Toughen up."

Gabriel laughed. "Or what? You're going to beat me up again like in fifth grade?"

"If I have to." The mayor lowered Molly to the floor. "I'm going to report that we made some progress and that you wanted a little time to think it over."

Gabriel escorted the mayor and Kendall to the front door and let them out. As he locked the door behind them, someone in the church basement screamed, "Fire!"

And a situation that could not possibly get any worse actually did.

28

Sam had been through turbulence before...even bad turbulence. But nothing had prepared her for this descent into meteorological hell. The problem was not the lightning or the booming thunderclaps, but the rims and rifts of air currents that seemed to attack the helicopter from all directions. One moment they were rising up and the next dropping down thirty feet only to be shot upward again. She was too scared to puke.

This violent display of nature forced her to consider that she might actually die in this helicopter. Despite that she had seen death often, and in fact was a member of the only healing profession authorized to deliver endings daily, she had not previously given much thought to her own death. She had been too angry and too focused on what someone else had done to her to take the kind of control necessary to imagine her own end.

But now Sam thought of what she would miss and what she had missed. Travel? A human life partner? Children she might have given life or love to, and now would never know?

Maybe these things. But her thoughts kept coming back to the smell of fur, the sound of paw-nails on hard floors, the clarity of gold-flecked irises in sunlight. She wouldn't miss the things she had never done. She would miss what she knew—her dogs, the shelter, and those who had toiled with her amid the sounds and smells of rescue and sanctuary. All those would-haves or could-haves and lives not chosen? What did they really matter now? Could it be that, whether by luck, coincidence, or destiny, she had been doing the exact correct thing all along?

Except even if that was true, she still could not avoid the conclusion that she had failed. The giant countdown clock sneered at her. She had given shelter but not sanctuary.

Never sanctuary.

In the hopes of some distraction from her own thoughts. Sam glanced at Tom, white-knuckling his armrest. He appeared to be experiencing the same physical effects of the turbulence and trying hard to keep it together. "I'm guessing I'm not looking too professional right now," he said.

"You seem to be doing fine."

"I'm trying to think of other things."

"Like what?"

Tom shrugged, but it wasn't convincing.

"Throw me a line," Sam said. "I'm sort of dying here."

"I was thinking that I miss my son. He would think this is really cool and if he were here I would try to act fearless for him. Try to be worthy..."

"He likes adventure?"

Tom nodded, and once again Sam could see the love this man had for his boy. "He likes movement, contact, activity, you know, signs of life. He'd love your shelter."

"He should come by...if we live through this." To the pilot Sam shouted, "Will this thing hold together?"

"Goodness, I hope so."

"A little more confidence right now would be great," she said weakly.

"We will be fine. Not as bad as I thought."

"Are you kidding me?" Sam asked.

"At least we're still vertical to the horizon."

Sam looked out the window and tried to see past the rain lashing the glass. "How can you tell?"

"Because we haven't stalled yet. We're almost through this," the pilot called back. "Just one more rift. Hold on."

"Crap. Not again." Sam gnawed on her thumbnail.

Tom unstrapped his broken watch and handed it over to Sam. "Keep this on until we finish this."

"I couldn't—"

"Take it. For luck."

Sam tightened the watch on her wrist and actually felt a bit better for reasons she could not explain. "Thank you. I promise I'll give it back when we land."

"Don't worry," Tom said, and smiled. "I know where you work."

A powerful blast of thunder rocked the helicopter. Instinctively Sam reached out to steady herself and grabbed the first thing she found. She discovered Tom's hand in midair already searching for her own.

29

When Gabriel reached the basement, he saw that Greg's shout had been slightly premature. There were no flames, but there was smoke.

For four hours an electrical outlet, wired when Eisenhower was president, had strained under the burden of two power strips attached to six lamps. In the 243rd minute of service, the outlet became so hot that it caused the wiring in the wall leading from the outlet to arc. The ancient "flame-resistant" insulation in the walls—made of some substance declared illegal under the building code two decades ago precisely for this reason—began to smolder. The smoke fought to escape the confines of the inner wall and found release in the same outlet that had started the problem.

"It's in the walls!" Sid shouted above the barking dogs.

"Open the cages," Gabriel ordered.

"Should we try to leash them?" Luke asked.

The priest looked across the rows of cages and the hundred dogs. "There's no time. Just open the cages and we'll try to leash them once they're upstairs."

"This ever happen before?" Greg asked.

Gabriel shook his head. "But only God knows how long it's been since these outlets have been used, let alone this much."

"We need to call the fire department," Sid said. He tried his cell phone but couldn't get service in the basement. "Got to do it from upstairs." Scrabble, Blinker, and eight other newly uncaged dogs followed him up the steps.

Within minutes they had released thirty dogs, then forty, but the smoke continued to build.

"We've got to get everyone upstairs," Gabriel concluded. "We'll need to see what the FDNY says when they get here."

"If the Guard lets them through unaccompanied." Luke spoke aloud what had been on all their minds. The Guard now didn't even need to break down the front door; it could step in right behind the fire department.

"I don't think we have a choice." Gabriel touched one of the walls.

Sid returned and announced, "Fire department is on the way."

Getting the dogs to follow Gabriel up the stairs and to the church sanctuary was no problem. The upper floor of the church and the sanctuary were still free of smoke, and the walls, for the moment, were cool to the touch. A dog's olfactory system is over one hundred times more powerful than its human counterpart. The smoke in the basement was not only irritating, it smelled awful, so the dogs were only too happy to get away from it. Only Hips needed assistance; Sid and Greg carried his wheelchair up the stairs.

Controlling the dogs once they entered the sanctuary, however, was a different matter entirely. They had been locked up for too long and the sudden freedom and excitement were overwhelming and irresistible.

Under the bemused countenance of a crucified Christ, the dogs began scent marking everywhere in the sanctuary. Then other dogs tried to cover those marks. Gabriel watched all of their antics without judgment or rancor. There was no point trying to catch them. He knew he could clean the smell of urine. Smoke damage, however, would be a much larger problem—if there remained anything left to clean at all.

Gabriel heard the sirens approaching and turned to face the crowd in the sanctuary—dogs chasing each other, Luke and Greg trying to leash as many as they could, Sid running to catch Louis, the isolation dogs surprisingly energetic and scratching to get out of their cages.

Then the first searching fingers of smoke poked through the wet towels they had used to seal the basement door. A debilitating fatigue overcame the priest. They were out of time and options.

Gabriel allowed himself a brief moment of despair and then he forced his mind to clear. His eyes landed on the stained glass image of Isaac and then the crucifix. In the juxtaposition of those two symbols of sacrifice, he suddenly saw a way forward.

"Greg!" Gabriel shouted. "You need to pull out these IV lines! Time to get the dogs outside."

"We can't," Greg said. "What if they're contagious? You'd be releasing this virus into the neighborhood."

"They're not contagious anymore."

"And who told you that? God?"

"The mayor of the City of New York. That's close enough for me right now."

"But what if she's wrong, Gabriel?"

"I just can't abandon these dogs in a house of God to suffocate or burn to death...not when they might also be a key to helping those kids who are still sick." He hoped his stated rationale sounded reasonable, because his real prayer was pathetically naïve and ran counter to all his actual life experiences.

"Releasing these dogs is a big call," Greg said. "And you won't be able to take it back."

"This is my church. I will take the responsibility."

"No," Luke said. "We share in this. We all take responsibility."

"Agreed," Sid said.

Greg was silent for a moment and then nodded his concurrence.

30

Kendall had to jog to keep up with the mayor as she charged toward McGreary in front of an angry crowd that had mushroomed to over three hundred.

"Stand your ground, Lieutenant," she commanded. "Let FDNY handle this."

"Was the city fire department your idea, Mayor?" McGreary pushed back. "A false alarm so you could send more of your own in and take control? It's not going to stop us. I have orders." As he finished his sentence, plumes of black smoke began to billow out of the church's basement windows. He pointed to the smoke. "This for real?"

"What's it look like?" the mayor snapped.

"Aw, crap," McGreary groaned.

The first fire truck and several ambulances pulled up beside the Guards' temporary command center. The fire chief jumped off the truck and ran to the mayor and McGreary while the rest of the fire crew began pulling hoses.

The chief acknowledged the mayor, Kendall, and McGreary with a curt nod. "What do we know about the fire condition?"

"Nothing," the mayor and McGreary answered in unison.

"The smoke just started," Kendall added.

"The news is reporting four people inside and a mess of dogs," the chief said. "That right?"

"Over a hundred dogs," the mayor answered.

"Shit," the chief spit. "And they won't come out?"

McGreary shook his head.

"And whose fault is that?" The mayor poked a finger at McGreary.

"I don't care whose fault it is," the chief said. "I'm gonna need the folks standing around the front of the church cleared away so we can get a line and smoke crews through that door."

"That's it then," McGreary said. "We're going in."

"You can't," the mayor protested. "It'll be a war. This is a church. If you start pushing those people, this time they will push back."

"I'm sorry, Mayor," McGreary said. "More than you know. But my overriding charge in this situation is to protect life and property. It seems pretty clear to me that there's no choice."

"The dogs in that shelter may be critical in helping to find a cure," the mayor said.

"I don't know if that's true, but if it is, then that's all the more reason to make sure they're secure." McGreary pushed past her and his men followed.

McGreary directed his troops to clear a perimeter around the church. Kendall saw that his own officers behind the barricades were getting antsy. The NYPD on one side of the fight, the Guard on the other, and over three hundred innocent protestors in the middle. Just one drawn weapon would mean disaster.

"Stand down!" Kendall yelled to his own officers. "NYPD, stand down! Do not engage. I repeat, do not engage."

McGreary caught Kendall's eye and nodded his thanks.

31

Andy observed the smoke coming from the church and for one blissful moment, he forgot about everything that had come before. No hard hands. No stinging slap. No grief pressing down on his chest. The smoke triggered no memory, no vestigial image embedded in his tortured mind. For the first time since he was eleven years old, Andy was completely and utterly forward-looking.

He left the group of protestors and ran to the church with a single objective—save the dogs.

Andy was within five feet of the narthex door and reaching for the handle when a rifle butt slammed into his cheek. He heard something in his face crack an instant before the pain blinded him and he collapsed to the sidewalk. Something salty, warm, and nauseatingly metallic leaked into his mouth. He knew that taste: blood.

Andy looked up and saw a blurred image of Owens standing above him, rifle butt raised, coming in for another hit.

"I told you we'd catch up," Owens sneered. Andy raised his arms to block the blow—or at least he thought he did. There was an unpleasant disconnect between what his brain said and what his muscles would do.

"Alexa," Andy whispered.

Then something took Owens completely off his feet. His rifle clattered to the concrete.

Andy heard a single shot before he went dark.

32

The rifle discharge was the only excuse the other Guard troops needed. All the frustrations of their current assignment, the monotony of perimeter patrol, the heckling by the crowd, and the pressure of the cameras combined in the worst possible way at the worst possible time.

The cops saw Kendall entangled with Owens and they forgot all about "stand down" and "do not engage." They tried to protect and assist their commanding officer and friend. The Guard advanced to stop them.

Then the crowd of protesters broke through the line of Guards like a baseball team in a dugout-clearing fight, and any semblance of control or order became a memory.

Hands became fists, protest placards became bats, and rifles became first barriers and, when that failed, bludgeons. The lines between aggressor and victim blurred. Members of the crowd—ordinary people caught up in the moment—became as energized and hostile to those in uniform as rock-throwers protecting their country from armed occupiers. The street and the sidewalk exploded with the sounds of confusion and physical violence.

McGreary shouted orders for the Guard to secure their own weapons and desist; the mayor found a bullhorn somewhere and was shouting orders to the NYPD to disengage, back away, and assist the fire department.

But it was too late.

And the cameras captured all of it.

33

When Gabriel finally took a breath and surveyed the scene before him, he tried to choke back his panic. The sanctuary had filled with smoke much faster than the basement—an inevitable consequence of warm air's rising. Gabriel heard everyone starting to cough and knew he needed to abandon the fantasy of other options.

"Are all the IVs out?" he called to Greg.

"Yeah," Greg answered.

"We need to get all the dogs outside!" Gabriel shouted. "Now!"

"What about leashes?" Luke asked between wheezes.

"We're out of time!" Gabriel slammed open the church door.

The act of opening the door sucked in a wall of fresh air, which was precisely what the smoldering heat needed. The first flames bloomed in the sanctuary and a deep and angry rumble started in the basement.

"Now, now, now!" Gabriel shouted.

Sid grabbed Louis and shoved the puppy in his coat. Greg waited by the door, urging the dogs to follow. He didn't need to, though. Nick, Scrabble, Blinker, and the strays from the park led every other dog in the church outside to momentary safety.

Over one hundred dogs ran through and among the crowd, excited to be free.

34

Owens was strong, but he was no match for Kendall in a street fight. Although Kendall wasn't interested in hurting the soldier, he needed to get to Andy and Owens would not quit. Kendall finally landed a hard blow to Owens's mouth that appeared to stun him. After that, Owens stepped back into the crowd.

With Owens in temporary retreat, Kendall tried to find Andy, but the street had fallen into confusion. He watched as the dogs ran out of the church and began moving as one, following some invisible current, heading east through the crowd. Wherever the dogs ran, the fighting slowed and then stopped. One moment members of the crowd pushed and shoved against angry soldiers or pulled away from frustrated cops. Then the dogs passed through and the humans paused to watch. Upraised arms and weapons were lowered, and shouts and curses were abandoned in mid-sentence.

In later interviews, those who had participated in the conflict tried to explain the change they'd experienced when the dogs ran among them. Most said it had just been the right distraction at the right time. But others implied that they'd felt something more; that seeing the dogs had reminded them of old promises to do better, or that it had simply been too hard to hold on to self-righteousness and anger in the face of such grace. Even McGreary would later admit to Kendall that he'd sensed something deep within him shift—a great unburdening: "Watching those dogs run free, it was like when the last bout of nausea from the worst stomach flu passes and you're finally able to get some damn sleep."

Whatever was happening to the civilians, police, and Guard, one person on the street in front of that church remained unaffected. Owens had returned and he was in the place that experienced combat soldiers call "the Gray"—the place where they hear and see nothing except for the combatant directly in front of them.

Kendall knew he was that combatant.

Owens drew his handgun and pointed the weapon at Kendall's head. McGreary tried to reach them but Owens and Kendall were too far away.

"Owens! No!" McGreary screamed at him.

Owens fired. He was no more than five feet from Kendall.

Kendall saw a muzzle flash and then the pack of dogs driving between him and Owens. He squeezed his eyes shut against the bullet's impact.

In his darkness Kendall saw his wife and daughter. He longed for more time with them and to know the look on Deb's face when she opened the wrapping on that bike, the quiet comfort of more family dinners and movie nights, the warmth of close walks, the different tones of his child's laughter. Then they were gone.

He saw his old partner.

Phoenix was coming for him one last time. Kendall's legs crumbled from the impact.

But it wasn't the bullet that brought him down; it was the force of one word.

Forgiven.

35

After almost all the life had run out of the sanctuary, Gabriel darted into his office. He grabbed Molly with one hand and Eliot with the other and ran for the narthex door. The flames curled along the sanctuary walls. The room was hot and filling with bitter smoke.

Gabriel glanced up at the stained glass image of Abraham and Isaac. Isaac's face was growing longer and more grotesque in the heat. The boy's eye began to droop down like a Dalí watch, his mouth a growing circle of darkness and silent anguish.

Gabriel forced himself to look away. He saw a human figure standing by a pew near the chancel. The smoke cleared for a moment and he got a good look.

Channa called to him. He sent Molly and Eliot out the door to safety with a prayer and then met his old friend in the aisle. When he reached Channa's spot, she was gone, but he heard whimpering from the floor. Hips's wheelchair tire was wedged under one of the pews. Gabriel caught the dog's eyes—big and brown, filled with fear and confusion.

Gabriel tried to undo the straps on the wheelchair but quickly realized that there wasn't enough time to take the contraption apart without tools. He hooked his fingers around the bottom lip of the pew and he pulled. Nothing. These pews had been bolted to the church floor for decades. His eyes found the hanging crucifix. "Not in Your sanctuary. This shall not be Your ram," Gabriel begged. He pulled at the pew a final time.

Not even a millimeter. The pew would not give up a creak or groan or the slightest whisper of indulgence.

Hips was in full panic now, clawing at the pew that held him captive.

Gabriel dropped down and cradled the dog's head in his arms. "I will not abandon you."

36

Kendall opened his eyes uncertainly, looking for blood and waiting for the excruciating pain, but he found himself whole and unharmed. The bullet never found its mark. Someone must have taken the hit for him—a person or one of the dogs in the passing pack. That was the only explanation. But the only one on the ground besides him was Owens himself.

McGreary appeared at Kendall's side as his soldiers surrounded Owens and confiscated his weapon.

"Where are you hit?" he asked, breathless.

"I'm...not."

"Are you wearing a flak jacket?"

Kendall shook his head.

"He was five feet in front of you."

"I know."

"So where the hell did that bullet go?" McGreary struggled to answer his own question. "He went down just as he fired. He tripped? Or something bumped him and he aimed high?"

"I don't know." Kendall looked around; wherever the bullet had gone, it hadn't hit anyone else, thank God.

"You sure have some damn good luck," McGreary said, pulling him to his feet.

37

Andy struggled to remain conscious. His left eye had swollen shut and his right could see only blurred images. He touched his cheek and winced as his fingers ran over the flap of hanging skin. An emergency medical technician was talking to him, but it all sounded as if it were coming from underwater. He felt softness beneath him and assumed he was on a stretcher.

Kendall's face appeared above his and then Luke and Sid were next to him.

"You're gonna be OK, Andy," Kendall told him. But Kendall's words lacked their usual conviction. "Just a nice scar to tell the girls about when..." Kendall's voice cracked before he could finish.

Louis popped his head out of Sid's coat and barked. Andy smiled—his attempt to comfort them all. "Sounds like music," he tried to say, but his words came out blurred and jumbled.

They pushed Andy's stretcher toward a waiting ambulance.

"You taking him to Riverside?" Kendall asked.

The EMT nodded. "We'll take good care of him. Promise."

Andy heard their voices, listened to their concern for him, and felt—maybe for the first time in his life—lucky. Perhaps that love had been there for him all the time and his hardest fight was yet to be, the one with himself, where he would need to accept that he was worthy of that love in real time. Everything that had happened before had brought him here. He was not merely the sum of his memories, but only a child born from them.

Andy tried to sit up on the stretcher and got as far as an elbow. He saw the dogs from the church joined together and running with one intention and in one direction.

He knew where they were going even if no one else did.

And he saw the crowd—the grieving, the curious, the sad, the amused, the angry, the fighters, the fallen, and the long-since beaten— follow them.

"The park," Andy whispered. Kendall leaned in and Andy grabbed his arm. "Get to the park."

"OK," Kendall said, but Andy knew it was only to placate him.

They lifted him into the ambulance.

"I'm going with him," Luke said, and jumped in.

Andy struggled to get off the stretcher but the EMT and Luke held him down. He needed to make them understand. "Another Mount Moriah…"

Andy could see enough through his one eye to know that Kendall didn't understand. None of them did.

"We've got to get him to the hospital," the EMT said gravely. "Like now." Without any further discussion, the EMT climbed into the ambulance and slammed the door closed.

As the ambulance began to move, Andy spoke the first words that came into his wounded head. "*Shema Yisrael, Adonai Eloheinu, Adonai Echad—*"

38

Sam saw the multicolored flashing LED lights below long before the helicopter actually passed over the shelter on the way to the park.

"Blue-and-white lights are police?" she asked.

"Yeah," Tom said, looking out the window.

"What about the red-and-white?"

"Fire."

"And the green?"

"There's nothing we can do until we get closer," Tom said.

"What are the green lights?" Sam insisted.

"Ambulance."

Sam tapped the pilot. "You have binoculars?"

The pilot nodded and handed Sam an old and battered pair. It was too difficult to make out any details at their current distance, but after a few more minutes, Sam was able to see the entire horrible scene more clearly—the fire devouring the church, the barricades, the FDNY pulling hoses, people fighting. She thought she saw someone on the ground outside the church, but then the smoke blotted it out. Sam just kept repeating the same two words: "My God."

The helicopter pitched to the left. Sam shifted the binoculars a few degrees and saw a huge pack of dogs running toward the park. Sam was sure it was her imagination, or the smoke, or the tears in her eyes, but she thought Nick was leading the pack. That couldn't be, she knew; Nick was too sick to walk, let alone run. She also saw a mass of people following or chasing the pack, but they couldn't keep up and were falling behind.

Sam panned the binoculars several blocks ahead of the dogs to the perimeter line. But it was what she saw three blocks farther east that made her stomach contract in a searing spasm. The Guard was forming a defensive line at the western entrance to the park that was already twenty strong. She remembered what had happened at the perimeter with Louis and then imagined it inflamed by several orders of magnitude.

Tom took the binoculars and scanned the scene below.

"How long till we land?" Sam called out to the pilot.

"Four minutes," he answered.

"Make it two," Tom told him.

"OK. But you won't like it. Hold on."

The helicopter plummeted. That was it. Sam's resolve folded. She turned her head and puked on the floor.

39

Kendall watched the ambulance drive off. He thought if he could figure out what Andy had been trying to tell him, then somehow the boy would be OK. But it had been gibberish, hadn't it? Another shard in a day that had long since splintered into incomprehensiveness. Still, something felt wrong. He knew he was missing a connection.

McGreary came up beside him. "He'll be OK, right?"

"I think so," Kendall said. He did a slow spin, taking in the mess surrounding them. Of course it all felt wrong; he would need to be dead inside to feel otherwise. But still... a hole tugged at him.

McGreary's phone buzzed and he lifted the receiver to his ear. After a moment he said, "But we don't know that... Who gave them that order?... These are my men and women... On whose authority?... Now?" And then a resigned, "I understand, sir."

"What is it?" Kendall asked.

McGreary's face answered before his mouth could. "By order of the governor, the dogs from the shelter are now all presumed infected. We are to obtain them as humanely as possible, but they may not under any circumstances cross into the park. We are establishing a second perimeter at the park entrance and keeping the public away. Firearms use is authorized for any dog who breaches. No exceptions."

Kendall shook his head in a mixture of disbelief and anger. "But you can't—"

"I'm with you on this one, Jim. I really am. But I've got no choice."

"I'll go with you," he said. "Maybe my men can help corral them before you need to go to weapons."

"I appreciate what you're trying to do. I wish you could join me, but I have orders to keep you and your men here. Maybe that's a blessing. I don't think you're going to want your hands anywhere near this one. This might be the stuff of nightmares."

"You're a good man, Ray. I believe that. You'll do the right thing if it comes to that."

Sid stepped up to them with Molly in one arm and Eliot in the other. "Have you seen Gabriel?" he asked.

Kendall gasped. The hole suddenly had a name and a face.

40

Gabriel examined the wheelchair apparatus again and almost laughed at his own stupidity. He reached down and unscrewed the air valve on the jammed tire. He heard the hiss of trapped air escaping. It was enough. The wheelchair rolled free of the pew. The device was now an unbalanced and awkward mess, but it still rolled well enough. Hips started for the door and then glanced backward, waiting for his rescuer to join.

"Go!" Gabriel shouted. Hips whined, looking between the priest and the door.

Gabriel tried to lift himself off the floor and felt something in his body give out. It was not unpleasant—like the fatigue that comes after thirty minutes on the treadmill. He dropped to his knees because his legs would no longer support him.

Hips took a step back toward Gabriel. The priest would not let that happen. He pulled off a shoe and threw it at the dog. "Go!"

That was enough. Hips ran out the door to safety.

"Thank you," Gabriel said. His eyes darted around the sanctuary. He wanted to remember it all. His gaze finally landed on the stained glass image of Abraham and Isaac above him. He watched the glass finally shatter from the heat. Isaac was free.

"I am the ram," Gabriel whispered. A smile brightened his weary face. He closed his eyes to the heat and smoke and embraced his victory. Then his old friend Christ dropped down from his cross on the ceiling and swept over him.

That was where Kendall found him.

41

The pilot landed as close to the front entrance of the park as he dared, adjacent to the space cleared for the convention party. "Wait for the blades to stop," he demanded.

Sam opened her door. "Can't. No time." She jumped out. Tom was half a step behind her.

They cleared the helicopter and ran between the faux Lincoln Memorial and Washington Monument. They made it to the park entrance on a sprint.

Twenty-five armed Guards blocked the entrance in the type of formation Sam had seen only in pictures of riots—shoulder to shoulder, their heavy batons held out horizontally in front of their chests. The dogs were still several blocks away, but Sam could see them coming. She couldn't identify the dogs from this distance, but several struck her as familiar.

Sam raced up to the line of Guards. "You can't hurt them! The dogs are safe! We have proof!"

"It was a vaccine!" Tom shouted. "The dogs aren't contagious. We need them alive," he yelled at anyone who would look at him. The stone-faced Guards would not respond.

"Please, listen to us!" Sam cried out. In her frustration she tried to jerk the baton out of the hands of one of the soldiers, but he was impossible to move.

Tom reached for her. "Don't, Sam. They'll hurt you."

Sam shook him off. "Let me go!"

McGreary's Jeep screeched to a halt in front of the line of Guards and he jumped out. "Step away, miss!" he shouted at Sam. "This is now a restricted area."

Tom ran up to McGreary. "Look, I'm the deputy mayor, Tom Walden. I don't know what's going on here, but these dogs are safe and we need them. Alive. Please."

"You have proof of that, Mr. Walden?"

"We're getting it. We are talking to the CDC right now."

"That doesn't help me, sir. The governor believes that if those dogs cross into the park, they will have access to the entire city."

"Bullshit! That's not why you're here," Tom said. "The governor screwed this up from the start, trying to protect his convention party, and now he can't back down without admitting it. That's what this is about—what it always was about!"

McGreary turned to his troops. "Stand ready! You have my orders, soldiers. I don't care what else you have heard today. I expect you to follow *my* orders. Do you understand?"

The soldiers, long drilled in command and combat, responded in unison: "Yessir!" Whatever feelings they had about their orders, these men and women did not show it.

Sam scanned the street; the dogs were just two blocks away. The leader ran with a familiar graceful strength. It was Nick! Scrabble, Blinker, and Monster ran behind him, along with all the shelter regulars and a mass of other dogs. The large pack dodged cars and pedestrians and leaped over obstacles, as if something in the park called to the dogs. They showed no signs of slowing.

Sam refused to stand around arguing with people who wouldn't listen. That was how she had spent her whole life, always out of place and too often ashamed even to be a member of this species. She knew that she had only one real choice.

Sam ran toward the pack.

She was still a block away from the dogs when Nick, relying on some impossible reserve of energy, charged ahead of the others. He bounded up to Sam, plunked his big paws on her shoulders, and licked her face. Despite everything that had happened, Sam felt a moment of elation. She hugged him tight and noticed with great relief that his eyes were bright and his breath smelled clean.

Scrabble, Blinker, and Monster ran up next. Then all the shelter dogs, the ones Sam had lived with and cared for, surrounded her. They had only a few moments of joyous reunion before the remainder of the dogs overtook them. Sam tried to stop them from pushing forward, but realized almost immediately that it was a lost cause.

Sam's twin demons of numbness and panic battled for control in her head. Then she heard her mother's voice cut through, as firm and as clear as if she'd been standing next to Sam. "Trust yourself," her mother said.

Perhaps she couldn't save these animals, but Sam vowed that she would never be the face of their Devil. The only thing she knew with certainty was that she had to get there with them.

Sam turned and, with Nick on one side and Scrabble and Blinker on the other, ran for the line of soldiers.

Of the thousands of images recorded that day, this one—of Sam running side by side with Nick, Scrabble, and Blinker toward the boundary of Guards, the rest of pack fanned out behind her—was the one that appeared on the cover of every New York and national newspaper and magazine. Sam often looked at that photograph in the years afterward and prayed that she had proven worthy of her running companions on that day.

The dogs were now a few hundred feet away from the Guards. Sam was nearly keeping pace with them despite her fatigue. All those years of running had conditioned her. But there was something else too. Sam felt part of a larger entity—powerful, feral, primitive, graceful, and purposeful. She had returned to an earlier form of her being and had never felt so utterly whole.

The first dogs, the fastest, charged forward to the line of Guards. Sam had no idea what would happen once the dogs met the batons, but she prepared herself to see the worst of humanity, knowing how horrible the worst could be. The nearly infinite number of images from an insane history of human-animal conflict sped through her mind: clubbed baby seals lying on bloodstained ice; lowland gorillas with their heads and hands removed; chimpanzees strapped to surgical tables; bulldozers full of dead pigs, sheep, and cows; dog carcasses lining the street following a rabies cull; caged dogs with their vocal cords sliced through.

The dogs met the Guards twenty feet in front of her.

"No!" she yelled. *Please*, she begged silently. *Give us sanctuary.*

McGreary called out three words. Sam's heart was pounding so hard in her ears that she wasn't sure she had heard them correctly. It sounded like—

"At ease, soldiers!"

The soldiers lowered their batons to their sides as one.

Most of the dogs stopped at the line. They sniffed soldiers, pawed the ground, and lifted their heads for soft scratches, playful pats, and utterances of affection that some of the dogs had not felt or heard in a few days and others in an entire lifetime.

Tom was so relieved that he nearly collapsed. Sam caught his arm before he hit the ground. That somehow turned into a hug and Sam didn't mind it at all.

The mayor arrived in a black SUV with blue bubble lights flashing. A few men in white lab coats jumped out with her. She ran to Tom, Sam, and McGreary, who stood in the center of two dozen excited dogs. "We have CDC confirmation," the mayor said breathlessly. "These dogs are no threat."

The mayor turned to McGreary. "I know for a fact what your orders were, Lieutenant. And this," she said, pointing to the scene of Guards and dogs playing together in small groups, "was not it. You have an explanation?"

McGreary smiled warmly for the first time since his assignment had begun. "Sometimes you've got to interpret and improvise," he said. "As someone very smart once told me, this is New York. We don't kill puppies in New York."

Nick and most of the shelter dogs surrounded Sam. Despite her human form, she was still their alpha. She had fulfilled her duty to keep the pack safe.

But, perhaps, only for today. She still had no long-term solutions and was no further along in her quest for a permanent sanctuary. Old voices tried to fill her head...voices of judgment, shame, and admonishment...familiar snickering. The countdown clock still loomed, accusing her of failure.

"Sanctuary."

She repeated the word. Now that her anger no longer gorged on her present, the word felt different in her mouth. She looked at her dogs...and really took them in this time. They were so happy to be near her. That counted for something. Perhaps she didn't need to find an abandoned farm in upstate New York to create her sanctuary. What if sanctuary was not about a specific place, guarded by a large lock from the outside world, but a feeling...a space that she had the power to create simply by choosing to be present for them? By caring? If that was so, then she could carry her sanctuary with her wherever she and the dogs ended up. The only thing really required of her was that she continue to love them.

And Sam could not deny that she did love them. She loved them so much that the thought of losing any one of them now for want of will was unacceptable. Their connection was so powerful that it sustained her just as much as she sustained them.

The recognition hit her as Nick and the others sniffed her shoes and jeans. These creatures offered her sanctuary in return. They always had. Sam saw the symmetry and felt its innocent beauty in a way that had been absent from her life since the days of her childhood animal tea parties. An injured dog, an angry daughter, a sick child, an abused teen, a grieving widower, a recovering drug addict, and a priest looking for understanding—they were all just seeking meaningful connections. They were all seeking sanctuary. In this most fundamental respect, no being was superior to another.

They were no less than equals.

42

Nine dogs—the nine Andy had originally led from the park—did not stop with the others. They continued through the Guards, straight ahead into the park. They ran past baited traps that held no interest for them. They crossed the ring of *Ailanthus altissima*, leaped through the narrow stone opening, and entered the cavern that was now their home.

There they joined others who existed so deep in the caverns of humanity that only the sins, songs, and sufferings of others could reach them.

And that is where they finally came to rest, waiting.

Book IV

And Thereafter

"The executive staff of the then-Governor of the State of New York ("the Executive Staff") exceeded their authority and the authority of the Office of the Governor when they employed executive powers in an attempt to eradicate the threat of rabies in Central Park. While the intentions of the Executive Staff may have been in the public interest, the means chosen to implement those intentions were contrary to the health and safety of the citizens of Riverside and the population of Manhattan in general. The decisions of the Executive Staff in this regard, while not the direct cause of the Riverside Virus, facilitated a series of events that both created the Virus and greatly exaggerated the response to the Virus. These decisions ultimately gave rise to the civil disturbance now known as 'the Riverside Riot.' There is no evidence that the governor was directly aware of the actions of his Executive Staff, although safeguards should have been in place in the executive office to prevent this type of inappropriate use of the executive's powers. It is our understanding that the safeguards recommended in this report are now being implemented."

Excerpt from *Report and Recommendations of the Senate Subcommittee on the Causes of and Response to the Riverside Riot*

The report was issued following the governor's nomination at the convention, but prior to the general election. The governor's celebration party in Central Park was canceled. The mayor resisted an eleventh-hour effort to draft her to run on an independent ticket, even though some polls showed she could take the majority vote. The governor failed to carry New York and lost the general election.

Daniel Lewis, working together with the CDC, was able to reverse engineer the Riverside Virus from the vaccine. No additional children became sick, and those who were ill received an antiviral drug Daniel helped create from the blood serum of several of the dogs who had been vaccinated and had developed immunity. With the knowledge that all the dogs exposed to the virus had been seen by Morgan, the city was able to isolate all avenues of infection. The dogs brought to the shelter during the crisis were reunited with their owners unharmed.

Daniel eventually returned to Cornell, where he resumed his research and lectured about the never-ending and always-evolving connection between emerging viruses and the way humans treat their animals. He was always on the lookout for evidence of renewed activity by VetMed and others and championed new legislation for rigorous controls on agricultural vaccine development.

Kendall worked closely with McGreary in the days that followed to return dogs, remove poisoned bait from the park, and clean up the mess that was now the Riverside Church. Kendall remained a commanding officer, and he had the respect and some say love of those he commanded. He was honored by his daughter's school on "Hero Day." His wife and daughter brought in a special cake in the shape of a Jedi Knight.

McGreary returned to the National Guard barracks with his troops. There was a brief and quiet investigation into why he'd refused the order to secure the Central Park perimeter in the face of the advancing dog pack. Following the investigation, and aided by the governor's insistence in media interviews that he had ordered the Guard to "above all, protect the welfare of the citizens of this great city," McGreary's actions were found to have been justified. Several months later he was promoted.

Owens was court-martialed and then dishonorably discharged for firing his weapon in a crowd of civilians during the riot. He fared better than Dr. Jacqueline Morgan, who was found guilty of involuntary manslaughter and sentenced to fifteen years in prison and a two-million-dollar fine.

Gabriel was buried next to Channa following a hero's funeral. Sid and Andy often met at the cemetery to discuss classical music and enjoy a bagel and coffee. They always brought Eliot and Louis with them. Eliot liked to sleep with his head resting against Gabriel's stone.

The Riverside Church was destroyed, but the insurance covered the cost of replacement. Rebuilding was a slow process, but the entire neighborhood joined the project. The mayor, with the approval of the diocese, made Sid the honorary head of the building committee. He decided against stained glass windows.

Sam lost the shelter. The smoke damage was too extensive and the property location too lucrative for an animal shelter. Instead the city arranged to lease Morgan's now-vacant hospital in partial payment of Morgan's fine, and that is where Sam set up shop. The new Finally Home Medical Center and Animal Shelter provided low-cost, city-subsidized veterinary medicine for the residents of the neighborhood as well as temporary shelter for lost, abused, and abandoned animals. Greg returned as Sam's chief of staff. He had five new employees to train. Luke also returned, but declined his salary. He didn't need it; Luke and his Vietnam War buddies had sold the rights to a smartphone app called Empyrean. As of today it has almost three million paid subscribers.

Luke and his friends also expanded Finally Home's presence on social media. They eventually commenced a very successful Kickstarter campaign for a sanctuary in honor of the children and animals lost to the Riverside Virus. With those funds Sam purchased an abandoned farm in upstate New York and opened the Finally Home Sanctuary for Animals and Children in Need.

Beth completed her government service and then stayed on to become the manager of the sanctuary. The rest of the dogs from the shelter went with her and never again knew the inside of a cage. The sanctuary became an award-winning animal education and child therapy center, Beth's home, and the final resting place for over two dozen cremation tins and one pendant made of dog tags.

Tom brought his son to the opening of the medical center and animal shelter. Nick wouldn't leave the boy's side. The boy was fine with that. Tom and his son came back several times. Sam eventually discovered that she loved the boy and, later, the man who came with him. Now Nick sleeps on the boy's bed.

Andy recovered quickly from his concussion. He studied hard and worked at the new medical center and shelter with the humans whom he considered his adopted family. He still spent many hours in the park with his other family. He took comfort in the fact that he'd once had no family and now had two. He never saw the one-eared dog again, but he finally finished his concerto for viola and violin in her honor.

He performed the full concerto for the first time in a hidden cave in Central Park before a small but adoring audience of stray dogs.

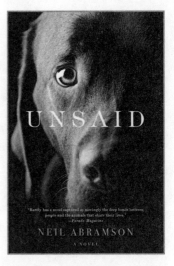